"A visceral, gut-wrenching, and heartbreaking take on the grieving process. I cried within the first fifty pages. You'll want to hug Tiger and never let her go. Kathleen has done it again!"

—TIFFANY JACKSON, author of *Allegedly* and *Monday's Not Coming*

"Magnificent. A beautiful, heartbreaking alleluia to survival."

—BRENDAN KIELY, *New York Times* bestselling coauthor of *All American Boys* and author of *Tradition*

"This story hauls you into its heart to live the pain in all its careening, messy, and miraculous glory. A brilliant, honest, raw look at what it really means to lose someone essential and make grudging peace with what is gained in the exchange. You will never forget Tiger Tolliver. Not ever."

—ESTELLE LAURE, author of *But Then I Came Back* and *This Raging Light*

"Gripping, powerful, and full of truth—an emotional level many novelists strive to reach, but few achieve."

—KAMI GARCIA, #1 *New York Times* bestselling coauthor of *Beautiful Creatures* and author of *Broken Beautiful Hearts*

# How to Make Friends with the Dark

## KATHLEEN GLASGOW

ROCK THE BOAT

A Rock the Boat Book

First published in Great Britain and Australia
by Rock the Boat, an imprint of Oneworld Publications, 2019

Copyright © Kathleen Glasgow 2019

The moral right of Kathleen Glasgow to be identified as the Author
of this work has been asserted by her in accordance with the
Copyright, Designs and Patents Act 1988

ISBN 978-1-78607-564-2
ISBN 978-1-78607-565-9 (ebook)

Interior design by Stephanie Moss

Printed and bound in Great Britain by Clays Ltd, Elcograf S.p.A.

Oneworld Publications
10 Bloomsbury Street
London WC1B 3SR
England

Stay up to date with the latest books,
special offers, and exclusive content from
Rock the Boat  with our monthly newsletter

Sign up on our website
**www.rocktheboat.london**

*...s with the Dar...*

"...owerful novel, *How to Make Friends with the Dark* dives ...to the heart of grief and healing with honesty, empathy, ...d grace."

—KAREN M. McMANUS, *New York Times* bestselling author of
*One of Us Is Lying* and *Two Can Keep a Secret*

"In this raw, powerful, and heartbreaking meditation on loss and grief, Glasgow writes with unflinching beauty. We meet Tiger Tolliver at her most broken—at her darkest moment—and yet, somehow, *How to Make Friends with the Dark* teaches us how to let the light in."

—JULIE BUXBAUM, *New York Times* bestselling author of
*Tell Me Three Things*

"*How to Make Friends with the Dark* is breathtaking and heartbreaking, and I loved it with all my heart. It's for all of us who have loved and lost and need to find our power again."

—JENNIFER NIVEN, *New York Times* bestselling author of
*All the Bright Places* and *Holding Up the Universe*

"A bold, fearlessly crafted story of loss and love. Kathleen Glasgow's prose commands the page with its trademark beauty and grace, and Tiger Tolliver is a character readers will root for every step of the way—and won't soon forget."

—COURTNEY SUMMERS, New York Times bestselling author of *Sadie*

"Kathleen Glasgow is the rare type of skilled storyteller that knows you have to hurt your characters before putting them back together. I loved every word of this lyrical and devastating novel."

—KARA THOMAS, author of *The Cheerleaders*

"A book as fierce, tender, and rare as its aptly named heroine, Tiger. *How to Make Friends with the Dark* is a gorgeously nuanced meditation on grief and family, and the incredible love that can pull you through the darkest of times."

—MEG LEDER, author of *Letting Go of Gravity*

"Beautifully written and profoundly moving. From page one, Tiger Tolliver grabs your heart with her pain, her courage, her humor—and she doesn't let go. Tiger, Cake, and Thaddeus (and Mae-Lynn, and Shayna, and Lupe, and LaLa, and Sarah, and Leonard, and June . . . all of Glasgow's deeply wrought characters) will stay with me for a long time to come."

—ALYSSA SHEINMEL, *New York Times* bestselling author of *A Danger to Herself and Others*

"Tiger Tolliver is so vulnerable and real, you'll want to turn your porch light on and have the spare room ready for her. In *How to Make Friends with the Dark,* Kathleen Glasgow's prose begs and pleads and grasps at the light, like a prayer."

—LYGIA DAY PEÑAFLOR, author of *All of This Is True* and *Unscripted Joss Byrd*

"Lyrical, devastating, witty and raw—this is Kathleen Glasgow at her best. Her fans will not be disappointed to fall in love with Tiger Tolliver, no matter how much she breaks their hearts."

—BONNIE-SUE HITCHCOCK, author of *The Smell of Other People's Houses*

*this book*
*is for the grievers*
*this book*
*is for the left behind*
*this book*
*is for every broken heart*
*searching for a home*

*Before*

I FIND THE BILLS BY accident, stuffed underneath a pile of underwear in the dresser my mother and I share. Instead of clean socks, my hands come away with a thick stack of envelopes marked *Urgent, Last Notice, Contact Immediately.*

My heart thuds. We don't have a lot, we never have, but we've made do with what my mom makes as the county Bookmobile lady and from helping out at Bonita's daycare. Come summer, we've got the Jellymobile, but that's another story.

You don't hide things in a drawer unless you're *worried.*

Mom's been on the couch since yesterday morning, cocooned in a black-and-red wool blanket, sleeping off a headache.

"Mom," I say, loudly. *"Mommy."*

No answer. I check the crooked clock on the wall. Forty minutes until zero period.

We're what my mom likes to call "a well-oiled, good-looking, and good-smelling machine." But I need the other half of my machine to beep and whir at me, and to do all that other stuff moms are supposed to do. If I don't have her, I don't have anything. It's not like with my friend Cake, who has two parents *and* an uncle living with her. If my mom is sick, or down, I'm shit out of luck for help and companionship.

And rides to school.

"Mom!" I scream as loud as I can, practically ripping my

throat in the process. I shove the bills back beneath the stack of underwear and head to the front room.

The scream worked. She's sitting up, the wool blanket crumpled on the floor.

"Good morning to you, too," she mumbles thickly.

Her short hair is matted on one side and spiky on the other. She looks around, like she recognizes nothing, like she's an alien suddenly dropped into our strange, earthly atmosphere.

She blinks once, twice, three times, then says, "Tiger, baby, get me some coffee, will you?"

"There's no coffee." I use my best accusatory voice. I have to be a *little* mean. I mean, come *on.* It looks like we're in dire straits here, plus, a couple other things, like *Kai,* are currently burning a hole in my brain. I need Mom-things to be happening.

"There's *nothing,*" I say. "Well, peanut butter. You can have a big fat hot cup of steaming peanut butter."

My mom smiles, which kills me, because I can't resist it, and everything I thought I might say about the stack of unpaid bills kind of flies out the window. Things will be fixed now. Things will be okay, like always.

We can beep and whir again.

Mom gets up and walks to the red coffeemaker. Coffee is my mother's drug. That and cigarettes, no matter how much Bonita and Cake and I tell her they're disgusting and deadly. When I was little, I used to wake up at the crack of dawn, ready to play with her, just *her,* before she'd drag me to the daycare, and I always had to wait until she had her first cup of coffee and her first cigarette. It was agony waiting for that stupid machine to glug out a cup while my hands itched with Legos or pick-up sticks.

She heaves a great sigh. "Shit," she says. "Baby! I better get my

4

ass in gear, huh?" She's standing at the sink, trying to turn on the faucet, but nothing is coming out. "The water's still crappy? I was hoping that was just a bad dream." She nods to the faucet.

"Pacheco isn't returning my calls," I say. Mr. Pacheco is our landlord and not a very nice one.

She murmurs, "I guess I'll have to deal with that today, too."

I'm silent. Is she talking about the bills? Maybe I should—

Mom holds out her arms. "Come here, baby. Here. Come to me."

I run so fast I almost slip on the threadbare wool rug on the floor and I go flying against her, my face landing just under her collarbone. Her lips graze the top of my head.

Mom trembles. Her shirt's damp, like she's been sweating. She must need a cigarette. "I'm sorry," she whispers into my hair. "I don't know what happened. What a headache. Bonita leaving, the daycare closing. I just . . . it was a lot all at once, and I guess I stressed. Did you even have any dinner last night?"

I had a pack of lime Jell-O, and my stomach is screaming for food, but I don't tell her this. I just keep nuzzling her.

My mother pulls away and laughs. "Grace," she says. Hearing my real name makes me cringe. "Gracie, that pajama top doesn't quite fit you anymore, baby doll."

I pull defensively at the hem of the T-shirt and cross my arms over my chest.

My mom sighs. I know what's coming, so I prepare my *I'm bored* face.

"Tiger," she says firmly. "You're a beautiful girl. I was just teasing, which I shouldn't have done. You should never hide *you*. You're growing into something wondrous. Don't be ashamed."

*Wondrous.* She and Bonita are crazy for the affirmation talk.

Cake likes to say their mission in life is to Build a Better Girl Than They Were. "You know," she said once, "their moms probably put them on diets of cottage cheese before prom and told them to keep their legs closed around boys."

I roll my eyes and groan. "You *have* to tell me those things," I answer. "You're my mom. It's in your job description."

Her face softens and I feel guilty. Once I overheard her say to Bonita, "I try to tell Tiger all the things I never got to hear, you know?"

And I always want to know, what didn't she get to hear? Because she's tight-lipped about her early, non-Mom, kidlike days. Her parents died when she was in college, and she doesn't like to talk about them.

My mother rummages around in the cabinets and somehow, somewhere, finds a lone can of Coke, even though I scoured the cabinets last night for spare eats. She takes a long, grateful sip and then wipes her mouth. She fishes in her purse for a cigarette.

"Go get dressed, Tiger. I'll drop you at school and then I've got a lot of things to do. Today is going to be one hell of a day, I promise. Food, Pacheco, the works. I'll make up for being out of it, okay?"

"Okay."

Mom heads out in the backyard to smoke and I hit my bedroom, where I frantically try to find something suitable in my closet of mostly unsuitable clothing. My mother thinks finding clothes in boxes on the side of the road is creative and fun and interesting and environmentally conscious ("One person's trash is another person's treasure!") and not actually a by-product of our thin finances, but sometimes I wish I went to school dressed

6

like any other girl, in leggings and a tee, maybe, with cute strappy sandals to highlight pink-polished toenails. Instead, I mostly look like a creature time forgot, dressed in old clothes that look like, well, *old clothes.*

I drag on a skirt and a faded T-shirt and jam a ball cap on my head, because the water in the shower is starting to look suspicious, too, so a shower is out of the question. I brush my teeth like a demon in the bathroom and splash water on my face.

Then, like I always do, I allow myself a minimum of three seconds to wonder: Who the hell is that? Where did *she* come from?

Because the dark and straight hair is nothing like my mother's short, light mop. My freckles look like scattered dirt next to her creamy, blemish-free face.

So much of me is from The Person Who Shall Not Be Named. So much of me is unknown.

But here I am, and for now I need to get my mother in gear, get to school, make it through zero period and the little five-day-a-week shit-show I like to call "The Horror of Lupe Hidalgo," which, if I survive, leads to Bio, and to Kai Henderson, the very thought of whom makes my heart start to pound like a stupid, lovesick drum, and who is one of the things I need to talk to my mother about.


In the car, she fiddles with the radio dial. My empty stomach is blaring like a five-alarm fire, so I scrape some Life Savers from the bottom of my backpack. Maybe lint and dust have some calories and I can last until lunch.

I'm sucking away when my phone buzzes. Cake.

*She up?*

*Yes! In car.*

*Thank God! You tell her yet?*

I glance over at Mom. She's muttering, trying to tune the radio in our ancient Honda, a car partially held together by duct tape and hope.

She looks tired. Maybe her head still hurts after all. Maybe it's the bill thing. Maybe I should get a job, help out. I could bag groceries at the Stop N Shop. Or bus tables at Cucaracha.

*Not yet,* I type.

*Just do it. Rip off the Band-Aid, Tiger. Then you can flee the vehicle and not have to deal with her until tonight.*

I don't answer. This is going to be a complicated issue, the Kai thing.

My mother is a little overprotective.

She is *not* going to be happy about me going to the Eugene Field Memorial Days Dance with Kai Henderson. Not because she doesn't like him, because she does. She's known him since he was a scrappy kid at Bonita's with bruised knees and a yen for butter cookies. She just doesn't like me . . . well, not being with *her.*

"Aha!" She grins. "Here's a good one."

She turns up the volume. Another song from years ago, nothing new, nothing I ever get to pick. She wrinkles her nose at the songs Cake and I play in our band, Broken Cradle, calling it a lot of experimental noise. It's *possible* I'm the reason it sounds "experimental," since I mostly bang away on the drums with no idea what I'm doing. I'm only there to back up Cake, who's basically a musical prodigy. And Kai, who looks dreamy and sweet, plucking his bass, his brow *furrowed,* like one of my novels might say.

Maybe it's the fact that I suddenly feel like my mother is always drowning me out that I blurt, "I'm going to Memorial Days with Kai Henderson."

As soon as I say it, I both regret it *and* relish it. I mean, what is she going to *do*? I'm *sixteen*. I can go to a dance like everybody else for once.

She turns down the music. "What?" Her voice is slow. "Since when? When did this . . . happen?"

I take a deep breath. "A couple weeks ago. He asked me. I'm going. It's going to be fun. Cake's going, too. Everybody's going."

"Wait," she says, again. "Kai? As in *Kai* Kai? Our boy with his head permanently buried in a medical textbook?"

I sigh. *"Yes."*

Silence. My heart drops. I knew it. I can almost count the seconds, so I do: ten . . . nine . . . eight . . .

"I don't know, Tiger. This is so sudden and we haven't talked about it. I mean, there's the drinking thing, probably an after-party—"

I interrupt her. "I don't drink, I don't party, I don't smoke. No one has ever felt my boobs except that one gross doctor, and I just want to go to a dance and *dance* like everybody else. For *once*."

"Do you . . . Is this . . . Is he your boyfriend now? Has *that* been going on?"

I can feel her eyes on my face. A blush creeps up my neck. *"No."*

I mean, not *yet*. Maybe. Someday. Like, after the dance, maybe. Isn't that how things work? You kind of slide into something? All I know is from books and movies and watching other kids at Eugene Field and remembering how it was with Cake

9

and the boy from Sierra Vista. I mean, what do I ever do without my mom anyway? Nothing. I go to school, sometimes I watch the skaters at The Pit, I come home, I read, I . . .

I sit in our small life. Watching everybody else. A bug in a jar.

In the distance, kids flood the parking lot and front lawn of Eugene Field High School. If I can just hang on until we get there, I'll have seven hours Mom-free. My stomach makes an unseemly rumble from hunger. I feel faint and dejected.

Why does one stupid normal thing have to be so *hard*?

"It's only a dance," I whisper. Tears form behind my eyes. My nose prickles. I'm starting to buckle, just like I always buckle. I buckled when she acted like gymnastics was too expensive, even though it was just a few classes at the dinky community center on half-worn mats. I buckled when Cake wanted me to take dance with her, when I had a chance to join after-school chess, all of it. The only thing I ever had was skateboarding, and that was four years ago, and then she took it away.

"I'm going to the dance with Kai Henderson," I say, my voice suddenly steely. "And you can't really stop me. And it would be wrong if you did."

My mom pulls into the lot, narrowly avoiding Mae-Lynn Carpenter, weighted down with her giant backpack. She glares at us before moving on. I don't think I've ever seen Mae-Lynn smile.

"Grace," my mother says. "We should talk about this later. It's a big thing. It's not as small a thing as you think." She puts her hand on my arm.

"No," I say, and then it happens. Tears, springing from my eyes. "It's *exactly* as small as I think. It's streamers and spiked punch and cheesy music and a party after. Something kids have done since the beginning of time, but never *me*. Not until now."

"Tiger, please," she says, but I'm already out the door, hoisting my bag over my shoulder, keeping my head down so no one can see me cry.

As soon as I take my seat in zero period, the texting starts, my phone buzzing insistently inside my backpack, starting a little war with the chaos happening in my unfed stomach. Those Life Savers weren't very lifesaving after all.

The noise alerts Lupe Hidalgo, much like the smell of tiny, frightened humans alerts sleeping giants in fairy tales.

Lupe Hidalgo sighs. Lupe Hidalgo stabs the point of her sharp, sharp pencil into the table. Lupe Hidalgo's legs are jiggling, the soles of her boots pumping against the black-and-white-tiled floor of zero p.

She glances at me, coldly, and then down at my backpack. She frowns.

There's some quick eye-to-eye action between me and the three other kids at our homeroom table. Tina Carillo looks at me; I swipe my eyes to Rodrigo; Rodrigo stretches his hands behind his head and rolls his eyes to Kelsey Cameron, who doesn't look at anyone, because she's too busy looking at herself in her phone and angling her head for a selfie.

Lupe tap-tap-taps the pencil. She bends her head to the right. She bends her head to the left. Her sleek black ponytail bounces against her back.

This is the signal that she's about to let loose on someone. The only time Lupe can focus is on the softball field. She's a senior headed to the U of A next fall on a full scholarship. The ability to throw a ball so fast and hard it's rumored her catcher, Mercy Quintero, ices her hands for hours after a game. The ability to nail a line drive into the soft stomach of an unsuspecting girl from Flagstaff.

Lupe Hidalgo is so good at softball it's like she's the only one on the team. I mean, I know I've *seen* other girls traipsing along the halls of Eugene Field with high ponytails and striped kneesocks on game day, their black-and-gray team shirts open and flowing, the fetching white fox mascot slinking along the game day T-shirt underneath, curling among the letters of *Zorros,* but for the love of God, I have no idea who they are.

Lupe Hidalgo is an eclipse. She slides over everything like a glamorous shadow, and even though you know it's going to hurt, you look anyway.

And I accidentally do.

In an instant, my heart is in my shoes. My stupid, dirty white Vans that I've markered up with stars and moons and a little facsimile of a cradle cracked in half, in honor of our band.

Lupe slides her glistening eyes up and down my body. Instinctively, I fold my arms across my chest. You never know when somebody, usually a guy, but sometimes a girl, is going to make a crack about your breasts.

*You have a beautiful body,* Mom always says. *Stop slumping.*

It's easy enough for her to say. *Her* boobs are like tiny overturned teacups on her chest, delicate and refined.

I force my mother from my brain. Our fight in the car didn't leave me feeling as triumphant or heroic as I'd have liked.

Mostly, now, I feel sick, hungry, and kind of scared. I resolve to not think of her any more today.

On cue, my phone buzzes. It's like my mother knows I'm trying to X-Acto knife her from my day.

I cannot believe I have sixteen million nerve-racking, day-killing things happening all at once.

Silently, I will Ms. Perez to stop bumbling around the front of the classroom and *start* already, but she remains obstinately unaware of the hell that is about to be unleashed on me and keeps shuffling papers around her desk.

Tina Carillo murmurs, "Here we go," and shrugs at me.

Lupe finishes giving me the once-over and growls, "Girl, what the *fuck* you wearing today?"

My body stiffens. The source and fact of my clothing has been an obsession of Lupe's since she rubbed mashed potatoes into my Hello Kitty tee in the third grade at Thunder Park Elementary. "Stupid cat," she'd said. "Dumb shirt."

Next to me, Rodrigo snorts and pulls out his phone.

"I mean, for Christ's sake, who do you think you are? Stevie fucking *Nicks*?"

Now, you might not be aware of the golden goddess of seventies music, the muse of a weird band called Fleetwood Mac, one of the strangest and most ethereal singers ever to float across a stage in six-inch heels, layers of velvet, and shimmers of lip gloss and fairy dust, but here in hot-as-hell Arizona, birthplace of our golden girl, we *all* know who Stevie is.

Lupe takes the hem of my unicorn-bedazzled T-shirt between her forefinger and thumb and leans close to my face. Her makeup is smooth and perfect, eyeliner spreading toward her temples like black wings.

"Girl," she breathes. I hear the slight pop of gum far back in her mouth. "Just . . . *no.*"

Kids around us giggle. One girl, whose name I can never remember, but whose face always looks like she just sucked a lemon, snaps a photo of me.

Super, now I'll be a laughingstock worldwide: #geek #weirdo #highschoolfreak #unicornloser.

My face burns, an instant heat that I know everyone can see. I'm awful at not blushing or being embarrassed, or not showing that I'm furious or frustrated. Mom calls this "a passion for life," but then again, my mother is the reason I'm being mocked at 7:25 a.m. in Room 29 at Eugene Field High School in Mesa Luna, Arizona.

Every day I go to school dressed like a miracle ticket hopeful from a Grateful Dead concert, and if you don't know who that is, look it up, and you'll see lots of confused people in tie-dyes and velvety skirts with bells at the hem trying to see a band made up largely of stoned dudes in dirty T-shirts and holey jeans who look like they haven't washed their hair since the sixties, when they started this nonsense in the first place. My wardrobe consists of old band tees, the aforementioned hippie skirts, men's pants, old suit jackets, and sometimes a hand-knit scarf, for "flair," my mom says.

I look away from Lupe and down at my clothes. I can't even pick my own damn *clothes.*

My phone vibrates. Instinctively, I kick at my bag, like that's going to make the buzzing, and my mother, stop.

Lupe looks at me and shakes her head. "Aw, your mama checking up on you again?"

She makes this sound like *Mm-mn-mm-nooooo,* and holds up her hand, flipping her wrist. Kelsey Cameron laughs. I glare at her, semi-betrayed. We aren't friends—I just have Cake—but still! We *share* this table with the demon that is Lupe Hidalgo. That should count for *something.*

*Sorry,* Kelsey mouths.

Lupe sighs and gestures in my direction. "I can't sit next to this. What if it rubs off on me? On this?" She glides her hands down her body, like she's a game show hostess. Lupe Hidalgo is mean and beautiful and even though she's wearing just a white T-shirt and black jeans and those boots, she's a shimmering, dangerous goddess.

I just don't understand how two girls can both be teenagers and yet one girl seems so adult, and knowing, and sexy, and the other, *me,* is like this piece of lumpy dough.

It's like a memo went out and only some girls got it.

I raise my eyes. Mae-Lynn Carpenter is across from me at another table, bent low over her notebook, the end of a pencil jammed sloppily in her mouth. The back of her shirt rises above her pants, revealing a downy patch of skin. Beside her, two girls are snickering at the bright white underwear peeking over the elastic waistband of Mae-Lynn's pants.

Girls like me and Mae-Lynn definitely did not get that memo.

I can feel tears brimming, because Lupe's got everyone's attention now, everyone except Ms. Perez, who's now writing something on the board.

If Cake was here, she'd have something snarky to say, but she isn't, and a thousand times a day, in situations like these, I think, *What would Cake do?* And I like to joke that I should get one of those bracelets, only it would say WWCD instead of WWJD, but Cake laughs that off. "You just need to yell more," she says. "Mouth off. Live up to your name."

Everyone loves Cake. Everyone admires Cake. She's five feet ten inches of awesomeness, bravery, and black and purple hair coiled in perfect Princess Leia buns. She's a bona fide rock star in the making and the sole reason I haven't been completely relegated to Nowheresville on the Eugene Field High School Ladder of Desolation.

I look at Mae-Lynn Carpenter again. She *is* the last stop on the High School Ladder of Desolation. They should probably just name it after her.

Mae-Lynn is wearing a pink sweatshirt with a kitten on it. A kitten with actual fur and an embossed pearl necklace. I swallow hard. At least I'm not that low. My unicorn might be bedazzled, but at least it isn't *furry.*

I adjust my T-shirt so that it's not riding up my belly as much. Lupe tsk-tsks.

My phone buzzes again. My stomach yelps. Lupe looks down at my bag, curious. "*What* is so important? I wonder. Did baby girl forget her lu—"

"*Lupe* Hidalgo and *Tiger* Tolliver, *are you* ready to learn today or *do I* need to send you *both* down to Principal Ortiz?"

*Finally.* Ms. Perez's voice booms from the front of the classroom. In an instant, you can hear the shuffle of phones being slid under tables, makeup bags being zippered, the clearing of throats. Ms. Perez, once she gets going, does *not* fuck around, even with only one month left in the school year.

Lupe tosses her head, her ponytail swinging, and swivels to face the front of the classroom, so her back is to me. Her shoulder blades press against her T-shirt, straining like wings beneath the cloth.

Lupe Hidalgo is so beautiful it hurts to look at her, so I look away, at the clock high on the wall, and begin my countdown to Bio, and Kai Henderson.

KAI HENDERSON IS READING the *Your World and You* text-book like nobody's business when I slide onto the rickety stool next to him in Biology. His "brow is knitted," as they might say in one of the books we read last fall in Lit class. I learned a lot of cool words in that class, like *provenance* and *skulduggery* and *mordant*.

I've barely cracked the Bio textbook all year, though. I don't fail my classes, or ditch, but I'm not a gold star kind of girl, either.

I have known Kai Henderson since we were eight years old, and everything was fine until that one day last November, in this very room, on the very same lopsided stool next to him, when he was pointing something out to me in that same stupid textbook, and somewhere in between *epicardium* and *myocardium,* he suddenly raised his head and our eyes met and *It* happened.

And when I say *It,* I mean *IT.* The thing you read about in books or see in movies. I always thought that it would involve something hokey like moonlight. Or fingers accidentally touch-ing inside a popcorn bag in a crowded movie theater, buttery skin on buttery skin.

I did *not* think it would happen in a Biology lab room that still stank of the cows' eyeballs we'd dissected a few days before. Cows' eyeballs are surprisingly springy and full of fluid, which spurts everywhere. In case you didn't know.

But it did. *Something* happened when I met his eyes. Suddenly they were no longer just *brown;* they were instead a gemlike and transfixing shade of *beyond brown with dazzling tints of mesmerizing yellow.* Suddenly the smear of acne across his jawline wasn't something I was embarrassed for, for him, but something I found tender, and wanted to *touch.* I mean, I hadn't *not* noticed that over the past year or so he'd kind of filled out, not a lot, just a bit, so that he wasn't quite like a bendy straw anymore.

He said, "The heart's really cool, isn't it? Like this beautiful and weird engine," and his breath had just a touch of mint toothpaste and he smiled this contented smile. Education is Kai's happy place.

His warm breath fluttered across my cheek, and for God's sake, I suddenly wanted to *taste* it. I mean, I had serious thoughts about those lips, and my whole world detonated in the space of three seconds.

And the thing is, the thing that makes me shivery, is that he started to feel the same way, too, because things got slightly different between us after that. Like, he got kind of quiet if Cake left the garage during our Broken Cradle band practice. He became very interested in adjusting his amp, like he even *knew* how to do that, because he *doesn't,* he can barely remember the chords Cake is always tossing his way, and there I was, just sitting behind the drums, tapping the sticks against the skins and trying not to blush as Kai looked everywhere but at me.

And when he walks me home from The Pit, and it's that time of night that has its own special kind of stillness, with just a couple of coyotes off somewhere howling? And when the skin of our hands kind of brushes every once in a while? I think I know *he's* thinking what *I'm* thinking, but we are both, as Cake has taken to telling me, "chickenshit."

19

Cake said, "Who better to have your first kiss with than one of your best friends, right? You *know* he's aces, you *know* there's nothing dark or creepy in *Kai, the Movie,* so why not kick back and enjoy?"

Cake even left us alone on her couch last week, saying she had to go water the plants for her mom, and there we were, suddenly afloat on the couch of panic. It was spectacularly hot and we were sweaty after sitting at The Pit earlier in the day, watching the skateboarders. We held cold glasses of grape Kool-Aid in our hands. It felt like hours as he leaned forward and carefully put his glass on the floor and then leaned back and said, "So . . ."

His breath smelled sugary from the Kool-Aid. That seemed right to me, that my first kiss might taste sweet and perfect. I could barely hear myself think, my heart was beating so loud.

And then Cake's Uncle Connor stumbled into the room, kicking over Kai's glass and collapsing next to him in a haze of weed, his socked foot resting in the oozing purple puddle of Kool-Aid.

He blinked at the television, and then at us, and said, "*Scooby Doo* is *still* fuckin' on TV? That is *crazy,* dudes. It's been like forty years.*"

We spent the rest of the afternoon watching Velma and the gang solve mysteries, along with Cake and her uncle, who never took his foot out of the Kool-Aid.

Now things are even more complicated, because Kai found out a few weeks ago that he's leaving at the end of the summer for some year-long schlepp in Germany, where he'll become a completely different person and probably fall for some completely cool and super-confident German girl with blunt-cut blond hair and red lips and bigger boobs than mine who will kiss him like it's no big deal. *Ja.*

*Nein!*

My face flames like a wildfire.

Kai looks up. "Hey, whoa, you're red."

And then, "Please don't tell me Broken Cradle is practicing today. You guys are killing me. I don't know how much more I can take."

I suck in a deep breath, forcing my voice to sound normal and not all *love me.*

"I'm sorry. You have to stay. If we don't have a guy in the band, people will assume we're socialist feminist lesbians—not that there's anything wrong with that—and we'll lose a key demographic in our quest for world domination."

"You don't need me for world domination. You have Cake."

"We need your sensitive backing vocals and awkward posturing. Your shoe-gazing and furrowed brow bring us the all-important cute-nerd-girl contingent."

Kai fiddles with his pencil, not looking at me. "I don't think the band has a problem with the cute-nerd-girl thing."

"You *guys.*" The drone is Taran Parker, who has wheeled around on his stool, carrying a whiff of pot smoke.

There's a weird triangular dusting of hair on Taran's chin, like he's deliberately trying to look like the spawn of Satan. I have pretty much hated Taran and his twin brother since the day they moved here three years ago from Phoenix. They stood in a lanky lump at the front of seventh-grade English as the teacher introduced them and Taran's eyes immediately zeroed in on me and he blurted out, "Dang, those titties!" Causing the boys in the class to erupt in laughter and me to slink down as far as I could go in my seat. If the floor could have absorbed me, I'd have been eternally grateful. So grateful I probably would have even agreed to just rename myself Floor. *Floor Tolliver.*

It doesn't have such a bad ring to it.

"You and you." He points a chewed-up pencil at us. "Kai-Kai and Tiger-Girl. Get a room already. You'll have a summer of sweet, sweet *liebe* before smarty-pants departs for *Deutschland.*"

I grab his pencil and throw it at him, but it sails over his head and hits Laizure, our Bio teacher, smack in his blue-plaid chest as he comes in the door, loaded down with his giant 7-Eleven coffee, briefcase, and seventeen thousand pencils in his shirt pocket. He gives Taran an annoyed look.

"Ding, ding, ding!" Laizure sings out, ambling to the front of the room. Ever since the school bell broke last fall, Laizure has delighted in doing the *ding-ding-ding*ing to announce the start of first period himself. "You know what I like when we have a mere four weeks left of school and a dance to look forward to? I like pop quizzes. Let's go, my little diploids! Let's hop to it. Let me give you something wonderful to remember me by, all summer long."

Kai whispers, "So, everything is cool about the dance and stuff? You said you were going to tell her."

Our faces are so close. If I leaned in just a bit more . . . My stomach makes an unattractive gurgle.

I rear back, startling us both. My stomach is all over the place, a hot little ball of hunger and heat. "Yes, absolutely," I whisper to Kai, trying not to invoke Laizure's wrath. He already thinks I'm lazy about learning, which I'm not.

"I'm tepid," I once told him.

"Nope," he said, handing me back yet another test with a big red D. "You're *lazy*, Tolliver. I can tell. I've been in this business a long time. You can't fool me."

"Absolutely," I tell Kai again. I mean *no*, of course, because of the fight this morning, but he doesn't need to know about that. Not yet. Maybe not ever. I'm going to this dance with Kai, whether my mother likes it or not.

I want this summer to be different, the beginning of new things for me, even if Kai is leaving in the fall for another country. He's a chance, a tiny, bedazzled chance for me to be someone different. Step away from my mom. Even if it's just at a dumb dance with crinkly streamers and lights hung sloppily from the rafters of a smelly old gym.

I concentrate on the quiz sheet in front of me, relieved to have the distraction.

"Hey," Kai whispers, nudging me with his elbow. "Meet you at The Pit later? Hang out at Thunder?"

I know it's dumb and cliché, but my heart soars when he says that. I nod. *Yes, yes, yes.*

I look back down at the quiz, filled with anatomical illustrations, all valves and arteries and tubes here and there and coils of things that seem vaguely disgusting, and I don't even care that I'm going to fail.

I don't understand the body and how it works, at all, but right now I know my heart is like a giant, colorful bird, flying right out of my chest and into the world.


Cake is waiting for me at our table in the cafeteria, nodding her head to the music on her earphones as she spreads her lunch out on the table.

The minute I sit down, she drags off her earphones and leans forward. "Did you tell her? She freak?"

I hold up my phone. Four missed calls and nine texts.

Cake whistles. "Damn. That's some serious momming."

She pushes a sandwich toward me. Then a baggie of apple slices. Then a baggie of hard Cheetos, because she hates the soft ones.

Cake always brings extra food for me. We don't even talk about it anymore.

Sometimes I'm so grateful for Cake I could burst. I bite into the sandwich. Cream cheese and strawberries. Not bad. Her mom is an A+ sandwich maker.

Cake says, "You've been crying."

I swallow a hunk of sandwich. "We kind of fought in the car about the dance. And then I saw Lupe, so the morning wasn't swell."

"At least it's done. Now you can move on. Now you can focus on other stuff. Right? Focus." Cake is big on goals. She has schedules for band practice, personal practice, when to research music schools, when to do homework.

On the table, my phone buzzes. Cake and I look at it, and then at each other.

She says, "Throw her a bone and answer it."

I feel a surge of defeat. "I was going to try to go the whole day."

*Meep—meep,* says my phone.

Cake shakes her head. "No, baby steps. It's been four hours since the fight. You have to answer it."

*Meep—meep.*

I sigh. My mouth is practically watering for the food in front of me. It's like my mom won't even let me *eat.*

"You do it. You check and tell me what she's saying."

Cake frowns and peers at the phone. Her expression goes from resigned to curious to . . . horrified. Her mouth drops open.

"Oh my God, what is it?" I ask. "Is it that bad?" My stomach starts to squeeze.

Cake takes a deep breath. "Tiger. It's . . . she . . ."

She flips the phone in my direction. "She bought you a dress. For the dance."

My mother bought me a *dress.*

I stare at the photo. At a dress draped over the back of our couch.

It's a monstrosity. It's a cross between Laura Ingalls in *Little House on the Prairie* and Isabel Archer in *Portrait of a Lady.* Ivory and lace, a high neck, and a sash.

A goddamn *sash.*

My mom's text reads, *It's so beautiful! I couldn't resist! Don't hate me!*

Cake says, "If we splattered it, and you, with cherry food coloring and then dumped a bunch of crushed watermelon on you, you *could* be a cool nineteenth-century zombie in that dress for Halloween, but for just going to a school dance? This is a *hard* no."

Two girls next to us lean over. "Oh my God, what is *that*?"

One says, "Gross. Are you actually going to let that touch your body? It's like a thousand years old."

"No!" I angle the phone away from them.

She didn't even *ask.* We didn't even *talk* about it. I don't even understand how we went from fighting about a dance to her *buying* a dress for the dance.

The phone starts ringing. I feel so angry it's kind of like I almost feel nothing, like I'm floating on a river of fire but I can't feel it. My stomach hurts from hunger so much I'm dizzy.

I swipe the answer button.

My mom's voice is very, very loud, and yet, to me, it sounds like she's calling from very far away, that's how angry I am. I'm embarrassed and alone on a little island.

The kids around us are watching me curiously, waiting.

Breathlessly, my mom says, "Thank you for finally answering! Listen, I'm sorry, but it's so beautiful, Tiger! It really spoke to me. You'll look so lovely and authentic at the dance, not all glossed up and plastic-y. And if we put your hair up—"

"I can't believe you did this to me." My voice trembles with anger. I can't help it.

Cake shakes her head at me, like, *No, no, not now.*

"What? Wait, *what*? Honey. I was just trying to—"

"You can't let me do *one* thing by myself. I can't do anything without . . . without you getting your fingers in it. Not even picking out my own stupid dress for a stupid dance."

Silence. Then her voice again, still loud, but a little cracked. "Baby, listen, it was just my way of saying I'm sor—"

*"Why can't you ever just fucking leave me alone?"*

It comes out too loud. Maybe even louder than too loud, because it hurts even *my* ears, and it hurts me somewhere deep inside, too. In fact, I think I screamed it.

My mother's voice says softly, "Grace."

I drop the phone from my trembling hands. The kids in the cafeteria have gone eerily silent and are staring at me.

Cake bites her lip. "Tiger. That was . . . not good."

I scrape the phone into my backpack and stand up, hitting

26

my hip against the table. I keep my eyes down. I don't want to look at anyone. I just want to get out of here.

"Wait," Cake says. "You're not okay. I'll come with." She gathers our lunch baggies.

"I have to go," I tell her. "I just have to get out of here. I'll see you later."

I rush out of the cafeteria with my head down, like I always do around here, hoping no one will notice weird June Tolliver's weird daughter.

And then I find the bathroom and cry in a stall until fifth period starts.

My phone doesn't ring again.


I work my library shift after school, part of my student contract, which is something they make certain kids at Field do if they don't have the most stellar grades. I think it's supposed to make you feel more invested in your education or something, having to work in the office answering phones, or in Shop, cleaning up wood shavings and making sure your fellow students don't sever an arm on a saw.

I'd like nothing more than to rush through this and get to The Pit and see Kai, but I don't, because I do like it here, sorting the collection, pushing the squeaky cart up and down the stacks. We have some books here that are so ancient they still have those little cards where the librarian hand-wrote the name of the person checking the book out and then ink-stamped the due date. The books even have slots to fit the cards, which I think is very cool. I like sliding the cards out and looking at the names and dates and thinking stuff like, *Well, whoever Tammy Frimpong was, she really liked* Island of the Blue Dolphins. *She checked it out thirteen times in one year.*

I'm not very smart at school, but I do like books, and reading, and maybe I get that from my mom, since she was a librarian before she had me. She was the special kind, though: an archivist, which is a person who figured out the history of things from old stuff found in boxes. She worked six floors underground at a university in Albuquerque, fitting spare pieces into stories. "You might see just a postcard, a photo, and a matchbook from a bar," she told me once. "But if I put those things together and do some research, I could find a love affair between famous writers, or political intrigue."

My mom was good at putting the stories of strangers together, even as she was refusing to tell me any details about hers.

Like the identity of my dad: The Person Who Shall Not Be Named. The person I think about all the time.

Like when I fix my hair in the morning and she comes into the bathroom and stands behind me, resting her chin on top of my head and smooshing up her short blond hair in the mirror, and there *I* am, pulling a brush through my boring, straight hair, so different from hers. Or the freckles that careen across my face, while her face is an unmarked sea of perfection. Does my dad have a planetary system of freckles across his face, too? Is he where I get my dark hair, my broad shoulders?

I think Monty Python and old stand-up comedy from the seventies is funny, and my mother thinks both of those things are tiresome and misogynistic, and yeah, I agree, but also, still *funny.*

If The Person Who Shall Not Be Named was shown a clip of

"Confuse-A-Cat" or had to sit through George Carlin's "Seven Dirty Words" monologue, would he laugh? Is a sense of humor a viable component of DNA? How about avocados and kiwis? One I like, the other I despise.

These are the things that often consume me as I stroll the stacks at the library.

That and kissing Kai Henderson, of course.

Cake texts me. *Are you okay?*

*Not really. Yes. No.*

*That sounds about right. I looked for you!*

*I was in the stall.*

*Ah, the crying stall. Where tears are shed in silence and shame.*

*That's the one. Tell me again about the kissing thing. Distract me. I think it might happen later.*

*NO.*

*YES. I mean, what do I have to lose now?*

*True,* says Cake's phone.

*Hold on. Let me take a break.* Cake has band in the afternoons. I can hear them, way, way across the school, an eerie cacophony of stumbling horns and tubas, interspersed with the occasional tinkling of a triangle.

I text, *We're meeting at The Pit. Thunder after. That's when it will happen. I think.*

*Plush.* That's the same word she used a few weeks ago, as she leaned back into the velvety pillows on her futon, holding her pink stuffed unicorn against her shirt. She'd put a black spiked collar around the unicorn's neck, Magic-Markered a heart on its fluffy white chest.

Cake's eyes turned dreamy as she thought about it, and then became a little sad, because she was still getting over that guy

Troy, from Sierra Vista. Troy was not, as Cake's mom Rhonda liked to say, "a gem."

*I don't know what to do with my hands,* I type.

*It'll be okay,* she answers. *Just remember to breathe, and to relax, because kissing is a fun and essential part of your adolescent development.*

*Ha ha.*

*It'll be a whole new you after this. You'll want to kiss everyone. Even Laizure!*

*That's gross and also illegal.*

*It's plush. You just fit, somehow. It's warm, and you feel like you're falling, but in a good way. Your body kind of figures things out for you. Don't worry.*

Last year, my mother took me and Cake to the dollar theater in Tucson to see a movie about a girl and boy who both have cancer. They go to Amsterdam to see a famous writer, but they really go to Amsterdam to have sex. Afterward, my mother took us to Bookmans, which is this huge and great used-book store, and I bought three books for less than ten dollars, which is a lot for us, and one of them was the book they based the movie on. We went for carrot cake and coffee after, and my mother said, "Girls, you don't have to go to a whole other country to have sex. Just do it on the couch when your parents go out for groceries, okay? And use protection."

I blushed, and I think Cake might have, too, even though she'd already had sex, though I'm not sure my mother knew about that and I wasn't going to tell her, because if I did, then she'd be all "Are *you* going to have sex?" And I'd never hear the end of it.

I read the book when we got home, all at once, in three hours. I cried. Even though they were both hurt, and sick, in the same, and different, ways, the boy and the girl seemed nice and tender to each other, and I liked that.

To this day, when Cake and I see a cute guy, one of us will joke, "I'd go to Amsterdam with him."

*Okay,* I type. I am definitely not ready for Amsterdam with Kai, but *plush* might be a nice place to start.

*Okay. I have to go back. We're butchering "Rolling in the Deep" right now. Can you tell?*

I smile. *A little. It sounds cool, though.*

*Text me right after you get home!*

I slide some books onto the shelf, my heart beating as deeply as the timpani across the school as they barrel through Adele's song.

My mom is not going to be happy about the mean thing I said, or that I'm ignoring her texts, or that I'm planning to come home late, without even checking in, but I need some space to breathe. And to kiss. I hope.

T HE LATE AFTERNOON IS my favorite time in Mesa Luna. It's when the sky starts ever so gently changing its colors, shifting into the prettiest thing I think I'll ever see in the world. Here, the world around me is messily alive. You haven't seen a sky until you've seen our moon hanging at night. It's how we got our name, in fact. A couple of miles out of town proper, there's a flat mesa, and if you're driving, or just out and about walking, on the right night, it looks like the moon is resting on the edge of the mesa, like a white plate on its rim on a table. Our big, white, beautiful moon hangs so low in the sky it's like you could reach out and touch it.

It's not nighttime yet, though. The day is still bright and hot and dusty enough when I get to The Pit, which is what we call Grunyon's emptied pool and the three home-built half-pipes on the land behind his house. His parents, Louise and Mary, run a coffee shop/diner/bookstore in a series of interconnected Airstreams on the property, which is probably highly illegal, but no one cares, because *coffee*.

There's an old eight-room motel there, too, that I think Louise and Mary are hoping to fix up someday, though I'm not sure who would want to stay in Mesa Luna. Tucson is better and not too far, and Sierra Vista has the Golden Corral buffet. We've got the moon, though, and The Pit, where I like to hang out and watch the skaters.

Grunyon and Boots and Chunk aren't at Eugene Field anymore. Boots and Chunk didn't graduate, but Grunyon did. They're trying to start a moving company called We Haul All. In the meantime, they skate and get high.

I bury my phone in my backpack. I *did* take a peek while I walked here: two missed calls, two texts, but I'm determined not to respond for a good couple of hours.

Grunyon pops up over the lip of the pool, blond curls springing from beneath his helmet. "Is today the day, Tiger T? You coming in? Or are you gonna spend another day buried in a book?"

Perched on a rock, I watch skaters rise and fall behind him, a smooth and beautiful wave of bodies. Even the sound of wheels on old pool plaster is cool: a little scrapey, a little promising. Grunyon sinks back down, disappears, pops back up.

"Well?" he says, grinning.

"Not today," I say with a shrug, like I always do.

Grunyon sighs. He's teetering on the lip of The Pit, bucking his board a little to stay up and not slip back down. "It's been years, T. That old arm is for sure healed by now."

Four years ago, my mother had a boyfriend named Andy. Andy was skinny and funny and I thought things I never should have thought, like *whole family* and *dad.* He bought me a skateboard and brought me here and my mom was weirdly okay with it for a while. It's like maybe she was playing *whole family* and *dad,* too.

I don't really like thinking about Andy, and what happened, and how he left.

I've never forgotten how free I felt, those moments I was lost in the air, before my board smacked down on plaster again. Before the very last time, when I landed and my arm shattered.

Lightly, I tell Grunyon, "Books are good. I can live life safely and without peril in a fictional universe."

"I think your boyfriend's here." Grunyon tips his head. "I'll get you back in this pool someday, Tiger Tolliver."

My heart does a little jump as Kai sits down next to me. "Hey," he says, shading his eyes from the sun. "I've got bizcochitos. You wanna walk to Thunder and hang out?"

I think I might see the tiniest hint of a blush creeping up his neck.

I think I might feel the tiniest hint of a blush creeping up mine.

I push my book in my backpack. "I'll go anywhere for cookies. You know me."

KISSING KAI HENDERSON IS exactly like Cake said it would be.

Plush.

Kai Henderson and I have been kissing for at least one billion hours under the white and perfect stars of Mesa Luna, leaning against the tentacled beast of a playground structure we all call the Command Center. It sits right smack in the middle of Thunder Park Elementary and has tube slides shooting out in eight different directions and a kind of high gazebo in the middle that you can hide in. Cake and I used to like to huddle up there together and tell each other stories while the other kids ran around at recess.

It took a little bit, and he was more awkward and shy than I would have liked, but I finally just kind of did it myself, because I remembered some girls in the bathroom at Field this one time, huddled up against the sinks winging their eyes with liner, asking each other why girls always wait for guys to kiss them first, to make the first move. And one girl, I think her name was Bettina, gave a sharp laugh and said, "'Cuz if a girl moves first, she's a horny sluuuuuuuut," and the way she dragged it out made the other girls laugh. One girl sighed, "Yeah, but if the dude goes first, he's all that, right?"

Maybe there was a dance that night, or a party somewhere, because another girl said, "Fuck that. Ima go get it myself tonight, am I right?" And they all fived down low, by their butts, and bumped hips. They weren't that much older than me, but they seemed so much more comfortable in their bodies.

I thought of those girls as Kai kind of weaved back and forth in front of me, his hands shoved way down in his jean pockets, and I got a little mad at him, and myself, for always waiting for other people to start doing the thing I want to be doing, like I have to ask permission, so I took matters into my own hands.

I did blurt out, "Can I kiss you?" to be on the safe side, and when I saw his face slide into relief, and start to lean down to mine, well, welcome to Plush Life.

I went out and got it myself.

His lips tasted like sugar from the cookies, which seemed perfect, and the way a first kiss, and all the kisses after, should taste. I've figured out where to put my hands, how to press against him slightly, how to breathe, all of it.

I never want to open my eyes again or come up for air. I want to spend the whole summer kissing him. Here, at Thunder Park Elementary.

There are things happening inside me that I don't even have words for, and I usually have words for everything, even if I don't say them out loud.

A shiver suddenly breaks us apart. A sharp chill rushes through me, when just a second ago, I was warmer than I'd ever been. My teeth start chattering.

Kai breathes heavily, his eyes unfocused. "What's wrong?" he asks. "You okay?"

"Fine, I guess. Cold. Weird." I wrap my arms around myself, but it feels odd, not so much cold, after all, as . . . well, weird.

The next shiver runs through me so hard it knocks the breath out of me.

I gasp. "Whoa," Kai says. He steadies my shoulders, his eyes crinkling in concern. "What was that?"

I try to catch my breath. "I don't know," I say, wheezing. "Maybe I should go home."

Maybe it *is* time to go home and make up with my mother. It's been all day and most of the night, after all. I mean, I'm not wearing that dress, ever, but *still*.

I lean down and paw through my backpack for my phone. Four missed calls from my mom, the last one just as we were starting to walk here from The Pit. Two calls from Cake, which is weird, since she usually texts. She didn't leave messages, which, also weird.

I listen as my mom's phone rings and rings. Finally, her voice mail picks up. "June here! Tell me something good, or don't say anything at all."

"Hi, Mom." I take a breath. "I'm sorry. I am. I'll be home soon, and you can yell at me all you want, okay?" I slip my phone into my backpack. Done. I've had my freedom. We can go back to our beeping, whirring machine now.

Kai's phone buzzes. It's been sounding on and off since we got here, but he's been ignoring it. He takes off the flannel shirt he's wearing over a T-shirt and wraps it around me. "Here. Just in case."

He kisses me gently, then pulls the phone from his back pocket.

I turn away, touching my lips with my fingers. I can still feel the heat of his lips on mine. I feel like people do in old books, you know, like when the writer says, "She was stirred by his actions," or some such thing.

I feel stirred by Kai Henderson. Plush and Stirred. That sounds like the name of a Victoria's Secret panty line or something. I make a note to mention that to Cake; she'll think it's funny.

I blow into my hands. It shouldn't be this cold in Mesa Luna in May. Maybe I'm getting sick. Maybe that means Kai will get sick, too, and we can lie around together, huddled under blankets, reading magazines, snuffling together, only I don't know where we'd do that, since my mom is so difficult—

Behind me, Kai makes a weird sound, like someone's punched him in the gut.

I turn.

His face isn't like it usually is, open and goofy and smiling, all Kai-like, glasses slipping down his nose, hair in his eyes.

His face looks like he's seen a ghost, or been told a terrible secret.

He says my name, and then he says three awful, horrible words that cut through me, make me cry out.

I beat his chest as hard as I can, until my fists start to ache, but I can't stop making him say those words.

I don't understand how he can say such cruel words to me, after what we were just doing, after all the plush-ness of us.

Out in the desert, the coyotes start up, one by one, howling and wailing, lonely in the dark, and they do not stop. They don't stop.

They never stop.

After

THE WOMAN ON THE bed in the hospital in Tucson is not my mother.

The brightness of the room stings my eyes. There are things hooked up to the person in the bed, the person who is not my mother. Things like tubes, and wires. Things you'd attach to a mechanical entity, a robotic experiment. *Not* a human being.

There are monitors and shiny lights and I feel like I should be hearing beeps or clicks, see crawling red lines across screens, just like you do on television or in the movies when you know there's still a chance a person can be saved. In the movies, some-one jumps on the hospital bed and starts pumping the dying person's chest, people shout, metal bins clang, there's a flurry of noise, and then *bam.* A red line slinks across the monitor.

But in *this* room, no one moves. Everyone is silent. Even me, because I cannot breathe.

One hour ago I kissed Kai Henderson in the playground at Thunder Park Elementary School and his lips tasted sweet from the sugary bizcochitos we'd shared.

One hour ago my very first kiss felt *plush,* just like Cake said it would.

But that's all gone now, every sugary and plush second sto-len. *Poof.*

Cake's mother, Rhonda, grips my hand so hard I think it might break, but I don't care. She can break all my bones if she wants. The pain feels good, because there are tsunamis of things happening inside me that I don't understand.

Finally, the young doctor in the baggy pants clears his throat. When my eyes meet his, he looks away.

I think I know what he wants me to say but the words seem too unbelievable. The words don't make *sense*.

I can't breathe. I feel like my chest is caving in.

The young doctor says, "I'm sorry. We tri——"

The rest of his words slice in and out of my brain, fragments of sound.

*But she was already.*

*It happens so.*

*Really isn't anything.*

*No predicting something like.*

Half-digested bizcochitos splatter down my T-shirt. The doctor winces. A nurse rushes over with a towel, patting my chest.

My chin is dripping. I don't care.

Someone hands me a scrub shirt. Without thinking, I drag it on over my vomit-stained T-shirt. Everyone looks uncomfortable, and I realize I was supposed to go into the bathroom and change out of the barf shirt and into the scrub shirt maybe, but no one tells me what I've done is wrong.

*This* is wrong. *This* doesn't just happen.

Someone comes with a bucket and slaps a wet mop across the floor.

The young doctor walks into the bathroom and closes the door. The nurse says hesitantly, "I'm so sorry. It's his first . . ." She turns her palms up.

I say, in a voice I don't recognize as my own, because it's something scratchy, and ghostly, and broken, "Mine too."

Cake's mom starts bawling, which makes me mad. *I* should be bawling, not the adult. The doctor comes back out of the bathroom, his face pale and resigned. He gives me a look. The body on the table isn't my mother, but he needs me to say it is. All of them do.

And I hate them all for trying to make me say it.

For wanting me to say it so they can move on, and save people who can be saved, while I can never move on, not *now*, and she will never, ever, ever be saved.

My eyes water. My eyes turn into lakes of water, but still I don't make a sound. I'm like that person on the bed in front of me: a machine, an automaton.

Finally, I whisper to the room, in my new and ghostly voice, "This isn't happening."

Cake's mom, Rhonda, murmurs, "Oh, Tiger." Wipes her face. Nudges me forward.

I let go of her hand and step closer to the body on the table. The woman smells clinical. Medicinal. Like sanitizer or something. She has the same spiky blond-and-silver hair as my mother, but it's flattened on one side, and there's a welt on her cheek, like she fell and hit something.

*My* mother smells good, like the oatmeal soap she uses in the shower. Like patchouli. Like the cinnamon she sprinkles in her morning coffee.

*This* person is different. This person died alone and has bruises, and must have been so, so frightened at what was happening, and she was alone when it happened, and I would never, never, never, not in a million years, have left my mother to die alone.

That's the sort of thing a bad daughter would do.

I open my mouth to tell them this, all of them, the youngish doctor with the stubbly face, the nurse with the rubber duckies on her shirt, Rhonda with her eye makeup smeared from crying, just like mine is smeared from crying.

I open my mouth to say: *That is not my mom. My mom is June the Strong. My mom drives the book bus, and makes jams and jellies from chiles and cactus, and read every single one of the Harry Potters out loud to me, long after every other kid's parent had given up, because those books were* long, *right? But my mom used to be a librarian, and she loved me, you see, she always said she would never lea——*

What comes out of my mouth is not those words. What comes out of my mouth is garbled and croaky, because I screamed so hard at Kai under the blazing stars at Thunder Park Elementary when he wouldn't stop saying those horrible three words to me that my throat is raw and swollen.

*Your mom. Died.*

Just like that. A pause between word number two and word number three.

The word I try to say, the word that chokes out of me, is *No.*

The nurse with the duckies on her shirt puts her hand on my arm.

I don't understand what's happening. Your mom can't be alive one minute and then the next . . . not.

Those things, I'm like those things you use to stoke a fire, what people used to use, those things with handles that kind of look like water bottles. *Bellows.*

My chest heaves up and down, like a bellows.

I want my mom to get up off that fucking table and hug me as hard as she can, even if it hurts me.

She doesn't.

44

"Mom," I say. "Mommy, *please.*"

I push her shoulder. The shoulder flops back, scaring me.

"Is that supposed to happen?" I whisper. No one answers me.

The nurse beside me says, "Honey."

"Don't say that," I bark, scaring myself even more. "That's something a mom says. And my mom is *there,* and you are *here.*"

The nurse takes her hand off my arm.

Behind me, Rhonda takes a giant breath. "Yes," she says desperately. "This is June Frances Tolliver and she lived at 344 Morales Road."

Lived. Not *lives.*

My mother is past tense. A kind of cement fog settles over me. I can feel everyone in the room start to breathe again, a giant wave of relief.

There's a great flurry of activity then, with nurses and attendants suddenly appearing and the doctor murmuring on his phone and no one remembers me. No one asks me anything else.

I turn and walk back into the waiting room in a daze.

Cake is waiting with two chocolate bars and a cup of soda. She must have gone to the vending machine. She's been crying, so there are black eyeliner streaks through her pale makeup, like tire tracks. Her Princess Leia buns are mussed, strands of purple hair clinging to her black sweater. Her dad's in the corner, talking with a frizzy-haired woman who seems very interested in me, taking notes on a clipboard, looking me up and down. She seems familiar to me somehow, and then I suddenly remember her, from when I first got here, and everything was blurry and there was so much talking, and moving around, and she'd asked me, a total stranger, "Where's your dad, dear? Is he here?"

I say, in my new hoarse voice, "Where's Kai?"

Cake answers softly. "He left."

I say, "He left?"

She nods. "He left."

"He just *left*?"

Cake's face scrunches up. "Stop saying that. It's freaking me out."

But I don't know what else to say.

Kai Henderson and his sweet, sugary mouth is gone. He drove me here in his mother's gray car with the comfortable seats. The seats in my mother's car are held together with duct tape. The seats in Kai's car are velvety and unripped.

I cried and he drove fast, mumbling under his breath.

He'd been the one to take the phone call.

*Your mom. Died.*

And now he's gone.

I touch my lips. The kisses disappearing, one by one, as though I dreamed them.

Cake turns and hugs her mother. The frizzy-haired woman pats Cake's dad's arm. His face is crumpled.

I'm alone. Everyone here has someone but me, because the only person I had is flat on her back in Room 142 across the hall from me, and she is no longer herself.

Somewhere far, far away, I hear a person crying. Nurses push wheelchairs, phones ring, things beep, and the intercom is noisy with words I don't understand. The whole world is a new language to me now.

It takes me a long time to realize the person crying is me, and no one has noticed.

## 11:04 p.m.

THE FRIZZY-HAIRED WOMAN AT the hospital who keeps asking Cake's dad all the questions is a social worker. Her name is Karen and I *so* cannot believe what she is telling me that she repeats it, twice.

"You'll have to come with me, Grace. I'm sorry, but since you don't have another relative to care for you while all this is sorted out, you'll be placed in an emergency foster."

Emergency. Foster.

I have no idea what she's talking about.

The only thing I can think to say is, "Tiger," and the frizzy-haired woman says, "What?" And I say, flatly, "My name is Tiger," because I bit a boy named Jaime Suarez at daycare for that name, and damned if I'm going to lose that now, too.

I bit a boy named Jaime Suarez because his nose was always running, and he was always crying, and my mother, who worked at Bonita's daycare, was always the one he ran to, clinging to her leg until she'd pick him up, wipe his nose, and sing to him. Something sad and pretty. She liked dreamy, folksy songs from the seventies. That day, she sang him a song called "Sam Stone," which is really about a dad who shoots heroin, but it sounds nice and kind of soothing when you're four, and not sad and tragic, like it does if you're older, and Jaime positively *sank* into my mother's body, and I exploded in jealousy and *sank* my teeth into his bare leg.

My mother was all I had. Other kids had dads. Aunties, uncles, grandparents, cousins. Sisters. Brothers. Even *stepparents*. All *my* life, it's just been us. No dad to plop me on his shoulders or cuff me on the head like the dads who picked up their kids at the daycare. I had a vague, mythical presence. I had: The Person Who Shall Not Be Named.

And I'd be damned if Jaime Suarez was going to take *my* mother from me.

Bonita had tugged me away, clucking her tongue. Mom iced Jaime's leg while he wailed. Bonita said, "Goodness, you're a little tiger for your mama's love, aren't you, Gracie?" And from then on, Tiger it was. All the little kids at daycare started calling me that, and it stuck.

Emergency *what*?

"Tiger," I say, louder, to the frizzy-haired woman. "And you can't . . . you can't just *take* me." I mean, *where*?

I live at 344 Morales Road, in a little peach-painted adobe with mammoth sunflowers draping the creaky backyard fence. I live with my mother, June, and it's just us, and it isn't perfect, but it's ours, and I want to yell, *You can't have me, I belong to her!*

But her isn't *her* anymore.

My heart, it turns black. A cold, wet chill falls over my body.

Everything, all the sounds in the hospital, the clicks and beeps and squeaky gurney wheels, get very echoey all of a sudden.

"I'm drowning," I say. The social worker doesn't bat an eye, but Cake's dad looks alarmed.

"Maybe we should get her something. A muscle relaxant. Something." He looks around for a nurse.

Cake starts to cry. "You can't just take her. She's like my *sister.*"

Her mom, Rhonda, spits, "This is ridiculous. This child's mother has *died,* and she should be with *us.*"

"I won't let you take her," Cake sobs again. She holds my hand tightly.

"I don't want to go with you," I say to the lady, my voice breaking. "Please. Just let me go with them." My heart surges at the thought of Cake's comfortable, weird house with all its record albums and ferns and iguanas in aquariums and old rock concert posters framed and hung on the walls.

My little house at 344 Morales Road will be empty now, and cold. A shell. And wherever this woman wants to send me, who knows what's *there*? What does that even mean, *emergency foster*?

Cake's dad murmurs, "Girls, please."

I am cold, I am hot, I am every possible feeling and temperature you can have at once. All I know about *foster* care is from movies and books, and it never ends well. They make you cook drugs and beat you and keep you in closets.

I think I might throw up again.

Karen the frizzy-haired social worker must have seen all this before, though, because she doesn't freak out or anything. She just says, "I understand this is a lot to take in, and we're all very, very upset, but this is going to happen, and I need everyone to calm down and understand that, okay?"

Rhonda sputters, "What are you going to do, call the police if we refuse to let you take her?"

Karen looks at Rhonda and says, "I will do that. I *have* done that. Is that what you want?" Her voice is sharp.

She looks around at each of us, then, like a teacher in elementary school making sure we all know the rules of the game before we start to play.

No one says anything.

"All right, then," she says firmly, taking Rhonda aside for some whispering. She even hugs her.

"This is surreal," sniffles Cake. "I mean, I cannot believe this is happening."

I say, "You and me both, sister."

Cake stares at me. "How can you make a joke right now?"

"I'm not joking," I answer. "I really can't believe this is happening, either. I'm so freaked out I can't even feel anything anymore. Look."

I push up the sleeve of the scrub shirt and pinch my forearm hard for as long as I can before Cake swats my fingers away. "Don't do that," she warns. "That's not good."

"I didn't even feel it," I tell her.

We both stare at the purpling skin of my arm. There are girls at Eugene Field who do far worse, and way more often, but no one likes to talk about it.

"Don't start that shit, okay?" Cake says.

She swipes at her wet face. "I will seriously kill you if you start that." She claps a hand across her mouth. "I'm sorry," she says, her voice muffled inside her palm.

"It's okay," I tell her.

I make a mental note that people are probably going to be afraid to use certain words around me now, like: *dead, death, dying, kill,* and *killing.* Maybe *morbid* and *mortal,* too.

It could turn out to be a long list.

"I have to pee," Cake says. "Do you want to come with me?"

"I'm just going to sit," I say. "Over there." I point at the long row of gray chairs underneath the window. On the wall, the clock says 11:04 p.m. I pull out my phone and text that time to myself. This morning I had one life, and now it's night, and I have another, and I want to record the very minute everything went to hell.

What time was I kissing Kai Henderson and what time, in that time, did my mother's brain betray her, and me? *A brain aneurysm.* Sub-something, the doctor had said, but I couldn't really hear, because my heart was exploding.

The doctor had used words like *rupture* and *instantaneous.*

My legs feel like cement, walking to the chairs. Will I always feel this way when I walk from now on, like something heavy? Rhonda is filling out papers at the nurses' station. That woman, Karen, is on her phone.

I'm facing the door to the room where my mother is, the body they *said* was my mother. Is she still in there, or did they move her already, and I missed it?

The last thing I ever said to my mother was a terrible, horrible thing.

The last thing I said to my mom was "Why can't you ever just fucking leave me alone?"

And then it hits me, hard, that she's done precisely that, and forever, really really forever, and suddenly I'm crying, great gushing waves that hurt my ribs and blur my eyes.

Only a bad daughter would say something like that to her mom.

I get up and run down the hall. I have to get away from them, all of them, even Cake.

In an alcove, I find a kind of niche between tall carts filled with plastic tubs and supplies, like cotton balls and swabs and gauze and bottles and jugs of strange liquids. I fit myself between two of the carts and cry. At first, I'm embarrassed, but after a little while, I realize that if anyone comes by, like a nurse or a doctor, they'll think nothing of it. Hospitals are filled to the gills with teary people, after all. I'm not any different.

I need my mother to come get me, to save me from the fact that my mother is dead.

I start to laugh, because that's terrible, and awful, and all my bones are shattering inside me and it feels like being stabbed from the inside out.

*My mother is dead, dead, dead.*

I'm a splitting atom, a human fissure, things I don't even have names for leaking out. Shit I should have studied in school, but didn't.

I can't feel my body, I can't feel my heart, I'm rising out of myself, watching as I separate into *the girl before* and *the girl after.*

"This can't be happening, this can't be happening, this can't be happening."

I'm whispering it, over and over and over, even as I know it *is* happening. Truly and definitely and terribly.

Down the hall, Karen is a watery, slow-motion vision, moving toward me with purpose and vigor, her frizzy hair lit from behind by the fluorescent ceiling lights. She's coming to rip me from one life to the next and I'm frozen in place.

I'm a girl-bug now, trapped in glass, watching everything on mute.

ONE MORNING, YOU WAKE up in the backseat of a small white car, surrounded by empty soda cans and crumpled plastic bags and all the other dirty shit that never gets cleaned out of the backseat of a car. Straw wrappers. Sticky old bags of fruit gummies. Flip-flops. Scrunched tissues. Single winter mittens and Styrofoam coffee cups and movie tickets from months ago. How did the movie tickets end up there? Slipped from a pocket. Fallen from a wallet.

You're on your side in the duct-taped backseat, cheek stuck to the vinyl, staring down at those movie tickets. Three little stained stubs amid a heap of trash.

You finger them. They're gummy from the last dregs of coffee that dripped from some Styrofoam cups. Things flip in your brain, like a movie reel: the Amsterdam teenage sex movie.

Why does remembering this stab you so hard? Why?

Through the window, the sun hits your face like a hot rock. You blink and wonder where you are, why you are in the backseat of this car, cheek plastered to vinyl, and then the world splits open again, wider than you ever thought it could, sucking your breath away.

Now you remember, now you know, now you know *everything*, like why the movie memory stabbed so much.

Your mother is dead.

You get out of the car and the sun hurts and the ground hurts and even the stupid air hurts.

You feel skinned. Like whatever held you together has been peeled away. You half expect to look down and see your heart hanging out, a slow-beating, nearly dead thing.

Your legs wobble and your mouth tastes dry and your mother is dead. They were all staring at you, in that too-bright room, silently willing you to say that the person on the table was your mother and she was dead so they could move on with their lives, while yours had just been stopped short.

You were kissing a boy when your mother's brain exploded.

It's very early and yet it's already so hot. The summer is going to be so brutal, you can tell already. Your body feels light, which is weird, because last night you felt as heavy as wet cement.

If you looked at yourself in a mirror right now, could you see pieces of bone close to the surface? Is this how it will feel every day from now on?

That you're walking around with barely any skin, your bones and heart open to everyone, now that your mother is dead?

Bits of the night before, just hours ago really, seep back into your skin. The frizzy-haired woman telling you she was taking you somewhere. Cake cried, and she grabbed onto you, and wouldn't let go, and finally the woman relented, and made Cake's mom and dad sign a piece of paper, and she had a nurse photocopy their driver's licenses, and said you could come here, and pack a suitcase.

"Just one, though," she told you sternly. "You can't take a lot of things. We won't know your permanent residence for quite some time. We've a lot to sort out."

You are to be, as the woman put it, "remanded to the custody of the State of Arizona by one p.m."

You slept in the car because the house was too empty and too full all at once. Her things were everywhere, bits of her in everything: the washcloth hanging from the shower faucet, the oatmeal soap in a brown, gritty puddle at the side of the sink. Everywhere you went, there she was, but she *wasn't,* and it was too much, and so you went to the car, a tiny, tight space that seemed somehow better.

Your friend Cake is still inside the house. She'd gone to bed with you, but you got up after you heard her start to snore. You were more tired than you'd ever been in your life, but you could not sleep in that bed, in that house, at that moment. You practically ran out to the car, avoiding the couch, where you think *it* must have happened.

Above you, doves shuffle in the cottonwood tree.

What was her name, the frizzy-haired woman?

Cathy? Kara? Karen.

Her name was Karen.

She's in charge of your life now. A total stranger. Your stomach coils in knots. You try to walk, to move, maybe even to run, but to where? To whom?

You can't move. Is this how it will be? Will even lifting a leg require great effort, and cause so much pain, all at once?

The blue door to your house opens and your heart quickens; maybe it was a lie, a stupid bad dream, and your mother will appear, blinking in the harsh morning light, a hand shading her face.

"Hey, you, what are you doing out here, talking to the doves? Come in and have breakfast, silly."

That's a thing your mother would say.

But it isn't your mother who opens the blue door.

It's Cake. She looks like a sad panda, her black eyeliner smudged in half-moons under her eyes. Her black cotton skirt is wrinkled.

She puts your pink suitcase at your feet. Her voice is soft.

"I packed you some stuff," she says.

"I was in the car," you answer. Your voice sounds muted. Girl-bug behind glass. Can Cake see you, trapped in there? Scratching your wings against the glass.

"I know. I came out earlier when I couldn't find you, but I didn't want to wake you up. I cleaned up a little inside. I couldn't get back to sleep."

Your friend looks so frightened. You think she is a little afraid of you now.

You think this might be the case. That you will scare people now.

Your friend says, "My mom's coming back soon. She's bringing coffee. Are you hungry? I think she's bringing muffins, too."

Your friend bites her lip. "Maybe you should change clothes," she tells you. "Before we go to that place."

You look down at the scrub shirt. Beneath it, your T-shirt is caked with vomit.

In the driveway of the small house where you have lived since the day you were born, you pull the scrub shirt off. You pull off the barf shirt.

Some of the dried-up vomit falls in flakes and chunks to the ground.

Cake says, "Tiger, hey, no," but you don't stop, you don't care that you're standing in front of your house in your giant bra that holds your giant boobs, the ones that Cake says aren't as big as you think they are, the ones your mom says will feed babies someday. She always adds, *If you so choose, that is.*

You kick the shirts into the dirt, pull down the too-long hippie skirt and kick that into the dirt, too. Your underwear is loose; the elastic is broken. You meant to tell your mom you needed some new ones, but you were waiting until the last minute. She'd find a sale, or scour Ted's Threads for a two-dollar package of unopened women's underwear. If the size was too big, she'd just say, "We'll wash them in hot, and shrink them!" If the size was too small, she was an expert at washing them in cold water, and then stretching them out by hand, and pinning them up on the line in the backyard to dry. You didn't like that, though. It made the underwear stiff and flat, like an unseemly cotton cracker.

*"Granny panties,"* Lupe Hidalgo liked to whisper in PE as you tried to change out of your clothes and into the red-and-white shorts as quickly as possible.

Cake's face is so scared. You push past her, into the small house, close your eyes as you pass by the couch, where you think *it* happened, open your eyes when you reach your bedroom. You know what you're looking for and where it is. Your mother treated clothes she loved well. She never just threw them on the ground.

It's there, just like you thought, hanging in the closet, carefully wrapped in a zippered bag. She'd been so excited for you to wear it to the dance and you'd hated it and yelled at her. And then she died.

Ivory-colored, pearl buttons down the front, high lace collar, and the goddamn sash. On the phone she was so happy about the dress. "You'll look so lovely and authentic at the dance, not all glossed up and plastic-y."

But the thing was, after years of wearing clothes from dirty boxes on the side of the road, you *wanted* plastic and gloss. You thought you should have had a chance at plastic and gloss, and shopping for a brand-new dress at Park Mall in Tucson, in one of those cute stores with blaring music and pouty girls behind the register, and kissing a cute and nice boy, even. All of it.

You will never forget the hurt in your mother's voice after you said the bad thing.

The way she said your name before you hung up on her.

In your bedroom, you pull the dress off the hanger and slip it on.

She was right. How did she know that it would fit so well? That the torso was cut to be somewhat loose, so your breasts wouldn't strain the fabric. It's billowy, and then drifts into the sash.

You will never take this dress off. It was all she wanted, for you to wear it, to look beautiful. And she didn't get to see you in it.

You hear footsteps and turn. Your friend's face is wet with tears.

She says, "Is that." No question mark.

You nod.

"Okay. If that's what you want to wear."

She blinks, considering.

She says, "Actually, it looks really good on you," and bursts into fresh tears.

She sniffles, "I swear we'll get through this."

You are silent. Whatever words you might have had left are

drifting away. Inside the glass, the girl-bug drops her eyes. She's tired now.

"I love you," Cake says.

She's crying hard. It kind of makes you angry, that she would cry. Like you should comfort *her*.

*Her* mother is driving somewhere in a nice silver car, with coffees in a cardboard tray, and warm muffins in a bag, and will arrive at any moment. And when your friend goes home to-night, and needs clean clothes, or someone to watch a movie with, someone to buy her the kind of underwear a sixteen-year-old girl would love to wear, someone to make her favorite food, which is homemade pizza with artichoke hearts and pineapple and garlic, that person will be there to do it.

*Her* mother is alive.

Your friend says, "I'm so sorry, Tiger. I'm so sorry. I'm here, Tiger. You aren't alone."

You wish you could speak, so you could tell her she's a god-damn liar.

## 16 hours, 1 minute

I T'S A TINY BUILDING with paneled walls and thick green carpeting and dusty window blinds in the lobby that clink against the glass. There's a hallway with lots of doors and faded posters with sad-looking kids. The posters say things like *A home shouldn't be hard to find* and *Fostering means family*.

It's getting late now. It was hard to get Cake's mom out of the house this morning; she lingered for a long time, looking through my mom's drawers and files, muttering, "She must have left *something*," even though Karen said we needed to be at her office by 1:00 p.m.

The loud clock on the paneled wall says 1:22 p.m.

Karen the frizzy-haired social worker is talking to another woman in the corner. Karen's not dressed in sweats and a hoodie now. She's wearing a nice beige skirt and a pink shirt with white buttons. She's holding a folder with my name on it, written in blue felt-tip pen.

*Grace "Tiger" Maria Tolliver, 12/5/2002.*

I'm a file folder now, a case, someone's *job.*

My breath comes in hiccups. Cake whispers, "It'll be okay."

"No, it won't," I tell her.

We stare at each other.

Cake drops her eyes. "You're right. I'm sorry."

Karen comes over. She does a double take at my dress.

"Pretty," she says hesitantly. "Different, that's for sure."

She says Cake and her mom can't come in, that it's time to say goodbye. Her voice is clipped, all business. She tells Rhonda, "Grace and I need to start some paperwork."

I say flatly, "Tiger. My name is *Tiger.*"

Karen nods. "That's right. My apologies, Tiger. I'm a little tired this afternoon. I know you are, too. We have a lot to do today, so I'd like to get started."

Cake's mom is still mad. She tells Karen, "This is ridiculous. I cannot believe she's going to foster care when perfectly nice people are *right here* to take care of her."

Karen gives the smallest of shrugs. She probably deals with this all the time. "I understand. I don't make policies, though. I just follow them."

Cake hugs me so hard I see spots. She smells like coffee and the banana muffins her mother brought to my house this morning. I just picked at my muffin, but Cake and her mother devoured theirs.

I try to make sure to at least seem like I'm hugging Cake and her mom, but the truth is that I really have no strength. My arms feel like licorice whips, loose and floppy, and I'm empty inside. At the hospital, people kept trying to give me candy bars and fruit chews, cardboard cups of weak tea, and I took each of those things and held them, but I didn't eat them.

The thought of eating now makes me remember that book about the little girl named Sal and her mother who went blueberry picking and ran into the bears on a hill. Every time Sal's mother dropped a blueberry into her tin pail, it made a sound like *kerplink, kerplank, kerplunk.*

I used to love it when my mother would read that book to me.

That's what it would sound like right now, if I ate. *Kerplink, kerplank, kerplunk.* Empty and hollow, because I've been carved out.

Cake and her mother leave. On the way out, Cake asks if they can stop for lunch somewhere and my heart aches; I want to go with them so much, and be normal again, and stop somewhere for salty fries and greasy burgers and sodas so cold and icy the outside of the cup sweats.

But it's just me and the social worker now.

She says, "I need some information from you, Tiger, and then we'll take you out to your foster."

My eyes swiftly fill with tears.

*Foster.*

Karen plucks some tissues from a box on the other woman's desk. "Follow me," she says, handing me a wad of pink tissues.

I've read those books in school, like Dickens, or whatever. Kids whose parents die and no one wants them. Bad things happen to them. They go to houses and the foster parents there are evil and beat them and starve them and make them rob and steal.

I follow Karen down the hallway to her office. She motions for me to sit.

She shuffles some papers on her desk and looks at me. "There's still time, Tiger, to tell me about your dad. He's not on your birth certificate, and it's okay if you're trying to protect him, but I need to know if he's out there. If you've got a blood relative, we don't have to do this, we can shut this process down now. Do you understand what I'm saying? I'm not sending you to summer camp, Tiger."

I wipe my face with the pink tissues. I never knew it was possible to cry this much, ever.

"I told you last night at the hospital, I've never met him."

"That's an awfully long time to keep a big secret like that. You were never curious? Never snooped around the house?"

Of course I'd asked my mom over the years about The Person Who Shall Not Be Named, but she always got squirrelly and shut down, and no kid wants to make their mom angry or sad, and she was all I had, so I just stopped asking.

*We are we and us is us,* my mother would say, braiding my hair, kissing the top of my head. *We don't need anybody else.*

"No," I tell her. "I love my mom. She's enough."

Is. *Was.* I will never get it right.

I push my fists against my eyes and hold my breath.

Karen says, "Easy, take it easy." She starts typing into her computer.

That's the only sound, for a long time. I rip the tissue into tiny pieces in my lap.

There's still time for this to be a mistake, for my mom, wherever she is, to wake up and start screaming in some room in that hospital, pushing aside the heavy blankets and ripping out those tubes and wires. It's happened in movies that me and Cake have watched with her Uncle Connor. He likes scary movies. It's not *implausible.*

That's another word I learned in English Lit last fall. Fusty old Mr. Hoffmeister wrote it on the board with a flourish and I copied it in my notebook, along with the other words that had jumped out at me from the books we read. *Inopportune* and *corporeal.*

Desperation licks at my skin. I try out some other words to calm myself down.

*Lapwing. Frazzled. Mezuzah.*

Karen finally looks up and says, "I have to ask these specific questions, according to policy, okay? Just say yes or no."

Her questions are rapid-fire and I'm so tired and confused I hardly have time to nod yes or no or say yes or no out loud.

"Do you have a sister, or a grandmother or grandfather, a cousin, anything? The law says you must live with a relative and that if a relative cannot be found, you'll become a ward of the state. Do you understand?"

I tell her, "My mother's parents died when she was in college. She was an only child."

I tell her, "Like I said, I don't know my dad, or where he is. My mom had a lot of secrets. She didn't tell me much."

Karen's eyes get very bright when I say that, but she tries to make her voice casual. "Like what?"

I stare at her. "She wasn't, like, a *drug* queen, if that's what you're hoping. Nothing like that. She read books and made jelly from cactus and just didn't tell me a lot of stuff, that's all."

Jars and jars and jars of her jellies and jams, neatly lined up in the shed behind our house. All for nothing now. My mother didn't cook drugs. She cooked strained prickly pears with pectin and lemon juice, that's what she cooked.

Karen blinks, like she's sizing me up. It could be sympathy, it could be suspicion, I can't tell. There must be kids who come into this office all the time with sad, awful stories, and maybe lies, too.

I say, "Don't you think it's a little crazy that I have to go live with complete strangers when adults spend a lifetime telling us kids *never* to trust strangers?"

"You're funny. Don't lose it. That'll help you."

She goes back to typing.

I go back to waiting, for what seems like hours. For what is, actually, hours, as Karen types, and gets up and goes to talk to the woman in the front office, comes back, makes phone calls from the phone on her desk, checks her cell, files papers, makes copies, takes my fingerprints, and looks through the suitcase Cake packed for me. She even gets down on her knees to take out each piece of clothing. She runs fingers all over the inside of the pink case and shakes out each piece of clothing.

"If there's anything in here I should know about, now's the time," she murmurs.

"Like *what*?"

"Dangerous objects, drugs, things like that."

I stare at her. "You got me. That tampon is really filled with weed and I'm an expert at using a mascara wand for a shiv."

She grunts. "Like I said, keep being funny. *That's* the best weapon you could have."

She folds my clothes, not very well, shuts the suitcase, and stands up, smoothing her beige skirt down and hauling a purse over her shoulder. "Let's go. I have to make a stop before we head out to your foster."

The car has a slight dent in the passenger-side door, and as I open it, Karen says, "No, dear. You have to ride in the back. Those are the rules. We're working for the state right now, not taking a joyride to the mall." She shoves my suitcase in the trunk.

There's a seal on the rear passenger door. *The State of Arizona.* A sunset logo.

I slide in. I have an excellent view of the back of Karen's neck.

I feel like I'm being arrested and that makes me feel dirty and kind of ashamed.

The air freshener dangling from the rearview mirror smells like lemon.

My mom's old white Honda has peace and love stickers over the bumpers. It doesn't smell like lemons. It smells like her. Cigarettes and coconut shampoo.

That's where I slept last night, which seems like such a long time ago. I wonder how long it's been, exactly.

My hands are shaking violently. I wish I had two other hands, so *those* hands could stop *these* hands from shaking.

Because my hands are looking for my mother, so she can hold me, and protect me, and make me not scared.

Tears slide down my face.

Karen sighs, looking back at me. "Tissues in the seat pocket on the back."

I wipe my face with the sleeve of my lace dress instead. "What's going to happen to my house?" My voice wavers.

Karen pulls out of the lot of the foster-care building. "Well, I don't know, dear. We'll have to contact the landlord. Box your things. Where you're going is temporary. Sometimes it takes moving around before we can place you long-term. To be honest, it can be difficult to home older children in the long term."

There's not much traffic. In a little while, we pass Randy Gonzalez's ranch. The horses are out, sleek and pretty, nickering in the gold afternoon light. I press a hand against the window glass.

Karen looks at me in the rearview. "We can take a minute," she says. "Want me to pull over? They're so lovely, aren't they?"

My mom brought me out here last week. She loves these horses. She packs bags of cold carrots and walks straight up to the fence and holds out a hand stuffed with orange sticks.

Once, she told me, "I used to ride a horse when I was little," but when I pressed her, she suddenly clammed up, said it wasn't important, and could I go back to the car and get the bag of carrots? She'd left it on the front seat. But when I went back to the car, there were no carrots. I turned around. She had the bag in her hand.

She was always doing things like that to me, distracting me from what she didn't want to talk about.

Just looking at the horses hurts. I shake my head. Karen says, "Suit yourself."

We stop at a fast-food place. "Hungry?" Karen asks. "It's on the State of Arizona." But I say no.

She pulls up to the drive-through. "Once, one of my cases was a little boy who'd never even had a milkshake before. He was amazed! He said, 'All of this, for me?' I think it took him a good hour to finish the whole thing, he went so slow and took such care with each sip. He was trying to make it last."

She smiles, but she doesn't actually seem happy about the memory, more like sad.

I think about that word she used. *Cases.* We are her job. Kids who don't have parents. Karen inches the car forward. I glance over at the big windows of the fast-food restaurant.

My heart drops. Taran Parker and his brother and Kelsey Cameron are sitting at a table by the window, staring at me, mouths open. Of *course* they are. It's a school day and school must be over by now.

Taran's eyes grow wide as he skims the State of Arizona seal on Karen's car. His eyes meet mine. *WTF?* he mouths to me. His brother shakes his head, half smiling. He looks . . . impressed.

Oh my God, they think I've been arrested.

Kelsey Cameron nods, laughing. *Yeah, girl.* I can tell, even through the glass. She lifts up her phone. I try to slide back down in the seat before she gets the picture, but I don't think I make it.

They don't even know. That my mom died. They don't even know. Last night seems like a billion years ago.

I peek up. Kelsey Cameron is checking the shot on her phone. #jailbird #prisoner #geekconvict #teenfelon

"What's going on back there?" Karen cranes her head in the rearview. "Are you going to be sick?"

She looks toward the windows of the fast-food place.

I'm down below the car window now, my butt practically on the floor and the seat belt choking me. There is no way I'm sliding back up until we are out on the road.

"Oh," Karen says softly. "I see."

When she gets her sack of food, the car fills up with the smell of the greasy burgers I wanted to have with Cake so much, and I feel queasy, so I crack the window. I hoist myself back up onto the seat as she pulls out onto the road.

Miles of cattle fencing, broken old houses set far back in the desert. Mesquite trees. The sky carving into ribbons of pink and deep orange.

After a little while, she says, "Not too far to the foster now." There are flecks of salt on the corner of her mouth.

The *foster.* The one who will have the face of an angel when Karen is there and the face of a beast when the door closes.

The longer we drive, the quieter the car becomes, the darker it gets outside, the darker I start to grow inside, that wet cement feeling sinking down on me again, the one that seems hopeless and finite.

I could get my phone. I could text Cake. I wouldn't be so lonely. I look around the backseat for my backpack. It isn't here, and my pink suitcase is in the trunk.

"Do you know . . . do you know what happened to my phone? And my backpack? Am I even allowed to have a phone anymore?" My voice is tiny.

Karen tilts her head. "I'll have to see. Sometimes, in situations like yours last night, at the hospital, things get shuffled around and lost, so I'll look into it, okay, dear? And yes, you are allowed to have a phone, as long as you can pay the bill."

Pay the bill. With what? I hold my breath. I don't want to cry again. My eyes are already swollen and salty.

I press my hand against the window. The stars are beginning to shine, tiny perfect pinpricks in the darkening sky.

If she was alive, my mother would be in our backyard right now, in her lawn chair, leaning back, her face glossy from the heat. She would say, "Sit with me a bit, baby."

And I would, our bodies curling together perfectly, as they always did.

My hand slides down the window and into my lap.

It doesn't matter where I'm going, who gets me now. They can kill me, for all I care.

## 22 hours, 4 minutes

THE YARD IS DARK and bare, with just a pockmarked saguaro and a gray mailbox on a wooden pole. I have no idea where we are, or how long we drove, exactly, and when we step out of the car, all I see is darkness forever. No other houses. Nothing.

Karen looks at her phone. "Georgia's a real believer in solitude and peace. Says it's good for the soul." She tries to smile, but I don't think she means it. I think she thinks this place is creepy, too.

The house is brick and painted gray. I can barely make it out in the dark, except for the bulb next to the front door.

I'm not breathing. I hope I pass out. I hope Karen has to drag me back into the car, limp and ash-faced, and deliver me to the hospital in Tucson, where I can be with my mother again. I pinch the folds of the dress's skirt in my fingers.

Karen says, "Listen to me."

The front door of the house opens. Over Karen's shoulder, a dark shape appears behind the iron screen.

Karen puts her hand on my arm. "*Listen* to me."

I drag my eyes to hers. They are blue, and concerned, and tired.

"It is for one night only, I promise. The next home is having a removal this evening, and I'll be here, first thing in the morning, to take you, okay? I just need you to follow Georgia's rules, and get some sleep, okay, Tiger?"

A *removal*. Like, taking a kid away, to make room for me? Are we chess pieces? Broken game pieces in a weird adult game?

She said, *the next home*.

I blurt out, "How many homes are there going to be?"

The iron screen creaks open. My heart skips. The woman, Georgia, calls out, "Come on, now. We held dinner for you."

Her voice is ragged. Not kind, but not mean. Flat.

"I can't answer that," Karen says, pulling my suitcase from the trunk. "One night, Tiger. One night."

I look around. Could I run? My fingers and feet itch.

But it's all just a velvety black dark everywhere I look. There aren't even any streetlights.

"Do you promise you'll come back?" I whisper. "Do you *promise* you will come and get me tomorrow?"

"It's getting cold. The other girls are hungry."

Georgia steps out onto the concrete patch in front of the house. She's wearing an apron, a gray sweatshirt, and jeans. In the small circle of light from the bulb, her face looks tired and lined.

"Do you *promise*, Karen?" She's going to leave me here forever. I know it. Beads of sweat pop on my forehead. I grab her arm and squeeze, even though she's an adult, and I'm a kid, and you *never* touch the adult first. Ever. I squeeze her hard enough to make her face pinch up.

"Yes," she says. "Yes, I do."

I drop my hand. She rubs her arm. I know she doesn't think I can tell how worried she is, but I can.

The last thing I say to her is, "You promised. And if you break your promise to me, you're lying to the daughter of a dead woman. Know that."

And then I take the handle of my pink suitcase from her and walk toward Georgia, and the silent, dark house.

I bite my lip until I taste blood, and I do not care.

THE AIR INSIDE THE house is hot and close, like walking into a sweater pulled straight from the dryer. The room is dim, just a lamp in the far corner, and a ceiling light with a weak bulb.

Georgia points to a corner. "Put your case there. I'll look through it later. Safety purposes. Go on into the kitchen. The girls will help you."

I hesitate. "The lady—Karen—she already looked through my stuff."

Georgia says firmly, "I take care of my own house, thank you."

She goes back outside and she and Karen begin talking quietly. I walk tentatively in the direction of the kitchen.

The light there is much brighter than the rest of the house and hurts my eyes after so much darkness.

Two girls sit at a round green plastic table in front of plates of creamed corn, white bread slathered with butter, and squares of dark meat. They run their eyes up and down my dress.

"Interesting choice of evening wear," the one with the blond hair says.

They're both wearing sweatshirts like Georgia. Plain, gray sweatshirts. It's so hot in the house already, and their faces are moist from the heat.

Brown Hair has nice eyes, round and sorry-looking.

"That's a weird dress," she says. "You just get back from a funeral or something?"

"No," I say quietly. "Not yet, anyway."

Blondie says, "You got blood on your lip. Here." She presses a forefinger to her own mouth.

I drag my laced arm across my mouth.

Then we all look down at the red smear across my sleeve.

Brownie says, "Ooookkkaaay." She points to a stool in the corner by the counter. "You have to eat there until you can show Georgia you know how to act. Your food is on that plate."

She adds, in a whisper, "Just eat it, okay? It doesn't matter, just eat it."

I walk over to the stool and slide onto it. On a paper plate is a piece of white bread and a spoonful of the creamed corn. No meat. A blue plastic cup of milk sits on the counter, its sides slick with sweat. The girls have glasses of milk and real plates.

The blond-haired girl says, "You get paper plates and a plastic spoon until she's sure you aren't a thrower, a screamer, or a stabber. And you better eat, because you won't get anything else until tomorrow."

I follow her eyes to the kitchen cabinets.

Every single cabinet has a padlock on it.

I look at the refrigerator. It has a padlock, too.

I look back at Brownie and Blondie, my heart sinking.

Brownie spoons some creamed corn into her mouth. "You don't get it, do you? Is this your first placement? Like, ever?"

I grit my teeth, nod.

Blondie makes a whistling sound between her teeth, then checks the doorway quickly, like she's afraid of letting Georgia hear. She leans across the table. "Some kids are hoarders because they never get enough food. Maybe lived on the street or their parents were druggies and never bought any food or anything and so they like to hide it, just in case. So some houses keep stuff locked up. I was with one kid one time? And his bio mom used to keep him in a dog cage? So she could get high without worrying about him wandering off and getting her in trouble. He got so used to eating out of a dog bowl, that's how our foster mom fed him. Even scrambled eggs? She'd put them in the bowl. He even slept on the floor. On a little pillow the foster mom gave him. I liked him. He was all right." She pauses. "I mean, it's not always the kids, though. Sometimes the fosters are just dicks, to be honest."

Brownie nods.

Blondie takes a small bite of her meat and winces. "Georgia is a big fan of boiling. It's her main culinary fallback. You'll get used to it."

"That can't be true." My voice shakes. I picture a little boy, huddled in a cage. Yellowy piles of egg plopped in a mound in a bowl. "About the dog cage. That's not true. You're just trying to scare me."

Blondie guffaws. Creamed corn sticks to her chin. "Oh man, you don't know the half of it. Just wait. Adults . . ." She pauses, and her eyes get very wet.

"They can treat kids like shit, is all." Her chin trembles, and a piece of corn drips onto her plate. She looks down at her lap.

Brownie's head jerks in the direction of the doorway.

There are footsteps in the hall.

"Start eating," she orders. *"Now."*

If I have to eat this food, I will vomit. If I have to cram creamed corn down my throat, and stuff dry white bread into my mouth, I will gag. "I can't," I tell Brownie. "I'm sorry, I just can't."

They start shoveling food into their mouths. I dig a spoon into my corn and move it around. Maybe Georgia won't notice.

She stands in the doorway, papers in her hand. I wonder if they are about me. In the light of the kitchen, her eyes look watery and unhealthy. I feel sick and decide to keep my eyes on my plate.

"You not hungry? The girls tell you this is all you get? I don't want you out here snooping around for food in the middle of the night. That's an infraction. Against house rules."

*Please don't let me cry in front of everyone. Please don't let me cry. Please don't let me—*

"You can at least drink your milk. The caseworker said you haven't had much to eat since yesterday." Her voice softens the smallest bit.

"Did you girls tell her the food rules?"

Brownie and Blondie nod, eyes down.

"Finish up, it's getting late."

I look at the clock on the wall. It's 7:30 p.m.

Georgia points to a laminated piece of paper tacked to the wall. "House rules," she says, walking to the sink. She turns on the tap, begins soaping some pots. "My house, my rules; you follow them, and you'll do just fine."

"I'm only here for tonight," I say quietly. "So I'm probably just going to bed and that's that."

When Georgia looks at me, I think I see the smallest flicker of a smile at the corner of her mouth. "Is that what the caseworker said?"

Blondie murmurs, "That's what they all say," but Georgia shoots her a look, and she shuts up fast.

The girls take their plates to the sink and Georgia steps to the side. Brownie dunks the plates in the water and Blondie rinses them. They move carefully, tucking the damp plates in the dish rack.

I slide off my stool. Georgia looks at me. "You're not going to finish your meal? At least drink your milk."

"I can't." I swallow hard, afraid of her dark eyes. "I don't . . . I'm not . . . I'm not feeling well. I think I'll just go to bed." I inch across the wall toward the doorway.

"No one goes hungry in this house and you eat what is provided to you. Drink your milk." Her eyes are not watery anymore. They are steel, and they are curious. She wants to see what I'll do. I wonder what *she'll* do.

Blondie and Brownie plead with their eyes.

The plastic cup shakes in my fingers as I lift it to my mouth. The milk is warm, too warm, now. It's full fat, and tastes oily. I keep my eyes on Blondie and Brownie as I drink.

They take the cup from me when I'm done and throw my plate away. The milk sloshes in my stomach in an uncomfortable way.

Georgia looks pleased. She folds her hands.

"Good night," she says. "Do your teeth and put your clothes in the hamper and I don't want to hear any fussing."

Blondie and Brownie push me out of the kitchen and down the dark hallway.

There's a plastic laminated list on the wall in the bedroom, too, and as Brownie sits cross-legged on the floor and sorts through my pink suitcase, holding up the clothes Cake picked out for me, Blondie taps the list.

"Bed is in fifteen minutes. Bathroom's in there. If you have to pee, go now, because she hates it if you get up in the middle of the night. She likes the night really quiet."

"It's not even eight o'clock," I say slowly. "Isn't it . . . kind of early for bed?"

They look at each other. Brownie shrugs. "Truth be told? I kind of like it. I get a lot of sleep. My life is better in dreams, you know? And I've been in houses where you got *no* sleep, if you know what I mean."

I don't know what she means, and I don't want to. I hold my stomach, as though I can keep the milk from sloshing around.

There are three twin beds in the room, each one with a dresser next to it. On top of each dresser is a lamp with a plain white shade and a small picture of Jesus. I blink and bite my lip. *Why a man?* my mom says every time we see an image of Jesus. *I mean, I like the idea of someone watching out for you, taking one for the team, but why always a white guy?* If she said it in front of Bonita, Bonita would cry out, *Where's my brown goddess?* And they would laugh together.

My heart tightens. I hold my breath.

Blondie catches me looking at the picture. She smiles. "Don't you think he always looks kind of annoyed? Always rolling his eyes all . . ." She folds her hands and tilts her head, thrusts out her hip, rolls her eyes back, like a sulky girl.

Kind of like Lupe Hidalgo, actually.

In spite of myself, and my gurgling stomach, I smile.

Blondie says, "I mean, I believe and all, just not in him. Something else. Something magical. A spirit, maybe. I just think there has to be, you know? After all *this*." She looks around the plain room. Her face turns sad.

"Nobody is up there looking out for us, Lisa. If they was, we wouldn't be here right now. We'd be in canopy beds watching *My Little Pony* and eating cheesecake all day long." Brownie shakes a Rolling Stones T-shirt at me. "Can I have this?"

She eyes my dress. "Something tells me your sartorial skills are taking a turn for the peculiar and you won't be needing it anyway."

*Sartorial.* Brownie would have fit right in with Hoffmeister's Lit class.

I nod and she murmurs, "Score," and keeps going through my things. She's skinny. My T-shirts are stretched out from my boobs and will hang off her, but I have a feeling she won't mind.

A heavy pang settles in my stomach. I sit gingerly on the bed. Brownie and Blondie, they must have seen lots of kids like me by now. They don't even seem to care.

How many people have seen Kelsey's picture of me in the State of Arizona car by now? Am I trending somewhere, people laughing at me in the backseat in my freak dress, my face swollen from crying?

#orphanarrest #littlehouseonthehomeless

The plastic alarm clock on one of the dressers says 8:15 p.m. And we're going to *bed*.

Blondie comes out of the bathroom with a shiny, clean face and dressed in a long nightgown. She folds up the gray sweatshirt and the blue jeans and places them carefully in her dresser drawer.

"Your clothes are in your bureau. They're just like these, so aren't you lucky."

She points to one of the twin beds on the far side of the room. "You sleep over there. Kendra gets the window."

Brownie—Kendra—looks up at me, her eyes suddenly fierce. "Don't fight me on that. Window is always mine. Right, Lisa?"

Lisa nods quickly. "Right." She slides into her bed, fits the blanket up to her chest.

The milk remnants in my mouth taste sour. My stomach turns. My forehead feels damp. I start to sway and brace myself against the mattress. "Why is it so hot in here?" My words slur.

Kendra strips off her sweatshirt and bra and slides on the Rolling Stones shirt. "You don't look so good," she says. "If you're going to yak, do it there, and do it in the toilet, and clean up, okay? She likes stuff very, very clean. I know this place is weird, but believe me, it could be so much worse."

Lisa sounds sleepy. "I lived in a place where the dad always came in to say good night and made you kiss him. On the cheek, but still. Creepy. And gross."

Kendra says, "Don't *scare* her. This is her first house."

"She needs to know," Lisa says, shrugging. "Why *are* you here, anyway? You run away too much or something? Your parents on the Ox cart?" She squints, looking at me intently.

I stare at her. I don't even know what that *means*.

I swallow the sourness prickling in my throat. I'm just a stupid girl who reads books and plays the drums and still sleeps with her mom sometimes and is actually kind of afraid of the dark.

Kendra says, "Oxy. OxyContin. That's what she's talking about. Painkillers. My mom's in rehab for the ninth time. I've been in care since I was seven. I'm going to turn eighteen in here, I know it. Oh well. Shit's the shit, I guess. Better than watching her sell our stuff for dope." She shrugs, like it's nothing, but her voice cracks a little. She hops on her bed, tucks her hands behind her head.

Lisa looks at me. "So? What's the deal?"

The coating of milk in my mouth, the squeezing in my belly, the damp and close smell of the house, boiled meat, creamed corn.

Black spots float in front of my eyes.

Kendra jumps out of bed and grabs my arm just in time to aim me toward the bathroom, pushing me in a beeline for the toilet bowl, which absorbs all the warm milk Georgia made me drink.

There's a sharp rap on the bedroom door.

"Everything is fine," Lisa calls out to Georgia. "She doesn't feel well. We're taking care of her."

Kendra wipes my face and then the toilet bowl with a washcloth. The small bathroom fills quickly with the smell of sour milk. She throws the washcloth in the sink.

"Rinse your mouth," she says firmly. "You'll feel gross all night if you don't. Sleep on your side, too, just in case. So you don't choke if it happens again."

She looks at me sadly. "My mom used to black out all the time from stuff, and you can choke on your barf if you sleep on your back or stomach. I spent a lot of time rolling her over and checking her breathing."

I rinse my mouth. The water tastes slightly metallic, and makes me gag again.

Kendra wipes at my dress with a tissue. "Just a couple of drops. Not too bad. There aren't any pajamas in your suitcase.

You gonna sleep in that? It looks old. I think it's growing on me, though."

I stagger past her, dizzy and sick. If my mom were here, she'd make me bouillon to drink and crispy toast. Tuck the red wool blanket around my whole body. *Like a burrito,* she'd say, and smile.

I settle on the bed carefully. My stomach hurts from heaving.

"My mom died," I tell them. The words hurt, coming out.

Not my throat. My heart.

My words hurt my heart.

"Her brain exploded. Last night. No, the night before. I can't remember now."

I can't remember now. I can't remember if my mom died last night or the night before. What is happening to me?

"She never kept me in a cage or anything like that."

I start to cry, but I wrap my arms around myself to keep from sobbing too loud and I roll my face into the pillow.

One of them, I don't know which, says softly, "Poor baby. That's horrible."

The lamps snap off, plunging the room into darkness. I hear the sounds of sheets and blankets being arranged, and then heavy, resigned sighs. Down the hall, Georgia shuffles around, murmuring. I realize she's praying.

*Thy Kingdom come. Thy will be done.*

Where. Is my mother. Is she . . . here, like on Earth, somewhere? Or somewhere else?

*On Earth as it is in Heaven.*

There are a lot of things we never really talked about. Like Heaven. Or death. Like, what happens *after.* What if she's somewhere . . . and she's scared? Alone? I saw a movie once and the ghosts were everywhere among the living, watching them from trees, looking into their grocery carts in the market. But the living never felt them.

My heart flops. Is it possible to have a heart attack at sixteen?

I roll over, tears sliding down my cheeks into the pillow beneath me. Kendra is on her bed, beneath the window, her knees drawn up under the blanket, trailing a hand over the windowsill, looking out at the stars in the velvety Arizona sky.

With no streetlights, you can see them, those pretty, promising stars, and the fat white moon, perfectly, through the solid black bars on the window.

Y OU WANT TO LAUGH at them. Maybe even *chortle,* another word from Lit class.

Because none of them, not the skinny brown-haired one, or the plump white blond one with the crooked teeth, or even that sallow, horrible, tall woman named Georgia, believed you.

They thought you were going to be here forever, like them. Or some of forever, however it works in this *foster system,* where maybe forever doesn't even exist anymore, because life is just one house after the next. One plastic cup of warm milk after another.

But there is Karen, stepping out of the State of Arizona car in the bright sunshine and walking purposefully to the heavily gated front door.

She's like your best damn friend now.

Knocking. You can see her from Kendra's window, through the bars, and you drag yourself, sick as you feel, but elated, from the narrow bed and throw all your clothes back in the pink suitcase without folding them. You toss a Poison T-shirt over to Kendra, who sleepily rubs her eyes.

The other one, Lisa, *Blondie,* is already dressed and making her bed. So neat and clean, that one. Hair smoothed flat over her ears, hands tucking the pale blanket under the slim mattress.

She looks up. "You were right," she says.

She tries to smile, but she's not happy about it, you can tell. She runs a hand over her bedspread.

And why should she be happy? She has more days, more nights, of bland, boiled food in the middle of nowhere. Black bars on the windows. Lists on walls.

And she thinks all that is *good,* which makes you shudder, thinking of where she must have *been.*

Georgia meets you in the hallway. "Well," she says, gravely, towering over you. "Sometimes I get kids two or three times, you never know. We might meet again."

She puts a large hand on your shoulder.

"I am very sorry about your mother, Grace."

Your real name stings a little, mostly because it was reserved for your mother, for those moments when she was pissed, or when she was very, very dreamy and sweet.

You look down, because the ocean is swelling in you again, and you don't want to believe Georgia means it, but you know she does, because you heard her long into the night last night, praying, and you know she believes some things very deeply.

You feel a little sorry for thinking bad things about her.

But then you remember she made you drink disgusting, overly warm milk, and the sorry feeling goes away.

You push past her, and don't care that the wheels of your pink suitcase tumble over her white sneakers.

In the back of Karen's car, as she says, "Ready?" you buckle yourself in and a little part of you wonders if your mother is watching all this, right now, like a movie ghost, but the thought hurts, and the girl-bug behind glass swats it away. You are carrying so many heavy feelings.

There just isn't enough room for them all.

## 47 hours, 15 minutes

THE FOSTER MOTHER NAMED LaLa doesn't look mean, and she isn't holding a wooden spoon, ready to strike me down if I don't cook drugs for her.

In fact, she's wearing a flannel robe, has thick black braids with strands of gray, and black horn-rimmed glasses with silver sparkles. She's fixed a plate, a *real* plate, ceramic, it looks like, of food for me and left it on the kitchen table. A glass of water. A fork with a cloth napkin. It is, to use another word I learned from a book, a lovely *tableau,* but I don't eat it. After Georgia and the sour milk, I don't think I'll ever eat or drink again, maybe.

I sit at the kitchen table while LaLa and Karen talk in the living room. LaLa lives on the outskirts of Tucson, where the land stretches out far and wide. Her house is very quiet.

I have my phone back. Karen took me back to the Children and Protective Services building after Georgia's to pick up paperwork, answer phone calls, and give me my backpack, which Cake had dropped off, and which had my phone. I'd left the backpack in Kai's car.

We were at the CPS building for hours, Karen doing her work, me sitting in a chair, watching her. "Things like this take a long time," she said with a shrug. By the time we left, it was already getting dark, and by the time we got to this new house, I was exhausted again.

In the kitchen, I start to text Cake.

But I don't—I don't even know what to say. What words am I supposed to use for . . . this?

Like, *Hi. I'm at a stranger's house. There is a yellow kitchen table.*

Like, *Hey.*

Like, *Hi. My mother is still dead.*

The front door shuts. Quickly, I type, *I'm alive.*

LaLa comes into the kitchen. I turn my phone over in my lap just as it vibrates.

LaLa sits down. "I like your dress."

"Thank you." My voice seems small. I rub a patch of lace between my fingers.

"I'm really sorry about your mom."

"Her brain exploded," I answer. Look at the lace of my dress, entwined in my fingers. The intricate pattern. If only I could disappear inside it. The phone buzzes again. I look down. Cake. *Talk to me.*

LaLa notices and says, "You can text if you want. Friends are important right now."

I turn the phone back over. Swallow hard.

There's a lot moving around inside me.

"I don't really understand it, you know? What happened."

The youngish doctor had talked about blood vessels and blood flow, but it was hard to concentrate on his words because my body was fracturing into millions of pieces.

LaLa looks sad. "I'm so sorry, Gra—"

"Nobody calls me that, except for my mom sometimes. My name is Tiger."

*We had such a terrible, terrible fight.* I wince, remembering. Hold my breath until the sharp pain passes.

"Got it. Cool name. Please eat, and if you can't that's okay, but I do want you to drink some water. You look dehydrated. I have some pajamas for you, too, if you need them. I'll bet you're exhausted."

My mouth feels grimy and dry, so I sip some water. "Am I the only one here?" I ask. I wonder if I will miss Brownie and Blondie, or if all the kids I'll know from now on will just bleed into one another.

She shakes her head. "Nope. I've got three, at the moment, plus you. Two littles and a boy a bit older than you. He's in Phoenix right now, but he'll be back soon."

"How long am I going to be here?"

"I'm not sure, exactly."

I bite my lip. How many times will I have to move now? Harry Potter went to his aunt and uncle's but he had to live under the stairs. He got Hogwarts, but he still had to go home in the summers. My mother always thought that was bullshit, Dumbledore sending Harry back to a horrible house. "He could have kept him at Hogwarts," she insisted. "Or even with Hagrid. He thought he needed to deprive him of love if he was going to do what he needed him to do. But I don't believe that. Not at all."

"I have essences that might relax you." LaLa ticks her fingers. "Sweet chestnut, lemon balm, star-of-Bethlehem. I could get you some drops. I'd have to get permission from Karen, though."

"Permission?"

"Yes. I can't give you any painkillers or even get your hair cut without asking permission first. Your parents still have rights."

"I don't think my mom is going to have much to say about giving me an aspirin, at the moment, do you?" I rub the lace harder between my fingertips.

LaLa sighs. "Sorry. I messed up there for a minute. I forgot."

There are tons of LaLas around Mesa Luna. Easygoing hippies with braided hair and worn clothes, with a tincture or a balm for everything.

But not for this. There will never be anything, ever, that can heal what I have.

LaLa snaps her fingers. "I always forget to say how this is going to work. Here goes." She takes a breath. "You live here and follow my rules. No fighting, no drugs, no drinking. In the background, Karen's working on finding you another place. I'm not long-term."

Fighting, drinking, drugs. I don't do any of those things anyway. But maybe I'll start, now that there's no one to care.

LaLa's house smells like ginger and incense, miles better than the boiled-meat smell of Georgia's house.

I'll have to get used to all-new smells. People. Rules.

I feel dizzy just thinking about it. My eyes fill up. I dig the heels of my palms into them until I see bright explosions of color.

LaLa says gently, "Let's do a tour, okay? It's getting late and I want you to rest. We've gotta keep it down a bit, though, because Sarah and Leonard are sleeping."

She leads me down a hallway, not to a room underneath the stairs, after all, but to a regular room with bunk beds, two wooden dressers, and a poster of Olaf the Snowman.

He's my favorite part of that movie, when he puts on the hat and sings about summertime.

I feel myself relax, just the smallest bit. This is going to be okay, I think. At least better than Georgia's.

LaLa whispers, "Sarah likes the bottom bunk. She gets a little anxious at bedtime because of where she was living in the past, so we have night-lights—" She points to the walls. There are three night-lights: a fish in a bowl, a duck, and the moon. In the bottom bunk, a Black girl with cornrows sleeps peacefully, two fingers jammed in her mouth.

"Sarah is ten," LaLa whispers. "That's your dresser, over there. You girls share my bathroom; it's the one down the hall with clouds painted on the outside. The door with the tree is the other bathroom."

She takes me down the hall to the cloud bathroom. "If you need tampons or pads or anything like that, look under the sink. Whatever you need, just ask, okay, Tiger?"

My voice is flat. "My mom died. Can you help me with that?"

LaLa says softly, "Grief is a process your body and mind have to go through, Tiger. There isn't a cure. But I *can* keep you comfortable and safe."

I fix my eyes on the floor. Faded rag rug. Scuffed wood.

LaLa sighs. "I've put some pajamas on the sink, right here. A shower and some sleep is going to help a lot, okay?"

She closes the bathroom door.

In the round mirror above the sink, the girl who stares back looks haunted, like she's been scooped out from the inside, like she's lost twenty pounds in a day.

I touch her face. I don't recognize her.

I think: *This girl is motherless. This girl has nothing.*

Tears stream down her haunted, carved-out face.

If my mother was here, she'd wrap her arms around me and pat my face dry and murmur, *You look tired, Tiger. Wash your face and get your book and go to bed. You'll feel better in the morning.*

Sometimes she sleeps in my bed with me, her back pressed against mine.

I don't understand how things are *keeping going* when she has just *stopped*.

If I close my eyes and wish hard enough, will she come back? Is this some cruel, weird trick by the universe? Like I've stepped into the wrong portal by mistake? That's always happening in books, after all. Maybe by yelling at my mother and telling her those horrible things, I set off some domino effect, tripped a wire in the cosmos, and changed my path and now I'm being taught a terrible lesson.

Maybe I've imagined the whole thing. Maybe all of *this* is not real, either. This strange and quiet house, after the eerie stillness of Georgia's, this kind woman with the black braids and sparkly glasses, trying to pawn her elixirs off on me.

The one thing my mom's told me over and over and over for years is *I will never leave you. I will always be right here.*

My mother might be a lot of things, but she isn't a liar.

This *has* to be a horrible mistake, a time warp of some sort, and it'll be over soon. It just can't be real: a life of locked cabinets and refrigerators, bars on the window. Sweatshirts and creamed corn on plastic plates.

I strip off the lace dress, relieved. Twist on the water in the shower. This is a tremendous, universe-gone-mad mistake. Because my mom *promised*.

When I get in the shower, I scrub myself until I'm just patches of red and raw skin. I shampoo my hair five times to get the horribleness out. I want to be clean when I wake up in the morning, when my mother comes for me, cup of coffee in her hand, her hair mussed, her eyes sleepy.

When I get out, I dry myself and hang my wet towels over the curtain rod because my mother didn't raise a total slob. I put the ivory lace dress back on because in the morning, when my mother comes for me, when the universe has been righted, she'll love that I'm wearing it. Her face will glow. She'll laugh.

She'll say, *How beautiful you look, Tiger.*

We won't remember a stupid fight about a dress, or any of *this,* whatever *this* is, because it isn't real, it can't be.

*This cannot be fucking happening.*

I find a new toothbrush in plastic beneath the sink, brush my teeth, glad to clean my mouth out after so long, and pad my way back down the hallway to the bedroom, where I climb the ladder to the top bunk, cover myself with the itchy wool blanket, and stare at the ceiling. My phone says it's 9:15 p.m.

I will myself to sleep, because when I wake up, it's all going to be a goddamn bad dream.

And we will be *we* again, the well-oiled, good-looking, and good-smelling machine.

## 2 days, 6 hours, 9 minutes

W HEN I OPEN MY eyes, I'm in a strange room, and my heart jumps. Not my bed, not my blanket, not my clothes, not my walls, not my—

And then *it* floods back over me. *It* wasn't a bad dream after all.

She's still gone.

The wet cement feeling settles on me again. It's hard to breathe.

I'm in a strange house.

My mother is dead.

I have no home.

Everything I knew is gone.

I start to cry.

"You want us to get LaLa?"

I look down from the top bunk.

Two Black kids, one super tiny and scrawny, and one stick-thin and tall, stare up at me with suspicious eyes, next to my open suitcase. My underwear and bras, everything Cake packed for me, spread all over the floor. The little girl, she's the one who spoke. I can tell. Her eyes are worried, even as she stands there, my underwear in her hands.

Jesus, first Brownie and now them. Is that what foster kids *do*? Rifle through each other's suitcases all the time?

The tiny one, the boy, says, "We didn't find any candy." He

has a blue basketball jersey on and matching shorts. His knees are as round as baseballs. "The hell you come here without candy for?"

"The hell," says the skinny one, the girl, only her "hell" is whispered, like she's trying it on. It's Sarah. I can see how expertly cornrowed her hair is in the light. I've never been able to do anything with my hair. I'm all thumbs.

"Don't you mess with me," huffs the boy. "I'll kick your ass." A bubble of green snot balloons from his nostril, but he doesn't notice. He punches his fist into his other hand.

Sarah repeats, "Don't mess." She tries to punch her hand, too, but misses.

They're just kids who've been abandoned, but I'm still a little mad they're going through my stuff. I should be nice, but what does it matter now? These kids are me now and I am them.

I wipe my wet face with the back of my hand and lean over the bunk and snarl, "I'm a ninja. My mom died. Her brain exploded. You put my stuff back in my suitcase or I'll take the both of you out with one kick."

The boy and the girl squeal and start tossing my things in the general direction of the suitcase before they run down the hall.

The ceiling over my bunk has old water stains. If I had a pencil, I would write *Kill me. Kill me now* inside them, like words inside cartoon text bubbles. Draw a girl with crosses for eyes and a limp body in an old lace dress. Or a girl-bug in glass, fluttering her crisp wings, waiting.

This isn't a bad dream. I am really, really, really here, and she is really, really, really gone.

It's like lightning, what tears through me then. I bury my

face in a pillow that isn't mine, that doesn't smell like anything I know, and cry myself back to sleep.

I sleep for so long that when I wake up, the small bedroom is dark again. Below me, the girl named Sarah snores gently in her bunk.

I climb down the bunk ladder and walk to the cloud bathroom, pee, wash my hands, brush my teeth.

It feels like it takes a million years to do all those things. It feels like it takes a million years to squeeze the toothpaste onto the red toothbrush, lift the brush to my mouth. I can't even look at the hollow girl in the mirror; my head is too heavy.

The house is very still except for the whir of a ceiling fan in one of the rooms. I stand in the hallway, listening, my heart pounding.

Maybe LaLa is a secret drunkard, and she'll burst from her room, hairbrush in hand, ready to punish me for leaving my bed in the middle of the night. Maybe, like Georgia, she has lists, secret lists I haven't seen yet.

I tense, waiting. *Drunkard*—that's another word I learned in Lit class last semester, along with *malt-worms*. Falstaff and Prince Henry and a face like "Lucifer's privy-kitchen."

But LaLa doesn't come flying from her room, face ablaze. Her door stays shut, and the house stays quiet. Maybe there are no Georgias here.

In the kitchen, a note on the yellow table that says, *Tiger, food in the fridge. Please eat. We have some things to do tomorrow.* I crumple it up.

The refrigerator is blissfully unpadlocked and stuffed with

food. Butter on a clear dish. Flats of tortillas. Grapes in a bag. Jars of sauces. This is more food in one refrigerator than I've ever seen, except for at Cake's house, and if this was any other time, I'd go to town on all of it. But not now.

I wonder if I will ever be hungry again.

There's an old-fashioned phone on the wall, the kind with glowing push-buttons that make noise each time you press them, like *beep-beep-BOOP*.

I want to hurt something. Someone. I want to slam the refrigerator door shut over and over and shatter the pert glass jars of sauce inside.

I grab the phone, and before I know it, I'm calling Kai Henderson.

I waited six damn months to kiss Kai Henderson. I waited practically my whole life to kiss anyone, for that matter, and he could not even stay in the hospital with me. He left me there, and drove away in his mother's car.

On that day six months ago in Bio, when I fell hard for him? I even went home and wrote it down: *10:46 a.m. in Room 11C, Bio lab, November 13th, Kai Henderson made me feel warm and weak.* I didn't know how else to put it, and I folded that piece of paper up a zillion times until it was just a small, tight square, and hid it in the secret compartment of my jewelry box.

Kai never seemed like some of the guys at Eugene Field who deliberately bumped me in the hallway, trying to get a squeeze on my breasts. He actually listened to Cake during band rehearsals, instead of the other guys she'd tried out, who talked over her and sighed loudly and quit in a huff.

We'd never even held hands before the kiss at Thunder Park Elementary. He'd only ever dated one other girl, Ellen Untermeyer, and that was way back in the eighth grade, when all of us were just amoebas with braces and pimples.

In the playground at Thunder Park Elementary, I learned you could kiss someone for a billion hours and they would still turn around and leave you alone in a hospital, your mouth still warm from kissing.

The jewelry box where I hid that note plays "Für Elise" and the netting on the ballerina's skirt is torn, but I still like petting it sometimes, because it's so delicate and pretty, and I guess that's just another goddamn thing I'll never see again.

The clock on LaLa's kitchen wall says 4:15 a.m. I listen to the *brrring, brrring, brrring* on the other end of the phone. My bones shake, electric with meanness. I can hold on all night until he answers. I have nowhere else to go.

Kai's voice is sleepy. "Hello? Who is this?"

I say, as coldly as I can, "The heart really is like a beautiful and weird engine, Kai."

There's silence on the line. Then he says, slowly, "Tiger? Where are you?"

"You just left me there."

"Tiger——"

"It's funny that I started liking you right when we started working on hearts in class, you know? I think that's irony, now. Is that irony? I'm not sure. I'm not really thinking clearly right now, you know? Anyway, is it ironic? Because I think you broke my heart. And what sucks the most? Is that you broke it right *after* it had just been broken in the *worst* possible way, you know? Like, you stomped on the pieces and made them even *smaller*. I mean, who *does* that?"

"I'm sorry. I didn't . . ."

His meek voice makes me even angrier. "All you had to do was stay. Just stay. Was that so hard? Do you even know where I *am*?"

I'm in a bad and mean place. I keep talking and the things I tell him make him cry.

Like: maybe *he* should have been the one to die, not my mother.

I want to hurt everyone right now. I want to break things so the world looks like how I feel inside: splintered into a million bloody and sharp pieces.

Kai Henderson hangs up on me.

I slide the phone back into the cradle. Through the window, the sun is rising in great pinkish waves over the sky.

Back in the bedroom, I clamber up to my bunk and wait, staring at the ceiling, my chest heaving up and down, up and down. I remember my phone and dig beneath my pillow for it.

I look at the text I sent myself the night my mom died.

My mother has now been dead for 3,294 minutes.

I can't be this way. I can't stay this way. I can't be this way. I can't stay this way.

I watch the seconds tick by on my phone's stopwatch, still running, until my eyes blur.

*"Are you there?"*

I whisper it, even though I'm sure Sarah won't wake up.

*"Please do something. Show me. Anything."*

But the only answer I get is silence.

## 3 days, 10 hours, 9 minutes

ALL THE WAY DOWN the hall, I can hear the little boy and the skinny girl fighting at breakfast. LaLa scolds them and they get quiet. Where is the other boy, the one LaLa said was older?

My jaw feels sore, like I was grinding my teeth in my sleep. How long have I been sleeping this time? What day is it? I check my phone.

My mother has been dead for 4,929 minutes.

I guess . . . I should go to school? 4,929 minutes ago was a Monday, wasn't it? It's hard to remember now. Sarah's dresser drawer is open, her plain cotton underwear, plain cotton T-shirts spilling out. Who buys her clothes now that she's here? Where does the money come from?

Such plain clothes. Little kids, they should have fun stuff. Sequined owls or something. Baseballs on their skirts if they want them. Jeans. My mother never liked me in jeans. She always said pants for girls were designed in a sexist way.

I finger the lace sleeve of the dress. I hardly even notice it now. It's like I've grown a new skin.

I text Cake.

*Don't know what to do.*

*OMG I'm so glad it's you. I was so worried yesterday when you didn't answer. Are you okay? Where are you?*

*I don't know. Some house. A lady. LaLa. Some kids.*

*LaLa? Sweet name. Are they all cool?*

I stare at my phone.

*I'm not sure that's at the top of my list of priorities right now, but yes, I guess. Sorry. I miss you.*

*I miss you.*

*I've never had a pair of jeans,* I type.

*That's a weird thing to say, but . . . I think you're right. You aren't missing anything, tho. They never fit right anyway.*

Then, *Are you okay?*

My heart surges with anger. How can I be okay? There *isn't* any *okay* anymore. What a *stupid* question. I almost type that, but I stop myself, and feel guilty, and take a deep breath, then, just:

*NO. I'M NOT. REMEMBER??*

*Right. Sorry. I'm sorry!*

*Am I supposed to go to school? I don't know what to do.*

*I think probably you don't have to go. I miss you.* 🖤

I type, *I miss her, too,* and then walk down the hall quickly, before I start crying again.

In the kitchen, they all stop eating and stare at me. I hold my phone to my chest.

There are oranges in a blue bowl, and a box of cereal, and a jug of milk on the table.

"Are you hungry?" LaLa asks.

Sarah has splotches of milk on her lips. My stomach twitches, remembering Georgia and the sour milk.

Sarah says, "It's good, and you can eat as much as you want, right? Even thirds! LaLa?"

The boy says, "Yeah. The last place I was at, they kept a lock on the fridge and there was a paper, too, that said what you could eat and how much. Like, just half an apple for breakfast, or one glass of soda for lunch."

Maybe the boy was at Georgia's, too. And who gives little kids soda for lunch?

Sarah nods vigorously. "One lady I had counted the food in the cabinets every night, and if something was missing, she'd make you sit all night at the table until you confessed."

LaLa says, "That's enough. Eat."

She rubs the boy's shoulder. "You can have whatever you want, Tiger. I can make you eggs and toast if you don't want cereal."

"I don't know how to get to school from here," I say. "Can someone take me? Is it a school day?"

I don't know what days are supposed to be anymore. What I'm supposed to be doing. Because a mom tells you that, usually.

*Get up. Eat. Pack your backpack. Brush your hair. Do you have homework? Stop texting and do your math. Should we have pizza for dinner? Look at you, you're getting so beautiful. Why are you so grumpy? Am I not allowed to call my own daughter beautiful?*

Behind my back, I twist my fingers together, hard, where LaLa can't see. The pain helps keep my tears in.

LaLa's hair is wound in a big, braided bun on top of her head, like some exotic pastry. "Don't worry about school, Tiger. We've got some other things to take care of. I'm going to drive the munchkins to school and then I'll be back." She starts putting lunchboxes in backpacks.

The little boy sticks out his tongue at me, so I stick out mine. He scowls.

When they leave, I peel an orange, press a wet wedge to my lips.

Nothing. It tastes like nothing.

Under the sink in the cloud-door bathroom, I find tampons

and pads. Towers of toilet paper. De-licer. Band-Aids. Bags of brand-new toothbrushes. Hair picks and combs and barrettes and hair oils and creams. I drink some water from a Tweety Bird paper cup. Brush my teeth. Spit out the toothpaste, rinse the sink. I'm following the routine in my head, all the stuff I'm supposed to do, but it feels like someone else is doing all these things and I'm just watching her from a distance.

I inspect LaLa's bedroom. She has a batik sheet spread across the wall over her bed, which is a thin futon on the floor. A record player. Lots of records on a shelf. A tiny table with candles on it. On the wall above the table she's pinned dozens of photographs of kids. All different colors, sizes. Some smiling. Some not. I wonder if I know any of them. Maybe I do, and I just never realized it, because I only ever really hang out with Cake, and Kai, and some of the guys at The Pit, and my mom.

My life was small, but it was mine, and now it's gone.

The other bedroom is the older boy's, the one who isn't here.

The first thing I see in there is a huge, dark poster. The face of a man, half-hidden, his dark skin floating from dark shadows. John Coltrane, it says. *A Love Supreme.* Another poster: KISS. Makeup, wild black hair. Probably Cake's dad would love these posters. They have a virtual record store they run out of their house, with loads of records and CDs and posters and memorabilia in a special room.

The blue bedspread is messy with earbuds and headphones and paperbacks, science fiction-y things with purple aliens and flying saucers on the covers. An electric guitar is in the corner. The floor is littered with boots and socks and flannel shirts and boxers, which makes me look away, embarrassed to see his underwear.

My room at home looks like this, too: stuff everywhere, piles of my mom's old records and CDs, underwear and bras on the floor. My mom always says, "This room is a veritable pigsty." She has to nag me to do laundry in the little shed behind our house.

I would do the laundry forever, all the time, if I could get her back.

I leave the boy's room, shutting the door tightly.

In the kitchen, I sit back down at the table, listen to the silence, which isn't really silence at all, because there are little things making noise that you never really notice. The hum of the refrigerator. The clock hands moving gently. A drip from the kitchen faucet.

Everything is happening outside of me and sounds very far away.

I pick at my cuticles until they turn pink and bleed. When the front door opens, I swipe them on my dress before Lala can see. The bloodstain from my lip on Tuesday, when I was at Georgia's, has dried to a pinkish streak on my sleeve.

"I'm back." LaLa looks at me curiously. "What did you do while I was gone?"

"Nothing."

LaLa's voice is gentle. "Tiger, would you like to change out of your dress? We have some appointments today. You might want to wear something else for them."

I blink. "This dress is fine. Where are we going, exactly?"

LaLa fills up a travel mug with coffee from the pot. It smells good. I'm so exhausted, and I want some, but I don't ask.

She sips from the mug. Her skirt today is long and brown and loose and she's wearing a pink tank top. "We have to go to the funeral home in Sierra Vista to make arrangements. For your mom. That woman, your friend's mother, Rhonda. She'll be there to help us. You."

My heart falls all the way down my body, past my knees, through my feet and toes and exits my body. *Arrangements.*

The girl-bug in the jar can barely breathe. She covers her face with her wings.


LaLa's old brown Volvo is hot and she apologizes for the broken air conditioning. She plays some Eastern music, the kind people listen to while they meditate, or get a massage. I suppose it's meant to be soothing, but the plucky strings and all that humming make me feel angry and sad, all at once, so I jam my thumb against her iPod and turn the music off.

LaLa doesn't say anything.

Rhonda's waiting for us inside the funeral home. The lobby's so quiet I can hear the soles of my Vans squish against the soft blue carpet.

Rhonda's eyes are red. She wraps me in a giant hug. "Tiger, sweetie, this is going to be hard, okay? Do the best you can."

*Do the best you can.*

Like this is a spelling bee and not a meeting about burying my mom.

The three of us sit in a room across from a man with pale, thinning hair and a turquoise bolo tie. He pushes brochures and papers at LaLa and Rhonda, who inspect them and ask questions I don't really understand. The air conditioner makes the sweat from being in LaLa's hot car dry on my body in a particularly itchy way.

LaLa tells Rhonda, "We need to make sure Tiger understands

everything today. They haven't been able to find her an advocate yet, so I'm going to do my best."

I guess we are *all* supposed to do our best today.

Rhonda answers sharply, "Of *course*. I know that. She's like my own *daughter*."

I know Rhonda is trying to be nice, but the "daughter" part . . . it stings. And . . . are they arguing about me? What is *that* about?

Now the three adults are staring at me, but I don't quite understand what they want me to do. I've noticed that since I became a teenager, adults respond to you in one of two ways: they wait for *you* to make the decision, like you should be happy they're allowing you a choice they're probably going to change anyway, or they just make the damn decision themselves because they don't trust you.

Right now, I can't quite tell what direction they're leaning in.

"Tiger." Rhonda's voice is soft. "Tiger, a few of the parents have gotten together and we're going to help out with the cost of the arrangements. So, we need you to take a look at these and let us know your thoughts." She nudges a heavy binder across the table to me.

The balding man taps the binder. "We have several options for all kinds of needs. Do you know what our deceased would have wanted?"

*Our deceased.* "She wasn't yours. You didn't know her."

"Of course." His face gets very pink. "My apologies. That was crass."

The binder is full of photographs of mahogany caskets and oak caskets, large, opulent steel caskets with puffy satin bedding inside, and plain caskets that just look like refrigerator boxes.

Everything seems very expensive. Where is this money going to come from? I flip the pages, getting queasier and queasier as I see how much everything costs. As I think about who goes in these things.

There are caskets with monogrammed initials and caskets with slots for photographs on the side and on the top. There are caskets made of poplar and bamboo. There are even double caskets, which means two people died together and will be buried together. There are caskets tiny enough for babies, with plump velvet pillows, and when I see those, my heart sinks in a way that feels hopeless and permanent. I push the binder away.

Rhonda asks, "Do you like any of those? We could do a simpler one, I think."

She points. "Like here. This?"

I try to imagine my mother inside that plain pine box, the lid closed, flat on her back.

That is the cheapest one in the whole binder. Four hundred and seventy-five dollars plus tax. More for bedding.

A thought occurs to me.

"Is she here?" I ask the man. His nose is shiny. "Right now?"

He nods carefully. "Yes. And we need to discuss that. If you'd like the option of a burial casket, or a service—a funeral—then we would need to start preparing the body now. And, of course, that has a cost, too."

My mother, well, her *body*, is *here*. She has a birthmark on her hip in the shape of a crescent moon and once she told me, "It's my superhero mark." When I asked her what her superpowers were, she said, "If I told you, I'd have to kill you." And then she chased me, and tickled me, and held me.

I'll never see her crescent moon superhero mark again.

It seems wrong to put her in a box and shove her underground and walk away. She made jams and jellies and grew irises and sunflowers and told me about periods and breasts and bras and how to properly wash my face and she brushed my hair and let me watch inappropriately sexy movies, because, she said, "Make love, not war, and the world will be an infinitely better place."

Thinking of all that makes my body swell with pain, and to keep it in, I actually hold my breath. The balding man meets my eyes. He must know that I'm about to cry.

He must see this all the time.

His voice is very gentle. "Cremation, too, is a very accessible way to honor our . . . *your* loved one. The remains go home with you, and you may decide later how to honor your person. In this situation, cremation may be our best path."

Rhonda explains, "Like scattering ashes, you know? This roadie friend of ours. He got cancer. His wife made pots. She put his ashes into a glaze and now he's a pot holding a rhododendron."

LaLa nods. "My friend Speedy died when I was fifteen. She was a real tough punk rocker chick. She was riding trains. Fell and got crushed. We hopped a train and scattered her ashes all along her favorite line."

"Earth to earth, ashes to ashes." The balding man crosses himself, which makes Rhonda frown. She likes to say she's a firm believer in the Church of Nothing. That used to make me smile, but it doesn't anymore. Not now.

"I can see June being okay with that." She clears her throat. "And that's . . . doable."

I'm not stupid. I understand that "doable" means money.

Now that my mother is dead, she's a price tag, which she wouldn't have liked, but I don't have much of a choice about that.

It's a funny word, *rhododendron,* and it ping-pongs in my head. I say it out loud, and everyone frowns at me, so I stare at my lap and fret some lace on the dress. I'm starting to get the wet cement feeling again, from having swallowed down my tears.

Before all this happened, I never knew trying not to cry would be actually, physically painful, but it is. My bones strain with the effort to keep all my tears in, because the last thing I want to do right now is cry in this stupid funeral home in front of this pink-faced man. In fact, the thing I most want to do, besides go *home-home,* is go back to that crappy, uncomfortable bunk bed in LaLa's house and stare at the ceiling and be left alone.

As everyone stares at me, waiting for me to decide, I begin to wonder what happens to bodies when people die, before they get put in silky caskets, and then into the ground, or in furnaces. Do they just . . . sit in a refrigerator? Is that where my mother is at this very moment? Being gently chilled inside a wall somewhere, like a packet of ham or wedges of honeydew?

Is it padlocked, like Georgia's fridge? The thought of a giant refrigerator filled with dead people, people we love, rips through me, and I laugh even though I don't mean to, because it scares me shitless, and everyone stares at me some more.

"She's overwhelmed," murmurs LaLa.

The photographs of cremation containers—*urns*—in the binder blur in front of me. There are plain vases, and elaborate vases, and fancy boxes for the ashes. There are so many.

Images of my mom, and fire, make me close my eyes tight. LaLa puts her hand on mine.

I close my eyes. I just want this to be over.

I snap my eyes open and point to the first box I see on the page, a white one, with a swirly red-and-green dragon on it. It's the cheapest one on the page.

"That one," I say.

Everyone breathes a sigh of relief, except for me.

"Can we go now?" I whisper. "Can we please just go?"


The funeral home was in Sierra Vista, about fifteen minutes from Mesa Luna, but a good thirty from where LaLa lives. On our way home, before we pick up the kids at school, LaLa stops at a café. It's cool inside. The walls are the color of mud. LaLa puts her purse, a big colorful bag, on the table. "I'm going to order us something simple. You haven't eaten in almost two days, Tiger. You need some protein."

The tabletop is cold under my hands. My skin is so dry I imagine it cracking and flaking off, bit by bit, until I'm just bone and gristle, and a great wind comes, and blows the rest of me away, until I'm nothing, not even a speck of a person.

That doesn't sound so bad. Disappearing. Not feeling.

The girl-bug in the jar flutters, nods her head. She taps her fingers on the glass. *Yes,* she seems to say. *What a good idea.*

Tears flood my eyes. I'm exhausted, and I can't hold back anymore. *Hush, hush, baby.* Coconut shampoo, her soft hair against my face. A bad dream.

My mom, burned to bits, stuffed in a small box. It's all a *horror.*

I don't want anyone in the café to notice me, but I'm powerless to stop it. So I do a kind of thing where I hunch my shoulders and lean forward and tip my face to the table. It's a complicated kind of breathing, but I manage not to make a sound or sob. My tears splash on the table.

"Oh God." LaLa sets two soup bowls down, finds a soft cloth in her bag, and wipes my face. "It's okay," she says gently. "It's going to be okay."

"No," I choke out. "It *isn't.*"

I meet her eyes. She doesn't try to correct me, or give me some crappy saying, and in that instant I understand. LaLa *knows*, but she doesn't want to say it out loud.

My life is going to be *shit* from now on. In ways I never could have imagined.

When we pick up the little boy and the girl, Sarah, they argue in the backseat. Sarah calls the boy Leonard. *Leonard,* stop poking me. *Leonard,* stop picking your boogers.

Leonard says, *You* stop.

LaLa looks at them both in the rearview mirror. "Guys, turn it down. Tiger's had a rough day."

I wrap my arms around myself. "I don't care. I really don't."

Truthfully? They can be as noisy as they want. Fine with me. Their noise just fills up all the empty space around me. Areas my sadness can leak.

When we get back to LaLa's, I walk straight into the house and down the hall, Leonard calling after me, "Where are you going? Where's she going, LaLa? And when is she gonna take off that weird dress?"

LaLa shushes him. From the top bunk, I hear the sounds of television, and clinking pots and pans as she starts dinner.

I text Cake, but she doesn't answer. Then I remember, *Oh,*

she's at band practice. She's at school, still. There's *school,* and *life,* and that's where everyone is. They are going on, and I'm just stopped, a girl-bug in the dirt, upended and pathetic.

I roll over, press my body against the cool wall. I'd like to become this wall, burrow in it, let the termites get me, ravage me from the inside out.

HERE ARE THE THINGS you think about when your mother dies:

That her skin was very soft. That you think you can feel it, still, when you close your eyes super hard.

That you're afraid one day you'll wake up and try to remember what her skin felt like, her cheek on yours when you were sick, and you suddenly won't be able to. It will be gone, *poof, kerplink, kerplank, kerplunk,* just like those blueberries in the pail after Sal ate them. That made your mom laugh, that Sal's mom kept picking the berries without knowing Sal was eating them all.

You're afraid the woman in the television show you're watching right now, crying as her daughter tries on wedding gowns, will never be *your* mother, and *you* will never be that girl standing in that gown for her in a ritzy shop, or any shop, for that matter, your face glowing. That's all done for, now.

If you ever get married, or go to prom, or graduate college, all that stuff that's supposed to make a life? There will be an empty chair where your mom was supposed to be.

Taking photos, wiping away tears, fixing the hem on your dress. Admiring your diploma.

If you ever have a baby, who will tell you all the secrets about fussiness and teething and walking and all that weird and scary stuff?

That if you have kids, they might wonder why they don't

have a grandma, just like you used to, before you realized how sad it made your mom, so you stopped asking.

These are the thoughts that make you suddenly jump off the couch, startling Sarah, who loves this show about picking wedding dresses, and you run to the toilet, where you heave everything you really haven't eaten in four days, gross yellow sticky stuff, until your stomach is sore and your jaw aches. You knew you never should have gotten out of the bunk bed.

LaLa holds your hair, just like your mother did when you were sick, but she isn't the same, she can't be the same, nothing will ever be the same, because wherever you go? There will always be this emptiness inside you and beside you, where your mom is supposed to be, and only *you* will know the emptiness. Other people won't be able to see it. They'll see *you*, moving around the world, just like before. You'll look alive on the outside but be dead on the inside, flicking your wings and watching everyone through the jar.

In the narrow top bunk, in the dress your mother bought for you because she thought you'd look beautiful in it, you hold the pillow over your mouth and sob and wish you could just die, too, because this emptiness is too heavy.

You're only sixteen, and you wish you'd known how to prepare for the sheer weight of it.

L ALA WANTS ME TO wash the dress, but I tell her no. LaLa
wants me to at least take a shower, and I say all right, but I
don't really wash myself. I just go through the motions of turning on the water, stripping off my dress and underwear and bra,
and standing there until I'm soaked. Then I get out. I don't even
brush my hair.

Today is the last day I will see my mother. It's called a viewing, and people will come, and we'll eat cold foods laid out on a
table, and people will pay their respects to her, and then they'll
take my mom . . . away. This is what LaLa has told me.

She asks if I want her to do my hair. "Just some brushing," she
says lightly. "Maybe pull it back at the sides? I have some cool pins."

My mom was forever petting my hair, braiding it, brushing
it. That's a *mother* thing to do, so I tell LaLa no.

"I can't go with you today," she says. "I'd have to take the
littles, and I don't think you want crazy kids running around."
LaLa looks sad as she tells me this.

She wants me to eat, so I nibble two crackers with peanut
butter and two slices of apple, chewing slowly, while Sarah and
Leonard eye me over bowls of Cheerios.

"Your dress smells," Leonard says pointedly.

"So what?" I answer. "It doesn't matter."

LaLa stands at the stove, sipping a cup of tea. It's a pretty cup,
with lacy designs. She has a lot of pretty cups, I've noticed, and

114

pretty, delicate things, like ivory-colored doilies over the back of the rumpled couch and stained-glass unicorns that hang down in the window, catching the sunlight. Sarah likes watching the colorful reflections of the unicorns against the far wall in the living room. LaLa's house has colors and softness. Georgia's was gray and hard and dark.

Sometimes when Leonard gets too antsy, LaLa makes him sit "crisscross applesauce" on the floor and watch the sand in an hourglass drift down. She says it calms him, and it does.

Karen the social worker is coming to take me to the viewing.

I check my phone. It's been 6,360 minutes since my mother died.

I type: *How many minutes is 50 years?*

If I live fifty more years without my mother, I will be sixty-six, an old lady, and I'll have lived 26,280,000 minutes without her, each one more damn lonely and horrendous than the last.

Cake texts, *You can do this. You can be brave.*

*No, I can't.*

I can't.

I run to the bathroom. Throw up the crackers and apple.



Karen and I have been sitting in her car in the parking lot of the funeral home for ten minutes. I know this because I've been watching the time on the dash over the front seat as she scrolls and texts on her phone.

I rest a hand on my chest. How is it physically possible for a heart to be beating so fast and a person *doesn't* die? I feel like I'm going to split open any minute.

Karen slides her phone into her purse. "It's time now, Tiger. We should go in. It'll be okay. Your friends are there. Your mom's friends, too."

"I wish everyone would stop saying *it will be okay*. It *won't*." I wedge the heels of my hands against my eyes, but it isn't any use. I cry.

Karen hands me a tissue. "It'll be like this for a long time, Tiger. You just have to keep keeping on, I guess."

My voice comes out sharp and ugly. "That sounds like song lyrics. That sounds *stupid*." I sniffle into the wet tissue and throw it on the floor of her car.

When I walk into the funeral home, Cake flies into me, hugging me so hard my ribs hurt. I miss her so much there's an awful ache inside me, but there's just too much ache for my mom, too, and it's drowning everything else out.

She leads me into another room, one with a lot of people. Karen pats my shoulder and goes to sit on a chair by the wall.

Cake whispers, "Are they mean to you where you are?"

I shake my head. "It's all right. It doesn't matter."

She leans down close. She's a good six inches taller than me. Her eyes are worried. "It *does* matter," she says.

Cake's wearing a black lacy dress with a black scarf around her neck and red barrettes in her hair. I feel a flash of anger. Does she think this is a *party*?

All around us, the room has gone quiet.

Everyone is staring at me. There are so many people; I don't even know all of them. They start walking up to me. "Paying their respects," Cake whispers.

Mr. Timmins, who runs Ted's Threads, holds his old felt hat in his hands and looks very sad. My mom liked to walk around his shop on hot days because it was air-conditioned, touching things like vintage velvet purses and rusty signs advertising soda pop.

He says, "I am very sorry for your loss. Your mother was a lovely, lovely woman."

Isabella who owns the Stop N Shop, who let my mom run a tab when things were hard, in exchange for some jams and jellies, is the next to appear in front of me. She touches my cheek. "Mija," she sighs. "Mi palomita. To lose your mama."

I can't help it. I say, "I'm sorry I'm crying so much," and she pulls me against her.

They keep coming, these adults with sad eyes and soft hugs, people I didn't realize even knew my mother.

Cake's mom, Rhonda, is crying, and so is Cake's dad, and even her uncle Connor, though I don't know why. Did he even really know my mom? He was usually hiding in his room when she'd come to pick me up at Cake's. I think he thought she was pretty. His eyes are glassy. He must be stoned.

Maybe I should start getting stoned, now that there's no one to care.

There are even some kids from school here, like Kelsey Cameron and Mae-Lynn Carpenter. Kelsey hugs me and says she's sorry. She smells like vanilla. She'll probably make some posts about me on Instagram later. #sad #poorkidnomom #orphangirl

Mae-Lynn is wearing a black dress with white buttons and a Peter Pan collar. I don't think I've ever seen her in anything other than a shirt and pants.

We've never even talked before, so I can't figure out why she's here, but she is.

She tugs at the edges of her hair. They're ragged with split ends. "I'm sorry about your mom."

She won't meet my eyes.

"Okay," I say. "Thanks."

She leans over and gives me the lightest hug I've ever felt, like she's a small bird or something, just barely putting her arms on me. Just before she pulls away, she whispers in my ear, "Welcome to the Big Suck. It's going to be really bad."

Before I can ask what she means, she's gone, melting into a thicket of people by the food table.

Cake says, "What was *that* about?"

"I don't know," I answer. "Weird." *The Big Suck.*

I'm starting to get really, really tired. The wet cement feeling. A thousand bricks on my chest.

A seemingly endless line of humans is waiting to kiss me, shake my hand, hug me, give me teary eyes. "I can't take this," I mumble to Cake, but she doesn't hear.

Randy Gonzalez from the horse farm puts his hand on my shoulder, which doesn't make me uncomfortable, just weird-feeling. My mom always called him "stately," and I think now I understand what she meant. He holds himself very still, like he's thinking deeply about things. He smells like all the old men around Mesa Luna, like aftershave and Three Flowers pomade.

"My deepest condolences, Grace. Come to the ranch sometime, and visit the horses, will you? They miss your mother. She came all the time, you know."

Cake and I look at each other.

"She did?" I say slowly.

Mr. Gonzalez nods. "Oh, yes, a few times a week. She'd stop the book bus on her way back. You were probably in school."

*The book bus.* What a funny way to put it. She drove the county library Bookmobile to nursing homes and houses way, way out in the desert, all by themselves with just dirt and sky around them. I went with her a few times, when I was little, but it was kind of boring, listening to her talk to very old people who lived in one-room houses about the new Danielle Steel she had in, or a nine-hundred-page biography of some British lord.

And then we'd visit the horses, which was fine. But I never knew she went without me. And often?

I wonder what other things my mother did without me. Who she talked to. What she . . . thought about things.

Suddenly, I wonder if my mother was lonely, and the thousand bricks on my chest become a million bricks, and I can't breathe.

Mr. Gonzalez says, "You're a very brave girl, Grace."

As he walks away, Cake whispers, "It's almost over. I think. You can do this, Tig. I know you can."

People come in waves. I can barely talk to them, I'm so overwhelmed.

There are some Eugene Field teachers here, like Laizure from Bio, who half slaps, half pats me on the upper arm, and Betty Bales, the Woodshop lady with the giant mole on her cheek, who always yells at me for not cleaning up the shavings on the floor. Betty Bales says, "I brought the casserole, over there. Black beans and potatoes. You just slice off a little square and warm it up and you'll be good to go, dear."

Betty Bales shrugs, her eyes filling up. "Or you can eat it cold, too. It's really up to you."

It occurs to me that Betty Bales might actually *like* me, to cook for me and come here, and so I start to wonder why she's always yelling at me about those shavings. They're just shavings. I mean, in the whole scheme of the world, they're just stupid wood shavings on the floor.

The school counselor, Walrus Jackson, is here. He's super big and used to play football at the U of A until he got hurt. Now he teaches history and hands tissues to crying kids in his office and tries to figure out who TP'd the mesquite trees on the front lawn of Eugene Field.

Cake says, "Hey, Mr. Jackson."

"Hello, Cake."

I wait for it. Usually, when he sees me, he says, "Hey, when are we going to start our own zoo?" You know, because *Tiger* and *Walrus,* duh.

But he doesn't say that today. Instead, he says, "Hello, Tiger. I am so very, very sorry about your mother. She was a wonderful person."

And his eyes are so nice when he says this, and his voice so soft, I can barely see him for all the tears.

"You can come talk to me anytime, okay, Tiger? About anything. My door is always open. You can even call me if you need to."

He hands me a small card. It has his name on it, and his school phone number and email. I swallow hard. What would I even say? *I miss my mom, Mr. Jackson. Bring her back, please.*

"Thanks." I squeeze the card in my fist.

"Be good, Cake," he says, flashing a smile at Cake, before he heads over to talk to Mr. Gonzalez, who's trying to balance a bowl of posole and a bottle of Fanta along with his cowboy hat.

People keep asking, *Do you need anything?* They say, *This is so awful.* They say, *She's in a better place,* and that makes me angry, because what does that make her place with *me*? Horrible?

Adults all look alike after a while. Bland and worn out.

The room has gotten kind of eerily quiet. People are disappearing into a door at the back of the room. Cake takes my hand.

Oh.

That's where she is.

Waiting.

Cake is watching Karen-the-social-worker on the chair by the wall, texting. She whispers, "You should be with *us*! This so sucks, Tig. My mom is calling everyone she can, trying to get you to stay with us."

"I can't," I say matter-of-factly. "I don't belong to you. I don't belong to anyone. Well, the state, I guess." I don't even really understand what that means. I kind of picture a piece of paper with my name on it in big black block letters being passed around by a bunch of serious-looking people and finally somebody stamps the paper *Orphan,* slides the paper in a drawer, and closes the drawer.

My eyes keep drifting back to the door at the end of the room.

Cake's mom appears in front of me, wringing a tissue in her fingers. "It's time for you, Tiger."

She means the door. The one where my mother is.

Cake says, "I'll come with, Tig."

But I say, "No."

My feet are like lead. My feet are like bricks. My feet are like cement blocks dragging along the floor. I can feel everyone's eyes on my back. What do they think about my weird dress? What will they say later about the crazy girl who wore a dirty, wrinkled, bloodstained old dress to her mother's viewing? In the corner, Kelsey Cameron is taking a picture of her plate of food.

#funeralgrub #orphaneats #sadjello

Maybe I'll turn into one of those mad girls from the Gothic novels I devoured all last, hot summer, the fan above my bed in my room whirring the hours away. I spent hours in a T-shirt and underwear, reading, my mother napping on the couch in the front room. In the hot months of June and July, we tried to go out in the Jellymobile in the mornings, before the small truck got too hot and close inside. Then we'd come home and eat cold pinto beans and slices of cucumber, and she would nap, and I would read and read, the storms and dark weather in the books cooling me off.

Those girls wandered cliffs in heavy dresses and moaned a lot. Their faces flushed scarlet when the man they loved was near. They turned ghostly when love was ripped from them.

Those girls never seemed to have mothers, either. They wandered endlessly, thirsty for love and comfort, with wind-tangled, wet hair and mournful coughs.

Maybe that's going to be my future.

I pause at the door. My heart beats so fiercely I can feel it in my throat. I think if there were not thirty people behind me, watching me, I would turn and run, because I don't want this moment to happen.

There are tall yellow and white flowers in vases in the room. Who ordered them? Or are there just always flowers in the room? My mom would know exactly what kind of flowers they are. Our backyard is filled with sunflowers and daises pushing up against the coyote fence. Aloe vera and herbs and tomatoes and carrots lined up in pots and tidy beds.

She's in the middle of the room, in the plain pine box Rhonda asked for, on a kind of stand. The plain box is just for the viewing, because my mom will be cremated later, and then her ashes put into the white box with the dragon on it.

Do they wipe out the plain pine casket after, or vacuum it or something, and save it for the next person with no money? Do they burn the box, too?

There are just too many details involved in dying. And the after. Maybe both. My head is spinning.

It's strange to see her again, and scary, because she's really, really gone. It's not a joke, or a nightmare, or a bad dream. There's no portal. It's all right here.

I have never heard anything this quiet in my life. My hands are shaking so badly I clasp them together.

She's *here,* but she's *not.* She looks like she's sleeping, but in a very formal way.

I'm trembling so hard my teeth are clacking together.

Someone gelled my mom's hair and combed it back. She would have hated that. She liked her hair spiky and messy. I tousle her hair, but carefully, like she's a doll.

Her skin is cool, and not warm and soft, like I remember, but waxy, and firm.

Someone painted her nails with clear, glossy polish. The star earrings look nice. A little bit of the hem on her dress has ridden

123

up, so I tug it down gently, and wonder who chose this dress, because it's too short and, well, not formal enough for death.

I feel like my mom should not be going to the afterlife with bare legs. It's like she's on her way to the Stop N Shop for some chips and dip. It must have been Cake. She and her mom must have gone back to my house and picked out the earrings and the dress.

"I didn't pick the dress, just so you know," I tell her.

Nothing.

"Open your eyes, Mommy," I say softly.

She doesn't.

"Why did you leave me?"

No answer.

"What am I going to do without you?" My voice cracks, and then my tears are dripping on her dress. I want to stay in this room with her forever, but I know I can't.

I put my head on her chest. It's a surprise and not a surprise there's no heartbeat inside her body. I breathe her in, deeply, trying to locate her smell, that nice and earthy thing, but it isn't there anymore.

She smells like hair gel and nail polish and something almost bleach-like.

I wrap my arms around her anyway.

A whole canyon forms in me then, immense and desolate.

And even though I know I'll never get an answer, I whisper it anyway, my words burying themselves against the flimsy cotton of her summer dress.

*Please don't leave me.*

*Please don't leave me. Please come back.*

*Please.*

I crack into so many pieces they will never fit back together, not ever.

The girl-bug in the jar folds her wings over her eyes. She doesn't want to watch.

In a little while, Rhonda and Cake come into the room and take me away.

## 5 days, 22 hours, 22 minutes

K AREN DRIVES ME BACK to LaLa's after the viewing, stacks of Tupperwared food next to me in the backseat.

"That was a lot to deal with today," she says, looking at me in the rearview mirror.

I stare at her. "You *think*?"

She frowns. "I'm sorry. I don't know what to say. I'm not too good at death."

"Like *I'm* an expert?" I say sharply.

She turns on the radio. Country music. The twang cuts into my ears.

We pull into LaLa's dirt driveway. Karen gets out of the car and takes a stack of Tupperware in her arms. I start walking to the house, lugging lukewarm black bean casserole and strawberry Jell-O and bags of Santitas.

"Tiger," Karen says. I turn around.

"I'm sorry, there's no good way or time to tell you this, but I've found a placement for you, a more permanent one, I hope, in Sierra Vista. Three foster kids, two parents."

My heart plummets. "How many times am I going to be *moving* from now on?"

She shakes her head. "I'm hoping this will be it for a little while, though I really can't say. There are just so many factors involved. They're prepping for you now, and we'll drive out on Monday morning."

Two days away. My heart spikes with fear, but then just as quickly quiets down. I've had praying weirdos, locked refrigerators, kids who paw through my suitcase, and my mom is *dead*. It's not going to ever get any worse than that.

"Okay, then, well, *whatever*, I guess. I don't care. I just don't care."

At the doorway of LaLa's house, I pause. Am I supposed to ring the doorbell or walk right in? I mean, I don't *live* here. I'm just a stupid visitor.

A visitor in someone else's life. One kid in a long line of kids who'll stand on this step with a stupid broken heart and a stupid, sad story.

I'm going to be a *visitor* forever now.

I stab the doorbell with my finger.

LaLa looks surprised when she opens the door. "Tiger. Honey. Come in. You don't have to wait outside."

I shove the food in her arms and walk straight to the bedroom, where I climb to the top bunk and promptly fall asleep. When I wake up, my dress is still damp from tears and sweat, and it's dark, and late, and LaLa's whispering with someone in the kitchen. I hang my head off the bunk to see around the bedroom door, which is slightly open.

LaLa murmurs, "Are you all right? Is there anything you want to tell me?"

The voice that answers is hoarse and tired. "Nah. It was the same old same old. He didn't do anything."

It's the older boy, the one she said was away in Phoenix.

He mumbles something I don't quite catch.

LaLa answers, "She's in her room. She had a hard day. The viewing was today."

The boy says something I can't understand. Why do boys always sound like they have rocks in their mouths?

Then LaLa says, "There's tons of food in the fridge if you're hungry."

"Can I go in the backyard? Then I'll go to bed, I promise. I'm tired, I swear. I just need to chill and stretch out after the drive. My back is super sore."

I roll back as they come down the hall. The light clicks off. The screen door to the backyard opens and closes.

I climb down the bunk ladder. I don't know why I'm going outside, except that teenagers are chemically drawn to other teenagers, and when another one appears, we're compelled to huddle together, like a pack of angsty and acned lemmings.

I've only seen the backyard once, through a window, because I've pretty much stayed in the bedroom all this time, but as I open the screen door, I suck my breath in.

LaLa's backyard *is* the desert, with lawn chairs and kid toys scattered near the house and then . . . darkness and the shapes of mesquite trees and prickly pears, whose flat pads always make me think of spiky ping-pong paddles. The moon rests in the sky like a perfect white paper plate, gentle and still.

I wish I could walk straight through the desert and take it in my hands.

The boy doesn't turn around. He's stretched out on a jelly lounger, and as I get closer, I can see the white cords streaming from his ears underneath a mess of long, thick hair. He's wearing an army jacket with a KISS patch. Maybe he's a regular shopper at Ted's Threads, too.

And I smell pot.

I thump him on the shoulder and he startles, dropping the

joint onto his lap. He tamps it out between his fingers, drags the buds out of his ears.

"What was *that* for? Are you trying to give me a heart attack or something?" He has eyes like a deer's, wide and brown.

"You aren't supposed to be doing *drugs* out here. Won't LaLa kick you out?"

"What are you, like a Goody Two-shoes or something?"

I blink.

Well, *yes*. Sad, but true. I've never had alcohol, much less smoked pot, or done anything beyond kiss for a billion hours at Thunder Park, and look how *that* turned out.

As Cake once told me: "You live a pristine, still-in-the-plastic-box kind of life, Tiger Tolliver."

Kids at The Pit smoke pot, and do other things during their parties, but not me. Mom always said that sort of stuff is no good, and that it turns you into a different person, and if you do those things long enough, pretty soon you'll get too far away from who you used to be, and it'll be hard to find your way back. To tell the truth, that's always kind of scared me. Not being able to find my way back to something.

"Don't worry about it," the boy says. "LaLa's cool."

He gets up kind of slowly, which makes me wonder how stoned he might be. He goes and gets me a jelly lounger.

He has a weird tilt to his walk, like someone bent him to the right and forgot to bend him back.

"Have a seat." He plops the jelly lounger down. Does he grimace a little? It's not that heavy.

"I already know your name. Tiger! That's a pretty cool name. I'm Thaddeus. Thaddeus Roach."

I lower myself onto the jelly. It's nice to lean back, and to breathe, and look up at the stars, which I feel like we always forget to do, you know? Even me, on my bed in my *old* room in my *old* house, scrolling my phone or reading a *book* about characters who look at the sky, instead of actually going out and looking at the sky myself.

"That sucks about your mom."

I don't think I'll ever get used to the sharp knife that runs down my spine when people say they are sorry. Or that it sucks. *I'm sorry to hear about your mom.* I must have heard that a thousand times today.

"Are *your* parents alive?" I ask. I'm not sure exactly how this foster thing works. We can't all be orphans. Maybe some of us were abandoned?

"My mom is, but not my real dad. She's remarried now. They're both kind of like the walking dead, to tell you the truth. Drugs and stuff, which is why I'm here. This is my fourteenth home."

Fourteenth home. I guess I'm going to meet a lot of kids like Thaddeus from now on, kids stitched together with unmatched thread, trying their best not to fray.

He points to the sky. His fingernails are painted pink. "Can you see?" he asks. "There. That kind of hazy mass."

I squint. Constellations have never been my strong suit.

Thaddeus starts talking about nebulas and clusters and black holes. He tells me black holes suck everything in, that they're basically vacuum cleaners in space. And once something is in, it can't get out.

"You still have a chance—I mean *the object* has a chance—to get away, while it's on the edge, just before the hole. But how long? Nobody really knows how long it takes to get sucked in. A blip? A nanosecond? Time in space isn't like it is down here."

"What's with the nails?" I ask. "Kind of a demure look for a member of the KISS Army."

"Oh." He holds his hands up, palms against the sky with its quivering white stars. "These. I was visiting my little sister in Phoenix. She likes to play nail salon."

I want to ask why his little sister is *there* and he's *here,* and what the deal is with his zombie mom and zombie stepdad, but I don't. I feel heavy enough right now, and a little selfish with my own pain, and I'm also kind of afraid of what the answer might be.

Thaddeus clears his throat. "No dad in the picture, I guess?"

"Yeah. I mean, obviously, there *was* one, or I wouldn't be here, but who he is or where he is, or if he even *is* anymore, is a question that was never answered."

"That blows. LaLa's cool, though. You could do a lot worse. I have. So, listen."

He leans over the arm of the plastic jelly chair. I dip my head closer.

"My advice to you is to split. Run. Get the fuck out. You don't know what's out there, what kind of people they might place you with. LaLa's great, but she's rare."

Thaddeus Roach doesn't even blink as he tells me this, so I fully believe the potential for hideousness might be real.

It's at this moment, so close to his face, the two of us, well, conspiratorial *orphans* together, and with thoughts that maybe *we'll* run away together, and he'll teach me the tricks of the street, like how to siphon money from someone's pocket at the bus station, or how to jam food in my jacket at the Quik-E-Stop, that I suddenly wonder what it might be like to kiss him, because I'm noticing that his lips are kind of attractively plump, and I immediately lean back on my own jelly lounger, because, my *God,* now that I've kissed one boy, am I going to want to kiss them all? And also, I can't believe I'm even *having* these thoughts, because my mom is *dead.*

I guess I kind of always thought that sort of stuff would take a backseat to death.

Death is kind of turning out to be a mean, weird bitch.

Anyway. I stop thinking about making out with a complete stranger and take a deep breath. "Thanks for the tip, but I'm not really Thelma, or Louise. I'm kind of a dork, prone to elaborate fantasizing, and I don't know the first thing about running away."

Thaddeus shakes his head. "Nothing to it, Tiger. You pack your bag and go, go, go. The street will teach you. I did it. Coupla times. Got caught, though."

I look up at the sky. How many stars are there, anyway? It seems impossible to comprehend all those tiny flares of heat and light. It's too complicated to think about, so I close my eyes.

My words come out suddenly, surprising even me.

"My mom . . . her thing was today."

Thaddeus says softly, "I know."

"I guess I just wanted to say that out loud. I don't know why."

"It's cool. I mean, *it's* not cool, but saying it is okay." He pauses. "What was it like? I was really young when my real dad died. Sometimes I think I can remember him, but then I think maybe I just made up the memories to make myself feel better."

I keep my eyes closed. I think of Mom in the plain pine box, on the table in the viewing room, and how my insides, my heart, seemed to expand and contract all at once.

How Rhonda and Cake had to come in and peel me off my mother. Pry my fingers from her thin summer dress. The way everyone sang along to her favorite song after. The dreamy Fleetwood Mac song with Stevie singing about a landslide and snow-covered hills and saying goodbye.

How Rhonda pressed the off button on the boombox and everything was done.

How I can't take *this* dress off, ever, not so much because Mom never saw it on me, but because now I think it's literally keeping me together. Holding my bones and heart and soul inside, because they're all split and shattered, and if I take this dress off, they'll spill out, everywhere, and I don't have the strength to pick up the pieces.

"I don't know how to describe it, exactly." Spots dance on the insides of my eyelids. My heart starts to hurt again. The smell of pot drifts over my face.

"Thaddeus. Can I have some of that?"

I just want to feel something *else.*

He hands me the joint. It's compact and papery. "I've heard people say you never get stoned the first time."

Thaddeus laughs. "That's *not* at all true."

It smells interesting. Rich. I bring it to my lips. I could be those kids, with wet eyes and sloped shoulders, giggling in the arroyo behind Eugene Field, lighting up and not caring who sees. I could be like that. I don't have anyone now who says I *shouldn't* be.

I hand it back.

"Not tonight?" Thaddeus murmurs, taking the joint back.

"Not tonight." *See,* I tell her in my head. *I didn't do it.*

"Thaddeus, how long have *you* been here, anyway? You're not really a foster, are you? You seem too comfortable."

Thaddeus bites his lower lip, like he's considering something. Then he sighs. "I've been here for five years. LaLa adopted me. It's complicated. We don't like to tell the littles about it, because then they think she'll adopt them, too, like something magical will happen and they'll never have to leave. It doesn't work that way."

He starts to say something else, but then he puts his earbuds back in, so I shut up.

I doze off for a little bit, and when I open my eyes, Leonard is there, poking my arm. He's snuggled against Thaddeus on the other jelly chair.

"We were talking," he grouses. "Pay attention, new girl."

Thaddeus says, "Leonard was just asking me how far the sky, like, the *universe,* goes, and I was telling him no one really knows."

"No," Leonard corrects him. "You got all weird and stuff and said we were just like a page in someone else's book."

Thaddeus chuckles. He takes a pull off the joint.

"You shouldn't be doing that around little kids, Thaddeus," I say sharply. "Cut it out."

Leonard shakes his head. "No, girl, he's got a subscription."

Thaddeus corrects him. "A *pre*scription. For my back. It got broke once and never healed right."

"Well, that must be a story," I say. "People don't just go around breaking their backs. Let me guess: Wild boar riding? Strenuous imitation of Beyoncé's dance moves?"

Thaddeus winces. "You're funny. Nah, just a dumb accident.

Len, we need to get you back to bed, brother. I'm going to pee, and then let's head in." He walks to the darkness at the edge of the yard.

Leonard's pajamas have a short red cape, which I fine oddly endearing. Maybe I'll start to like him. Maybe the three of us can be Oliver, Sissy, and Pip, and overcome the awful obstacles that have befallen us, cheerfully blacking boots and running through the streets with pails of ale. People will write books about *us*. I picture the three of us, our silhouettes embedded in a cameo brooch.

Leonard squinches his eyes at me. "Where did you go just then? You have a distraction problem, don't you? I have that. Eddy Etchdey. All my parents are always telling me that, and teachers."

*All my parents.*

*Eddy Etchdey.* I smile. Like ADHD has a name. Like ADHD *is* a little kid, running wild, popping balloons.

"I do have a distraction problem," I admit. "My m— Anyway, someone I used to know told me I suffered *flights of fancy.*"

Leonard stares at me. "You weird. Fancy can't fly. Fancy's not *a bird.* Anyway, listen. About Thad. I heard La talking about it on the phone. His stepdad did it. Like, stomped on him. You know." He slides from the jelly lounger and hops up and down hard, saying *Bam! Bam! Bam!* He adds in some kicks. Sand flies up, stinging my eyes.

*"Stop,"* I say, not just because of the sand stinging my eyes, but because of the stinging awfulness of what Leonard has just said. It can't be true. I try to get the image of *that,* a parent doing that, out of my head. I swallow hard.

I miss my mother so terribly, and our quiet, kind life together.

Leonard says simply, "Yeah, well, it's a bad world, you know." He's starting to look very sleepy. I wonder how *he* got to LaLa's, what *his* broken-back story is.

He murmurs, "Thaddy says we're just stories in somebody's book and every time they turn a page, that's when new stuff happens. But I think we're like one of those snow balls. You know, shake 'em up and everything gets all messed up and the snow-flakes cover everything and nothing goes back where it was."

Is that it? That I'm stuck in a bizarre snow globe of grief now, someone controlling my destiny with just one tiny shake? Leonard sighs on his jelly lounger.

The stars are fading. Pink and orange begin to climb up the horizon. It's never really occurred to me before that stars are always shining, they don't "go out" when night ends. You just can't see them, because of the sun. I feel stupid all of a sudden, that this thought has never occurred to me before. I should have paid more attention in school. Too late now.

Thaddeus comes back and scoops up a sleeping Leonard.

"We should go in," he says quietly, and takes him inside the house, me following. I head to the room I share with Sarah, and try to sleep, but I can't. I just keep thinking of the horribleness of what Leonard said, and the horribleness of my mother's viewing, and what's going to happen to me, and where I'm going to end up, and my stomach starts clenching, and I start to sweat and panic.

My loneliness is like the black hole Thaddeus was talking about, sucking everything in.

Once, for my mom's birthday, I begged Cake's mom to drive me to Tucson to Whole Foods, so I could buy my mom's favorite coconut shampoo; it was expensive, almost nine dollars a bottle, and Whole Foods was the only place that sold it. I helped Bonita at the daycare for two weeks every afternoon to earn enough money for the shampoo, the frozen Sara Lee cheesecake with strawberries, the candles, and the fancy card with a dancing Chihuahua that we picked out at the Red Store, which is what Cake's mom called Target. It was a running joke to her. She calls Walmart the Blue Store.

My mom cried when she unwrapped the pink tissue paper. She said, "Tiger, you are the *best* girl."

No one is ever going to say that to me again.

I think of the favorite way she liked to fall asleep, when the two of us shared a bed: back against back, "like bookends," she said. Our spines pressed together, warm and firm.

I always fell asleep right away when the two of us did that.

I remember that for all my wanting a dad, or at least the story of a dad, I never didn't want *her,* I never didn't love *her,* I never didn't love the well-oiled, good-looking, and good-smelling machine.

In the top bunk, in a stranger's home, I'd give anything at this moment to have her back, because I don't think I can live without her. And I don't want to.

The black hole glistens. The girl-bug pauses, considering, rubbing her wings thoughtfully.

*What you had left to lose is already gone,* she whispers.

*All my parents,* Leonard had said. How many has he had? How many more locked refrigerators and cups of too-warm milk and plates of boiled meat am I going to have before this is all over and I'm . . . what? Spit out on the sidewalk? Eighteen, with a dented pink suitcase and . . . nothing?

My brain spins. There are so many things in LaLa's house.

There's probably aspirin I can swallow. Something sharp I can use.

A kind of bleak quiet settles over me. Something weirdly warm and calm. Like fog over the moors in one of my books.

The girl-bug waits, her wings flickering.

I suddenly understand the girls at Eugene Field who take to razors and broken glass, and even those kids who went a little further.

It's like Thaddeus said: if I go in the black hole, I'm in forever.

My fingers are trembling so badly, but I manage to text Cake.

*I'm not in a good place. I'm freaking out. I'm having thoughts.*

Cake answers, *OMG, what?*

*Like bad stuff. The S word. I feel so bad, Cake, I feel so, so, so, so bad.*

That's what Cake and I called it, after what those kids had done two years ago. We were in Davidson Middle School and didn't know them. They were older and went to Eugene Field.

It happened in quick succession, first the one girl, Tonia, and then two boys, Harvey and Crash. Wrists, hanging, gun.

Cake types, *DON'T.*

*My mom is dead, Cake. I don't have anyone. They found me a place in Sierra Vista. I leave on Monday.*

My phone buzzes. I'm breathing so heavily I start to hiccup, and can't even say hello to Cake.

Cake says firmly, "You shut your mouth right now about the S word, do you hear me? You're my best friend, and I fucking love you, and I will *not* let you die. You have *me.* And I'm awesome. And we will get through this, somehow. I don't know *exactly* how, because we're just stupid kids, but somehow, we will, okay?" Her voice cracks.

"There's a boy here, like, our age, and he says I should run away."

"Hmm. A guy. Well, what the hell does he know! He doesn't *know* you. You're as tender as a baby *chick,* for God's sake."

"I know." I pause, and hiccup. Just talking to Cake is calming me down. "His stepdad, he beat him, I guess. Broke his back."

"That's . . . that's not going to happen to you, okay?" But her voice shakes, just the same. We both know it's uncharted territory, where I'm going.

She says, "And that's terrible. That's disgusting. People are *shit.* How could a person *do* that to a *child*?"

"I'm just so tired, Cake."

"You poor thing. Here, I'll calm you down, okay?"

I scooch down in the bed and pull the itchy blanket over me, putting the phone next to my head on the pillow. I know what's coming, and I'm grateful.

Cake is extremely musical. When she was born, her parents took her on the road with them. Everybody thought Rhonda was going to be washed up, that she wouldn't be able to sing anymore, lugging a baby around, but she proved them wrong. Cake was born and they bundled her up and took her on tour until she was eight years old, when they decided to settle in Mesa Luna, where Rhonda's brother, Connor, lived. I've never been anywhere but Mesa Luna and Tucson, but Cake's been all over the world.

Britney Spears taught Cake her ABCs, Gwen Stefani taught her to dance, and she went on a massive tour with Billy Joel that ended in Tokyo, where he brought her out onstage and she banged out "Only the Good Die Young" on the piano in front of fifty thousand people. She was seven. Her dad filmed the whole thing from the stage. If you have patience, you can find this performance on YouTube, and it's hilarious and totally cool at the same time. At one point, Billy just throws up his hands and lets Cake do all the singing, too. Those six minutes? They paid for whatever music school is going to grovel for her when she graduates Eugene Field.

There's some shuffling, and then Cake starts playing a variation of Beethoven's "Ode to Joy." If you haven't heard that piece played on solo violin, then I urge you to head over to YouTube right now and start listening, because it's beautiful, and sad, and then happy, and perfect in its own confusing way.

I have no idea if Cake ever messes up notes, or makes noises that shouldn't be made. I don't have a musician's ear, and I bang the drums in Broken Cradle like a toddler on Kool-Aid, and my mom always tells me that's fine. "Listen with your heart. That's all that matters."

You know what best friends do? They know what you need without you having to ask, so when Cake finishes, she just starts again.

And I listen to her play that piece over and over, the music an ocean that washes the bleakness away and rocks me to sleep, far, far away from the black hole.

## 6 days

T HE BUZZING OF MY phone pulls me from a deep sleep. I answer blearily. It's Karen.

"Be ready tomorrow morning at 8 a.m., bags packed, okay?"

"How long am I going to be there?" I mumble sleepily.

"Anything could happen, and a lot of it depends on you. On your behavior."

I test her, remembering what Thaddeus said about *taking off.*

I say, "What if I run away, what happens then?"

She doesn't even bother to be nice and call me Tiger.

"Grace," she says, her voice growing steely in a way I don't like. I'm instantly sorry I said anything. "Don't think about that. One, I've been at this a long time, and I've seen a lot of kids with a *lot* of problems, and please believe me when I say you wouldn't last a day on the street. Two, you run away? You'll get picked up in a hot second and thrown into juvie, and everything you've seen in movies about juvenile detention? It's true. And sometimes? Real life is even *worse* than the movies. You're sixteen years old. You have two years until you're legally responsible for yourself. Keep your head down, get better grades, and take care of yourself, and someday you and your friend Butter can rent an apartment together like Laverne and Shirley. Okay?"

"Her name is Cake," I answer meekly. "And I don't know who Laverne and Shirley are."

"They were best friends on a TV show when I was a kid

and they had their own apartment and twin beds and Laverne drank milk and Pepsi mixed together and all her clothes had a giant cursive *L* on them, which I absolutely adored, and Shirley had a boyfriend named the Big Ragu and I wanted to be just like them when I grew up. Be ready at 8 a.m. I'm very cranky in the morning and I don't like to wait for people." She clicks off.

Down the hall, I can hear them in the kitchen. Silverware clinking. Laughter.

When I walk in, everyone gets quiet. LaLa dishes out some sort of rice and vegetable concoction. Finally, Leonard sputters, "How long are you going to let her wear that dress, La? It's starting to smell."

I look down at the dress. As far as I'm concerned, it's never coming off. It was the last wish my mother had for me, whether she knew it would be the last one or not, and I'm going to wear this dress as long as I need to. Maybe forever.

LaLa says, "People mourn in their own ways, Leonard."

I slide into a chair. Thaddeus smiles at me and pushes a plate in my direction.

Leonard chews his rice thoughtfully. "I don't know what that word, that *mourn,* means."

"It means she's the saddest in her heart that she's ever been in her life, now that her mom is dead," Thaddeus answers.

We read a Charles Dickens novel in class once and the mourning women wore heavy black dresses made of something called bombazine. They wore those dresses for two years, until the sad period was over. But that was mostly for husbands, I think. I don't know how long they wore the bombazine dresses if their mothers died, or their children. Maybe years. And back then, people were always dying, one after the other, *kerplink, kerplunk,* because everything was dirty and hard, so maybe some women lived their whole lives in heavy black clothes, grief turning into a permanent kind of perfume.

Leonard says matter-of-factly, "*I* don't even know my real parents. They took me away when I was a baby because my daddy left me on top of the car when I was just borned and I fell off. He was high." He shrugs and takes a huge drink of milk, like being left on top of a car is nothing.

Sarah squeaks, "*My* mom is in the hospital, she's always been there, and my father lives in Flagstaff, but he doesn't give a shit about us. That's what he always told me and my sister, Pookie. 'I don't give a shit about you. Now get the hell away from me.' And finally, we did. We lived in a cardboard refrigerator box at the corner of Salter and Fifth, right by the 7-Eleven, and we used to eat the leftover hot dogs people threw in the trash."

I stare at Sarah, surprised at the filthy words and depressing meaning coming out of her mouth. She's *ten* years old.

She gnaws her carrot, blinking at me. This is just *life* for her, and Leonard.

Parents not wanting you.

My mother is overprotective and secretive and sometimes overbearing, but at least she loves me like nobody's business.

Everyone at the table is quiet, chewing.

I look down at the mound of sticky rice and sautéed carrots and slick mushrooms on the plate Thaddeus gave me.

The girl-bug corrects me. *Loved,* she whispers. Not *loves* anymore.

. . .

After everyone has gone to bed, after I hear Sarah begin to snore, and Leonard begins to hum in his sleep down the hallway, I decide to go outside, to the jelly lounger, to the stars.

Thaddeus is out there, his legs wrapped in a blanket, his earbuds in. I stretch out on my lounger. I wish I'd brought a blanket out, too.

Sometimes Kai and I would share earbuds in the school library, sitting on the carpeted floor between the stacks, and that was nice, the way our heads were so close, like the music went through his body into mine.

I can barely remember what he and I used to listen to together, now. I guess it doesn't really matter. I probably would have listened to trees being cut down if it meant I could be that close to Kai Henderson.

I shake my head to clear the memory. It just adds to my loneliness and I want to try and stay away from the black hole as much as I can. Last night scared me, how calm I felt, thinking about killing myself. The S word.

Lizards and prairie dogs scuttle in the brush in the darkness of LaLa's backyard. In just a couple of hours, I'm going to my third brand-new place in six days.

The feeling that rises up in me then is overwhelming, and I wish I could hear my mom's voice. I sneak a peek at Thaddeus.

His eyes are closed. He's not paying any attention to me.

I pick up my phone and call my mom's number. I have no idea where her phone actually is, because I haven't been back to the house since Cake and I went to pack the suitcase and I fell asleep in the old white Honda.

The minute I hear her voice, a hot kind of lonely washes through me.

"I miss you," I say quietly. "I wish you were here."

Where is her phone? What's going to happen to our things, our little house? What's going to happen to the jams and jellies on the pine shelves in the backyard building, waiting to be sold from our truck this summer? The Jellymobile. That's what everyone in town calls it. The half-dead, rumbly former ice cream truck my mother bought from a guy named Canyon on Craigslist and spent hours fixing up and painting. There's a giant, sexy saguaro cactus on the side with red lipstick and a cowboy hat. It's completely embarrassing and humiliating to drive that thing through Mesa Luna and then park it by the side of the road, waiting for tourists from Kentucky and North Dakota to stumble upon us, exclaiming about prickly pear jelly and mesquite apple jam, but it was our life together.

What's going to happen to our piles of books and photographs and blankets and clothes and chipped mugs and the collection of painted rocks in the backyard? Would our things end up in boxes tossed by the side of the road, pawed through by hungry people who needed clothes and coffee cups? Will I see someone in a grocery store in Sierra Vista wearing one of my mother's shirts someday?

I haven't checked my voice mail since it happened. I see a few from Cake, and several from my mom's friend Bonita.

I press the first message. Bonita's voice is sad. "Mija. Oh, my mija. It's Bonita. Oh, Tiger."

My eyes fill up. Bonita's crying. She and my mom loved each other so much, like me and Cake. I still hate that Cake wore that too-fancy dress to the viewing, but she's my best friend, and it won't come between us.

"Honey, I wish I was there. I wish I could come, but my mama is so sick. She's just not getting any better. I'm going to send some money. Not so much, but a little, okay? To help. I know June was running—"

The message beeps, ends. I press the second voice mail.

"It's me, again, Tiger. *Gracie.* Listen, you need to listen to me very carefully. Rhonda called me, okay? She told me what's happening, all that foster business. Oh, mija, I have something to tell you. Please forgive your mama. She thought she was doing what was best, but I kept telling her and telling her to be straight with you about your daddy and her past and you know your mama, always digging in her heels. Listen, he's out there. She said she was gonna write you a let—"

*Beep.*

Third voice mail. My heart is pounding so hard and my hands are shaking so much the phone slips out of my fingers and into the dirt. It sits there, glowing. *Your daddy.*

*Listen, he's out there.*

Thaddeus pulls his earbuds out. "Dude, Tiger. You okay? What's up?"

He brushes off the phone. His fingernails are dirty. He made a mud kingdom with Sarah and Leonard earlier in the day. "What's happening? You look sick. Breathe. I'm right here. I'm right *here.*"

Haltingly, I say, "He's out there. My dad. He . . . exists."

Thaddeus frowns, puts the phone on speaker.

146

Bonita's voice rings out in the desert air. "Ay yi yi. These stupid phones. You shouldn't be going to any foster place, you hear? She said she was gonna write a letter, but I don't know if she did or not. Oh, honey. I am sorry. Just remember, she had her reasons."

Somewhere in Texas, Bonita heaves a great sigh. Her little pug, Luther, yips in the background.

What Bonita says next sends a giant shock wave down my spine.

*His name is Dusty Franklin and he used to live in Albuquerque, and then Austin, and then Socorro, and then I don't know.*

Thaddeus says, "Holy crap."

We stare at the phone, which is no longer a phone, but an alien, a stranger, a Magic 8-Ball, the past and the future all rolled up into one.

Dusty Franklin. I have a father and his name is *Dusty Franklin.*

Thaddeus and I look at each other. Then we run inside the house and wake up LaLa, who rubs her eyes and listens to me ramble and then asks me to repeat what I said. I'm shaking, so she makes me lie down on her bed.

"This is a *lot,* do you understand, Tiger? You've had a *lot* to deal with in the past week. Your soul needs you to rest."

Dusty Franklin, Dusty Franklin, Dusty Franklin.

The thought of an actual, tangible father, that mythical piece of my DNA enjoying avocados while spurning kiwis, is almost too much to bear, so I do what LaLa asks.

The bed is warm with the heat from her body and it settles me. LaLa puts her glasses on. She listens to Bonita's messages, one by one. Thaddeus takes off his giant neon-yellow sneakers and stretches out next to me.

At the end of the bed, LaLa looks back at me. I can't read her face. I can't tell whether she's happy or sad or worried. She gives me back my phone.

"I'm going to go make some calls. Stay here."

I want to call Bonita back and ask her everything, everything, but she's probably asleep now.

*I have a dad.*

I have a dad.

Dusty Franklin, Dusty Franklin, Dusty Franklin.

I do some quick work on my phone.

It's taken sixteen years, which is roughly 8,409,600 minutes, for me to find out my dad is alive, and that he has a name.

The clock says 4:24 a.m. I keep staring at the numbers as they change. 4:25. 4:26. 4:27, like I'm in a trance. Every minute that passes is possibility now.

Because in less than four hours I'm supposed to be going somewhere new.

But if I have a dad, I can go live with him, right? I don't have to stay here or go to strangers. I don't want to think about anything else but that, not about where he's been, or why my mother never told me anything about him, or anything. I just want him to be as he is, right now, a kind of beacon.

When I open my eyes, it's because LaLa is shaking me awake. Thaddeus is still asleep. The sun is coming up.

LaLa's voice is tired. "Okay. I woke Bonita up. She doesn't know much, or if she does, she's not spilling anything to me, but I gave her Karen's number. She says there might be a letter somewhere, but who knows. At least we have a name."

I sit up and smooth my hair. "Let's go, then," I say firmly.

"Let's go . . . find him. I mean, I like you, and thank you for taking care of me, but he's my *dad.*"

She smiles and shakes her head. "You're welcome, but nothing doing, honey. I've got little kids here, and big ones, who need some sleep. Karen's on it. I talked to her. She's doing some investigating. I mean, we don't know who he is, where he is, *what* he is. There are a lot of legal implications."

She takes a breath. "It could be a disappointment, too, Tiger, and you need to prepare yourself for that. But if it's disappointing, it doesn't have to be devastating, does that make sense? Life has *this,* life has *that,* and then something else comes along again, like a wave. We ride the waves. You go down, you go up, you go down, sometimes you just drift."

I know she's right, so I nod slowly, but my whole being aches at that moment to meet the biggest secret my mother ever kept from me.

Dusty Franklin, Dusty Franklin, Dusty Franklin.

## 6 days, 12 hours

I T'S MONDAY.

They put the Sierra Vista home on hold. All LaLa would tell me is, "There are some developments."

I'm waiting to hear from Karen about my dad. Sarah and Leonard are home from school and watching *The Octonauts* when there's a sharp rap on the front door. I'm so beside myself that I rush to answer it, even as LaLa suddenly calls out in a sharp voice, "No, Tiger, let me."

But it's too late.

The woman at the door has a no-nonsense look and a big shoulder bag stuffed with folders. "May I speak with LaLa Briggs, please?"

Over her shoulder, I see the car. The seal on the back passenger-side door.

And then Sarah starts screaming.

My tongue feels wooden. *They're here for you,* the girl-bug croaks. *No,* I tell her. *Not yet. Not until tomorrow. I have a dad.*

*No,* says the girl-bug. *Not yet, you don't.*

But she's wrong, because it isn't me the woman wants, it's Leonard.

The woman says his full name. Leonard Louis Lamont.

Leonard starts to cry. The woman eases past me.

LaLa knew this was coming. She must always know, because

she suddenly has a brown suitcase with happy face stickers on it, and Leonard's Batman backpack.

Thaddeus appears in the hall doorway. His face is grim. Sarah rocks back and forth on the couch. *You can't have him, you can't take him, you're always taking us away.*

They seem brave most of the time, but not now.

"I need everyone to calm down and follow the rules, please. Leonard." The woman lowers her head to look at him. Tears pour down his face, but he doesn't make a sound.

"I've got a nice house for you. There's even a pool in the neighborhood. I'll bet you like to swim."

He shakes his head. "No, thank you. There are sharks in the water."

*Make that girl stop screaming,* says the girl-bug. *She's hurting my bones.*

I walk over to the couch, put my arm around Sarah. She buries her face against my chest.

Thaddeus kneels down in front of Leonard. "Be strong, buddy. You remember what we talked about? The bad stuff?"

Leonard whispers, "All superheroes were sad kids. The sadness made them strong and then they rose up and helped people."

"You'll rise up, Len. You'll find your power. We'll see each other again, I just know it. Brothers always find each other, right?"

Leonard sniffles and nods. He keeps his eyes on his shoes. Frayed, plain sneakers.

I hope someday Leonard has millions of sneakers that are brand spanking new, so clean they squeak.

LaLa hugs him, but he's gone stiff; there's a flatness to his eyes. Thaddeus ruffles his hair.

"Goodbye, Leonard," I say. "I liked meeting you."

"Goodbye, smelly girl. Change your dress, okay? It stinks."

The social worker stands up, collecting Leonard's things. LaLa signs a form and hands it back to her. "Come with me, Leonard. There's an ice cream cone out there with your name on it."

Sarah wails. Leonard looks over at her.

"Don't take any shit, Sarry. I'll see you on the flip side. You'll find Pookie. I know it."

And then they're gone.

Thaddeus's shoulders sag. He walks away quickly, to his bedroom. In a few minutes, he turns his music on, loud.

"What the fuck." I try to catch my breath. "They just . . . come like that?"

*"Language,"* LaLa says, sitting down on the couch and stroking Sarah's hair. "It is what it is. Kids are moved around, sometimes with no rhyme or reason. They're great kids, but they also have great big issues that can't be resolved in a week or a month, and it's hard to find families who are in it for the long haul. Leonard's going to some people who have experience with his issues, and can help him, much more than I can."

The social worker's car starts up in the driveway.

If I don't find something out about my dad, and soon, I'm going to be like Leonard, and like Sarah, who will probably be taken any minute now, too, moving from strange house to strange house for years, until finally we're too old to take in.

LaLa flutters her fingers over Sarah's back, very lightly, until Sarah, exhausted, falls asleep in her lap. "It's like raindrops," LaLa explains softly. "You do this to women in labor. It distracts them."

She pauses. "Sarah's sister was taken away by a man who gave Sarah a bag of potato chips and a Coke and told her to wait by the trash can and he'd be back for her. He never came back. Neither did her sister. When people leave, it's very hard for her."

I touch Sarah's kneecap. She's wearing shorts and a Pinkie Pie T-shirt. Her knee is a little scraped from a game she played yesterday with Leonard.

"She's next," LaLa murmurs. "In a few days. And then we'll get some more. There's no end to sad children in this world."

I guess I'm one of them now.

I text Cake. There's really no other way to put it, so I just say: *I have a dad. The social worker is coming over soon to talk about it.*

It only takes a minute for her to respond. *WAIT WHAT WHAT? A DAD? BE RIGHT THERE. I'll ditch band.*

Pause.

*Oh, wait, I don't know where you live now, and that makes me really sad.* 😂
*Me too.* 💜

I look up. "I don't really know the rules. Can my friend come over? She's nice, I swear."

"Of course," LaLa says. "The same things apply that I told you about before. No drinking, drugs, or sex, and be mindful of Sarah and Thaddeus's space."

LaLa gives me directions. Within an hour, Cake shows up with coffees from Grunyon's moms' café.

The first thing she says when I open the door is, "Holy cannoli, a *dad*?"

"It seems so," I answer, and let her in. We hug, and I feel safe, for just a minute, like everything is going to be okay, because Cake is the last thing I have left from my old life.

Thinking stuff like that stings and I have to blink really fast to keep myself from crying.

Cake hands me a coffee. "This is *huge*. How are you feeling?" She peers at me intently.

I take a sip of the coffee. "Lost. Kind of excited. Scared. Sad."

"Okay, well, like, what's his *name*? What do you know? Oh my God, details!"

"His name is Dusty Franklin. That's all I know. The social worker is coming today to tell me more."

Cake squints. "Dusty Franklin? That sounds vaguely like an alcoholic country singer from the fifties."

"Or a singer in his fifties from a vaguely alcoholic country."

"Can you *be* vaguely alcoholic? Pretty sure you have to be all the way alcoholic to be an alcoholic."

"Alcohol makes you sing country. In a vague way. Long into your fifties."

We grin at each other, and everything is like it used to be, when we'd just ramble about nothing, being silly, but then her smile dies, and mine does, too, and we come back to where we are: a stranger's house, and one of us has a mom, and the other doesn't anymore.

When Sarah woke up, she and LaLa moved to the kitchen table, where they are now surrounded by yarn and glue and coloring paper, making a lion.

Cake whispers, "This doesn't seem so bad."

LaLa smiles up at us. "I'm LaLa," she says.

"Cake."

"Cool name. You and Tiger are a perfect fit."

Cake says, "Seven years and counting. From pigtails to fishnets."

154

LaLa smiles. "I remember those days with my friend Speedy. We went from jelly doughnuts to belly rings in the blink of an eye."

I walk Cake down the hall to the room I share with Sarah. I almost say, "Let's go to my room," but this isn't my room. My room is in a house I'll never see again.

Cake looks around. "Where's the boy?"

I gesture across the hall at Thaddeus's closed door. From behind it come the pretty trumpets of Chance the Rapper.

Cake whispers, "Is he cute?"

"Not really on my mind right now, Cake," I say.

"Just asking."

She glances around the small room.

"Remember when we were little, and we begged my dad to make us bunk beds? Weird that you have them now."

She looks closely at me. "You're still wearing that dress, Tiger."

"I know."

"Do you plan to take it off any time soon?"

"No."

"Is this because of the fight?"

I bite back tears. Cake heard what I said to my mom in the cafeteria. She heard how horrible I was.

Cake says, carefully, "Your mom would forgive you, you know. You know that."

The girl-bug whispers, *She would, but she can't, not anymore. So we will wear the dress, because you don't know anything about this. You are a girl with a mother.*

Cake and I stare at each other.

"Okay, then," Cake says finally. "But if you start feeling

weird again, like the other night, the S word, promise you'll tell me, okay?"

I nod.

Thaddeus appears in the doorway to the room, his eyes red. I can't smell pot, so I know he's been crying.

"Hey," he says.

"Cake," I say. "This is Thaddeus."

I turn to Thaddeus. "Thaddeus, this is my best friend, Cake. She actually knows Billy Joel. And Billie Jo Armstrong. Not Billie Holiday, because she's dead, but pretty much any famous Billy you could think of."

Cake says, "Billy Bragg, for instance. And I did meet Billie Jean King once, too. Also, are you the one who told my friend to run away? Because that would rip me apart."

"Sorry. Just trying to prepare her."

"Well, prepare *less,* okay? I need her."

"Okay."

I start talking to ease the tension. "Cake's parents are in rock and roll. They do both quite well, as a matter of fact. The rock and the roll part. So does Cake. Cake, tell him all the instruments you play."

But before Cake can tell him, LaLa comes to the door of the bedroom, her face serious.

"Karen's here, Tiger."

"This is it," Cake says, taking my hand and leading me down the hall, Thaddeus following us.

In the living room, I try to gauge the news by Karen's expression, but she's poker-faced, a trick she's probably learned by being in the lost-kid business.

Karen looks at Cake and Thaddeus. "Sorry to bust in on your

little party, but I have something serious to talk to Tiger about. Can we have some privacy, guys?"

I shake my head. "They can stay."

Cake links arms with me and Thaddeus. He kind of blushes when she does that. "Yeah," Cake says. "We're staying. We're her family, too."

"Well." Karen digs in her gold purse and brings out some folded pieces of paper.

The look she gives me sends bolts of fear through my heart. Her face looks funny, almost like . . . almost like *she's* the one who's scared shitless.

"What?" I say, my voice hard. "Just *say* it."

She takes a deep breath. "Tiger, the first thing we try to do in this situation is find relatives for children whose parents are unable to provide care. We didn't have your father's name at the time, but now we do. Dusty Franklin. *Dustin* Franklin."

Cake says brightly, "You *finally* have a dad. This is good. This seems good. Right?"

We look at each other.

I can tell we're both remembering the same thing. The first time I went over to her house after we met in third grade, her dad made us cupcakes. I thought that was the best thing in the world. He was nice and funny and smelled like sugar, and when my mom came to pick me up, I said, "Gabe is coming, too. He can be my dad, too." My mother kind of laughed and so did Cake's dad, but I got mad when they told me it couldn't be that way. I cried.

That day, Cake said kindly, "He's *mine*. But you can borrow him until you find yours, okay?"

In LaLa's cozy living room, Cake is grinning. I guess I *have* finally found my dad.

Dustin Franklin. *Dustin. Dusty.* I test it out. "My dad . . . *Dustin.*"

Everyone is quiet until Cake asks Karen, "So, what happens now? She goes with him? Like, have you *talked* to him? Where is he? When is he coming?"

"Not so fast, Cake." Karen still has the funny look on her face. "It's more complicated than that. Tiger's father *can't* take care of her."

"Why not?" I don't mean for my voice to sound so desperate, but it does. "Is *he* dead, too?"

"He's not *dead.*" Karen looks me straight in the eye. "He's currently in a correctional facility in Springer, New Mexico, serving six to ten years. By the time he gets out, you'll be over eighteen."

I try to form words, but I can't.

I finally have a dad, but he's locked up, like a precious, yet also criminal, gem.

Thaddeus has words, though. He's taken the papers from Karen, and is reading something very official looking, with a State of New Mexico Correctional Facility logo in the top corner.

"Dude killed somebody with a car?" His eyes are wide and disbelieving.

Karen nods. "Alcohol was involved. And not a death, but an injury, and Mr. Franklin had several incidences before the one in question, so his sentence is appropriate. Mr. Franklin . . . your *father* . . . has a lot of . . . history. Addiction to alcohol, multiple arrests for things related to intoxication."

Cake breathes, "Yikes."

Thaddeus's eyes darken as he turns to me. He is, at this point, my sole expert on all things foster-home-related, so of course when I see the darkness in his eyes, my stomach drops, because this can't be good.

He mutters, "So you *do* have to go to that new house, then. Remember what I told you, okay? Just remember."

About leaving. Running away. I think of Sarah and her sister, Pookie, scrounging for hot dogs in the trash can outside 7-Eleven. Sleeping in a cardboard box.

Pookie never coming back.

Dusty Franklin. My dad's name is Dusty Franklin and he's in prison, where he'll be until I'm old enough not to need him anymore. Where he'll be while I get funneled through home after home after home. Thaddeus told me LaLa's was his *fourteenth* home.

I feel sick and disappointed, dizzy and confused. I'm realizing that the things my mom kept from me while she was alive might be more complicated than I ever thought.

"Did my mom know about all this?" I whisper. "Like, where he is?"

Karen looks at me steadily. "Dustin indicated they were in contact over the years, yes."

So, he *was* there all along, alive. Messing up, but still alive. A thing. A person. A presence I could have known. Avocados and comedy. Freckles and dark hair.

"I might throw up," I say softly, but it's weird, because I don't feel sick from sadness or being scared, I feel sick because I'm *mad,* and I don't know how to feel about being *mad,* because that would mean being *mad* at my mom, and she's dead, and you can't be mad at dead people, can you? Isn't that wrong? But I *am,* because someone should be helping me with this, like a *mom,* because I'm just a kid.

I stare at all of them. Cake bites her lip.

Thaddeus says, "Holy crap, she's flipping out."

LaLa says, "Sit down, Tiger. Sit. I'll get you some water."

I don't want to sit. I want to break something.

The girl-bug is beating the glass with her whisper-thin wings.

Cake says, "Just breathe, okay. Take it easy."

*She knew all along.*

Thaddeus says, "She probably had her reasons for not telling you. I know that sucks, but it's true, okay? Adults are always lying."

"This is like a giant soap opera." Cake collapses on the couch, taking the papers from Thaddeus. She starts reading.

Karen hoists her purse over her shoulder. "Tiger, I know this *does* seems like a soap opera at this point, and I'm sorry."

"Can I see him, at least?" My voice is sharp and hoarse. "I mean, now that I *know* about him, when do I get to meet him? You can't *keep* me from him, right? I mean, unless . . . unless . . ."

Unless he doesn't *want* to see me.

The girl-bug picks at a bruised wing. *Not like he ever tried.*

That's right. He's known about me all these years, a walking piece of his cellular structure, and never come to see me. Or written a letter. Or tried, I don't know, *anything,* to know me.

I'm not sure where to put all this anger that's cresting inside me, because it's fighting with my sadness.

I hold my breath. Ball my fists behind my back.

"Let's discuss that later." Karen pauses. "Dusty's given me a little bit more information regarding your remaining family that changes your immediate circumstances."

*Remaining family. Immediate circumstances.*

Thaddeus says, "Holy shit, this is getting worser by the minute."

"More worse," Cake murmurs.

"You do have paternal grandparents, but dementia is a factor for both of them, so they won't be able to care for you. However . . ." She trails off, handing me a piece of paper.

I stare down at a grainy image of a woman's driver's license. Well, not a woman-woman, like my mom's age, but like a *young* woman, a college girl or something. She's scowling, like she doesn't want her picture taken. Her eyes are puffy. But no one ever looks good in ID photos, right? Even in my Eugene Field ID, I look at least ten pounds heavier and my eyes are half-mast, like I'm falling asleep.

"What the hell is this?" I shout, my heart thundering in my ears. "What are you *telling* me?"

"You have a sister. A half sister. She's your father's daughter. Her name is Shayna Lee Franklin, she works as a waitress in Hawaii, and she's twenty years old. She'll be here by the end of the week."

Cake blurts out, "A *what* and a *who,* now?"

"What does that mean, exactly, 'she'll be here by the end of the week'?" I ask slowly.

"It means she's agreed to be your guardian. As your half sister, she's your nearest blood relative who can care for you. She's . . . family." She gives me a big fake smile, like this is the best news ever, even though she knows it's probably not.

I hold the paper closer to my eyes, like there's a secret buried in the photo that can only be revealed by close-up inspection.

And, in fact, there are a few clues to be had.

Shayna Lee Franklin has curly dark hair stuffed into a messy ponytail.

Shayna Lee Franklin has a nose that's a little too round at the tip and dark eyes.

Shayna Lee Franklin has a cleft in her chin that mirrors the dimple in my cheek.

*She's your father's daughter.*

"I can't believe this," I say, and everybody in the room looks like they can't believe it, either.

I have a sister and I know this to be true because she looks *just fucking like me,* right down to the apparent smattering of freckles across her face.

Kiwi, avocado, Monty Python, and the ability to look half-asleep in any photograph, even if you've consumed a gallon of coffee beforehand, is glaring up at me from the State of Hawaii, 1444 Holamoana, Apt. 102, Honolulu, Hawaii, 5'6", 115 pounds, organ donor, expires January 12, 2025.

## 7 days, part two

A FTER KAREN LEAVES, LALA takes Sarah out shopping, and as soon as they're gone, the three of us race down the hallway to Thaddeus's room and fire up his laptop, because if there's anything teenagers love more than jumping to conclusions and creating drama . . . well, there *isn't* anything we love more than jumping to conclusions and creating drama.

Cake sits on the extra chair next to Thaddeus at his desk. I take a spot on the bed, after carefully sniffing it for boy odor, and pushing shirts and sci-fi paperbacks out of the way. "How many flannel shirts do you own, anyway, Thaddeus?" I ask.

"Twenty-four," he answers matter-of-factly. He cracks his knuckles. "Let's do it. Sister or dad first?"

Cake ponders this. "Sister. We know where Dad is right now, but Sis is on her way, so we need to do some recon to prepare. Dad's not going anywhere."

She turns to me. "You have a *dad*. That's so *excellent.*" Her eyes glitter with happiness.

The way she's smiling, it's like I've gotten a dog, or a new, pretty bracelet. "*Cake.* He's in *prison.* Let's not forget that part."

Cake shrugs. "Minor detail."

"Hawaii," I say, changing the subject. "Her driver's license says Honolulu."

Thaddeus scrolls through pages of Shayna Lee Franklins on

Facebook. It makes me wonder how many Tiger Tollivers or Grace Tollivers might be out there, all variations of me.

Maybe one of them can loan me *her* mom.

I stare at Thaddeus's ceiling. He's covered it in posters: Minecraft, Wu-Tang, Thelonious Monk.

I have a sister. She's a waitress. She's twenty, which means she was four when my mother had me.

Did my mother know about her? That seems like kind of a rotten thing to do, being with a married guy, especially one who has a kid. *Was* he married when they were together? Why would my mother do that? Maybe she didn't know, and then she found out, and that's why she left him.

Bonita told Karen there might be a letter. Maybe in the house? But we share everything. Wouldn't I have found it by now? I mean, I found the overdue bills.

Where would she put something like that, anyway? A letter that says, *Dear Tiger, Sorry about lying to you your whole life, but your dad's name is Dusty Franklin and you have a sister. My bad for not telling you about them!*

My head starts to hurt, and a swell of missing Mom rises in me.

I roll toward the wall so Cake and Thaddeus can't see the tears running down my face. I never thought I'd get so good at silent crying. This whole dad thing is not turning out how I'd hoped.

My *life* is not turning out how I'd hoped.

Imagine always wanting something for such a long time, like to know your dad, and suddenly you get it, along with a whole bunch of other information you didn't even know you were going to need, but it's all jumbled up, and some of it is missing, and you can't put it together, yet it's what you asked for.

The absolute worst part is, I don't even want it anymore, because to get it, I lost the thing I loved most in the world.

I close my eyes. That feeling, the black hole feeling, is creeping close to me. I hold my breath to make it pass.

A sister. A dad in prison. No home. Living with strangers. My mom gone. I can't take much more.

Orange sparks flutter on the inside of my eyelids. I feel ready to explode.

Cake says, "Here. Stop."

But she's not talking to me. She's talking to Thaddeus.

I let all the air out of my body, slowly, so Cake and Thaddeus don't notice, my head aching.

They get quiet. I sniffle and roll back over, craning my neck to see the page they're staring at on Facebook.

*This* Shayna Lee Franklin says she lives in Boise, Idaho, not Hawaii. But the photo is definitely her, though she seems happier here than in the driver's license photo. She's smiling at least, and in braids, not a ponytail.

Shayna Lee Franklin's page is mostly photos: blurry flashes of people and colors—crowds at music festivals, the insides of bars with people huddled together for group shots, red eyes, sweaty faces, hoisting glasses and bottles. Beach scenes with endless sea and sand and gloriously fit young kids wearing giant sunglasses lolling around.

It seems like my half sister has two looks: grumpy and ash-faced, slumped at a table and ignoring the camera, or hopped up, her mouth roaring and eyes blazing as she flashes devil horns or the peace sign, a bottle of beer always nearby, an amazing sunset behind her, wearing only a half T-shirt and a pair of bikini bottoms, her wet braids snaking from the ball cap on her head.

She might look like me, but she definitely does *not* act like me.

Cake says, "Well. This is interesting. Didn't that driver's license say she was twenty? She totally has a fake ID somewhere."

"Is that . . ." Thaddeus peers at the screen. "Is she pierced?" He points to her belly button.

"Niiiice." Cake nods.

"Stop looking at my sister that way, you pervs," I say weakly.

Cake says, "That's funny. Look at you, all protective already."

Shayna Lee takes loads of selfies: flecks of sand on her cheeks, mixed with her freckles. Hanging out with her friends, a sea of bikini'd girls with ankle bracelets and cute butterfly and pinup-girl tattoos.

*This* is who's going to take care of me? This twenty-four-hour party girl?

"I don't feel well," I tell them. "I feel weird and lost. Empty."

Thaddeus stops scrolling. "She doesn't look so bad. It could be so much worse."

Cake stares at him. "Her mom is dead, and her dad, who she didn't even know existed until practically an hour ago, is in prison. How could it be any worse?"

Thaddeus sets his mouth in a grim line. "Believe me, I know worse. This isn't it."

Broken backs and druggy parents. My dad's a drunk in prison. My half sister romps around an island paradise in a bikini, swilling beer and getting skin cancer.

*Welcome to your new world,* flits the girl-bug.

Is this what a panic attack feels like? I can't breathe. I feel jumpy, like I'm bouncing around inside my own skin.

This girl at Eugene Field, Janey Simpson, used to have panic attacks all the time. She would start sweating in English Lit while we plodded through *Catch-22* or some other old-white-guy book about stuff that had nothing to do with our adolescent lives, and she'd have to go to the nurse's office and spend time on the cot. It seemed like a good idea, so I tried it once, too, because even though I love reading, I don't like talking about books in class, because teachers always seem to *kind of* listen to your opinion, but then they just bust in with "Okay, but . . ." and then tell you what *they* thought, which is the thing that would appear on the test, and my God, who tests you on a *novel*? The whole idea of reading a novel, or a poem, is to come up with your own ideas about it. You can't test somebody on that. *You* might think eight hundred pages of going after a white whale is a metaphor for the human condition, but I found that whole business tedious, and I bet if you were honest with yourself, you'd admit you did, too. A *whale*, for God's sake. *For eight hundred pages.*

But Mr. Hoffmeister, who I actually like, would have none of it. He shook his head and said, "I think not, Tolliver. Sit. Back. Down."

I have a sudden pang for Mr. Hoffmeister and his horn-rimmed glasses and polyester shirts and *I think nots.* Sometimes Cake and I see him in Cucaracha, one of our favorite restaurants, sitting at a table by the window, reading a thick book and drinking a blue Icee, with a bowl of green chile chicken stew in front of him, and Cake giggled, but I thought it was kind of sweet and interesting that a grown man wasn't ashamed to drink a sugary blue kids' drink in public.

Cake strokes my hair. "Oh, Tiger, don't cry. I mean, okay, *cry,* but really, this all might be okay, right? You have a *sister.* She's going to take care of you! That's gotta be better than a foster home."

She turns to Thaddeus. "No offense."

He shrugs. "Blood family can be just as bad, but I'll keep my fingers crossed."

"You're a beacon of positivity."

Thaddeus shrugs. He looks back at the screen, mutters, "How did she end up in Hawaii, of all places?"

I gulp and try to catch my breath. "I mean, what is *happening*, you guys? What did I do to deserve this? Who is this . . . this *person* here?" I point to that girl, my *half sister,* on the screen. "What the hell is going on? Does that look like a mother to you? A person who could take *care* of me?"

Thaddeus turns around. "I don't know," he says slowly. "I mean, this is all horrible and everything—like, your life has really helled out this week. And I don't know what to say about your dad, but at least you have *her.* You have *something,* right? I mean, would you peg LaLa for a mom if you just saw her at the grocery store? You'd just think she was some hippie freak, all into her teas and swishy skirts and shit, but she's nice. That's all that matters, to me. And the truth is . . ."

He trails off, picking at one of his pink-painted nails. His shoulders slump.

"The truth is, you don't have a choice anyway. She's blood. The state gives you to blood before anything else, no matter what. Even if you've never met them before and even if . . ."

He meets my eyes.

"Even if they kick the shit out you so hard they break your stupid back. Who knows? Babealicious here might turn out to be a really good thing."

Cake frowns. I wonder what she thinks about what Thaddeus just said, if it makes her stomach feel as sick and hot as it makes mine feel.

She sighs. "He's right, Tig. I mean, what choice do you have, really? At least we'll still be together, and there won't be a Sierra Vista, right?"

Slowly, Thaddeus says, "Well, you don't know if they'll stay here. I mean, her sister could take her anywhere. She's family."

My heart sinks.

LaLa's car chugs into the driveway.

"Okay," I say. "Whatever. I give up. I'm really tired. I'm going back to bed."

I leave them there and walk across the hall to my shared room. I feel like I weigh a million pounds, all of it soaking wet.

I wish I could ask somebody to hold me, or hug me, or tell me everything was going to be okay, and that I could trust them when they said it, but the only person I know who could do all that is gone, gone, gone.

So I pull the blanket over my head and call her, over and over, on her phone, wherever the hell it is, just to listen to her voice.

HERE ARE THE THINGS you think about when your mother dies:

Will she visit you? You know, like *show up*.

You've seen movies like that, where dead people appear to the living, to comfort them. Maybe frighten them, too, if the living person was cruel.

You don't think you could handle something like that, like if you were brushing your teeth and spitting out toothpaste and suddenly you saw your mom's face behind you in the bathroom mirror, tired and ghostly. Cracked lips, bleary eyes.

Maybe if she came in a dream, or something, that might be better.

You read a book once where a girl traveled the whole length of time and the universe looking for her dead mother, only to find her, and to have her mother say, "I don't want to go back."

Like, what the hell was *that* about?

You think there must be reasons for what happened, but what they are, you can't figure out.

How does a brain just . . . explode? She wasn't sick. She had a headache. Just a headache.

You'd fought over a dance in the car, you fought over a dress on the phone, you said terrible things, you ignored her texts, you kissed a boy instead of going home, and somewhere in those hours, those minutes, those seconds, your mom *was,* and then she *wasn't.*

It makes you breathe hard to think about all of that, that maybe she had a split second where she was so, so scared, alone and dying, and the last thing you said to her wasn't *I love you,* but *Why can't you ever just fucking leave me alone?* And that maybe those words were what she thought about, as it happened.

It makes you feel like your chest is being crushed when you think of how scared she must have been.

That the last words she heard on this earth were mean, and they were from you. Her *daughter.*

You can never, never, never, never, never, never wash that away.

The guilt that waves over you is hot and makes you feel very, very small. The wet cement comes again, pressing down on you. The girl-bug cries out.

The last minutes of your mother's life, she probably thought you *hated* her.

The black hole hums, waiting. Hungry.

I PUSH YOGURT AROUND THE bowl, trying to make it look like I've eaten something, but I don't think LaLa is buying it.

"Do you want to talk about anything, Tiger? This is a big deal, a sister and a dad, all at once."

Last night I thought about messaging Shayna Lee Franklin on Facebook. Friending her. It seemed like something sisters would do. My hand hovered over the "Add Friend" button for a long time, too.

But I didn't message her or friend her. And I noticed she didn't to me, either. I mean, what would I say? *Hi. You get me, now that my mom's dead. By the way, is Dad cool?*

It's all so complicated, and I wish I could ask Mom what to do, or how to feel.

But I can't.

It's been seven days. Ten thousand six hundred and eighty minutes.

LaLa is still looking at me. I change the subject. "What about school? Am I going back to school? It's Tuesday. What am I supposed to do all day?"

And tomorrow, and the next day, all week. *Forever.*

Thaddeus slumps into the kitchen and pours some coffee into a travel mug.

"I don't know if that's such a good idea," LaLa says hesitantly.

"It might be a little overwhelming. Maybe you should wait. There are only a few weeks left anyway, right?"

"Three," I say.

School ends in three weeks, like it always does, with the Eugene Field Memorial Days Dance, the one I was going to with Kai Henderson. The whole reason for the dress that I'm wearing at this very moment.

It might be good to go back. I'll have Cake. I'll know the routine. The sounds, the old lockers, the ones they'll be tearing out this summer, creaking open and then slamming shut. We're all getting clear backpacks instead of lockers.

Kids chattering, the clicking intercom, the smell of different shampoos and perfumes and colognes mixing with teenage hormones and angst to create a highly specific and unholy odor that I'm told is called "the Best Years of Your Life."

If I stay here, I'll be in my bunk, staring at the ceiling. Or on the couch, staring at the television. Or looking at LaLa looking at me with her sad, sad smile. I don't think I can take that.

Thaddeus says, "I could take her on my way to work. Let her go. She's not a prisoner."

LaLa frowns. "Let me text Karen."

I stare at Thaddeus. "Wait, why aren't *you* in school, anyway? You're not eighteen."

"Soon enough. Just a couple more months. I do correspondence." He sips his coffee and grins. "School and me didn't get along in person."

LaLa looks up from her phone. "She says it's fine. No reason you can't go back if you feel up to it."

Thaddeus jingles his car keys. "Let's roll."

LaLa says, "Hold up, let me make you some lunch. And don't you want to . . . change your clothes?"

I look down at the dress. It's getting dingy and some threads are starting to hang from the hem, but I can't take it off. I just can't.

"No," I say. "I'm good."

She starts fussing with sandwich bread and slices of cheese, but the thought of eating makes me feel sick again. "No, that's okay," I say quickly. "You don't have to make me anything. Cake always has extra, anyway."

I leave the kitchen before she can argue, grabbing my backpack from the bedroom. Thaddeus is waiting outside in the car.

As Thaddeus drives, I look out my window at cottonwoods and mesquite trees, the miles of cattle fencing, mountains like soft clay against the endless, endless blue sky. Fat, cottony clouds that never seem to move. A tiny part of me, just a smidge, is opening up, being out of the house, out of the bunk, in a car, moving. I can breathe. I might be in a musty old car, but I can breathe out here.

We pass by Grunyon's moms' coffee shop and The Pit. No one's there right now, because of school or work, but come three o'clock, it'll start to fill up with skaters, bodies rising and falling in the air, and watchers.

Thaddeus says, "You go there?"

I nod. "Yeah. I don't skate, though. Just hang out."

I look down at my hands, folded against my stomach. I stretch my fingers out, think of Lightning, the skateboard Andy bought me all those years ago, the feel of tape and grit against my palms as he showed me how to work the board. Do my feet twitch, all of a sudden, at the mention of skateboarding? Like they have a life of their own? Like they can remember those few times I felt weightless and free, beautiful and promising? Those few times I was just any other kid?

Before I broke my arm and my mom took it away.

I shake my head, hard. It doesn't matter. I'm spare parts now. A series of phantom limbs pieced together with tears.

I text Cake: *I'm coming to school. Meet me by my locker.*

*What? Wow, ok.*

Thaddeus looks down at my phone. "That your friend, from yesterday? The tall one?"

"Yes. Why? You interested?" I turn my phone over.

"No! I mean, not that I couldn't be, she seems cool and all. It's just . . ." He hesitates. "I don't . . . really know how that stuff works. I've never had a girlfriend." His face gets pink.

I sigh. "I'm not really a pillar of wisdom. I've never had anyone, either, so I think if you're just nice, and cool, that's all that matters."

Thaddeus gives me an amused look. "You use weird words. 'Pillar of wisdom.' What's that all about?"

When I was little, if I was being noisy, my mom would say, *Please keep it down to a dull roar.* When I asked lots of questions and she got tired of answering, she'd say, *What am I? A pillar of wisdom?* She had sayings for everything.

*Had.*

I bite my lip. "Nothing. Just a phrase I heard once."

Thaddeus says, "Anyway, girls always say they want nice dudes, and then they go for jerks, like my mom does. Every time, when I was little, she'd go, '*This* one is different. *This* one is nice.' They never were. Like, why couldn't she just take care of *me*?"

I look over at him.

Thaddeus is kind of handsome, underneath all his hair and that ball cap guys insist on wearing all the time, even if they don't play ball or watch sports. And it seems like he's got some muscles, not that it matters, but who can tell under the baggy flannel and the loose T-shirts he's always wearing?

I rub the lace on my dress thoughtfully. I can't fault Thaddeus for what he wears; I guess we all have our costumes, our armor.

"I'm sorry about your mom. But I swear that not everybody goes for assholes." I frown, though, because, I mean, Cake did. With Troy, the guy from Sierra Vista. And Kai didn't turn out to be such a gem, either.

Thaddeus slows down to let some quail skitter across the road.

"It's hard, like, getting close to people. Because of my life. I have a lot of problems . . . like, if I think people are mad at me, I start . . . I just do stuff. It's hard to explain." He keeps his eyes on the quail.

Ahead of us, the parking lot of Eugene Field looms, kids milling around, lugging backpacks, huddling by the trees and the old, cracked fountain with the statue of Eugene Field clutching a book and pencil to his chest. He was some famous poet once, and wrote weird rhymes for kids.

Thaddeus pulls into the lot. "Man," he murmurs. "I do not miss high school."

We sit, watching kids make their way to the entrance.

I hold the door handle. I could just tell Thaddeus to drive

away, take me back to the house, to my bunk, to nothingness. Or I can get out and melt into the crowd of kids, emptier than I was eight days ago, the last time I was here.

It's now or never. I open the door.

"See you later," I tell him. "Thanks."

As I get out of the car, Thaddeus says, "Good luck."

I concentrate on the big double doors that lead into the school, trying to make a straight line right inside. If I can just get to Cake in the hallway, waiting by my locker, it will be okay.

All around me, kids jostle and joke, look at their phones, laugh.

Nervously, I look around the hallway, but I don't see Kai. At first I feel relieved, but then I realize he'll be in Bio.

At the lab table we share, because we're partners.

Bio is second period. Zero p is first period, with Ms. Perez.

The last time I talked to Kai was that phone call, when I was mean, and made him cry. I wonder what he'll say to me. How he'll act.

Maybe this isn't such a good idea after all. My stomach starts to knot.

Cake isn't by my locker. I text her. *Where are you?*

*Running late. Overslept! Sorry! I'll see you at lunch, okay?*

I spin the dial on my locker, then pretend to rummage around for something inside. Grab a notebook just to have something to hold.

Behind me, it's gotten really quiet in the hallway. My heart starts thudding.

Whispers. *Mom dropped dead. I think she got sent to one of those homes. Oh my God, what is she wearing?*

I'm not the kind of girl who has loads of friends who'll run to her and hug her at school after a great tragedy. It's not that things suck for me, though I guess they could be better. I just really only have Cake, is all, and now she's not here. My life was already small, and it's getting smaller by the minute.

I scrabble around my locker for a pen, just so it looks like I'm busy. My fingers are shaking.

I try not to look at the photo of me and mom on the inside of the locker door; I'd forgotten about that, and in my rush to avoid the photo, I accidentally slam the locker door shut a little too loud.

When I turn around, a bunch of kids are staring at me. At the dress. At the #orphangirl.

I'm just so *sick* of everything, I shout, *"What?"* Watch them scatter.

It feels good, shouting that way. Scaring people. I start walking to zero p.

With every step, I get heavier and heavier, though. I think of the table in zero, with Selfie Kelsey and I-don't-care Rodrigo and timid Tina and horrible Lupe Hidalgo. All of them looking at me. Or, maybe even worse, *not caring.* I think of listening to Ms. Perez droning on at the board, and then sitting in Bio next to Kai, and how awful that's going to be, and I already have so much awful inside me at this very moment.

I can't take any more awful. I'm stuffed to the gills with awful. This was a terrible mistake.

Oh Jesus, now I really *am* Janey Simpson, and it's not a good feeling. I'm panicking and sweating. I have to get out of here.

I jam my notebook and pen in a trash can. I start hustling, keeping my eyes on the exit doors at the far end of the hall. If I can just make it, if I just make it home, my *actual* home, everything will be all right, I can curl up in my bed, put my headphones on, wait for my mom to come back from driving the Bookmobi—

In an instant, my face is wet.

There won't be anyone there. Of *course.*

I should tattoo this on my freaking hand so I can remember it forever: it's only *me* now.

"Tiger! Tiger Tolliver!"

Walrus Jackson catches up to me, holding his blue tie against his chest, breathing heavily.

"Tiger, you run fast. You ever think about trying out for track? I think I'll mention it to Coach Archer. Good Lord, I'm winded."

"Look at my boobs, Mr. Jackson. Do you honestly think running track is going to work for me? Listen, I've gotta go."

I think I see the smallest smile flicker at Mr. Jackson's mouth. "Tiger, I'm not allowed to stare. At you. Or any girl. Moving on."

"Can I please just go? I really need to leave."

Mr. Jackson says firmly, "In a moment. Your care worker called me this morning to say you'd be back. I gather it's not going well today? We should work out a plan for your return, I think. Take things slow. One step at a time. Do half days instead of full. Like that. How would that be? Here. This might be a good start."

He holds out a card to me. It says "Tuesday/Friday, 4 p.m., Room 322, Eugene Field, *GG.*"

"GG? What is this?" I ask.

"Grief Group. For teens. We're trying to think of a better name." He smiles. "I gather it was started before I got here, when there was some trouble. I run it now, though."

*When there was some trouble.* Walrus Jackson and I look at each other. He means when the three kids died by suicide. That.

"How are you *doing,* Grace?" And because he uses my real name, I think he means *Are you going to kill yourself, Grace? Are you going to wrist, hang, gun?*

We stare at each other for a long, long moment.

Adults always say they want you to tell them how you feel, but when you do, they mostly just tell you to try to feel *another* way, one that requires less work from them. I bet in this Grief Group everyone says how they feel and Walrus Jackson tells them things like "Well, what if we try *this*?" "Or *this*?" They probably draw their feelings with crayons.

It would be nice if once, someone would just say, "Girl, you are in the *shit* and you will not be getting out soon. So here's how to make friends with the dark."

Kind of like how at my mom's viewing, Mae-Lynn Carpenter said everything from now on was going to be a giant suck-fest for me. *The Big Suck.* At least *she* was honest.

My voice cracks. "My mother *dropped dead.* That's how I'm *doing.*"

Walrus Jackson's eyes get soft.

I swear to God, there should be a manual for dying, or for death, and if I ever write it, Chapter One will be: Do NOT cry when someone else's person has died, because then *they* will feel guilty, or mad. *You* lost nothing.

My hands ball into fists behind my back, crushing the Grief Group card where Walrus Jackson can't see.

He takes a deep breath. "You're welcome to join our group, Grace. I think it might help, but no pressure."

I spit, "Who are the other kids in the group? Because I'd like to know who else in this school is flailing around in a lava of grief, because I sure didn't see any of them this morning, when everyone was whispering and giggling about this . . . this *dress* and my *mom*."

And, just like that, from the corner of my eye, I start to notice kids peering out the round windows of classroom doors at me, curious. I have to get out of here.

I start walking before Mr. Jackson can say anything else, folding my arms tight against my chest, counting the big black and white tiles as I go to keep myself from crying again. If Mr. Jackson calls after me, I can't hear it. There are too many waves crashing in my brain.

I push open the double doors as hard as I can, the sunlight nearly blinding me. When I shade my eyes, hoping to see a magic path, or a beam of light telling me where to go from here, there's Thaddeus Roach, leaning against the emptied Eugene Field fountain. He lifts his hand in kind of a sad greeting.

"I thought maybe it might not work out, so here I am, just in case."

As he holds the car door open for me, he grins. "Looks like you're coming to work with me."

For the first time in more than seven days, I feel a spark of happiness and relief. I jog down the front steps, dropping the crumpled GG card in the trash can on my way.

"I JUST HAD A FEELING," Thaddeus says when we get in his car.

"Thanks," I say. "I kind of felt like I couldn't breathe all of a sudden. I've been feeling that way a lot lately. I just can't imagine why. Hmm . . ." I pretend to tap my chin in a thoughtful manner.

Thaddeus grimaces at me. "You don't have to be funny, Tiger."

I shut my mouth and look out the window at the desert and the mountains, the bright, bright blue sky. I close my eyes and let the sound of the wheels on the road lull me. What if my sister doesn't want to live here? Can she just take me back to Honolulu with her, no questions asked? Or anywhere, for that matter? I've never lived anywhere else or gone anywhere else. My mom moved here from Albuquerque, after whatever happened with *Dusty Franklin,* me squirming around in her belly, and that was that.

It's still weird to think about, that I have a dad. That he exists. That's he's out there.

And that he never tried to find me.

Before I know it, I'm texting Karen, the social worker.

*Hi. Did my dad even say anything? About me? When you told him?*

She answers right away. *I thought you were at school today.*

*It didn't work out.*

182

*Okay.* And then: *Dusty was somewhat confused at all the news. As you can imagine. He offered his condolences.*

*Did he use that word,* condolences? *Or did you?*

*It was his word. He was quite sorry to hear of your mother.*

My father, Dusty, used the word *condolences.* I like that. It makes me think he was a reader, at some point, like maybe we'll have something in common someday, other than a few cellular similarities.

*Did he ask anything about me? Like what I'm like? Does he want to see me?*

*Dot dot dot.* Karen is typing.

*Texting might not be the most productive way to talk about this. In the long run, Tiger, therapy is probably warranted. For all of you. Whatever happens.*

*All of us?*

*You and your sister. And dad, maybe, someday. You're going to have to learn to live together if this is going to work, Tiger. She'll be here soon.*

My sister will be here soon.

My stomach flip-flops. I've never had to learn to live with anyone but my mom, and it seems overwhelming and unfair that I have to learn how to live *without* her at the same time I'm learning how to live *with* a complete stranger, especially a long-lost, belly-pierced sister.

Karen says, *Talk to you soon. I'm with another client right now.*

"Client" stings, too. I slump lower in my seat. Thaddeus turns up the radio, some hip-hop station. I close my eyes. *"Dear Mama"* by Tupac Shakur is playing.

I grind my fists into my eyes. "Thaddeus, how much longer?"

He says, "Here."

I take my hands away from my eyes, blinking. My head hurts so much now. I'm so tired. We're driving down a long dirt road toward an enormous iron-and-wood arch with prancing horses. I sit up, my heart racing.

I say, "Really? Here?"

He stops at the gate, presses a code, and the gates part. Thaddeus pulls into the lot, parks the car.

"Yeah," he says, grinning. "Here. I love it. It's my happy place. Come on, get out. It's almost time."

Never in a million years would I have guessed that Thaddeus works at Randy Gonzalez's horse ranch. There are a couple of long white trailers arranged around the lot, and some buildings farther down the road, next to a rambling, rose-colored hacienda.

I get out of the car.

Thaddeus stands next to me. "Listen," he says softly.

I don't know what he's talking about, so I wait, the warm desert air still and quiet. We stand there for so long, so quietly, that I start to get jittery. I'm getting my wet cement feeling back. The song on the radio about the singer's mom made me sad and now I want to return to LaLa's house, and retreat to my bunk bed. Sleep for a thousand more days.

Then I hear it.

It starts slowly, in the distance, an echoey sound like rain or soft thunder.

The soft sounds of nickering, hooves in the dirt.

Then they appear, stepping from a thunderous cloud of golden and shimmery dust, cantering by the fence in a tight herd, manes flying, the muscles of their bodies wild and rippling. A mosaic of coal gray, earthy brown, sleek white, jewel black. They're like something from a fantasy book, a magical movie, a dream. The horses my mother had always loved.

I stay.

## 7 days, 11 hours, 50 minutes

THADDEUS TAKES ME INSIDE one of the white trailers and plunks down behind a junky desk. He starts checking voice mails on a huge, blinking phone. He seems completely at home, whirling around on the rolling chair, taking notes, pressing buttons.

I slink to the window. The glass is warm from the sun. I can see them from here, inside the circular white ring, pacing and prancing.

The first time my mom stopped by the side of the road to show the horses to me, I was young and kind of scared. They seemed so big to me then. They liked my mom, letting her pet them and stroke their manes. Sometimes she'd lift me up so I could pet them, too. Their fur was warm from the sun, and velvety.

These horses, the ones in the ring, they seem a little volatile. Pent up. They kick around the pen, snort, flick their tails.

I feel a little more alive than this morning, watching them. They are ready to do something, to *move.*

Two men and a woman enter the ring. They're wearing boots and hats and have ropes and something that looks kind of like a whip.

They work the horses, putting them through paces and exercises. Thaddeus makes phone calls and then fixes us coffee from a machine in the corner. He hands me a mug and stands next to me at the window.

"Awesome, right? I love it here. So much better than the grocery store where I was before. I know working inside a stupid trailer isn't the coolest, but I talk to people from all over the world on the phone and stuff. Mr. Gonzalez is kind of famous. Some of the horses are Arabians, which are pretty special. Did you know that?"

I shake my head.

He stretches and yawns.

"I'm gonna go to the main house and get a sandwich. You wanna come, or should I bring something back for you?"

"I'm not hungry. I'll wait here."

After he leaves, my phone buzzes. Cake.

*What happened???*

*I guess I wasn't ready,* I text back. *Thaddeus brought me to work with him. At the ranch. With the horses.*

*That's cool. Hey, what's your mom's full name and her birth date? I'm gonna do some digging.*

Last year, Mom and I made her birthday cake together, a lumpy, three-layered thing, each layer dyed a different color: red, green, blue. It was delicious and disgusting at the same time. She'd eaten two pieces, one after the other, and then sighed happily. "I'm so old," she said, touching my cheek. "Will you take care of your old mom someday? Make my tea? Put the blanket on my decrepit legs?"

"Of course not," I'd answered, cutting myself another piece of cake. "I'm going to be out with all my boyfriends, partying it up. I'm not gonna have time for old people like you." I flipped my hair like Selfie Kelsey Cameron in zero p.

My mom laughed.

My mother's birthday falls between Thanksgiving and

Christmas and she likes to say, "I spend two months of the year gaining ten pounds and ten months trying to lose it."

I tell Cake the date, and give her my mom's full name, June Frances Tolliver.

And then I wonder: Is that even her real name? I mean, maybe it's not.

I know nothing about her childhood, except that she rode horses, and that later she went to college, and her parents died, and she became a librarian.

I look back down at my phone. Cake is typing . . .

*Cool. Gotta go. Band prac. I'll call you later.*

I sit at Thaddeus's work desk and cruise the computer. His Facebook page pops open. Photos of boys, Thaddeus with them, making devil horns, playing guitars. A little girl with hair the same color as Thaddeus's, in a yellow swimsuit in a pink baby pool. That must be his sister. The caption says, "Jax thins she's a mermad." I peer closer. In the background beyond the baby pool, beer cans are scattered in the dirt. A skinny black dog on a chain. Broken plastic toys.

In the search box, I type *Shayna Lee Franklin.*

*Aloha, friends and lovers. It's been real. About to fly into the great unknown. Adventure and new life await.*

My heart skips a beat. Photos of puffy clouds taken from an airplane window. A selfie of my sister in her seat, the blue sky and clouds behind her, her eyes wide, smudged with black liner. Red bandanna over her dark hair. Pink gloss across her lips. A half smile. She's so pretty.

*You have a beetiful soul, Shay!!!! Love you!!!!!*

*The universe works in mysterious ways, babe, we'll miss you on the beach!!!*

*Come back soon and tell us all about your adventure.*

A beetiful soul. My sister has a beetiful soul.

I type, *How long does it take to fly from Honolulu to Tucson?*
*Eight hours and ten minutes, one stop.*
Shit.

Thaddeus slouches back into the room, holding a paper plate with a sandwich and some potato chips. He holds out the plate to me, but I shake my head. "Skin and bones," he mutters. "You're gonna turn into skin and bones soon, girl."

He glances at his computer, sees that Facebook is open. "Oh, wow. Is that new?"

"Yeah, she's on her way here. Pictures from the plane and everything."

He blinks. "It'll be okay." He gnaws on a potato chip.

I look at the way he sits on the other chair, slowly and carefully. Think of his little sister, Jax, in her dirty backyard, in her pink baby pool.

"Thaddeus, what happened? I mean, like, after the thing. To your back."

His voice is low and he keeps his eyes on his plate, pushing chips around with a finger. "My stepdad tried to say I fell down the stairs of the apartment building, but doctors can figure that stuff out, you know? They aren't stupid. He was always, you know, like, hitting me and stuff. Mostly when my mom wasn't there. He'd say I fell out of bed or something. He got sent to jail. He and my mom weren't married then, anyway, and they sent her to rehab, because she was all strung out. They both were, all the time. And the state took me away. My mom gave me up. Then they got back together and had Jax."

His voice is shaking.

"Like, when I said I had problems, earlier? I can't be touched

188

a lot, because my brain thinks somebody's gonna hurt me again. Does that make any sense? It's why school doesn't work for me. Too much shit, and shouting, and calling me poor and all that crap, you know? Makes me mad, and then shit happens. Oh, no, please don't," he says, turning to me, pleading. "I'm sorry I said all that. Please don't do that."

I take big gulps to stop crying. "I was trying to be quiet about it," I say. "I've gotten really good at the silent cry since . . . you know. I could probably win a silent crying contest."

"Again with the jokes," he says. "You don't have to joke about sad stuff."

I ignore what he said, wiping my face with the dirty sleeve of my dress. "How can you go back and see him, though? I mean, doesn't that kind of kill you?"

He shrugs. "My little sister. I just go up, you know, keep an eye on things. My mom doesn't make great life choices, is the only way I can put it."

Thaddeus starts moving papers around the table. I look at the soft tangles of hair against his stooped back, the way his skinny legs are bent awkwardly. How am I only just now seeing that Thaddeus's entire body is kind of twisted? No wonder he smokes pot. He must be in so much pain, inside and out.

Yeah, he'd get picked on in school, for sure. I know exactly which group he'd be in, and what would be done to him. The only reason I'm safe is Cake, and her coolness.

"Aren't you afraid of him, Thaddeus? Aren't you afraid he'll do something again, like, to her? I don't know if I'd be able to do that. See someone who'd done that to me."

Thaddeus rolls his chair next to mine and scrolls around my sister's Facebook page. Beaches with red-and-gold skies. Digging money from a stained and crinkled waitress apron, looking tired. Standing in a line of pretty girls with glossy faces and minidresses, bridesmaids holding colorful flowers.

When he finally speaks, his voice is mild. "I love my sister more than I'm afraid of *him*. Sometimes you'd do anything to protect your family. It's just something you know, deep inside."

Hundreds of Shayna Lee Franklins, scattered all over the blue-and-white page.

Legs stretched out, gritty with sand, toes buried. A selfie, her face sunburned and smiling. Tiny shells on a string around her neck.

A living, breathing, magical sister.

## 7 days, 21 hours

THAT NIGHT, FROM THE lower bunk, Sarah says softly, "You going to your family soon?"

I skipped dinner when Thaddeus and I got back. LaLa wanted to talk, but I came straight to the room, and sat on my bed in the dark as she and Sarah and Thaddeus laughed and chatted over dinner down the hall.

It was a weird kind of lonely, listening to them. Like they'd made a temporary family, and I was just a giant blob of sadness plopped down in their midst.

I clear my throat to push down the sad.

"Yes. My sister. I don't know her, though. It's kind of . . . complicated."

I feel stupid right after saying that. Sarah's already lived a way more complicated life than I have; I don't know why I don't just explain things to her. She might be ten, but in some ways, she's not. I mean, she lived on the *street*. In *cardboard*.

"Are you scared?"

I look down at her over the side of the bunk. She's holding the edge of her blanket up to her chin in a worried kind of way.

"Honestly? Yes. I'm scared. A lot."

"I wish we could be sisters. I mean, I have Pookie, but I don't know where she is. She got taken. You seem nice, even if you do sleep all the time."

Her eyes glisten in the dark, like she's about to cry, so I climb down the bunk ladder, holding my cellphone carefully with one hand. I've become very protective of the phone. It's the last thing that holds the absolutely true sound of my mom's voice. Part of me is afraid I might lose that sound inside me.

"Can I come in?"

Sarah scooches over. I fit myself next to her and stare up at the springs on the underside of my mattress through the bunk slats. I try to consciously breathe deeply, just like my mother did when I was sick, so that Sarah can feel me being calm. Maybe it will calm her down, and she won't cry. The world is full of tears, and I'm starting to drown.

She's so thin her bones poke through her light summer nightdress. I try to imagine her, and Pookie, sleeping in a cardboard box by a convenience store. If she's ten now, how long ago was that? One year, two? Three? When *I* was seven, I was mostly concerned with collecting toads and lizards from the backyard. I had a big aquarium my mom got from Mr. Timmins's junk store, and we filled it with dirt, and leaves, and a small dish of water. My toads and lizards didn't last very long, because of course they wanted to be out, and not in some glass tank in a backyard, but I remember laying their still bodies out on a patch of dirt and watching, day after hot summer day, as their skin hardened and bits of grayish bone appeared.

Sarah could have been doing that, but instead she was eating somebody else's germy leftovers from a trash can.

"How long did you live in that box, Sarah?"

She screws her eyes shut, thinking. "I don't know. I'm not good at time. A while." She pauses. "Sometimes people gave us money. Pookie knew how to count money and we'd get a soda or something. That tasted good. When the store closed, we bathroomed in the alley in the back."

"Didn't . . . didn't anybody ever try to help you?"

"Pookie said we had to be careful or they might take us away from each other, so if someone asked a lot of questions, we went and stayed at another store a few blocks away. Pookie is twelve but she has boobs, so people think she's older. Her boobs aren't as big as yours, though."

I fold my arms across my chest.

She screws her face up, like she's thinking really hard. Finally, she says, "Pookie might not be twelve anymore. She might be older. Like I said, I'm not good at time. But she used to be twelve."

"I'm sorry about your sister," I say.

"It's okay. That nice man gave her a home. He just didn't have room for me, is all. I wasn't good like Pookie, anyway. That's what everyone always told me. My dad said, 'The big one has the brains, the little one is dumb as a sock full of rocks.' "

My stomach rumbles in a sick way and I close my eyes. "Sarah, no," I whisper. "No, you're lovely. You're really cool. Also, your dad is a total *dick.*"

"I'm sorry about *your* mom," Sarah answers matter-of-factly, as though she hasn't heard me at all. "She died."

I wait a minute before answering, because the stabbing in my chest is so sharp.

"Yeah," I say. "She did."

"She might come back. Your mom." Sarah sounds hopeful. "Like in my book LaLa reads to me. Like this."

She takes my hand and presses her mouth to it. "And then the princess wakes up," she says, pleased. "The love makes her."

*And then the princess wakes up.* I do feel like that. Asleep, underwater, beneath my veil of wet cement. A walking ghost.

I want to tell Sarah things don't work like that, that dead is *dead,* and once they take the body away, it's gone forever. But I don't. She's just a kid, and a kid with a horrible life, and if she needs fairy-tale hope, then she's going to get it from me.

"Maybe you're right, Sarah. Wouldn't that be neat?" I say cheerfully.

She falls asleep. Her warmth is pulling me in, but it's also reminding me a little of my mom, and how comforting it was when she slept with me in the same bed.

Hands shaking, I text Cake. The dark is crowding me again. *Lonely. Scared.*

After a minute or two, the phone vibrates.

Cake says, *Love you, T. Deep breaths.*

Then she sends me sixty red heart emojis. I know because I count them, each and every one, twice, until I calm down. Who knew heart emojis were the new sheep-jumping-over-a-fence?

But still, long after I realize Cake's slipped away from me into her own sleep, I feel them: one after the other after the other after the other, tears sliding steadily down my temples and through my hair, pooling on Sarah's SpongeBob pillowcase.

And I whisper it, just in case she's listening, wherever she is. *Please come back.*

HERE IS WHAT YOU think about when your mom dies, and you try to go to sleep:

Will she come tonight, to your dreams? You've read books about parents visiting their kids in dreams. Those movies with dead people in corners, in pockets of mist, sitting on the limbs of trees, watching.

Harry looks in that mirror and his parents are there.

From now on, whenever you feel a light breeze on your face in an otherwise still room, is that her? Her hand grazing your cheek.

From now on, will you listen more closely to the world, to its sounds, in case she's trying to talk to you? Trying to send a message.

A whisper while the teakettle rumbles. Your name floating in a crowded, noisy room, drifting inside the chatter of strangers.

It seems like a safe place that she could visit you, in a dream, so every night you say out loud, but very quietly, so as not to wake the little girl in your room, *It's okay. I'm not scared. Please come back.*

Even the girl-bug stops her pacing and waits hopefully.

But your dreams are just slabs of gray and black, lumpy clouds of nothing. No people. No music. It's like you enter a room, the door closes, there's no light switch.

Just you, stumbling, feeling your way around, looking for her hand to hold on to.

## 8 days, 4 hours, 35 minutes

I WAKE UP. I DON'T remember any dreams. Just darkness.
LaLa's house is quiet.

Sarah sighs in her sleep. Her body against mine is sleep-sweaty.

I fell asleep clutching my phone to my chest.

It's 1:56 a.m.

I do the numbers on my phone.

It's been 11,795 minutes since my mother died.

Like lightning, missing her rips through me.

## 8 days, 10 hours

LALA SIPS HER TEA. "I talked to your guidance counselor, Mr. Jackson, yesterday. He called. I wish you'd told me you left school." Her voice is firmer than I'm used to.

The oatmeal is chunky in my throat. I gag, avoiding LaLa's eyes. I'm so tired I can barely keep my eyes open. I wonder if this is it, if she's going to yell at me, finally, be *that* foster mom.

She sets her cup down on the table. "Mr. Jackson spoke to your teachers, and the principal, and everyone thinks that school might be a good idea, like, the *routine* of it, but that maybe you should start slow. Half days. Take it easy. See how it goes."

I think about yesterday, and the kids staring at me. Me shouting in the hallway. Maybe I *don't* want to go back.

"Do I have to?"

"You don't *have* to, but it might help. Mr. Jackson mentioned some sort of counseling group for some of the kids, too."

GG. Grief Group. The card I threw away.

"He thinks you should attend at least one session. I can't make you, but Karen thinks it's a good idea, too, and will discuss it with your sister."

My sister. Yesterday, she was looking glum and on a plane, which was supposed to take eight hours.

"About that," I say. "Where is she? When is she getting here? Does anybody *know*?"

LaLa shrugs. "She's 'en route,' is how Karen put it. I'm not sure what that means. I know it's hard, with everything up in the air."

Thaddeus slumps into the kitchen, his long hair tangled over his shoulders. He yawns. "You coming to work with me today?"

LaLa waits for me to answer.

Part of me really wants to see the horses again. It felt peaceful out there, watching them. If I stay here, it will just be me and LaLa. She'll be in her room, sewing something, and I'll be . . . on my bunk bed, sleeping again. I feel like if I sleep any more, I'm just going to sink somewhere I won't be able to crawl out of.

Maybe I should try school one more time. I can not look at anyone, keep my head down, like usual. At least I'd get to see Cake. Have a tiny piece of normal.

*There is no normal,* snorts the girl-bug.

"I guess I'll try it again. Maybe today will be better."

Thaddeus nods. "Sure thing. Let me shower and I'll take you on my way."

LaLa clears her throat. "Speaking of showers, I have to be honest. The dress situation is getting a little unsanitary. It's not that I don't think you should wear it. I think I can intimate your reasons for wanting to wear it. But if you choose to keep wearing it, especially to school, you should keep it clean. The last thing you need is kids making fun of you, you know?"

"They made fun of me before, even when my mom wasn't dead." I stare at her.

LaLa gives me a long look.

"You need protection," she says finally. "Come with me."

In her room, she opens the double doors to her closet. It's stuffed with cool-looking clothes, like shimmery flapper dresses and shiny alien costumes. "It's my other job," she tells me. "I

198

design costumes. I have a lot more in storage, but we should be able to find something in here."

She sorts through some boxes. "They shoot a lot of Westerns out here, natch, so I've got tons of cowpoke stuff. Here. Let's start with a hat. This goes perfectly with that dress. It's a replica of the one Blondie wears in the Clint Eastwood movies. I used it for this movie about a girl who gets work at a ranch after her parents die. The lead girl stole the original, but I can't blame her."

She holds it out to me. The leather is soft in my fingers. "Great, huh?" She places it gently on my head. It feels snug and perfect.

She tugs at the brim. "This little peak here, it's called a telescope crown," she says, tapping the top of the hat.

"I started making clothes and costumes when I was about your age," she says. "I liked being different people. Dressing up my friends, watching them become brave inside costumes, become new people. It's amazing how just a little bit of fabric can change your life."

LaLa rustles around the bottom of the closet, pushing aside boxes and bags until she finds what she's looking for. "These should do it. Get rid of those yucky old sneakers."

I pull on the pair of thick black socks and the thick brown boots she hands to me. When I stand back up, the boots feel good and solid on my feet.

In fact, I feel like I could kick the whole world to smithereens in these boots.

LaLa says, "This hat looks *perfect* on you. Suits your bone structure." She smooths my hair over my shoulders.

I get a funny, sad feeling then.

This is the sort of stuff a mom says and does. Picks out clothes, smooths your hair.

"You've got a great face," LaLa says. "And a real spirit. I can feel your essence."

Embarrassed, I look down, pick imaginary lint off the dress.

Down the hall, Sarah calls for LaLa.

LaLa murmurs, "Be right back."

In the full-length mirror in her room, the hat on, the tie pulled tight under my chin, the solid boots, and my dress dirty and ragged, I try to imagine myself as some sort of desert warrior. A pained, sad, awful-looking desert fighter girl, so different from the quiet girl in the hippie skirts and faded T-shirts featuring rock bands no one listens to anymore.

That girl is gone. She was softer and hopeful. Maybe this girl will get me through.

My phone buzzes. Cake.

*Thinking about you. On computer, looking up your mom and dad.*

I type back. *Did you find anything out? I'm trying school again today.*

*YAY. I found out your dad was a history teacher.*

*Really?* I try to imagine this, but it's hard. I don't even know what Dusty Franklin looks like. All I can picture is a disembodied head with a striped tie and brown pants standing in front of a whiteboard, but that doesn't help with the *other* picture, the one of a crumpled guy in a gray jumpsuit sitting on a cot in a cinder-block cell.

*Yeah. I found some articles about the accident. The thing. That.*

*Oh.* The drunk-driving accident that sent him to the correctional facility in New Mexico.

*So I guess he was kind of an alcoholic. He had a lot of priors. That's what the articles say. "Priors."*

200

My mom drank wine sometimes, but always just a glass, and always with her friend Bonita after a long day. She told me, "I like the taste. I don't overdo it. It's a social thing, but it's not something I want you doing, ever. You have to trust me on that. We'll talk about it when you're a little older."

I guess I can guess now why she didn't want me to drink. Maybe that's why I never got to go to anybody's parties. People asked Cake, and Cake asked me, but Mom always said no, and I was too afraid, or maybe just relieved that I could always blame it on her. Eventually, Cake stopped asking.

*A history teacher,* I type.

*Yeah. I'll print out some of the articles at school if you want and save them for you. Gotta go. See you soon.*

After Thaddeus drops me off, I keep my eyes straight ahead, ignoring the sidelong looks and whispery giggles as I walk to the front doors of Field. *The desert warrior needs no one. She walks a path of loneliness and heartache.* Head straight to my locker. Put the brown bag LaLa shoved into my hands inside. It's weird to bring a lunch. I got so used to Cake bringing me something to eat.

I tense up, listening for any whispers behind my back, but there's nothing. Just the sound of kids shuffling around, sneakers squeaking on the floor. Maybe the hat and the boots are protecting me, after all. A shield.

In zero, Lupe isn't there, and I feel relieved. Kelsey Cameron leans over. "What was up with you in that car? Taran says you went to a foster house. Is that true?" Before I can answer, Tina Carillo puts her hand on my arm and says, "I'm really sorry about your mom."

Besides Walrus Jackson, she's the first one at school to say something nice to me about my mom and it takes me by surprise. I knit my hands together super hard, super hurtful, so that I can stop the swell of tears behind my eyes. "Thanks," I say softly.

Ms. Perez claps her hands together. "Okay, people. Hats and hands, hats and hands." That's our cue to take off ball caps and whatever else is on our heads, to put our phones away, and put our hands on the tables. I drag off the hat LaLa gave me and slide it onto my lap. It feels good to hold it, to have something to concentrate on, because all of a sudden, I can feel Mae-Lynn Carpenter's eyes on me from across the room, hard and dark, and her voice from my mom's viewing rings through my brain.

*Welcome to the Big Suck.*


It isn't until I'm halfway to Bio that I remember Kai will be there, and I stop up so short in the hallway a couple of kids bump into my back. I mumble, *Sorry,* and drag myself the rest of the way to Bio, slinking close to the lockers lining the walls.

Kai's rickety stool is empty. I slowly sit down on mine. Taran Parker whirls around in front of me. "I saw you. At the food place. That car. Where you at now? It was only you and your ma, right? I'm sorry about that."

His face is super serious and it occurs to me that I don't think I've ever seen him *not* smiling. He looks, I'm sorry to say, like someone died.

*Funny,* says the girl-bug. *Aren't you a comedian.*

"I don't know. I mean, with a lady. A person. Like, a foster mom." I decide not to say anything about my sister.

My face flames up. I look at the clock. Three minutes until the start of class. Where is Kai? I just want to get this over with.

Taran nods gravely. "Is it cool there? Is she nice? My ... I'm ..."

His voice drops off. He pulls at the buttons on his flannel, not looking at me.

"I'm really sorry. That's all."

He spins back around.

I'm not used to a non-sarcastic Taran Parker, and so I don't notice Kai at first, standing in the doorway, one hand holding the strap of his backpack, staring at me.

My heart jumps right into my throat as we lock eyes. Then he looks away, walks to the front of the classroom, taps Marshall Gleason on the shoulder, and nods in my direction. Marshall gets up and lumbers back to the stool next to me, sliding on with a sigh. He opens his *Mad* magazine and ignores me.

I stare at the back of Kai's head.

My lips sting where once they tasted sweet with his mouth, with sugary cookies. With thinking the summer would be full of kisses. When I thought I was going to be one kind of girl for the summer.

I grit my teeth. Laizure starts writing on the board.

Beside me, Marshall Gleason whispers, "Dude, I am sorry about your mom, and about whatever is up with that Kai guy, but please do *not* cry, because that is *way* beyond my skill set."

*Welcome to the Big Suck,* chortles the girl-bug. *Not so funny now, huh?*

Cake waits for me in the hallway after class, her face grim.

"What now?" I ask.

"I'm sorry," Cake says. "The funeral home called my mom, because she's the one who paid for the services." She puts her hand on my arm.

My heart sinks.

Cake's eyes get wet. "Your mom. She's ready. They said . . . they said we can come and get her ashes."

H ERE IS WHAT HAPPENS when you call the funeral home to arrange to pick up your mother's ashes.

"Hello, this is Leanna Linkletter of Linkletter and Family Funeral Home, and who am I speaking with, please?"

*Me.*

"And what can I help you with today?"

*You can help me with this person, the woman, my mother, my mom. She's there. You called me. June. June Tolliver. That's her name. Was her name. Sorry.*

"Thank you. The remains of June Tolliver are available for pickup today. We are open until 6 p.m."

*Okay.*

"Please bring photo ID. Thank you, goodbye."

*Click.*

Just like that. You'll pick up what's left of your mom like picking up dry cleaning or stopping for milk on the way home. A task to check off. An unexpected chore.

You will click off your phone and stand in the dusty parking lot of the high school, your tall best friend next to you, wondering what she should say to you.

Finally, she says, "We should go."

In her car, which her parents paid for, and gave to her for her birthday, you think, *No one is ever going to buy me a car.* And then you feel guilty, because that's petty.

You think: *Not that my mother had money for that anyway.*

Your friend says, "Do you want to listen to music?"

*No.*

"Do you want something to eat? We're going to miss lunch. I have our lunches in my bag."

*No.*

"Are you nervous?"

*Please be quiet, please.*

Your mind races, because you don't know what to expect, because there isn't a manual for death, though you are really, really, really starting to wish there were. What did they call those starter books for little kids a long time ago? *Primers.* There should be primers for death, so you could connect all the dots, like shock to sadness to ashes to sadness to shock to *alone.*

#dyingfordummies #deathmanual #aprimerforpain

When you get to the funeral home, the lady at the front desk asks for your ID, so you give her your school ID. At first, she seems hesitant and so you say, *I mean, you are not NOT going to give me my mom, you know?* And she shrugs in kind of an ashamed way and hands you some forms.

You sign the forms.

She gives you a blue velvet bag with a golden drawstring. It is square-shaped and surprisingly heavy.

You'll find out why it's so heavy later. It isn't all ash in there, you know. There are bits and chunks of bones, too, like a strange little archaeological site you could puzzle out, if you had the time.

And there isn't just one box, like you thought there'd be. There are three.

The lady tells you three death certificates and a coroner's official report will be mailed to you in a few weeks. She says if you want additional death certificates, they'll cost twenty-five dollars each.

Your friend says, "Isn't three plenty?"

The lady gives you a pitying look. "Well, hon, this was your mom? I'm real sorry. Well, if she had bills in her name and all, like the telephone or a utility or a credit card, they are going to want to get paid and you will tell them, *But my mama's dead,* and I am sorry to tell *you,* they will say, *Prove it.* And you have to send them a certificate. They won't take copies. Has to be official. Most people, they end up getting at least ten, if they have the money."

"What a dumb rip-off," your friend says.

And that will be another thing that should go in the primer. Bills. Who does that for all the kids whose parents disappear or die? What about this phone? Your only lifeline to your friend and your mother's voice? Karen said you could have a phone if you could pay for it, but with what?

And what about your house? Mr. Pacheco, the landlord, might have tolerated your mother's penchant for paying rent late for many years, but he won't tolerate *no* rent, and he's just the type of sour man to throw your things in the arroyo, where they'll be trampled by javelinas and stomped into suitable beds by coyotes.

"I am truly sorry for your loss," the woman says. She pulls a blue plastic bag from behind her desk. "Her clothes and earrings and things."

Oh. So, they . . . take those off. Before it happens.

Your friend takes the bag for you, because your arms are full of boxes of your mother.

You carry her against your chest to the car and hold her that way all the way home.

You are numb.

You think you might cry again, maybe, because the fact of her being reduced to a series of medium-sized boxes, after being so much in your life, such a *presence* . . . well, it takes all your breath away. It's kind of incomprehensible that a human can be, after all that living, just . . . ash. In boxes.

Your friend asks you, "Are you . . . Do you . . . want to spread her ashes somewhere? I guess that's a thing to think about."

You remember what Rhonda and LaLa said about ashes: the roadie rhododendron pot, spreading Speedy's ashes along her favorite rail line. You picture yourself flinging your mother's ashes in Lake Powell or making a somber trip to Mexico to drop them in the sea. Your mother never said anything about what she wanted, and it doesn't seem right to just guess for her.

And if you let the wind or water carry her ashes away, you won't have her anymore.

You understand now why some people prefer burials and cemeteries: they have a place to visit. To feel sad. To sit and cry, to know the person, or what is *left* of the person, is still, some-how, physically *there*.

Like wearing the lace dress, you can imagine yourself carry-ing around your mother in her white boxes with the red-and-green dragons inside the blue velvet bag for all eternity.

You tell your friend, *I can't think about that right now. That's too much.*

"You don't have to decide anything right now. We'll just go home."

You want to ask, *Where is that?* But you don't.

The ride is very quiet, though she says she's hungry, and stops once for burgers and salty fries, ignoring the lunches in her backpack. The sounds of the wrapper crinkling in the car sound like rain. The ice knocking in your soda cup sounds like rain.

You don't mind.

Your phone lights up. You look down. It's the boy orphan.

*Hang in there.*

You hug the boxes of your mother tighter against your body. You are only sixteen, and this should not be happening to you, that what's left of your mom is in bits and pieces, ash and burned bone.

You think about what the boy texted. His simple, kind words.

All your life, you've loved words and language, even if you aren't that great at school. You've loved weird words and smart words and beautiful words and awkward words, all of them. *Podunk. Mastermind. Effluvium. Macrosomatic. Hullabaloo.*

But there isn't a single word in the universe that you can think of that would describe the way you feel right now.

## 8 days, 16 hours

KAREN'S CAR IS IN LaLa's driveway, which is strange, since she hasn't texted me or anything, but what's stranger is when Cake and I walk by the car, I notice a blazing pink duffel bag stretched out across the backseat. Is Karen going on a trip? She doesn't seem like a pink kind of person.

Cake stares at the pink duffel bag and her eyes widen. She says, "Oh, holy hell," and my heart freezes.

This is *it*.

In the driveway, we stare at each other.

The front door swings open. Sarah shouts, "She's here! Tiger, your *sister* is here!"

Cake stares at me and I stare at Cake. Two deer, frozen.

"I'm not ready," I say.

"Too late. It's happening."

"I can't."

"You don't have a choice."

She puts her hands on my shoulders, turns me toward the house. Nudges me forward. As we walk, Cake murmurs, "Stay positive."

LaLa, Thaddeus, and Karen have grim faces. A ponytailed, skinny girl in a tank top and cutoff jeans, with a flannel shirt tied around her waist, is pacing back and forth in front of the couch, listening to something on her phone. She looks frustrated.

Karen says, "Shayna Lee?"

At the sound of her name, the ponytailed girl—woman? What are you when you're twenty, anyway?—turns, and blinks at me.

Time stops. I don't think anyone in the room is breathing, including Sarah.

The very first thing my brand-new sister says to me is "What. The nutballs. Are you freaking *wearing*?"

## 8 days, 17 hours

M Y SISTER'S CAR BROKE down somewhere in Utah. I have no idea why she would be in Utah, or why she decided to make coming to get me a kind of road trip for herself. I *thought* she was coming directly here.

She ended up taking a bus to Tucson, where Karen picked her up. She's hot, and sweaty, and dirty, and in a bad mood. She frowns at me in the living room.

"My mom bought it for me. For a dance," I say quietly.

"You can dance at a time like this?"

I freeze. I can't tell if she's joking or not, and she's looking at me, quite frankly, as though I'm some sort of annoying insect; like she's figuring out how to swat me away if I sting her.

I guess we aren't going to hug, or anything like that, because she doesn't make any moves toward me, and I don't make any toward her.

I guess I thought our first meeting would be a little more *sisterly* than this.

Shayna abruptly turns to LaLa. "Where's the bathroom? I think I need to freshen up before we hit the road again." LaLa points down the hall.

Once we hear the bathroom door close, Thaddeus says, "Oh. My. God."

I clench my Boxes of Mom closer to my chest.

"That was awkward," Cake whispers.

"She's tired," Karen says. "This is going to be stressful and overwhelming for everyone. Let's just take it step by step."

The toilet flushes.

Shayna saunters back into the room, her face brighter. She claps her hands together.

"Well," she says. "What happens now? I'm brand-new at this. Do I need to sign some papers or something? For . . . her?"

I get a cold feeling in my chest. I'm not a puppy from the pound.

Thaddeus gives me a small shrug, like, *Give her a chance.*

Maybe he's right. I mean, what did I think I was going to get, Jennifer Aniston? Some sort of cheerful angel who hugs me right away and does my hair and giggles secrets in my ear?

Shayna crosses her arms across her chest and juts her hip, inspecting her nails. I'm glad her eyes are looking down. I can look at her freely.

I wish for a fleeting moment that I could freeze everyone in the room, especially Shayna, with some sort of superhero power, so I can circle her slowly and inspect her for signs of me. I want that time to suss her out, like she's a rare artifact or a precious object. We're blood, after all. What things do we share?

Karen is talking quietly on her phone. Shayna looks up, blows out her cheeks.

Her eyes fall on me, finally, "So, you're *you*. There you are. In a very weird dress."

"It's nice to meet you, too, I *guess*," I reply snarkily. Thaddeus sucks in a breath.

"This isn't going well," he murmurs.

My sister regards me.

Karen clicks off her phone and clears her throat. "Let's get this show on the road, Tiger. LaLa's packed your suitcase and I have another client in a few hours. We can talk more about expectations and procedures in the car."

Shayna pastes a big smile on her face, suddenly noticing the blue velvet bag I'm holding. "You have a present for me? That bag is so pretty! Thank you!" She moves to take the bag.

I say, "It's my mom."

The room descends into an awkward silence.

Shayna jerks her hands back. "*Right.* Moving on. Thank you, everybody, for taking care of my little sister. I'll be assuming the reins now. Don't worry, everything will be just fine. Just super."

She slides the red sunglasses perched in her dark hair down over her eyes and moseys out the front door to Karen's car.

I stand there, slightly freaked out. She's literally only four years older than me and she's going to be taking *care* of me.

I can't even move.

I miss my mother so much right now it's loud inside me, like the worst thunder, the kind that shakes the windows, shoves the sides of your house, makes you feel unsafe. It's so loud I don't even know if it's LaLa, Cake, or Thaddeus who says, *It'll be okay.*

All I know is, I want to scream so hard it will tear their ears off. Because it will *never* be okay, never ever ever.

Like a zombie, I turn to go, ignoring Cake's attempt at a hug, Thaddeus telling me to call, LaLa and her whispered *Be brave.*

*Brave,* says the girl-bug. *What's that?*

. . .

214

Outside, the three of us climb into Karen's car, me in the back, as usual. My sister's pink duffel bag emanates a perfumy smell. I hold my Boxes of Mom tight to my chest.

No one says anything for a long time, until Karen finally breaks the silence. "I've been out to your house to check on things, Tiger. We need to stop at the grocery store on the way. You've got no food."

Shayna says slowly, "About that. I kind of blew a lot of money on a tow and motel in Utah, so I'm a little short."

"Why were you even in Utah?" I ask, suddenly and sharply.

My sister doesn't turn around. "Seeing friends. Bought a car, but it turned out to be a dud. Fancy that."

Karen says, "We've got a food card set up right now, until we can get some paperwork done and get you both in the system for benefits." She goes on about Social Security payments for orphaned children, a monthly allowance from the state, paperwork for medical and rent needs. "It's going to move slow. It always does."

Shayna grunts. "I spent a lot of money on the plane ticket here." She glances back at me. "I hope you're worth it!"

I think she thinks she's making a joke, but it's not a good one, and I'm already feeling sensitive about the dress comment, and maybe the fact that she hasn't been, well, *sisterly* to me so far at all, so what comes out of my mouth is kind of a shout.

"Sorry about your stupid money, but no one *asked* you to come here anyway."

"Actually," Shayna retorts, shoving her sunglasses on top of her head and leaning back to glare at me, "somebody *did* ask me to come here, as a matter of fact. To save you, apparently."

"Save me from *what*? My mother's dead—you can't save me from *that*."

"Save you from the orphanage, of course. If I wasn't here, that's where you'd be. Because God knows you can't count on dear old Dad. You know, *our dad*. Or, as I like to call him now, inmate number 24491. The one who left me and my mom for your mom. That's a whole two years I'll never get back, by the way, so you *could* be a little more grateful." Her voice cracks, and she turns back to the front seat, dropping her sunglasses back down over her eyes.

"They don't even have orphanages anymore," I spit. "Just foster homes. Rent-a-parents, right, Karen? You just have no idea at all what this is. At *all*." Tears of anger and confusion spring to my eyes.

"Girls," Karen says firmly. *"Enough."*

Neither my sister nor I say anything. I hold my Boxes of Mom tighter and look down at my lap. The dad comment hurt. I'd never really thought, in all my years of hoping for a dad, thinking about him, that he might actually have another family, a kid even—one who might have gotten really hurt, too.

And here she is, in front of me.

And I'm pretty sure she hates me.

*She hates me,* I text to Cake. *This is all horrible.*

*She doesn't! You're un-hateable. Relax. Give her a chance.*

Karen says quietly, *"Girls.* I don't think this is a good conversation to have right now. Let's all take a deep breath, get some food, get back to Tiger's house, and begin the transition into the home space."

I mumble, "I never even *knew* him. It's not my fault."

Shayna frowns. "Yeah," she said. "Well, I *did* know him. We had a whole little family and then your mom came along and *kaboom.*" She flutters her fingers and turns to the window.

It suddenly seems like my mom's life before me left an awful lot of wreckage. It's like I feel guilty now for something I had nothing to do with.

What Thaddeus said, about leaving, getting out, it's a dark thought, but it's starting to roam around the corners of my brain.

Karen pulls into the parking lot of the Stop N Shop and hands Shayna a card, like one of those gift cards you get for a store. There's a picture of the Grand Canyon at sunset on it. "You two go and get what you need for the house, food-wise. This card will have money put on it the fifth of every month. It's to be spent on groceries. To sell this card or to sell items purchased with this card is punishable by law. You can't buy toothpaste, toilet paper, tampons, or anything like that. Only food items. Here's the PIN."

She hands Shayna a piece of paper.

"Score." Shayna grabs the card and hops out of the car.

Karen gives me a *look.* "Go with her, Tiger."

I run to catch up to Shayna in the parking lot, keeping my Boxes of Mom tucked tight under my arm. The Stop N Shop is nice and cool inside and Shayna sighs with pleasure. "It's *hot* here. I had no idea how hot it was going to be. Jeez."

"It's going to get hotter," I mumble.

Shayna swears, which makes me smile.

She gazes around the Stop N Shop like she owns it, hands on her hips and her sunglasses on her head. Her tank top is pulled up a little and I glimpse the simple silver ring in her belly.

I'm torn between being fascinated by her and hating her.

Shayna grabs a cart and heads down the snack aisle, stopping at rows of chocolate cakes and doughnuts and Twinkies. She shovels boxes of Little Debbies into the cart.

Then it's a twelve-pack of Diet Coke. A bag of potato chips. A box of Lucky Charms. Ten yogurts (*10 for $6!* shouts the sign). Frozen egg rolls. A bag of frozen Tater Tots. When we hit the dairy aisle, she thumps a gallon of milk into the cart. My God, how does she stay so skinny?

"Have you ever heard of vegetables?" I finally ask, exasperated.

Her glance is withering. "Are you some kind of health nut?"

"No, just a human being who knows the value of a lentil and some broccoli." We round the corner to the produce section. I dump a bunch of broccoli and a bag of carrots in the cart.

She tosses me a head of limp iceberg. "Happy now?"

I hold my breath for an instant. Kiwis are right there. What will she do? Exclaim in delight? Or groan in disgust?

She pokes one with her finger. "So gross. Like a testicle."

Not *quite* the most elegant answer to my DNA question, but close enough.

She shudders, pushing the cart forward to the dry aisle, where I add bags of lentils and black beans.

Shayna eyes them. "I'm not much of a cook. This isn't going to be like *Chopped* or something. I'm easily distracted. Like, I *burn* things. Cooking is not my thing."

"Lentils and black beans, you can make a bunch at once and freeze them for later. And they're cheap, see? But good for you," I say. "My mom taught me to cook. She was good at it. When we had money." My voice breaks. I pretend to examine some sale cans of peas so she can't see my face.

She murmurs, "That's cool."

I drop a bag of rice in the cart, mentally adding up what we've spent so far, like my mom taught me to do, and I almost tell Shayna we should quit while we're ahead, but I have a feeling she won't care, because she's heading for the rows of Hershey bars at the checkout counter.

She dumps a bunch on the conveyor belt. Lady Spinoza is working the register. My mom always liked her. They used to joke about getting old, stuff about gray hairs and creaky knees. At my mother's viewing, she pressed me so hard to her chest I could practically smell her lungs.

Lady Spinoza dips our items over the scanner slowly, scrutinizing Shayna while talking to me. "I heard they had you in a home, eh? And now this, who is this?"

I swallow. "My, um, my sister."

Lady Spinoza whistles. "Ay yi yi. That sounds like a big story, eh?"

I nod.

Lady Spinoza tsk-tsks. "She doesn't look much older than you, Tiger. Two young girls on their own. Goddess help us all."

She tips her chin at Shayna, who's chewing a fingernail with an expression of utter boredom on her face. "You better take good care of this little one, sis. I loved her ma."

Shayna spits out the fingernail and slings our bags in the cart. She tells Lady Spinoza, "It's not a competition, *sis*."

Lady Spinoza raises her eyebrows at me as Shayna stalks away. "Watch out for that one, Tiger," she whispers.

In the parking lot on the way to Karen's car, though, when I catch up to her, Shayna digs out a couple Hershey bars from the endless bags of snacks and hands one to me, like a tiny, sugary peace offering.

The chocolate tastes good.

. . .

Karen walks around the house making notes on a clipboard while I unpack the groceries.

It's been a long time since our refrigerator and cupboards have been this full. Sometimes, just a couple of times, when I was a lot younger, before she got the Bookmobile gig, I can remember my mom making food just for me, not for herself, and just drinking tea while I ate.

I know now that she was stretching food. That she was worried.

I swallow, gripping a can of tomato sauce so hard it feels like I could crush it.

Shayna's looking at her phone.

Karen says loudly, to get her attention, "A caseworker will be doing home visits over the next several weeks. Someone should be assigned soon. I recommend some counseling as you two ease into the situation. It's going to be complicated, but I don't think it's impossible, not with some hard work."

She looks pointedly at Shayna, who is now watching the foggy running water from the kitchen faucet with distaste.

"I want to commend you, Shayna, for taking on Tiger's care. I hope you don't take it lightly. I'm not asking you to be her . . . *parent*, I'm asking you to be her guardian, her caretaker, with all that implies."

Shayna shuts off the water. "I can dig it. No problemo. Curfews, chastity belts, I'm down with the whole parenting thing."

Karen says, "*Shayna.* This isn't a joke. This is a child's welfare."

My sister holds up her hands. *"Kidding."*

Karen sighs. "Tiger, if you need anything, give me a call or a text. You have my number. Rhonda is assuming the cost of your phone until you and Shayna are on your feet."

I nod. I wonder what Thaddeus and LaLa and Sarah are doing. If my bunk is already occupied by some other sad and lonely kid. I look around my small house.

I haven't been here since the day after she died, and I can smell her, everywhere, in every corner and speck of dust.

One moment she *was,* and the next moment she was in the hospital, and she *wasn't.*

It feels good to be back in my familiar house, but also horrible, and now I am a mess inside. I can barely understand what Karen is saying about guardianship papers, parenting classes, and court-ordered something or other. I just stand there, holding my Boxes of Mom, Karen's voice sounding far, far away.

After Karen leaves, Shayna jerks a thumb at the faucet, bringing me to. "What's up with the water from hell?"

"I don't know. It was like that in the shower, too, before . . ." I pause. "I think my mom might have missed last month's rent and the landlord won't fix anything until he gets paid."

Shayna shakes her head. "Oh, no, hell no. That's not gonna play here. You have the number? What's the name?"

I find it on my phone. "Gilberto. Gilberto Pacheco. He won't pick up, though. He never does."

"He'll pick up. I'll telepathically will him to do so." She laughs to herself.

She takes my phone, presses his number. "Forgive me for the card I'm about to play, little sister, but this shit cannot stand."

"Yes, hello, is this Gilberto? It is? Well, this is Shayna Franklin and I'm Grace Tolliver's sister. That's right. Grace Tolliver. Yes, the *child* whose mother just *died*. *In the house you rent to them*. No, no, you listen to *me*. You're going to get over here and fix these shitty pipes stat or I'm calling the health department and, hell, maybe even the police, to report the unsanitary conditions that you have *forced* a *child* to live in for—" She mouths to me, *How long?* I shrug, not sure, so I just hold up ten fingers.

"*Three* weeks, *Gilberto*. She can't drink the water, she can't take a shower in the water, and oh, Gilberto, she *needs* to take a shower. Don't even get me started on this bizarre, grimy dress she's wearing. I've got the health department on speed dial, Gilberto. I have an itchy finger, Gilberto. How many properties you own? Let me start Googling you—"

She winks at me in triumph. "Super. I'll see you then."

I have to admit, I'm impressed.

"Boom," she says. "Now show me the bathroom. I have to take a monster dump. I've been riding in a bus for like a million days and there was no *way* I was going to dump in that lady's house with all you guys waiting in the other room."

I point to the bedroom. "Um, okay. I don't think I needed to know that, but okay. In there. Turn left."

I sit on the floor because I'm afraid to sit on the couch. Maybe she was there . . . when it happened.

Thaddeus texts me: *How is it?*

💩 🙁 I type, *I mean, like literally* 💩. *That's what she's doing right now. TMI! TMI! Also, two new kids. One's a crier. One's a hitter. I miss you already with your smelly dress.*

*Thanks a lot.*

*Hang in there. You want to have coffee this weekend?*

*Sure.*

*Don't forget. I'm here for you if you need me.*

Shayna's back, so I put my phone down. She's changed into extremely formfitting pink velour Victoria's Secret pajama bottoms and a white tank top and pink hoodie.

I tug at the hem of my dress. She seems comfortable in herself, which unnerves me. I felt comfortable in my body when I was a little kid, but somewhere around eleven or so, when I started to get these boobs, I started feeling less so.

Shayna tilts her head in the direction of our kitchen.

"This," she says, waving a hand. "This redness. Explain."

When I was twelve, my mother decided to spruce up the kitchen area by painting the counter and the wall red, but she also decided to paint everything *on* the counter and the wall red, so now we have a red kitty jar, a red toaster, a red coffeemaker, and a red microwave.

When Cake saw it for the first time, she said, "This is like a kitchen of death, June," which made my mother spit out the coffee in her newly red coffee cup.

"My mom. She liked brightening stuff up," I say.

There's a knock at the front door.

Our landlord, Gilberto Pacheco, stands sheepishly on the other side, holding an enormous, rusty tool kit in one hand and series of complicated-looking pipes in the other. He does a double take when he sees my sister in her skin-tight pink outfit.

He steps around her gingerly, like she might bite. Who knows, she might.

To me, he says gravely, "I am very sorry about your mother, Tiger. I am now here to fix the water pipes." He hustles into the bathroom first.

Shayna chops a bunch of iceberg lettuce in a bowl, opens a few packets of the Little Debbies, and plops down on the couch. "Dinner and some downtime," she announces, clicking on the remote. "My favorite time of day."

*Everybody Loves Raymond* pops on the screen.

I stay, cross-legged, on the floor, listening to Mr. Pacheco grunt and groan in our small bathroom for the better part of an hour before he moves to the kitchen.

My sister says nothing to me. Raymond's wife yells at him, and so does his dad, and his mother whines. Those are the only sounds, except for Mr. Pacheco and the echoey pipes.

Without my mom, this house doesn't seem like a home anymore. It's just a small adobe house with one bedroom and one bathroom, at the end of a long dirt road, with a red kitchen and mammoth sunflowers starting to poke through the dirt in the backyard. When my mother was here, the scuffed wood floor was charming and rustic, the cracks in the walls meant the house was aging in a poetic way. With a little paint, my mother turned the slivers along one wall into the green stems of flowers, and so we have daisies and roses and lilies trellising to the ceiling. The leaks in the roof when it rained meant the drops chiming into our pots and pans were an orchestra, and not an annoyance, or a potential safety hazard.

But now, as I listen to Mr. Pacheco clanging pipes and swearing softly, it all looks lonely and disheveled. And poor.

And I know it sounds cliché, but it's true: love makes everything seem better, and love isn't in this house anymore. Not that I can feel, anyway.

Not yet.

I feel like I'm drowning.

The girl-bug stirs. She's been sleeping. *Unknown quantity,* she whispers, motioning with a wing to my sister, on the couch. *Anything could happen.*

Raymond whines to his wife and she whines back.

This is the way it's going to be, I guess.

It takes Mr. Pacheco another hour to fix the pipes in the bath and kitchen, with a lot of swearing and banging. Shayna makes him drink a glass, just to be on the safe side. He starts to ask about rent, but she herds him out the door and plops back down on the couch.

I head into the bathroom. I place my mother's velvet bag carefully on the top of the vanity. I place a washcloth over her oatmeal soap. Cram her shampoos into the corner of the shower. Strip my clothes off.

I don't cry. I just stand beneath the water, letting it cascade over me.

I haven't eaten a real meal in so long my ribs are starting to press through my skin. Maybe I'll gradually disappear into nothingness, my skin floating away, my body morphing into bleached bone in the desert. The animals will get me. I'll become something else entirely, maybe, and not this terribly sad girl.

Where do people go when they die? If my mother is somewhere, where is she? If we have souls, what happens to them? Do they just . . . float somewhere? Like vapor? It makes me dizzy, thinking about it all.

When I get out, I find some yoga pants and a loose T-shirt, grab the hamper, and scoot by Shayna on the couch. She's flipping through channels and muttering.

The washer and dryer are in the backyard in a small building. My mom said that a potter used to own this house in the 1960s and used the outbuilding as his studio, which is why there's running water for a washer and electricity for a dryer and two big, dusty windows. There are a lot of artist types in Mesa Luna, weavers and painters and jewelry people. There's even a woman who makes paintings out of bottle caps, painstakingly applying them to wood or canvas. You think it's just bottle caps, but when she's done, there's a pattern, and an image. She's actually really famous. She was on the *Today* show once.

It's a pain to walk out here to do clothes in the winter, when it's cold, but it beats having to drive to town and hope the Spin Cycle is open, which it often isn't. It's also where my mom stores our jams and jellies in the winter, since it stays cool. I open the shed door and rows and rows of bright jars on shelves stare back at me. Around this time of year, my mom would be checking out the Jellymobile, testing the engine, the tires, getting it ready for the summer. I look out the tiny window of the shed at the Jellymobile, tucked under its winter tarp in the backyard.

I put my dress in the washer and reach back into the hamper and pull out the Boxes of Mom.

"Look," I say to her softly. "I'm doing the laundry. You didn't even have to ask."

The Boxes of Mom say nothing.

I dig into the hamper, come up with a fistful of her clothes.

The smell of her surrounds me and makes my heart beat faster.

Do you wash the clothes of a dead person? What do you do with their clothes? Keep them in the closet, pushed way off to the sides? I know my mom used to get all our clothes from thrift stores, but it feels weird to think of someone wearing *her* clothes.

Like, what if I run into Lady Spinoza at the Stop N Shop and she's wearing my mom's gray T-shirt with the faded tulip on it?

A giant tsunami of hopelessness swirls through me then: What if, in the end, all we are is a bunch of dirty clothes and gritty bits of oatmeal soap, to be thrown out and left on the street? I don't want that to be true, but maybe it is. Maybe that's just what a person's life ends up being.

Maybe that's how small our lives really are, no matter how much we try to make them big while we are alive.

I look at the boxes. "What should I do?"

The Boxes of Mom stay silent.

I wash her clothes.

I stay in the shed through the whole wash cycle and the dry cycle, folding everything up very carefully and putting it all back in the hamper. I take off my yoga pants and T-shirt and slide the dress back on. The blood on the sleeve is just a pink stain now.

The Boxes of Mom go on top of the folded clothes.

Shayna's half-asleep on the couch when I get back in the house. She sits up, rubbing her eyes, then yelps. "Shit, my makeup." She's rubbed her eyes into raccoon eyes.

While she's in the bathroom, I hop into the bed, hiding my phone under the covers. The sheets and blanket smell musty and unused. I should have washed and changed them, too.

When Shayna comes out, her face is pink and scrubbed. She looks even younger without any makeup.

"I'm going to sleep." I pull the blanket up to my neck.

Shayna looks around the room. At me. At the one bed.

"I'll probably just fall asleep out there. I have my bag." She points to a sleeping bag in the corner. A pink pillow that matches her pink duffel rests on top. I look through the doorway. To the couch. We only have one bedroom and my mom and I shared for years, until I turned thirteen and she said we should split up, that I needed my space. At first, I was a little put out. I liked sleeping with my mother, the two of us reading until we were drowsy and fell asleep with the lights on, but after a while, I understood, and I started to make the room my own, painting each wall a different color: blue, lilac, purple. I had glow-in-the-dark stars on the ceiling and skate posters, and when Cake came over, we could close the door and talk about her boyfriend, the one who broke her heart.

"I don't know about the couch," I tell her hesitantly. "That's where my mom slept. Also, just so you know, I think it might be . . . you know, where she maybe—"

Shayna holds up a hand. "Say no more."

She sighs. "This place might be a little too small. Don't get me wrong, I'm feeling the whole southwestern rustic kind of thing, but space-wise, it's a little tight," she says. "Probably we'll have to talk about that. When the time comes. If things work out."

*If things work out.*

She gazes around the room at our stuff, my stuff, my mom's stuff.

I feel protective of my mom suddenly, like I want to scoop all her tiny glass bottles of patchouli and her raku bowls of earrings into my arms and hide them.

"Maybe I'll sleep out back. You know, all rugged-like, the great outdoors, etc., and all that shit. I've slept in my car at rest stops. Lots of time on the beach out in Hawaii. It's no biggie."

I don't say anything. She can learn on her own about bugs and cicadas and coyotes.

Shayna picks up her sleeping bag.

"Well," she says. "Ciao." She leaves. The back door opens and closes.

I get out of bed and take my mom's boxes out of the hamper and put them on the floor of our shared closet and close the door, but that feels like I'm putting her in a time-out or something, so I settle for the top of the dresser, covering her with one of her flimsy scarves from Ted's Threads.

"Good night," I tell her, turning off the light. I lie down and stare up at the ceiling. One by one, my glow-in-the-dark stars pop out above me.

But alone in the bed, and in the house, I start to feel weird. Wobbly inside.

If she was still alive, I'd be listening to her in the other room, humming to herself as she prepared the couch for bed. Scooching herself under her blanket, cracking open her book.

I'm wiping away tears when Shayna stumbles back, clutching the pink pillow and her sleeping bag. "It's cold out there. What the shit? It's *May*. And it sounds like the jungle or something."

"Javelinas," I sniffle. "They come up through the wash." Can't she see I'm crying? Shouldn't she notice my voice is broken and weak?

"The *who* and the *what*, now?" She pees in the bathroom, leaving the door open. I look away as I answer her.

"The wash. An arroyo. You know, like a river. Only dry. They fill up when it rains, though. And javelinas are kind of like nasty pigs. Boars."

"That's hideous. And why would they call it a *wash*? That's dumb."

She comes out pulling up her pink pants. She shakes out her sleeping bag *on top of the bed,* way over on the right side, at the very edge. She hops up, slips down into her bag, mumbles good night. In a few minutes, she's snoring.

I stare at the glow-in-the-dark stars on my ceiling.

The moon burns through the window, full and bright.

Next to me, Shayna shifts. I can't believe I have a sister, and that she's in my house, snoring next to me. Big life events are supposed to happen over time, and in a certain order, like birth, school, marriage, death. And your parents are supposed to die when you're older, not when you're young.

*That's* the way life is *supposed* to work.

The universe is supposed to be kind and wait until you know things about life, like how to open a bank account, or purchase a vacuum cleaner, or get a job, and to eat responsibly, *not* Little Debbies for dinner, and the universe shouldn't let your parents *die* when *they* are still young, either. You're supposed to grow old, so old you get sick of people exclaiming how old you are and turning the television *down* when you want the volume *up,* and then finally you just get tired of no one listening and not being able to hear *Grey's Anatomy* and *that's* when you die.

I feel like I've had fifty-seven million giant life things happen in the space of nine days, and suddenly, being back in my own house is both comforting *and* overwhelming. I don't know whether to be relieved or still scared. Sleep or stay awake.

I feel myself sinking into the familiarity of my musty, unwashed bed, the comfort of my own sheets and blankets. My phone lights up and I see the words, *You there?* And a moon, a star, and a tiger, but I can barely lift my hands to respond. Thaddeus's words drift before me in the darkness of my room: *Good night.*

I fall back and back and back into a grayness that tightens like a spider's silk around me.

## 10 days, 12 hours

I WAKE UP TO SUNLIGHT on my face, my walls of many colors, my skateboard posters, my familiar soft, pilled blanket.

I'm home.

For a minute, my whole body is a golden, glowing thing, because I can hear someone walking outside my bedroom door, moving things around in the kitchen area. I smell fresh coffee.

It *was*. It *was* a terrible dream. A nightmare. A *something*. Like when Dorothy wakes up and sees Auntie Em and starts babbling about Oz and Auntie Em is like, *wtf, Dor?* But she's kind to her anyway, because she thinks Dorothy's just hit her head.

Maybe I just hit my head.

The door opens.

"Mo—"

But the person holding the chipped red mug isn't my mom. My eyes flick to the dresser.

My mom is in her boxes, under the silk scarf from Ted's Threads.

It's the other person, the strange one. My sister. Her hair on top of her head, mussed and dark. She's sipping from her mug and scratching her butt through her pink velour pajama pants.

"Jeez Louise, I thought you were *never* going to wake up. I even went through your stuff to see if you'd, like, *taken* something. I mean, you don't seem like the type, but who knows, right? Grief does weird shit to people."

Shayna blinks. "Are you okay? I was just joking. Say something. You were asleep for *almost two days.* Your friend, that tall girl, she came by and we couldn't even wake you. She said you were probably traumatized and sleeping it off. Seriously, I was worried."

I look at her. "Really? You were worried?"

"Yeah." She shrugs. "I didn't come all this way for nothing, you know. I didn't come out here just so you could up and die——"

Her face drains. "I'm sorry. I can be really stupid."

I tell her it's okay, because I'll probably be getting a lot of that. I try to smile.

"Good," she says, triumphant. "That's what I like to see. A smile. Now, you missed some days of school, which is fine, but we have bigger problems on our hands."

"Like what?" I scooch up in bed.

"Like the fact that your mom hasn't been paying any bills." She leans over and flicks the light switch. "We got a letter that this is *jussst* about to get turned off. We need to get down and pay it in a few days or it's dunzo. I have a little money, but not too much left, and I don't know when you'll start to get whatever it is the state is going to give you or even how much that's going to be. I called that caseworker but she didn't call back." She stares at me carefully.

"I'm not sure there are a lot of job prospects for me in Mesa Luna. I just want to say that up front. We might have to make some . . . changes."

My heart squeezes.

"I have some friends in Boise. They bought an old motel by a ski resort. But that's so much snow." She shudders. "It could be fun, I guess. And I know people in Portland who do artisanal cheese and raise ostriches, but it's so damn gray up there. Not even an ostrich can make up for gray skies."

The last thing I want is to leave Cake. Leave the little I have, the only place I've ever known, but the job thing is true. My mom had to cobble stuff together. A lot of people who live here commute to Tucson or Sierra Vista, or they're on welfare, or they work for themselves, like the artists and people like Grunyon's moms, who run the coffee shop/diner/bookstore and are trying to start some sort of alpaca farm in their backyard with dreams of alpaca scarves, mittens, and hats, though neither of them knows how to make that stuff. Yet.

"I'm not ready to ditch everything for ostriches and weird cheese," I say tentatively.

My sister and I stare at each other.

"Well," she says. "You think about it. I know stuff is rough. It would be hard. I'm gonna go sit outside. Get some sun." She turns.

Outside. My brain is working overtime through my two-day-sleep fog, through my fear that we might move.

Outside.

"Shayna!" I yell so loud she jumps, coffee sloshing from her cup and onto her pink pants.

"Dude! Turn the volume down!" she shouts back, flicking brown liquid from her pants.

"No, but, Shayna, outside, outside!" I'm waving my hands.

"What? *What's* outside?"

I try to kick the blankets off me, get tangled, and half roll onto the floor.

"Jesus, that dress. Still with the dress?" She shakes her head.

"Never mind that." I pop up, pushing hair out of my face. "Outside. The Jellymobile. It's May, Shayna. It's time for the Jellymobile."

I don't think I've smiled so hard in months.

I N THE BACKYARD, SHAYNA stares at the Jellymobile. "Um," she murmurs. "Hmm."

"Don't you just love it?" I say to Shayna, brushing dust off the sexy jalapeño pepper in her cowboy boots. There's a nick in her big red-lipsticked smile that we'll have to paint over, and her crown of strawberries and red chiles could use freshening up, too.

"My God," my sister says. "Is this for real? Is this real life?"

"Well, yes," I say. "*Mine.* Five days a week in the summer. That's how we make some money."

"All day?" she asks. "Like, sitting in this truck. And people really buy this stuff?"

"Well, sometimes seven days, depending on how much we made. And sometimes we sit outside, under an umbrella, but yeah, mostly in the truck. We move around town, or over to Sierra Vista, week to week, change up our stops."

"And it *worked*? Like, you made money?"

"Some. Enough. She drove the Bookmobile for the library, too, and worked at a daycare."

"I'm almost afraid to ask," Shayna says hesitantly, "but here goes. Where are these mythical jams and jellies? And who, where, what, why, and when do they happen?"

I open the door to the outbuilding so she can see the shelves packed with jars, neatly lined up and waiting for a spritz of gingham around the lid, tied with bright yarn.

Shayna whistles.

"And your mom made all this? How long does it last?"

"She does it during the winter, mostly. At night. It can last for like two years if it's sealed properly. We usually move it into the kitchen in the summer and store it in crates, because it can get hot out here."

"Why didn't she just sell it online? Wouldn't that be easier than sitting in a truck all day?"

I shrug. "I don't know. She seemed to like it. We hung out together. She met people. Sometimes, they'd buy more when they got home, wherever that was. I mean, she had business cards and stuff, and then she'd just mail it out after they sent her a letter saying what they wanted and a check."

Shayna runs her hands over the truck. "You know, this thing would totally fly in Portland. They love any kind of truck that sells something you can eat or drink."

"Well," I say slowly, toeing the ground. "We don't live there." Is she really thinking about making us move?

*Us.* What a weird thing to think, that we are an "us" just because we've been thrown together. I feel like you need to earn "us-ness." Or it's built in. Like with a mom.

"Well, we have to keep some options open, right?" She walks around the Jellymobile, disappearing for a moment. "There must be a permit or something for this, right? Any idea where she kept it?"

"You can check inside. She kept stuff like that in the desk in the front room."

Shayna's phone vibrates. She frowns. "Shit."

"Who is it?" I ask.

"Nobody. It's just Ray. I have to take this. I'll be back." She pushes the latch on the backyard fence and walks down the alley.

I text Cake. *I'm showing her the truck. We have no money. My mom wasn't paying bills.*

*OMG. June's Jams. The Jellymobile. Also, you were OUT COLD.*

*I know.*

*You must feel good being back.*

*Yes and no.*

*I'm not sure your sister is a jams kind of girl, but maybe?*

*Do you want to come over?*

She texts me back a sad face. *Can't. I'm filming my performance video for that camp.*

*I thought you didn't get in.* There's some violin camp in Massachusetts that Cake wanted to go to this summer for three weeks, but she got put on a wait list.

*They had two kids drop out so they're picking from the list. I have to submit a new piece, though.*

She types, *I was going to tell you, but then all this happened. I mean, I'm not going to go! I won't leave you. I just want to do this video. It's good practice for when I apply to music schools and stuff.*

*You should go. If you get in.*

I don't think I've ever texted anything so slowly in my life.

*Oh God no. Hey, let's hang out Sunday, okay? I'm thinking we could dig around the house, maybe see if your mom left something.*

*Okay.*

*Okay.*

I sit down on a lawn chair, the sun warm on my scalp. Cake away for three weeks.

This is like a whole summer of leavings, all of a sudden.

Shayna comes back, her face grim. "Let's do this," she says with determination. "I need to work off some steam."

I notice that her hands are shaking a little bit. "Are you okay?" I ask. "Who is . . . who is Ray?"

"Just a guy. It didn't end well. Not even worth talking about."

"Was he your boyf—"

"I said, not worth talking about. You got a tool kit or anything? We're probably gonna need to get air in these tires, too."

She leans down and feels the tires. She won't look at me.

Ray. Something about this worries me. She doesn't seem like a girl who would get upset about a guy, not the way she handled Pacheco. She seems like somebody who doesn't take any shit.

"You gonna help or not? This was your idea, after all."

I head into the shed to get cleaning supplies and the tool kit.

We spend a lot of time cleaning the truck off, which means I get to listen to Shayna swear. A lot. Completely and utterly transfixing combinations of words that I never even knew existed. Probably, if my mother knew her, she'd have found this hysterically funny.

Which makes me wonder: *Did* my mom know about her? Shayna was four when I was born. I watch her wipe beads of sweat off her forehead as she runs a sponge over the back bumper.

What would my mother think of her, of this? Of us, together. Was my mom ever going to tell me about all this . . . this stuff from her pre-me life?

And how much does my dad, *Dusty Franklin,* currently languishing in a minimum security facility in Springer, New Mexico, know about my mom's life? I mean, don't people in love share secrets? They must have been in love, right? I mean, there was *me,* after all.

Or maybe I was just an accident.

Before I can stop myself, I blurt out, "Shayna, maybe we could call Da— Dustin, sometime? Would that be okay? I think he might know some stuff. About my mom. Like before she had me and all. She never . . . she didn't really talk about herself all that much."

I don't feel right calling him "Dad" in front of her. After all, he did that, *was* that, with her, not me. I feel like she owns that part of him.

Shayna's inside the front of the truck now, dusting off the dash. "I'm not sure that's such a good idea right now."

"Why not? I mean, you must have the number—"

"It's very complicated." She winds the dust rag into a tight ball.

"Why? It's not like he's going anywhere soon."

"Let's just drop it. I'm here. Isn't that enough for right now?" She's getting annoyed.

"I don't understand why you're getting mad. I just want to ask him some questions about my—"

She throws the balled dust rag down and tightens the scrunchie in her hair. Her voice comes out fast and angry. "Maybe I don't want him to talk to you, okay? Maybe there's that. Maybe I don't think he should get a damn reward for bad behavior, how about that? I'm already out here cleaning up his mess, just like I've always cleaned up—"

She looks at me.

My face is burning. I bite my tongue as hard as I can without drawing blood.

"I didn't mean it that way." She jiggles the Jellymobile's keys and doesn't look at me. Her voice is soft.

"I'm not a mess."

"I'm sorry. I'm a little stressed. This is stressful on me, too, okay?"

"Do you even want to be here? Because you can just go. Really, just go." My heart's beating so fast I can hear it in my ears.

"Of course I want to be here. You're my sister. Blood is blood."

"I'm not a mess," I whisper.

"No," she says. "You're not."

She sighs. "I have a stupid quick mouth, okay? I'll try to work on that. Let's just get this going, all right? We'll talk about Dad later."

She sticks the key in the ignition, drowning out any answer I might possibly have mustered anyway. The Jellymobile spits and coughs but finally chugs to life, rivulets of smoke blooming in the tiny desert backyard, sending up clouds of dust.

The girl-bug blinks and blinks. *A mess,* she says. *A mess!*

Blood is blood.

T HE NEXT MORNING IS Saturday. Shayna and I tiptoe around each other, not saying much in the Jellymobile. On the way to what is my mom's favorite sell-point, Shayna stops at Grunyon's for lattes. I see some kids from school inside, so I duck down a little in the front seat. The alpacas, John, Paul, George, and Ringo, stare at me steadily from beyond the fence with their sleepy eyes.

Shayna stays in the Airstream a little longer than necessary, gazing at the alpacas through the window. I can see her standing there, sipping one of the coffees, and I wonder what's got her so fascinated with John, Paul, George, and Ringo.

At the sell-point, we unload our cooler of water and lunches and snacks, and I show her how to set up the hand-painted sign next to the truck, how to use the credit card machine, how to log sales in my mother's favorite ledger.

We unload the jars, arranging them inside the truck on the shelves. Shayna takes a long time making the jars look *just so* on the front counter of the sell-window.

And then we wait. There are fans inside the truck to keep us cool, and a small air-conditioning unit hooked up to a petite generator.

It takes about five minutes for Shayna to whine, "This. Is. Boring."

"I brought books." I hold up two Stephen Kings, and *Pride and Prejudice.*

She heaves a deep sigh and sips water, adjusting the brim of one of my mom's hats. I'm not sure how I feel about her wearing something of my mom's, but I stay quiet. I guess I want to keep things on an even keel after yesterday. I feel like we were close to something dangerous.

"There are reservations out here." She gazes at the landscape. Dry desert, blue sky, white puffs of clouds.

"Yeah."

"Are there a lot of Native kids at your school?"

"Some. My friend . . . Kai. He's half Navajo and half Japanese." It still hurts a little, saying his name.

Shayna whistles softly. "That's a helluva combination. Is it rough for him?"

"I don't know." I think about the question. We've all been in school together forever, and Mesa Luna has lots of different kinds of kids, because it's the only high school for miles, so tons of kids get bused in from other dinky towns, but maybe there are problems I never really noticed.

"I mean, he never says anything about it, anyway."

"Well, did you ever ask him?"

"No, I mean, he's just *Kai*. His skin color doesn't matter. His character does. We listen to the "I Have a Dream" speech every February during Black History Month." I like listening to MLK's voice streaming from the speakers in each classroom.

Shayna snorts. "That's some very hunky-dory peace-and-love shit, Tiger, but his skin color *does* matter. And he's not Black; one ethnicity isn't like, one size fits all, you know? You can't just pretend color doesn't matter because you think it *shouldn't*, because you were born with white skin and privilege. And you can't pretend to not notice racism because you listen to the one famous Black guy every single year. That's not *enough*. There are terrible, terrible people in the world. Kai's life will *always* be vastly different from yours." She takes a sip of water.

"Also, there was a significant pause between the words 'My friend' and 'Kai,' so it sounds like there's something going on there. He your boyfriend?"

My face reddens. "No! It's not—"

Her phone pings. She looks down. "Dude," she says softly. "You. Will. Not." She starts texting.

"Who is it?" I ask.

She grimaces. "Ray."

Ray again. Maybe I can get more from her this time.

"Is he *your* boyfriend?"

"Like I said, it didn't end well. He's not quite ready to say ciao."

"Why not? What happened? What's he do for a living?"

I went too far. Shayna gives me a look and changes back to me. "How far did you get with the Kai guy? You got all red, so I know there's a story there." She's looking curious now.

I slide my hat down over my face.

"There's nothing to be embarrassed about. Sexual intercourse is the bomb." She laughs.

"Stop! We didn't do that! We just kissed! And then my—"

"What? And then *what*?" Shayna leans forward, tugging her skirt down a little.

"Nothing. I don't want to talk about it."

*Don't cry don't cry don't cry*

"You kill me. Why are you so embarrassed?" She pokes me in the shoulder and then leans out the window suddenly.

"Company. It's go time."

Relieved, I show her the ropes. The couple who emerge from their camper have southern accents, they comment on the dryness of the heat, want to know how long we've lived here, what's in the jams, how long can they be kept unrefrigerated, do we have a website, how lucky we must feel to live out in all this wide-open beauty.

It goes on like this for the next couple of hours. Cars pull up every fifteen minutes or so; people get out and buy jams and drinks from the cooler. And Shayna can *talk*. I'm impressed. They love her, all these people, hanging on her every word. They think she's funny and friendly. Someone tells her about her chemotherapy, and Shayna darts out from the truck to hug her. A man says he's buying jelly for his brother, who's broken a hip and lives in San Diego. They'll eat jam sandwiches, just like they did when they were little, he tells us. He's old. The brim of his straw hat is cracked, and his car makes an unpleasant sound as he drives away. I wonder if he'll make it.

Shayna clucks her tongue. "Poor old dude," she murmurs. She checks her phone. "Ray! Gah." Her fingers fly.

Watching her, I feel happy and sad at the same time, because she's like my mom in that way: people open up to her, they spill their souls.

On the way home, she's very chatty. The money makes her happy, I think. Or maybe relieved.

She decides we should get pizza and watch movies, so we pick up some frozen ones at Stop N Shop with the card Karen gave us. After my shower, when I'm sliding pizza slices onto plates, she comes out of the bedroom in her sexy pink pajama outfit and settles on the couch. She has no problem sitting there, but I still do, so I tuck myself on the beanbag my mother got me

245

when I turned twelve. It's purple and yellow and reminds me of a cupcake.

Shayna flips through the channels until she finds a movie with a lot of car crashes and bad language and we stay that way, watching movie after movie. I don't eat much of the pizza, but Shayna doesn't seem to notice.

I'm thinking, while pushing pizza around on my plate, that I kind of feel okay about things, about *her,* and *us,* that things might be fine after all, like, baby steps, I guess, even if it takes a while, when my sister drowsily raises her head from the couch and peeks over at me.

"I might drive into Tucson tomorrow. Borrow your mom's car, okay? I need some wheels. Just to have a look around. That was cool today, out in the truck, but I don't know if that's totally me. We should keep our options open, okay?" She gives me a searching look, then drops her head back over the armrest.

I tear the pizza crust into tiny, tiny, tiny bits.

## 12 days, 16 hours

C AKE STARES INTO MY closet. My sister's in the front room, watching *House Hunters* and enjoying a close, personal relationship with a bag of potato chips.

Cake says, "I can't believe you never even looked in here. You weren't the least bit curious?"

I hold my pillow against my chest, trying to sniff the air subtly. My mourning dress is taking on a kind of salty, deep smell. It might be time for another wash.

"No. You knew Mom. There didn't seem to be a point in snooping around. She was . . ." I search for the right word. "Intractable." Another word from Hoffmeister's class.

"True," Cake agrees, gently pushing some of my mother's clothes to the side of the closet. "But maybe there are clues in here. She must have kept *something.*"

Cake has spent considerable time Googling my mom's full name and birth date. She'd called, on a whim, the University of New Mexico archive, where my mom used to work, and talked a woman named Laura into telling her a little about my mother.

"She cried when I told her your mom was de——" Cake stops talking, glancing back at me, her face frozen.

We stare at each other. "You can say it," I tell her. "It's not like it's not real if you don't say it. You know?"

"It's hard to say," she says, biting her lip. "I don't want to make you . . ." She stops.

"Sad?" I say. "Too late."

Cake says, very softly, "Okay."

We stare at each other again.

"Dead," Cake says firmly. "She cried when I told her your mom was dead."

"There," I say, trying to joke, even though hearing the word coming from her mouth hurts. "That wasn't so bad, was it?"

We both know it is, but it's like a hurdle we have to jump, I guess.

She turns back to the closet. "She was her supervisor and said your mom was really nice, and a hard worker."

Her voice is muffled from inside the closet. "She said your mom had a boyfriend. That must have been your dad, and that they fought, and your mom left without notice and she never saw her again."

"But," Cake says, emerging with a bag and inspecting the contents, "she also said your mom said she grew up in Phoenix. Did you know that?"

I shake my head. I guess I always thought she was from Albuquerque.

Cake looks up from the bag. "I mean, do you think she had a *will*?"

I look at my Boxes of Mom, as if to ask her, *Did you?*

Of course, she doesn't answer.

"Does a will cost money?" I ask Cake.

"I think so."

"Then I don't think my mom had one."

We smile at each other. "Good point," Cake says.

Cake pulls out paper bags labeled *Christmas lights* and *Halloween* and then crawls so far into the closet I can only see the soles of her Mary Janes.

She backs out on her knees, the bottoms of my mother's dresses falling over her face. "Here," she says breathlessly. "Look through here."

"Those are just me," I say, eyeing the brown shoeboxes she pushes toward me. "I've seen those boxes before. It's just old school photos of me and stuff."

Cake does a quick run-through to make sure. She holds up my kindergarten picture. Missing teeth, puffy pigtails, that awful desert vista backdrop with the jackalope. Then she brings out a photograph of our class in the third grade, the year she moved here.

"Mrs. Hervey." Cake nods gravely. "She was the *worst*."

Mrs. Hervey was always telling Cake to sit down, but Cake was *already* sitting. She was tall, even when we were eight. And Mrs. Hervey refused to call her "Cake," only "Katerina," and so Cake refused to call Mrs. Hervey "Mrs. Hervey" and called her "Mrs. Mean" instead and it was not a good year, except for the fact that Cake became my friend.

Cake stacks the shoeboxes and reaches deeper into the closet. Her voice is muffled by clothes and darkness. "I can't believe you never snooped around. You're, like, the most incurious person I know."

"That's not true! I read," I say defensively.

"Incurious about real life, then."

I shake my head. "Again, not true. I just didn't have a lot of chances."

Cake looks back at me.

"You know how Mom was."

*Was.* It burns my mouth that I said that, that I made her past-tense.

"I know. I'm sorry."

She comes all the way back out and swipes some hair from her face. "I would have been all over this, though, looking for some clue."

Here is what I want to say to Cake, but I don't have the courage: *Maybe I don't want to unravel this mystery just yet.* I've been through the biggest thing you can go through, losing a parent, and I'm not sure I can handle knowing more than I ever thought possible about my mother, especially if some of it turns out to not be so, well, *good,* like the possibility that she'd wantonly and knowingly stolen a married man from his family.

It's very hard to think of your parents as *people.* Full of bad checks and bad decisions, fistfights and broken hearts, all of it.

Because if they can't goddamn take care of themselves, how will they take care of *you*?

And I've already met enough kids with parents who can't take care of them. Or don't want to. And if my mother's only problem was that she wanted to take *too* much care of me, well, then I was lucky.

There it is again. *Was.*

I feel really tired all of a sudden. Like I want to be alone in my room, and not talking, and not treating my mom's life like she's an episode of *Forensic Files* or something.

"Cake," I say. "When are your parents coming back?" They dropped her off to go shopping in Sierra Vista.

She grunts from deep in the closet. "I don't know."

The ends of her purple hair are tangled against her shirt.

250

Suddenly I remember the first time her mom let her dye her hair, when she was twelve. Cake had been having a tough year. Some kids were bullying her pretty hard that fall because of her weight gain, and she was starting to get angry, talking back. Rhonda brought home the dye and did it herself: bright pink with chunks of lime green. For some reason, having that unusual hair gave Cake some sort of strength. Kids looked at her differently, with a kind of awe. Some kids still tried to harass her, but she *felt* different, that was the thing. Kind of like what LaLa said, that people can get braver when they have on armor, like different clothes. Or dyed hair, in Cake's case.

My mom kind of disapproved of letting her have dyed hair so young, but Rhonda said, "Sometimes you need to let them make their own decision, June. They need to find a safe way to rebel or to feel special. I'd rather she start dyeing her hair than smoking weed or hurting herself because she feels hated."

In all my life, I've never gotten to choose my clothes or even my hair.

I sink down farther in the bed.

Cake emerges from the closet, a dust bunny stuck to her cheek. "Here," she says. "This looks promising." She hands me a wide blue box.

I slide the lid off the box. On top, in round childish writing, someone has written, *Property of June Tolliver. Open This Box Under Penalty of Death.*

Inside are photographs in plastic baggies, a manila envelope, and a folded square of newspaper. I shake open the envelope. Gold and silver medals fall out, along with some brightly colored competition ribbons. I smooth them out and read the cardboard tags on the back.

*1st Place, Dressage, June Tolliver*

*1st Place, Beginner Novice, Eventing, June Tolliver*

There are so many awards. Some of the ribbons are huge, with big satin rosettes at the top. I run my fingers over the raised horse and rider on the front of one. In the baggies, there are photographs of a girl, sweet-faced and smiling, wearing a velvet hat with a roundish peak and a chin strap, and a cute businessy-looking shirt and jacket. She's hugging the neck of a beautiful horse. She looks insanely happy. I peer closer at the smiling girl in one photo. My hands start shaking.

The loopy handwriting on the back of the photograph says, *June, age 9. Phoenix Invitational.*

I touch the girl's face, my *mother's* face, with my finger.

I've never seen my mother as a child.

She has a giant, shit-eating, I-just-won-this-whole-thing grin on her face. My mother, a happy little girl who rode horses. No wonder she loved the horses at Randy Gonzalez's ranch. She'd grown up with horses. She'd loved them since she was a little girl.

My heart hurts, and my eyes burn with tears. I look at the Boxes of Mom and think, *Why couldn't you have just told me this, this one memory? Why?*

Cake's breath is warm on my cheek. "Whoa," she says, taking the photograph from me. "Your mom was *adorable.* You have the same cheeks."

As I rifle through the shoebox, my mother's childhood reveals itself: horses, and a red-brick, ranch-style house with a pool, and a curvy slide, and two nice-looking people named Ed and Crystal. My grandparents. The ones who died when she was in college.

Ed wears glasses and has two pens in the pocket of his shirt, always, and Crystal has blond hair, like my mom's, and she's always holding a cake with candles, or handing my mother a Christmas present, or standing next to a big piece of meat on a grill outside.

Grandparents mail you ironed dollar bills inside birthday cards, one for each year you've been alive. Grandparents give you butterscotch candies and soda when your parents aren't looking. They raise you, at least as far I've seen in Mesa Luna, when your parents die, or one disappears, or maybe one drinks too much or gets hooked on drugs. There were always a lot of grandparents on parent-teacher conference day at Davidson Middle School, shuffling into the building in fuzzy slippers and too-big checkered shirts, squeezing awkwardly into those seats that attach to the desk.

Ed and Crystal seem like nice people, from the photographs, and I feel a longing for them that I've never felt before.

My grandparents. People who kept pens in their pockets, liked barbecue, and bought my mother a horse named Charlotte.

Which I learn because there's a newspaper article folded into a tiny square, about one of my mother's wins, that she and Charlotte were on their way to some sort of championship in Texas. When the reporter asked about the name of her horse, my mother said, "Well, I named her after a character in my favorite book, *Charlotte's Web*. You know, the spider? The spider and the pig are great friends, just like me and my horse."

"Whoa," Cake breathes. "This is intense." She paws through the box, but there isn't anything else to see. We've looked through all of it. I stare at the photos of my equestrian mother, and my grandparents, while Cake crawls back into the closet and shuffles things around. She comes out, sweaty and satisfied.

"That's it," she says. "The rest of the shoeboxes are just shoes. Who knew your mom liked shoes so much? Also, now we know the names of your grandparents, which is going to help. We can Google them."

I carefully refold the newspaper article. *Area Girl Canters Her Way to Great Things.* My mother went from a chubby, wet-cheeked baby to a slim girl with medals and ribbons and a horse, and then her life . . . stopped. Until me.

There are no middle school photos. No more ribbons after a certain year. No high school photo. Prom. Graduation.

I ask the dragon boxes, "Who are you? What happened from the time you were ten until . . . me?"

Cake holds up her hands. "Wait, who are you talking to?"

I point to my mom's boxes on top of the dresser. "June. She's over there."

Cake breathes in deeply, considering.

Then she says, "Not that I'm criticizing, but I just want to clarify: First, the dress, and now . . . talking to your mom's ashes? Do I have everything clear?"

I feel weird inside, not as empty as I could, or as sad, but not happy, either. I give Cake a half smile. She's a good friend, to do all this for me.

"Yes, I talk to my *dead* mom now."

Cake grimaces at the word and brushes the dust off her knees. "Good to know. But, like, if you decide to do weird experiments with electricity and, like, other people's body parts or something, to bring her back? I'm not sure I can be the supportive best friend. I just want to state that up front."

"Noted," I say.

"I'm gonna go wash my hands." She closes the bathroom door.

I hear a car pull up outside and the slams of two car doors. Then angry whispering. I put the photographs down.

"It's *ridiculous.*" A man's voice. Cake's dad. "She's *going* to go."

"She's sixteen. She can make her own choices, good or bad, and then live with them. She doesn't want to leave her friend." Rhonda sounds pleading, like they've been talking about this too long.

Talking about Cake, I think. About the camp.

"We have done everything we could for this girl. We have helped with money, we've helped with food, we've helped with car repairs, we're paying for her *phone,* and I love her, I do, but at some point, she is holding *our* daughter back. Our very, very talented daughter. She cannot turn down this camp again. She was lucky enough to get another chance to apply after turning them down last year."

Rhonda murmurs, "Tiger had mono. They've always been so close. Frankly, I think it's nice our daughter has the heart she does."

Cake was accepted to the music camp in Massachusetts? I didn't know that. I didn't know she got in last summer, too.

I was so sick for a month. Cake stayed with me as much as she could, wearing a mask and rubber gloves, so my mom could do the Bookmobile and Jellymobile. She joked about her hazmat fashion. We watched oodles of television and listened to records and took naps and I held her while she cried about Troy, the guy from Sierra Vista.

And what are they talking about, money and car repairs?

Did they give my mom money and I didn't know?

"I mean, Rhonda, come on. I'm sorry June *died,* and I miss her, I do, but our daughter is going places. What, is she not going to go to college because her friend can't afford to? We need to start pushing her to think of herself first. It's time."

That is something Cake would do. The college thing. I haven't really thought about it, not in the real sense, only abstract. But she would. She would stay behind for me.

The toilet flushes in the bathroom. Cake comes out.

"What?" she says. "You have a funny look on your face."

"Your parents are here."

"Oh, cool." She puts her earbuds and phone in her backpack.

"Hey, what happened with your music camp?" I ask, keeping my voice mild. "You get in?"

She doesn't look at me. "I haven't heard back, and I'm sure I won't get in, but it's no big deal."

My friend is lying to me about something that she should be happy about.

She's lying because *I'm* unhappy, and have a dead mom, and she thinks *she* shouldn't be happy.

"Cake," I start to say, but Shayna breezes into the room.

"I'm gonna hop in the shower and then head out to Tucson, okay? Not sure when I'll be back."

She shuts the bathroom door. The shower starts running. There's a knock at the front door.

"Cake!" her mom calls. "Let's go! We're meeting Connor for dinner in fifteen minutes."

Cake hoists her backpack on her shoulders and we walk out to the front room.

Her mom is picking up stray bras from the back of the couch. "How's it going, honey? Things seem a little . . . messy around here." She dangles two purple bras in front of me. Cake's dad sighs heavily.

I try to ignore the fact that he was just bitching about saving my mom and me from, well, *everything,* and concentrate on Rhonda.

"My sister is making herself at home," I say lightly.

It's true. The house is starting to get Shayna-fied: bras on the bathroom door handle, the couch, eyeliner pencils on the vanity in the bathroom. Lipsticked coffee mugs and dirty plates on the kitchen counter. Copies of *Cosmo* all over the floor.

She even shoves her own clothes in my hamper. If I didn't do laundry, or the dishes, or straighten up, I don't think they'd get done.

Rhonda folds the bras and puts them on the couch. "You doing okay? Staying brave?"

I look at her. What does bravery have to do with *anything*? My mom is dead and I'm supposed to be brave? It's like I'm not allowed to even cry now that the funeral is done and my sister is here and, well, this is life now.

Because crying would make people uncomfortable, I guess.

"Sure," I say flatly.

Rhonda frowns and hesitates, like she wants to say something, but she's not sure what.

"Why don't you come stay with me tonight?" Cake says, watching me and her mom. She uses her extra-cheerful voice. "Your sister's going out anyway."

"Cake," Gabe says impatiently. "Let's go. I'm hungry."

That would be nice, to be at Cake's comfortable Earthship, with its ferns everywhere and low lights and music always playing in the background.

But now I would feel weird. Like I was just taking something else from them. Keeping Cake from being Cake.

"No," I say. "That's cool. I'll be fine."

Rhonda hugs me. I let her for a few seconds, but then I gently disentangle myself and step away. Gabe claps his hands. "Well, kid, let's get a move on, okay? Maybe we can give that new piece a whirl when we get home, all right, Cake?"

Inside the bathroom, Shayna's humming a song softly. I hear the whir of her electric toothbrush.

I can't always run to a better life, like Cake's, and hide. This is my life now. Bras on the couch. Cleaning up spilled coffee grounds on the floor.

Cake nods. "I'll text you," she calls on her way out.

I go back into my room, slide onto the bed, draw the lid back over the photos and medals.

My mom's whole life, small enough to fit in a blue hatbox.

H ERE IS WHAT IT feels like when your half sister leaves the house you used to share with your mother.

You listen to the silence.

You wonder when she's going to come back

You wonder *if* she's going to come back.

What if something happened to her what if a car hit her what if her car hit another car what if she just kept driving in the car and never came back and gradually the sky would get darker and darker and the stars would pop and here you'd be, waiting.

Alone.

Once, you left the house and went to school and your mother died.

Your heart squeezes. Your fingers tremble above your phone.

You press her name.

*What time do you think you'll be back?*

She's been gone three hours, twenty-two minutes, and eleven seconds.

You wait.

The girl-bug blinks, waiting. Whispers, *If you lose* this *one, you are really shit out of luck.*

No answer.

*Is everything okay? Do you know when you'll be back?*

No answer.

*Getting worried.*

No answer.

You pace around the house. Laps around *the couch,* where it must have happened, and you get more and more panicky, black dots swimming in front of your eyes. You move back to the bedroom.

You should call the police. Report her missing. But you don't even know where she went. You don't even really know anything *about* her. And she's an *adult.* Well, adult-*ish.*

You call. Voice mail. *I'm just getting worried, I haven't heard from—*

God, you're stupid. What a freak. You end the voice mail.

The front door to the house opens just as tears spring from your eyes. Your sister appears in the doorway to the bedroom, holding the phone to her ear. Her hair is mussed and her eyes are red.

You stare at each other.

"I'm right here," she says softly. "Okay?"

You nod.

Okay.

## 13 days, 10 hours

S HAYNA IS STILL ASLEEP when I leave for school the next morning. I thought she might wake up in time to take me to school, but in the end, I texted Cake. *Don't know what she did last night, but my sister isn't getting up. Give me a ride?*

In the car, she says, "Maybe she parties or something. I mean her FB was full of beer shots."

"I haven't seen her drink one thing while she's been here."

"Well, she's only *twenty*. Maybe she went to a meet-up or something. Somewhere. To . . . meet people of her own . . . ilk." Cake laughs. "She seems cool. I think this is gonna all work out. Probably just growing pains. Like when a person has a baby and has to learn how to understand which cry means what, like hungry, sleepy, change me. Your sister has to learn all that stuff."

"I'm not a baby," I say. I smooth the lap of my dress and adjust my hat.

*No,* says the girl-bug. *You're a mess to clean up, remember?*

Cake frowns. "This cowgirl slash butter-churner outfit? How much longer is it going to last?"

"I don't know," I say lightly, looking out the window. "Maybe my whole life. You'll leave and go away to camp or college and I'll still be here, forever, a loser, wandering the streets of our dusty town in my musty old dress and Clint Eastwood hat."

Because I'll spend my whole life missing my mom, and so

I should dress like it, just like the women in Dickens's books. Dirty and sad and hollow.

"That's a weird thing to say," Cake says slowly.

She pulls into the Eugene Field parking lot. "What do you mean by that, anyway?" She looks at me, her face hurt. "I'd never leave you like that. You're my best friend."

"Everybody leaves," I mumble. "But I'm just being dumb. Forget it."

Tentatively, she says, "You seem mad at me or something."

"Just forget it."

We walk the lot in silence, enter the hallway in silence. I feel shitty for saying that, but I also feel shitty for thinking Cake should stay with me forever. Or that I'm holding her back somehow.

Her poor, orphaned friend.

Cake says, "Well, see you at lunch, then, I guess."

I watch her go, her shoulders slumped, her skull backpack swaying against her hip.

I open my locker and see the photo of my mom on the door. A little slice of pain runs through me at the sight of her smiling face. My eyes start to feel hot, and wet. I press myself against the wall of metal.

*Oh my God, her clothes.*

*She's still in that dress.*

*I'm going to die.*

*Don't say that word!*

Giggling.

*Oops. My bad.*

Slowly, I turn around, my heart on fire.

Ellen Untermeyer is standing with a group of her friends, and Kai Henderson is next to her, looking down at the ground. He mumbles something, and tries to take her elbow, but she shakes him off and whispers in her friend's ear.

Ellen Untermeyer was Kai's girlfriend in the eighth grade, the *only* other girl he ever kissed in the world besides me, a girl he claimed slobbered like a teething baby, and if I had to describe my feelings at this moment with emojis, they would be:

And his face would be this 😳 and Ellen Untermeyer's face would be this 🐺.

"*What* did you say?" I try to keep my voice from shaking.

Really, the whole world, at least the world inside the hallway, stops. Like, needles screeching across records and car tires skidding across blacktops in an endless movie-montage loop kind of thing. I mean, kids stop walking and start clustering around us.

"Girly fight," some guy in a leather jacket says, and laughs.

"*What* did you *say*?" My voice sounds hard, and faraway.

"Oh my God, Grace. Please. You can't take a joke? I mean, have you *looked* at yourself?"

Ellen Untermeyer called me a jackass freshman year *in front of the entire English Lit class* for pronouncing *hyperbole* incorrectly, and even though I always felt her eyes burning into my body whenever she'd catch me standing with Kai in the hallway at Eugene Field or on the knoll at The Pit, I never much paid attention to her after that.

Her beady little eyes are exactly like mean raisins, if raisins could be mean.

I look at Kai.

Kai keeps his eyes on the ground.

I'm so furious at him. Hurt and filled with fury, that he would . . . just *stand* here. Like he just *left* me at the hospital.

"You just left me there," I say.

It's out before I can stop it, my voice small, almost pleading.

He looks up. "I *said* I was sorry."

"My mom died and you just left me there."

Oh God. My voice cracks. Some girl in the growing crowd of kids covers her mouth like she feels sorry for me.

"Graaaaace . . ."

Ellen Untermeyer's voice is like a slice of lemon in the air, tart and sharp as she drags out my name.

"Grace, *get over it,* already. Move *on.*"

Ellen Untermeyer tosses her amber-colored hair over her shoulder. She's that type of girl: smart in school, and never lets you forget it, but it's also kind of her curse, because people hate her for it, so she doesn't have too many friends, and she acts like she doesn't care, but you know she totally does, and that just makes people like her even less.

Something about the way her lips purse in that moment tears through me like a lightning bolt. I realize she's never been touched by true harm, or she wouldn't give me that look.

She's never felt carved out, hollow, weighted down.

She's never felt the way I've felt for the past thirteen days.

Standing there in the middle of the hallway, smug in her unsmudged life.

I walk over and slap Ellen Untermeyer in the face as hard as I can.

And then, astonished, I hold my palm up and look at it, like, *Hey, what are you doing here, you crazy, face-slapping piece of flesh?*

I'm almost more astonished at how good it felt. To hit her. To hit something. *Anything.*

I'm breathing hard. I want to hit everything now. Kick everything with these kick-ass boots. Because it felt *good.*

Maybe this will be my lifesaver, my grief talent: I'll be a world-famous girl boxer, fighting her way out from her mom's death by reducing horrible people to pulp.

*Awww, shit,* says the crowd. People start clapping. *Fight fight fight.* Kids hold up their phones.

#griefgirl  #schoolfight  #girlfight  #madgirlwalking #dangdogyoufiercegirl

I have so much adrenaline I can barely see or hear anything, blood pumping through me thickly, urgently. I think I hear Cake shout, *Tiger, no.*

Because I have my hands up, and I want to go after Ellen again.

Ellen, who is cupping her right cheek with both hands like it's a Fabergé egg, which are these intricate gold eggs made for Russian royalty a long time ago, one of which even had a teeny tiny replica of a royal coach inside, something I learned about while watching *Antiques Roadshow* with my mother, who is now dead, and whom I am supposed to *get over.*

Ellen Untermeyer wails and calls me a bitch. Her friends close ranks around her, cradling her like a lost kitten. Kai stares at me. *Jesus, Tiger, what's wrong with you?*

That makes me even more mad, because now I'm a mess *and* wrong, so I shove him as hard as I can, which sends him reeling backward into the crowd, his glasses flying off and skittering on the ground. There's the sound of glass crunching.

Someone in the crowd says, *Oopsie.*

And then Walrus Jackson is there, pushing kids aside and shouting, "Oh, no, no, not in my school, no, uh-uh, and Tiger Tolliver, you will stop with all this *right now,* do you *read me*?"

But I'm all hands and nerve and blood and shame, all the kids staring at me, Kai Henderson on the floor, feeling around for his glasses that kids keep kicking away, because kids are shitty like that, and that makes me feel even *worse,* so I fight Mr. Jackson, my fists crashing against his white button-up shirt, until he moves behind me and wraps his arms around me and *picks me up* and carries me down the hall like a wild, kicking doll.

## 13 days, 11 hours, 39 minutes

I PRESS THE ICE PACK Principal Vela hands me against the palm of my hand, which is now swelling up.

I hit Ellen Untermeyer in the face so hard I knocked out one of her teeth, which is sitting in a plastic baggie on Vela's desk.

Principal Vela sighs and rests her chin on her hands. "This is grounds for *expulsion*. Do you even realize the gravity of this situation, Grace? You may be having the worst crisis of your life, but that is no excuse for violence, do you understand?"

I nod, tears poking my eyes.

"Grace, I know right now you feel the worst you have ever felt, but as time passes, you'll begin to feel some peace."

She's talking like my mom is a lousy boyfriend that I'll get over after a few weeks.

*Stay strong. Be brave. Time heals.*

I can't even breathe, I want to scream so loudly. My head pulses.

Principal Vela takes the Eastwood hat off my head and throws it on her desk. "We respect rules here. We do not wear our hats indoors."

She checks her watch.

"*Where* is your sister? It's been an *hour*."

"I don't know," I whisper. My hand actually really hurts now that I'm not so full of adrenaline anymore.

She calls my sister again from her phone, leaves another terse message.

Her voice softens. "Is everything all right? With the sister, I mean? You can tell me."

"Her name is *Shayna.* She eats cake for dinner."

Principal Vela frowns.

We stare at each other.

There's a soft rap on the door. Ms. Delgado, the school secretary, pokes her head in. "I've got the sister here. Send her in?"

Principal Vela nods and leans back against her desk. Her office is filled with Eugene Field banners and books and plaques. She and my mother liked each other. Every year, she would buy prickly pear jam to send to her son in Fort Collins, Colorado.

Shayna breezes in wearing cutoff jeans and a tank top, her hair still damp from the shower. She's enveloped in a cloud of coconut shampoo. My mother's shampoo.

Another thing that means nothing to her, but the world to me. I mean, she could go to the Stop N Shop and pick up some goddamn Garnier Fructis, for God's sake.

I wish I could cut off my nose so I don't have to smell it.

I press the ice harder against my hand.

"Sorry I'm late. I've been a little under the weather. Hey, slugger, how are you?" She bends down to look at my swollen hand. "You got quite a left hook there, I guess."

"I don't find any of this funny, Ms. Franklin, and I'm surprised that you do." Principal Vela's voice is sharp and disapproving.

My sister plops down in the chair next to me.

"I didn't say it was funny. I'm just trying to make my sister feel better, that's all."

"Our school counselor has spoken to the other girl's family. They're using the word *assault,* which might mean we have to call the police."

"Call the police because my sister slapped their daughter in the face? That kind of just sounds like high school to me, and girls. You know how girls are. We can be wicked mean."

"Ellen Untermeyer has lost a tooth." Principal Vela picks up the baggie.

My sister leans close, inspecting the pinkish-white tooth through the plastic. Then she pulls her phone out of her purse.

"Well, that's not the worst thing in the world." She starts tapping the phone. "From what I see on her Instagram account, she's got buckets of money. She can get that fixed. This is a really interesting Insta account, by the way."

She holds the phone up to Principal Vela, who squints.

"Look at this post, in particular."

Principal Vela blinks rapidly. Her face changes. "Oh, Lord."

My sister chuckles. "See what she says there? That's a picture of my sister in the cafeteria two weeks ago, crying the day her mom died. I mean, she wasn't dead *yet,* that happened later, but something upset her, and she was crying, and this girl, this Ellen what's-her-name, took a photo of it and put it on Insta. What did she call my sister there? Oh, right, she hashtagged her #crybaby #freak #mamasgirl. That seems like . . . bullying."

"We have zero tolerance for bullying," Principal Vela says firmly.

"Hmm," my sister says, fingers working her phone. "That's funny. Because when I search Insta using some of Ellen Unctious's tags, and then find some other Eugene Field kids, I see a whole *lot* of pictures of my sister, with a lot of not-nice things said about her, and I see a lot of stuff about other kids who go here, and some pretty messed-up photos, like this one of a kid getting his face pushed in the dirt. See here, this little guy."

She holds the phone up again.

"What was that about zero tolerance, again?"

Principal Vela says angrily, "Nevertheless, your sister hit Ellen Untermeyer, causing her bodily injury. There are witnesses. Her parents could sue us and you."

"Tell me why you did this, exactly." My sister looks at me coolly.

"Because . . . because . . . because she told me to get over it. Like, get over the boy, the one we talked about." I sniffle. "He was the one who took me to the hospital the night . . . the night it happened, and then he just . . . left me there. But she . . . *Ellen* . . . really meant . . . get over my mom . . . dying. And they were laughing. About my dress."

And Cake and I . . . no, *I* fought with Cake because this is turning out to be the Summer of Everyone Leaving Tiger.

"Wow," my sister says, turning back to Principal Vela. "It sounds like my grieving sister was provoked. That must really hurt, don't you think? When your mom dies and some girl in the hallway, at school, in front of a crowd of kids, tells you to get over it. And you know what's like a *knife* dragging across the wound? If that girl is standing right next to the boy who gave you your first kiss and then ditched you *the night your mom died.*

"Do I have that right?" Shayna asks me. "The kissing and the ditching?"

I nod.

My sister holds up the phone again. "I've been texting with Cake Rishworth, who kindly forwarded me texts from six people who swear that Ellen Untermeyer started the fight by picking on my sister, and while I don't condone violence, I do take into account that my sister is one screwed-up piece of motherless kid at the moment, and if she forgets her p's and q's and lashes out when some nasty girl baits her, well, maybe *I'll* just sue that nasty girl for harassment, seeing as how she took pics of my orphaned sister crying in the lunchroom and posted them on social media, a post that has now reached 4,452 views. The poor little kid eating dirt at your school has 9k views."

My face is flaming from a mixture of embarrassment, fright, and shame, and, um, well, *pride.*

The phone rings on Principal Vela's desk. She tells us to wait outside.

In the reception area, my sister inspects my hand, which is turning a plump purple. "Sorry I took so long. I was gathering evidence. Getting my Olivia Benson\on, if you will."

"Thanks," I say. "I'm in deep shit, but thanks."

"You're in the shit, but I don't think it's that deep. I think we have room to negotiate, here. I haven't watched ten seasons of *Law and Order* for nothing, you know."

She gives me a half smile, like we're in this together. A team. Blood is blood.

From behind her desk, Ms. Delgado motions to my sister. "The principal would like to see you, Ms. Franklin. Just you." She gives me the hairy eyeball and I sit back down.

"Just me?" my sister says, standing up and straightening her shorts.

"Just you."

"Well, dang, ain't I lucky?" My sister goes into the principal's office.

Ms. Delgado stares over her sparkly silver glasses at me.

"Your mother," she says. "She would not like this behavior. Punching and kicking and wearing dirty clothes. Is this the girl she would want you to be?"

I look down at my lap.

#failuregirl #baddaughter #mess

M Y MOTHER WOULD HATE the way Shayna drives. She's one of those drivers who's perpetually distracted, yet never seems fazed by the prospect of a grisly death. She keeps her phone in her lap, glancing down every time it pings. She checks her face in the rearview, brushing strands of hair off her cheeks. The coffee from the gas station we stopped at is wedged perilously between her legs.

"Please don't kill us," I say desperately, cradling my hurt hand. "I might be in mourning, but that doesn't mean I have the desire to shuffle off this mortal coil."

"That's from a play, right? I was checking out all the books in your house. You a big reader?" She takes a drink of coffee. "Stop clutching your pearls. I've been driving since I was eleven. I know what I'm doing."

"What do you mean, you've been driving since you were eleven?"

She gives me a slow side-eye, like she's thinking very carefully about what to say. She still hasn't told me yet what happened in Principal Vela's office.

"Dad," she says finally, her voice flatter than it was before. "Daddy. *Dusty*. He was a drinker. A bad one, but you probably guessed that by the prison thing. He went up and down with it. He taught me to drive. At first I thought he was just being a cool dad, but then I realized it was so when he was on a bender, I could pick him up at the bar after my mother fell asleep."

I try to picture Shayna that young, driving some sort of junky car late at night, peering over the steering wheel into the dark streets. For some reason, even little Shayna, with her hair in an innocent ponytail, is still wearing the ultra-tight Victoria's Secret tracksuit, which is not a totally pleasant image.

I still have no idea what my father looks like, so I can only picture a dark-haired man slumped on a curb outside a dingy-looking bar, stray dogs licking his pant cuffs and snuffling.

"Eleven? That's kind of awful. That must have been really hard."

Shayna shrugs. "That was in a small town in Kansas. It was what it was. We didn't live there very long. He'd have a job, then get fired, and we'd move on."

Tentatively, I ask, "Were you . . . did you live in . . . Albuquerque? Where he met my mom?"

Shayna keeps her eyes on the road. "No. He took off after he lost a job in San Antonio and we didn't see him until after all that. I don't remember. I was really young."

She changes the subject. "So, about your pugilistic tendencies."

My heart sinks. "Yeah. I'm sorry. Am I expelled? Do we have to pay for her teeth? I'll get a job to help. I guess I can . . . maybe I can bag groceries at the Stop N Shop."

"No, not expelled. You have to stay away from that girl, Ellen Fullermeyer—"

"Untermeyer."

"Whatever. You have to write her a letter of apology, which, if she posts on social media, I will personally go over to her house and rough her up myself, and you have to go to some grief group with some counselor who sounds like a character in a book for kids."

"Wait, what? Walrus? Walrus Jackson?" The Grief Group. *GG.*

"That's him. He seems nice. You have to go to at least six sessions, two a week, or her parents will make us pay the dental. They weren't too happy when I brought out my evidence that she provoked you, or about all the shitposts she puts up about kids on Insta."

"I should tell him I'm sorry, too."

"Who?"

"Kai. The guy I pushed. The kisser-ditcher." I don't tell her about the phone call where I made him cry.

"I think you get a pass right now. There will be plenty of disappointing lovers in your life, trust me. And Ellen Untermeyers, too, unfortunately. Mean girls multiply like guinea pigs the older you get." She takes a big swig of her coffee and grimaces, pulling over to the side of the road.

"Here." Shayna tosses the car keys in my lap. "You drive. This coffee is horrid. I'm getting a headache."

The keys are warm from her fingers. My mother's keys: the gold house key, the silver car key, the matted rabbit's foot. I rub the tawny fur. She said her mother gave it to her on her seventh birthday. But maybe that was all a lie, too.

"Can't," I say, throwing the keys back. "No license."

"*What?* Not even a learner's permit?"

"Nope."

"How long have you been sixteen? I was out at the DMV the same *day* I turned sixteen. I couldn't *wait* to legally drive."

"My mom didn't want me to, yet. She said I had lots of time."

Cake doesn't get it, either, but she got used to it, the way my mom would restrict certain things.

Shayna presses the keys back into my hands. "Welp. No time like the present. Hop along, cowgirl." She climbs over the gearshift toward the passenger seat, and if I don't want to get crushed, I'm going to have to scramble under her to the driver's seat. Our hips collide mid-crawl and she laughs.

Briefly, I think, *Oh, so this is what it's like, laughing with a sister, getting tangled up together in a car.*

It feels nice. Almost . . . comfortable.

I sit there, absorbing this feeling, until Shayna blurts out, "What are you waiting for? Let's go!" and that nice feeling's gone. Poof. *Kerplink, kerplank, kerplunk.*

Nervously, I pull the seat belt on, trying to favor my good hand. I rest my hurt hand on the steering wheel.

It's a whole other world in this seat, on this side of the car. There seems like so much . . . responsibility. My heart thuds in my chest. "We probably shouldn't do this," I say nervously. "I mean, look at my hand. And I don't have a license or even a permit."

Visions of eighteen-car pileups, mangled metal, and blaring sirens swim through my brain, even though we're the only car on the road.

"A woman without wheels is a woman without freedom," Shayna says. "Now shove that key in the ignition and let's get started."

She points out everything in the car: what all that stuff is on the dash, the weird letters on the gearshift, the parking brake, lights, windshield wiper, gas pedal, all of it. She tells me how to adjust the mirrors, how to reverse, and how to, well, *drive.*

I have a sister, and she's teaching me how to drive a car, like sisters do. Like family does.

My heart kind of jumps with happiness.

I pretty much instantly forget everything she's telling me, so it's a bit rocky at first, and I'm so excited to be doing this that I just ignore the dull pain in my swollen hand.

But she doesn't yell or anything, she just patiently corrects me as I jerk forward and back. She keeps repeating, "No worries."

I finally relax, though I check all the mirrors obsessively approximately every half second. It feels kind of like being in a small cloud, just drifting. I mean, a *metal* cloud capable of major injuries, explosions, and decapitation, but a cloud nonetheless. A cloud under my complete control. And I'm having completely insane thoughts, like *I could drive to Kentucky! Where is Kentucky? It doesn't matter! I could just go there! Right now! Kentucky is an attainable dream!*

Shayna's resting her head on the headrest, watching the landscape.

She's so pretty, with the sun shining on her face.

Which is a weird thing to think, because I can also see traces of me when I look at her, and if I can see some of me, well, then maybe that means I might be, well, kind of pretty, too. Not that I think I'm not, it's just hard to tell. My mom always says I am, but she's my mom, so she has to; it's in her job description. But she also follows that up with, "But it's your insides that really count," because that's in her job description, to try to build my character, which is a very mom-ish thing to do.

Or it was, at least.

Truth be told, I don't think there's anything wrong with wanting to be pretty, or look nice, or take care of your hair and skin and wear pink if you want to, whoever you are. If you feel good about doing all those things, won't you just naturally feel good about yourself? And then you'll feel good about being in the world? Confident, I guess? Is that a bad thing?

As I look at my pretty sister, and see a little bit of me in her, I realize what I'm really seeing is glimpses of future me, Future Tiger, somewhere way down the road after high school and college and a little more life under my belt. It's scary to think about.

Is that a cat on the road? What is that? Jackrabbit. I slow down to a crawl. The jackrabbit glances at me over his shoulder, like *Dumbass, this road is MINE.*

Shayna murmurs, "Cake said your mom was a little overprotective."

I wait for the jackrabbit to saunter away. What was Cake doing talking to my sister about me?

"I guess. I mean, that's not a crime or anything." Does my voice sound madder than it should? I press the gas too hard and we jump forward.

"Easy," Shayna murmurs.

"I mean, it makes me crazy sometimes, sure. Like, no camps or classes or dances or anything. She didn't even let me stop going to daycare until I was eleven and Cake's mom yelled at her. I've never had any friends but Cake. And Kai, a little."

Shayna grunts. "That sounds kind of extreme."

I frown, watching the road. "Yeah. Like when her boyfriend, this guy named Andy, he took me out skateboarding, and I really liked it, she got really weird about it. She let me do it, but then I broke my arm and she freaked out. They broke up over it."

Shayna glances over at me. "Really."

"Yeah." Things are coming back to me a little. After everything happened with Andy, I tried not think of him anymore because it was too sad, and I didn't want to be mad at my mom for making him go away, but talking to Shayna is bringing things back.

Like the way Andy was tall and lanky and bought me a board with rainbows and glitter on it and taught me shuvits and took me to The Pit, like I was any kid. Like it was a normal thing to take a kid out skateboarding, without it being a huge deal, like it always was for my mom.

I liked Andy a lot. He was really graceful in the empty pool; all the kids were kind of in awe and that made me feel special, because he was with *me*. And then one day I went up, and then I went down. My mother yelled at him and he yelled back, which surprised me. It was a big fight.

*You use her so you don't have to live, June. And that means she never gets to live, either. What are you so afraid of?*

I'd been listening from my room, my arm heavy with a plaster cast.

He didn't come back after that.

"I thought for a little while they'd get married, and I'd have a dad and stuff, but that didn't happen." I bite my lip.

"Well," Shayna murmurs. "Just because you have two parents doesn't mean everything is peachy keen, you know? Sounds like your mom *was* pretty overprotective."

"Well, sure, but she was my *mom*." I catch myself. *Was.* She *was* a mom. She was crazy and protective and kind of stifling, but I'll never have that again.

And then all of a sudden, I'm thinking about *mom* as a verb, not a noun, and I start flipping out.

There isn't any more "momming" to be done. There's no more mom to tell me what to do, like homework or flossing my teeth, or how to do it, like "Tiger, make a schedule for your math quizzes." "Tiger, you rinse after you floss and not before!"

And there won't be a mom to see Future Tiger, after high school, or maybe college, with a little bit of life under her belt.

Shayna isn't a mom. She eats Little Debbies and lettuce for dinner and thinks nothing of spending hours on the couch watching *Law & Order* reruns, which is helpful in certain situations, as I now know, but not all.

Moms don't do that. Moms kiss you good night and you know exactly where they're going after that: to the couch, to lust after Anderson Cooper or curl up with a dirty book.

I will be in the dark forever, feeling around for a light switch and never finding it.

My breathing starts going very, very fast. My face is wet in an instant.

I don't understand how one minute things are okay, and the next, I'm in this blender of shit.

Shayna sits up, all business. "Pull over. Let's switch. Take a breather."

This time, we don't crawl over each other. We each get out of our separate doors and walk around the car to the other side.

In the driver's seat, she digs in her leather pack and hands me a crumpled tissue. It still has a faint purple lipstick smear on it.

She shrugs. "My nurturing skills are a tad undeveloped."

She gives me a halfhearted pat on the shoulder.

We drive the rest of the way home in silence. At the house, she tosses her phone on the bed and goes straight into the bathroom. I curl up under the covers.

Suddenly, I miss Sarah and LaLa and Thaddeus and Leonard, and LaLa's tidy little house. I wonder where Leonard is and if he's okay, and my heart starts to ache, because I remember Thaddeus's broken-back story, and Sarah's sister, how even your own parents can treat you so cruelly.

Shayna's phone vibrates. I sit up, glance down at it.

*You are not the one in charge here don't forget that.*

Before I can stop myself, I pick up her phone.

Ray.

My heart beats fast. What does he mean? That sounds . . . awful.

I look up at the bathroom door. She must be changing, or fixing her makeup. I scroll up.

*I'm asking for the billionth time: leave me alone. I'm telling you for the billionth time: I don't want to be with you anymore.*

*You don't know what your talking about You can't manage without me We know what your like*

*Stop it*

*How can you do this to me I saved you*

*Please just stop I have a new life I said no*

*Your not the one in charge here*

Shayna snatches the phone from me. "What are you doing? This is private. I don't look at *your* phone."

"I'm sorry, it lit up and—"

She frowns at me. "This isn't something that concerns you. I'm handling it."

"He seems mad," I say tentatively.

She drops her eyes. "Just don't worry about it, all right? There's nothing to know. I'm handling it."

"You said that already."

"Whatever." She tightens her ponytail. She's done her eyes up in solid black and her face is smoothly powdered. "I'm gonna go out for a little bit. Don't eat all my snack cakes."

She turns to go, pausing at the door.

"Listen," she says. "I wasn't trying to bad-mouth your mom or anything. I mean, I *want* to, because of the whole stealing-my-dad thing, but not for keeping an eye on you. Like, my mom practically shoved me out of the house every day, you know? Well, I guess you don't."

I stare at her. I don't quite know what to say. She has such a weird habit of moving from one subject to another very quickly, and I'm still stuck on the texts from Ray.

"I mean, part of me thinks maybe your mom ditched my dad precisely to protect you. So you wouldn't grow up like *me.* You know? I'm not saying he acted like a monster or anything, but it wasn't the greatest life for a kid, Tiger."

She looks uncomfortable. I think of her driving that car at night to pick him up. Did she have to help him to the car? How did that make her feel? I try to imagine that, being eleven and driving down a dark street looking for your dad, instead of being at home and, I don't know, watching television or dancing to videos on YouTube or something. Stuff like Cake and I did when we were eleven.

I feel almost sorry for her, my sister.

Shayna says, "I'll see you later, Tiger. Take some ibuprofen and go to sleep. Put some more ice on your hand if you need to, okay?"

She turns to go.

"Wait," I say.

She looks back at me.

"Do you know, like, what time you might be back?"

I'm feeling a little panicky again, like last night.

"I'm not sure," she says. "My phone will be off for a bit, but

I'll check it when I can, okay? Don't worry. I'll text you when I'm on my way back."

"Okay," I nod. "Okay."

After a little while, I doze off. My phone buzzes me awake.

Kai says, *That was really immature today. I mean, you could have been expelled. Ellen isn't the greatest person in the world, but you didn't have to hit her.*

Me: 😢 🔪

*We kissed once, Tiger. It's not like we were officially together.*

Me: 🐅

*I SAID I WAS SORRY. You were practically stalking me anyway. Always hanging on me in Biology. So desperate for attention.*

The thing that happens to my heart right then is deep and hot. It's a cut that is not going to heal.

*I hope your mom dies. Then you'll know what it's like.*

*Wow. Just, wow. And to think I even defended you to Vela.*

My face flames.

*Wait, that was you? You were one of the witnesses?*

*Yeah. Cake told me I needed to step up, so I did, and she gave me your sister's number. But I'm done now. You said horrible stuff to me that one night, Tiger.*

He's right. Shame floods through me, and then I start thinking about what Shayna said, about how his life is probably harder than I know, and I was too selfish, or stupid, to see it, and I say the only thing I can think to say:

*I'm sorry.*

I start to cry, so I put the phone down. I'm horrified by what I said, in the same way I was horrified by slapping Ellen Untermeyer, but perhaps this *is* the new me: a merciless, mourning girl who lashes out.

"I really liked Andy," I tell the Boxes of Mom. "I think maybe you loved him."

No answer.

"Why was my dad a secret?"

Silence.

"I drove today," I say softly. "I kind of liked it. I'm going to do it again, okay?"

No answer.

"I'll be very careful," I assure her. "But I also want to have fun. I mean, not too much, because I'm just so super sad right n—" My voice catches. I press the heels of my hands to my eyes, as hard as I can.

I have no idea how I am going to live with such a giant piece of sadness in my body all the time, knowing it will never get any smaller.

I cup my bad hand against my chest and rub it tenderly.

I miss my mother holding me. Hand rubbing my back, fingers smoothing my hair.

The girl-bug shakes out her wings. *Stop it. That hurts, don't remember that. You can't get it back. Time to let go, like everybody says.*

The room gradually goes dark as the sun goes down.

Who would ever guess that it isn't your bones or your blood or your heart that keeps everything humming along inside you, it's your freaking *mom,* and when she's dead, it all disappears.

You're just an empty dress crumpled on the floor, nothing inside to hold you up anymore.

I wait and wait and wait, fighting sleep, until my phone buzzes.

In the dark, I read, *On way home. See you soon.*

I T'S FRIDAY AFTERNOON, 3:30 p.m., and sweltering hot in the basement of Eugene Field.

I was suspended for four days and now here I am, on a Friday afternoon, standing outside Room 322 for my first mandated Grief Group therapy session. I'll have to go two times a week, Tuesdays and Fridays, for six sessions.

My sister is supposed to pick me up later. She was in a bad mood this morning, looking at the water bill while chewing her cuticles, ruining her pink polish. "It's like your mom stopped paying *everything*," she said.

I sipped my coffee slowly, thinking about what Cake's dad had said about giving my mom money. I didn't want to tell Shayna that.

I was waiting for her to notice, too, that there was a big manila envelope from the State of Arizona on the table by the door, addressed to "Shayna Lee Franklin, Guardian." It had been there for a few days, gradually getting lost under circulars, bills, and flyers for yard landscaping.

She'd sighed and gulped her coffee, checked the temperature forecast on her phone.

"Ah, holy fuck, one hundred degrees and I'll be out in that truck." She looked like she might cry, and that scared me. I'd been out there all week with her on my suspension, making some money, but not as much as my mom and I had. She'd barely said anything to me when Thaddeus picked me up for school this morning. Her phone had buzzed and when she saw who it was, she dipped her head in her hands. *Ray.*

It wasn't so bad, coming back. A couple of kids stared at me and whispered, but I ignored them. Ellen Untermeyer wasn't in school, and Kai kept his distance, choosing a seat at the front of Bio again and sitting far across the cafeteria as Cake and I ate lunch silently, still in our weird fight.

And now I'm here.

Room 322. In the basement, by Betty Bales's wood shop. Also known as the old detention room, before they decided detention didn't work. Now they do something called "quiet reflection," which involves yoga and soft music in a stifling trailer outside, behind the cafeteria.

It's weird to walk through the school hallways with practically no one there. Empty lockers. Empty classrooms. I wonder how I'll feel, coming back here next fall. Junior year. When all the smart kids with money will have to start thinking about college and "life after." Like Cake.

Like her dad said, she's going places, and I'll just be holding her back.

I would say it'll feel like losing an arm when Cake goes, but I already feel like I've lost most of my body anyway.

Walrus Jackson opens the door of 322, startling me. He's not wearing his normal nice white shirt, dark pants, and nice tie today. School is out for the day and he's changed into khaki shorts, a plaid short-sleeved shirt, and Birkenstocks.

"Hello, Tiger. I'm so glad you could come this afternoon."

We look at each other like we both know what made me

come here, but we aren't going to talk about the Slap Heard Round the World.

"We're waiting for just one more and then we'll get started. Go on in, take a seat."

Inside, there are three kids in chairs arranged in a circle. One girl is bent so far over her desk writing that her dark, straight hair obscures her face, so I can't tell who she is, but when she looks up, I have to stifle my gasp.

Mae-Lynn Carpenter. She gives me a weird smile, like, *I told you so.*

And there is Taran Parker from Bio, the one who made fun of my boobs, with his brother, Alif, who has never made fun of my boobs, but has also never acknowledged my existence.

Taran looks almost ashamed when he sees me, but his brother barely flicks his eyes at me before going back to his phone.

That day, when I first came back, Taran said he was sorry about my mom and then he tried to tell me something but he stopped.

He must have been telling me *this.* That he comes here. That he and his brother are like me. Giant blobs of sadness walking around in the bodies of teenage kids.

They sit like most boys do, halfway down the chair with their legs spread and feet way out on the floor, giant sneakers blocking my way to the chairs; I have to step over their feet.

Mr. Jackson checks his watch. "Let's get started. I'm not sure where our other member is. Do you all know Tiger?" He slides into his own chair.

Alif and Taran barely nod. Mae-Lynn gazes at me.

"I went to your mom's viewing. Do you remember? It was

nice. I liked the song, and the singing. Nice touch. Homey. My mom didn't do anything for my dad."

She's keeping her face as stiff as possible, but I think I see her mouth tremble, ever so slightly.

She's a girl-bug in a jar, too.

Mr. Jackson says, "Boys?"

"I know you," says Taran. He gives me a small wave. "Bio lab, and you hang out with the rocker chick and in the back of cars with official state seals." He grins.

Taran's brother, Alif, grunts. "That girl, her friend, she blazes on the bass." His eyes skim over me. "What's up with the dress? Are you, like, Aimless or something?"

We all blink at him. "What?" I say.

"Aimless. You know, those people who don't use electricity or drive cars. They wear old-timey clothes."

Mae-Lynn says, "*Amish,* you dolt. You mean *Amish.* Not *Aimless.*"

I say, "Actually, I *am* a bit aimless, if you want to know the truth. And yes, that's my friend Cake. And my mother bought this dress for me to wear to the Memorial Days dance, only she didn't ask me first, and we had a fight, and then her brain exploded, and now she's dead, and I slapped Ellen Untermeyer and that's why I'm here."

Weirdly, I feel relieved to say all that aloud. I mean, nobody here is going to look at me strangely, or walk on eggshells, if I say *dead,* because they have people who are *dead, dead, dead,* too, or they wouldn't be here.

Alif says, "Ohhhhkaaaayyyy. That's a lot to work with."

Mae-Lynn purses her lips. "God, I hate Ellen Untermeyer. I bet it felt good."

"It did," I admit. "And now I kind of want to punch a lot of things, to tell you the truth."

I look at Mr. Jackson. "Am I going to get in trouble for saying that?"

"No," he says. "You can say whatever you want here. But there are better ways to express your anger."

Mae-Lynn says, "When my dad finally died? He was sick for eight years? I took all his jars of medicines and pills and bandages and all of it and burned it in the backyard. It smelled horrible and made my mother cry and the neighbors called the fire department, but I didn't care."

Her eyes blaze.

"I'm not allowed to have matches or lighters anymore."

Taran snickers.

Mr. Jackson clears his throat. "Enough. Tiger, it's pretty loose here. We talk about what's on our minds, whatever is weighing on us most heavily at present. What we try to remember, most of all, is that grief slips into every part of your life, every day, every minute. Is there anything you are struggling with right now that you'd like to talk about?"

We all stare at him.

Alif says, "There goes the Walrus again. Always with the giant questions right off the bat." He turns to me. "Of *course* you're fucked up, right? It's been four years for us and every day still sucks ass."

His brother nods his head. "Yep. It doesn't go away."

"Peachy," I say softly. "Thanks for the heads-up." But it feels good to hear them say it. Everyone else outside this room is telling me to *be brave* and *go on*, like what I'm feeling is something I'm just supposed to get over, like stepping over glass in a parking lot, or waiting for stitches to heal.

Mae-Lynn flicks her hair over her shoulder. "The way I like to think of it is, when my dad was sick? That was my Sick Life. I had eight years of Sick Life, which meant chemo and hospital beds in our living room and my mom turning into a walking ghost. Now that he's gone, I have Grief Life, which is horrible in its own way. Sick Life lasted pretty much half my life, but it still ended when he died, you know?"

She sniffles but doesn't cry. "But Grief Life? That's forever. And it's going to really suck. It *does* suck. That's the Big Suck I was telling you about."

Taran and Alif nod. Taran says, "Your mom, she died real sudden, right?"

I nod slowly.

"Yeah, that's what I heard. Our dad, too. Truck flipped on the interstate. One day we got up and went to school and every-thing was fine and then we came home and our mom was on the kitchen floor, crying, and there were policemen making coffee in our kitchen."

His voice gets scratchy. Alif reaches out and takes his brother's hand.

Which makes me kind of want to start bawling, two brothers who act like dicks most of the time, holding each other's hands.

"We take care of her now, it feels like. But it's a lot. It's a *lot.* Our grandma moved in. After, to help us. But now she's sick, too. She's got a bad back and a lot of pain. Takes a lot of pills."

Alif wipes his eyes. Taran covers his.

Taran and Alif crying has freaked me out a little. They always walk the halls with a lot of swagger, flannel shirts untucked, those impossibly giant sneakers shuffling on the black-and-white floors, half sneers on their faces. That dumb comment about my boobs that Taran made in the seventh grade, the comment that made me start hunching my shoulders and carrying my books close to my chest.

I've always kind of hated them both, but I can't now.

They've been carved out, too.

Mae-Lynn touches my shoulder and I jump. "They're totally right. Sometimes it feels like I'm taking care of my mom now, instead of the other way around. How's it going for you?"

I look around the room. It smells like chalk and dry-erase markers and rubber and sadness.

"I don't . . . It was just me and my mom. My dad, I didn't know him. I mean, I still don't. He's in prison. I have a half sister and she came out to take care of me."

Taran says, "Dang, girl, that's rough. Prison? Shit."

Mr. Jackson clears his throat gently. "Mae-Lynn brings up an excellent point. We can't forget that the surviving parent is grieving, too, and that's hard, isn't it? Because you are the child, and someone is supposed to take care of *you*. Are there things we can do in this situation? How can we tell our mom or our dad or our grandma, 'I'm feeling overwhelmed in my sadness and I need you to help me, listen to me'?"

Alif snorts. "Shit, I tried that and Mom just started crying."

Taran says, "She's a mess. And you can't tell Grandma anything. She's all zonked out on her pills."

Mae-Lynn says, "Maybe we should have business cards that say that, Mr. Jackson, and we can just hand one to our moms when stuff gets bad. How would that be?"

Mr. Jackson grimaces at her and looks at me. "You have some

very hard things to deal with, Tiger, especially since you're grieving and adjusting to a new family member in a caregiver situation. You have to process your grief *and* get to know someone at the same time. And that can be stressful, and cause things, like acting out, or panic attacks. A lot of survivors have post-traumatic stress disorder."

"I thought that was just for veterans," Alif says, picking at his nails.

Mr. Jackson shakes his head. "No, it's for any life-altering traumatic event. You want to forget, but your mind won't let you. The smell of a person's clothes. Maybe seeing a car the same color as they had. Things can set you off, make you panic, disoriented."

I think of my sister, that night she was late, how scared I got, like somebody else was going to disappear from my life, too.

Mae-Lynn nods. "I can't even watch TV anymore because even seeing a hospital in a show makes me freak out."

The door to 322 flies open, slamming against the wall.

I suck my breath in.

Lupe Hidalgo stands in the doorway, her girlfriend, Breisha Walters, by her side. Lupe's wearing her glossy dark hair in two braids and is dressed in a sheepskin vest over a tie-dyed T-shirt even though it's a billion degrees outside. My heart practically stops. She wasn't in zero p this morning, so I thought I'd dodged a bullet on my first day back from suspension.

I was wrong, but also . . . Lupe Hidalgo is *here*. Lupe Hidalgo is in the Big Suck with us, but why? How?

We watch as she kisses Breisha goodbye. From the corner of my eye, I can see Taran and Alif nudging each other, because of course some guys have to be all weird if, like, girls are *queer*.

"Grow *up*," Mae-Lynn tells them.

"Did ya miss me?" Lupe asks everyone, grinning wildly. Her eyes are wet and pink, but I don't think it's from what Mae-Lynn calls Grief Life. Maybe Pot Life.

Mr. Jackson says, "Lupe, we do have rules, like being on time. I'd like you to respect and follow them."

She salutes him with two fingers. "Will do, Walrus. Now, where were we?" She gazes around the room. Her eyes land on me.

Her face falls. "Oh, right. Oh, hey. Yeah. That's right. You're in the shit now." She looks over at Mae-Lynn. "Sorry. 'Grief Life,' tm."

Mr. Jackson says, "I think this might be a good moment to do some reflection."

He stands up, passing out single sheets of blank paper and black pens. "I'd like you to take five minutes or so to write down something you remember about your loved one that you miss the most. We don't have to share. But the point is, you have a space to remember something, a moment."

I look at the paper. I *knew* it. I just knew we were going to have to write something.

I can barely get a handle on everything I've just heard, from kids I barely know, about terrible things they feel, and he wants me to write about my mom. How am I supposed to pick just one single thing out of the millions of memories I have?

Next to me, Lupe hunches over her paper, covering it with her hand, like we're working on tests and she doesn't want anyone to cheat off her. I'm wracking my brain, trying to think of who her dead person might be, because I've seen her parents come to school on game days, but I can't come up with anything.

Maybe I *did* know about Mae-Lynn's dad, like maybe she was out of school for a couple of weeks, and when she came back, she was even more quiet than usual, and started sitting by herself in the cafeteria, instead of with her math-y friends. She's always been on the outer edges, too. Taran and Alif are popular and not in my orbit, and also kind of mean, so I stay away from them.

Maybe I should have been better about seeing her. Seeing Mae-Lynn's sadness.

But you don't realize what it feels like, this hole, this *missing*, until it happens to you.

Everyone is writing away.

I'm just drawing empty squares on my sheet of paper, one after the other.

There are five of us, but how many more kids at Eugene Field are walking around every day carved out and hollow and I have no idea? How many of us are ghosts, going home to oatmeal soaps that will never be used again? Shirts that still hang in the closet after months and years?

I think of Thaddeus. How many kids here go home to parents who are fucked up and do bad stuff, like hit them? And then they come to school like nothing's happened.

This whole place is swimming with pain.

I look at my sheet of paper, packed with empty squares. My head spins.

*Write something you miss.*

I can't. There are too many, because I still miss all of her. She hasn't been separated into parts, yet, into tiny pieces of memory. She's still whole to me.

My tears make big wet spots on my blank paper. I put my pen down.

"It's all right, Tiger. We're friends here. Everything stays here," Mr. Jackson says softly.

Mae-Lynn reaches out and pats my hand.

"Everything in good time," she says. "Because this shit is going to last forever."

I look over at her paper.

She's written: *making my toast with a pat of butter in the shape of a heart; reading Little Women to me over Christmas when I was nine even though it made him more tired; buying me my kitty; snoring during football games; being my goddamn dad.*

M AE-LYNN CARPENTER KEEPS A bottle of rum in her backpack.

This is what she produces in the arroyo after Grief Group, after Mr. Jackson has driven away in his shiny red pickup truck, after I've texted my sister to tell her something I never even got to tell my mother.

*Be home later. Going to hang out with some kids for a little bit. I'll get a ride.*

Shayna texted back, *Should I give you a curfew? I'm new at this. JK. I have to go see some people myself 2nite. See you on the flip side.*

I feel a little let down that she didn't, like, question me more.

Moms would want to know when you would be home, who you were with, what were you doing. Like, they make you *work* for that little bit of freedom.

I don't have that anymore.

In the arroyo, Taran and Alif are digging cans of beer from their backpacks. Lupe Hidalgo is practicing windups with an imaginary ball.

Mae-Lynn holds out the rum. "Don't worry," she says. "Walrus *did* ask us what we were going to do to feel better, right? This is it. It's Friday. Woo. Par-tee."

I hold the bottle in my hands.

Alif is lighting something that is *not* a cigarette. He winks at me.

Lupe sees me looking at him.

She laughs. "You have always been such a *nice* girl, Tiger Tolliver. Are you scared of a little weed?"

"She's not nice anymore," Taran says. "She's here because she busted that Ellen chick's teeth in."

"Yes and no," I say quietly. "I busted *one* tooth, but I was *provoked.*"

Mae-Lynn nods at the rum bottle in my hand. "If you want some, go ahead. If not, pass it on, okay? I have piano practice in an hour."

My mom always said not to. My dad's in prison for drinking. That's, like, a thing that can be hereditary, right? Drinking a lot.

But my mom is dead. Shayna isn't here. I don't even *know* my dad.

It's what kids do.

The girl-bug stirs. Tilts her head, waits.

I twist the lid off and take the tiniest sip. It tastes disgusting, and I cough, and give it back to Mae-Lynn. Taran and Alif laugh.

"It gets easier," Taran says, inhaling. "*That.* And *this.*" He makes a gesture toward his beer, and then to all of us, arranged in our various slumps in the arroyo. A lizard darts across the sand and up the wall of the arroyo.

He passes me the joint. Cake always told me she heard too many horror stories about her parents' rock-and-roll friends dying from overdoses to try drugs, even something as minor as pot. "Gross," she said once, mock-shivering. "Not for me."

If I texted her right now and said, *I'm smoking pot in the arroyo with Taran and Alif and Lupe Hidalgo and Mae-Lynn,* the first thing she would say is, *No way!* and then, *Shit no, STOP. I'm coming to get you right now.*

She would. That's the thing. She's always been saving me. Maybe this time, I just want to float, and see what happens.

I handed it back in Thaddeus's yard, but this is different.

I'm in a different world now.

I inhale.

The girl-bug hides her eyes behind her wings.

It burns my throat, and I cough a little, but I inhale again before Taran leans over and slips it from my fingers.

It doesn't take long before I can feel it. It's like a long, slow, warm wave of water that starts at my toes and threads up my body, relaxing all of me.

"This is weird," I say. "I feel marshmallowy."

Everyone laughs.

Mae-Lynn leans close to me, like we're good friends. "So, Grief Life," she says. "It's hard. It never stops. I cry in Claire's when I go to Park Mall for earrings. I cry in debate prep. I cry *during* debate. I cry in the shower. I cry opening a can of tuna for my cat. I'm surprised I haven't drowned in my own tears."

Alif leans back on his elbows. He's that type of lanky boy who seems comfortable everywhere, even in an arroyo covered in graffiti and with used condoms littered all around. Maybe he's even responsible for some of those. I've heard stories. He catches my eye and I look away quickly.

Alif says, "I started bawling the minute I tried on my suit for Memorial Days, like, *Dad would have told me what a handsome dude I was.*" His eyes fill up. "I cry in fuckin' Woodshop when the sawdust is flying and the saws are going. Everybody is so fucking freaked out thinking they're gonna saw off a limb that nobody even notices me."

His brother says, "You never told me that."

Alif shrugs. "I know."

Lupe Hidalgo sighs loudly. "Listen, Tolliver, here's the thing. It sucks. I mean, *it sucks!*"

That last part, she screams as loud as she can, her whole body as stiff as a madwoman.

"But the thing you need to realize is that no matter what the Walrus Jacksons tell us, no matter how touchy-feely, *let's tell each other our deepest feelings* kind of stuff he throws at us, the fact of the matter is that you are gonna walk around for the rest of your life with a huge hole in your heart. Like, Grand Canyon big, girl."

It doesn't escape me that none of us would be talking to each other this nicely if we weren't all in the Big Suck.

I start crying, but quietly. Mae-Lynn pats my shoulder.

I take a sip of the rum again. Now I feel like a particularly chatty marshmallow, what with the rum *and* the weed.

"Lupe," I say, hiccupping a little. "You didn't say in the meeting. Why you're here. Who you . . . you know. Lost."

Taran and Mae-Lynn and Alif get very still.

Lupe looks up from her phone. Her eyes have grown very dark.

"Everybody knows who I am. Don't you?"

They are all looking at me. I shake my head. Slowly, I say, "To tell you the truth, you've always scared the hell out of me, so I try not to know too much about you."

She ignores that.

"Don't you remember?" she asks. "The three?"

She looks down, kicks the sand with her sneaker. I can barely hear what she says next, her voice is so quiet.

"The kids who died. By suicide. One was mine. My brother. Crash."

She slowly raises two fingers to her temple. "Bang, bang," she whispers. Everyone is silent, until Alif suddenly stands up and walks to the edge of the arroyo.

I swear that I can't breathe. I swear that I will never breathe again. I can't look away from Lupe's face. She has an expression that's the saddest thing I've ever seen and I cannot even think of a word for it.

Mae-Lynn swipes tears from her cheeks.

"Don't worry," Lupe tells her. "It wasn't me that found him. People always want to know that, even if they're too scared to ask. But it means I'm different than you guys, too. Your people didn't want to leave you, you know?"

"Lupe, that's not true," Mae-Lynn whispers.

She says, "You don't know. You don't know how it feels, when someone goes *that* way, and you never will."

Lupe shakes her head, hard, like she's clearing something away.

There's a crunching sound in the parking lot behind us.

"Oh, shit," Taran blurts out.

I turn around. A sheriff's car has pulled into the lot. Mae-Lynn shoves the bottle of rum at me. "I can't," she whispers. "I have piano. My mother will kill me. Please."

Without thinking, I slide it into my backpack.

The sheriff's car does a perfect circle in the parking lot and then drives back out onto the road. Taran and Alif start laughing. "I almost pissed my pants," Lupe Hidalgo says. "Holy moly."

The boys hoist up their backpacks. My whole body is shaking from fear. Lupe says, "We're headed over to a party. You wanna come?"

I hesitate. I mean, I could. Because no one's waiting for me.

But I'm also starting to feel a little woozy, so I shake my head.

"I can't," I say. "I have to get home."

Mae-Lynn says, "I have piano practice."

She looks at me. "Me and my mom can give you a ride, if you want."

"Okay," I say. I watch as Lupe and the two boys walk to a beat-up gray truck, Taran sliding into the driver's seat. They peel out, Lupe giving us devil horns out the passenger-side window. She shout-laughs at me, "This doesn't mean I like you, by the way! You're still dirt on the bottom of my shoe!"

Mae-Lynn and I start walking across the parking lot, toward the school steps. She says, "I didn't really have any friends before this. It took my dad dying to get those guys to talk to me. Weird, huh?"

I nod.

"I mean, they only talk to me on group days, not during regular school or anything. That's okay, though. I get it. High school hierarchy and all that."

We sit down on the steps of Eugene Field.

After a while, Mae-Lynn says, "I don't mean to be a pill or anything, but I just feel like you should know. Mr. Jackson means well and all? But I don't think he's ever actually had anyone die, or he wouldn't even say half the stuff he says, honestly. I walk around like my skin's been removed, cooked, and put back on me. That's how I feel. Like a walking piece of hot, bloody meat. My hair is falling out. I make myself puke up my meals. It's like my mom is on the other side of the swimming pool, and we're both underwater, and I can see her mouth moving? But I can't understand a damn thing she's saying."

She shakes some Tic Tacs into her hand and tosses them to me.

"Sorry for talking so much," she says. "I don't really have anyone to talk to about this stuff. There's only so much I can say in GG. This is kind of a relief."

A white car pulls into the parking lot and honks. Mae-Lynn starts walking, so I follow her.

"I mean," she says earnestly, "half the time, I can't even believe I'm walking upright.

"So, I just want you to know," she says, turning to me. Her eyes look like mine when I see myself in the mirror every morning: hollow, lifeless.

"This is what I meant when I called it the Big Suck: it's all bullshit, and it's never going to feel any better."

When Mae-Lynn's mom pulls into our driveway, I see that Mom's car is gone, which means Shayna is still gone, too. I'm relieved, because I'm a little drunk, and since I've never been drunk, I'm not sure how this would play out with Shayna, like if she'd pull the parent-y card finally and what? Ground me or something? I never even had that with Mom. I never had the chance to. Maybe Shayna would just laugh it off.

My phone pings. Woozily, I look down. Cake.

*How did it go?*

*It was okay. Good, I guess. Hard to explain.*

*Who was there? Tell me!*

I open the door to the house, drop my backpack on the floor. I flop down on the beanbag. Should I have water? Coffee? Sober up? Go to bed?

*I'm not sure I'm supposed to tell you. Like, maybe some of them want it to be private. I heard some really sad stuff.*

*Oh. Yeah, I get that. I can see that. Do you think it helped?*

*I don't know, CAKE. I don't think what I have can be cured in one session, you know?*

*Sorry! You don't have to bite my head off.*

I don't want to fight anymore with Cake, so I tell her the truth.

*I'm sorry. I drank alcohol. In the arroyo. With them. After. I don't know what to do now.*

I almost type "affer" because that's the way the word sounds inside my head.

*Oh God, really? Are you going to throw up?* Cake has never had alcohol, either. *Hold on, I'm Googling.*

*Okay, it says drink water and take ibuprofen and go to bed. Maybe put a bucket next to the bed or something.*

*Okay.*

I stagger up, drink a glass of water, can't find aspirin, and am almost in bed before I realize I have the bottle of rum Mae-Lynn stashed with me. I stumble to the shed and tuck it inside some old milk crates with tarps in them and make my way back to bed, where I pretty much pass out as soon as my head hits the pillow.

H ERE IS WHAT HAPPENS when your mother's death certificates come in the mail.

This shit is scary. This shit hasn't been covered in Grief Group yet.

You think things are okay, not great, because "great" won't ever be a thing again. But you and your sister are kind of humming along, working the Jellymobile together on the weekend. She's still doing it during the week. You still have one more week of school left, but four sessions of Grief Group left, which extends after school is out for the summer.

You feel like you are always behind, spinning your wheels. The universe doesn't wait for you to catch up anymore.

You just keep your head down. Thaddeus tells you to stay quiet, make nice with your sister, with school. He'll get you a job over the summer at the ranch, he says. You wish you could go back and see the horses, but there hasn't been time. You dreamed of them once, the way their beautiful hooves flew in the dust, made hazy, beautiful clouds.

Your sister is always busy, it seems. Spending a lot of time at the coffee shop/bookstore/diner. Suddenly very interested in being Louise and Mary's friend. "They have an interesting setup over there," she said one day on her way out. "I think I need to pick their brains."

Every day you go on, just like everyone tells you to, and every day, you feel more and more invisible.

When the death certificates come, they're in a large manila envelope. *City of Tucson Medical Examiner* is stamped in the corner. There's no letter. No *Dear Miss.*

They look strangely like the achievement reports you got at school during grade time at Davidson Middle. Boxes checked off. Measurements and percentages and a lot of words you don't understand. Everything is online now. Your mom had to log in to see how you were doing. Your sister will have to do that now.

They also come with a 911 report.

Because just before your mother's brain exploded, she had been on the phone with Kai Henderson's mom, Sue.

Which you hadn't known before. Because neither Kai nor his mom came to the viewing, and his mom didn't come to the hospital that night.

*Caller: I was on the phone with my son's friend's mother and she suddenly stopped speaking. I think there's something wrong.*

*Caller: I thought my son might be over there, with her daughter. We were on the phone and I heard something. I think she might have fallen. She hasn't hung up yet. I'm on a different phone right now. I can hear breathing on the other line. It doesn't sound . . . right.*

You stand in the red kitchen and spread all the papers out on the counter, one by one by one.

*Caller: Can you please send someone out right away? This isn't like June. I'm quite worried.*

These were the last moments of your mother's earthly life.

*Caller: I can't believe this is happening. Please help. Are you sending someone? What's happening?*

The information blurs in front of me.

"The deceased was found . . ."

*The deceased.*

"The deceased was found face-down on a couch in the home. The deceased showed signs of . . ."

*Face-down on the couch.*

Your body goes cold. You actually leave your body. Part of you is above, watching the other you read these papers, watching that sad girl in the weird and dirty lace dress and boots hold strange papers with trembling hands.

*Face-down on the couch.*

"Upon examination, the deceased displayed . . ."

You'd had a fight that morning. You'd kissed a boy for what seemed like hours in a park, and she'd been here, dying, and alone.

You run a finger down the medical examiner's report until you find a name, and a number, and with shaking hands, call that name and number. Dr. Marisa Matthews.

You don't expect her to *pick up.* On television, medical examiners are always so busy helping to solve interesting and complicated murders, dabbing creamy stuff under their nostrils as they examine a particularly rancid corpse. You figure you will leave your message and that will be the end of it. You will have *tried.* Who is going to call back a kid, anyway?

But there she is. "This is Dr. Matthews."

"Hi." *Stupid.*

"Hello? This is Dr. Matthews. Who am I speaking to, please?" Her voice is brisk. You picture short hair, wire-frame glasses, a no-nonsense color of lipstick like peach or light rose.

"This is Tiger Tolliver."

There's a pause. "Do I . . . know you, Tiger Tolliver?" She sounds amused. Everyone finds your name funny.

"You . . . worked on my mom. I got the certificates in the mail today. The report."

Another pause. When she speaks again, her voice is less edgy. "My condolences. Is there something I can help you with?"

"So, it says here, and I remember in the hospital, that she had a brain aneurysm? Like her brain exploded?"

Dr. Matthews speaks very carefully, like you are a child.

Because you are. You're a child and you feel like everyone is trying to get you to be an adult. Working. Moving on. Grief Group.

"That's one way to put it, I suppose. Do you have a specific question about that?"

You pinch your thigh through the lace dress. Cake isn't here. She won't see it.

You need something to keep you grounded during this conversation.

"Well, we had a fight that day. About a dress she wanted me to wear for a dance."

Dr. Matthews chuckles softly. "I might remember something like that happening with my own mother."

"I didn't want to wear it."

"My dress showed too much cleavage. My mother made me wear this awful shawl. I left it in the limo when we got to the dance."

"I'm wearing the dress now, though. I haven't taken it off since she died." Your voice is barely above a whisper.

Dr. Matthews says kindly, "It would probably be okay if you wanted to wear something else now, Tiger. Or when you're ready."

"I know," you say. "Anyway, I was just wondering, like, when that happens to your brain, do you die right away? Or is it, like, very slow? Because that fight, it was the last time we ever talked and I was very mean to her, see—"

Your voice breaks.

"It's just us. It's always been just us and so she was all alone when it happened and we'd had that fight and I just—"

That's it. You didn't know what else to say. You stop at *I just.* You're crying. Maybe you should hang up the phone.

Dr. Matthews asks, "Are you asking me if your mom suffered, Tiger?"

"I don't know."

"What's your mom's name, Tiger? I'll look for her file. I know the forms are probably very confusing for you."

"June Frances Tolliver."

You hear typing on the other end of the phone. She says, "Okay, I found her. Let's see. There are two types of aneurysms. One is slow and can be survivable, and one can be instantaneous.

"Your mom had the second type. The only way I can describe this is for you to imagine that you're sitting in a room and the lights are on, and then they go off. The lightbulb doesn't flicker, you don't hear a pop, everything just goes . . . dark. Gone."

The lights are on. The lights go off.

You look around the tiny front room, at the couch, at her desk, with her cups of pencils and pens and pads of paper. The sunlight outside is fading.

She had probably puttered around. Maybe she'd been reading on the couch, waiting for you. You didn't fight out loud very often. Sometimes, when it's just two people like that, you keep

308

a lot inside. You have to, or the well-oiled, good-looking, and good-smelling machine will break down.

Had she felt lonely? Worried about why you hadn't called her back? And then the lights went out?

A few times, during summer storms, the lights suddenly snapped off. You might be in the bedroom reading, cozy under blankets, and the monsoons would start, the trees would whip, maybe a line would go down somewhere, and poof, darkness.

Your heart would leap in your throat, and the first thing you would do is call out, "Mom?" And she would answer, because she was never far from you.

That's the way she'd planned it, you are learning. To never be far from you. To not lose you, you think, like she'd lost her parents.

Only, the universe had other plans.

*It's all bullshit,* Mae-Lynn had said. *It's never going to feel any better.*

"Are you there, Tiger?"

"Could she . . . like, did she know what was happening? Was she in pain?"

Dr. Matthew's voice is firm. "No. Like I said, as brutal as it sounds, everything shuts off. If I had to choose a way to go, this would be it. It just happens. A lightning strike to the brain that turns everything off at once."

"But why?" you ask. "Why does that happen?"

"No one knows, Tiger. Not really. The body is an amazing machine made of intricate systems. You can wander around in there for days, poking this, poking that, trying to figure out reasons for *why* and *how,* and sometimes you do."

She takes a breath.

"And sometimes the lights just go out. And we don't know why, because as much as we study and study and study, the universe is always smarter than we are. There will always be unknowable things and we have to make peace with that."

Always the universe, against you.

"Tiger? Is there anyone with you? Do you have someone you can call after me? I have the number for a crisis line."

"My dad's in prison. My sister's not home. I'm all alone."

Did she call out for you, when it got dark?

You weren't there. You weren't there to answer her.

The walls of the small house are closing in on you. You're being crushed. On the last day of your mother's life, you had not been there for her.

You blurt out, "Do you believe in God? I mean, or something? Like that?"

There is such a long pause you wonder if you've been disconnected.

"Hello?" you ask tentatively.

She says, "I'm here."

Then, "Yes, I do. And I believe your mother is in a lovely place. I think she's being taken care of, and I think she's watching over you, and she wants you to know how much she loves you."

You close your eyes.

"I'm worried about you, Tiger. Let me get that crisis line number, okay? I think you need to talk to someone."

"There's a group, like for teens. A grief group. At my high school. I'm in that."

"I'm glad. It's not good to keep things bottled up."

Dr. Matthews hangs up. You sit on your bed, staring at your

Boxes of Mom, the medical examiner's report in hand, listing all the ways you were a bad daughter.

Such a long list.

Wanting nicer, more expensive clothes. Wishing you had a dad. Wanting to go to camps. On vacation. More food. More everything. Mostly you kept it inside, but sometimes, like with the dress, it was too much to keep in, and now she's gone.

You pinch your thighs. Cake doesn't answer your text. Thaddeus doesn't answer your text. Why didn't you ask Mae-Lynn for her number? She would know. She would know what you are feeling right now.

It is dark outside, and dark in the house, just like it must have been when she died. Dark in her head. Dark in her heart.

You feel dark in your heart, too. You feel like that darkness is going to split you apart.

It is thirty steps to the outbuilding. The girl-bug hops up and down. *You'll feel better.*

Mae-Lynn had tossed it to you when the sheriff's car showed up.

It's still there, buried under the tarps in the milk crate. Shayna wouldn't find it here. She never does laundry. It feels like it's always going to be you, you, you, telling her how to raise you, what to feed you, how to make money, how to be.

Why do *you* have to become the parent?

The first sip is horrible, burning your mouth, carving a raw path down your throat.

The second sip is better, but still.

Under the laundry sink, you find some cans of Coke, sparkling water. Stuff your mom had left over from your last birthday party.

What a party. You, your mom, Rhonda, Cake, Bonita.

Other kids had sweet sixteens and quinceañeras with cakes and streamers and DJs and bouncy houses and credit cards and shopping trips and plastic and gloss.

You have always been lonely and you have never admitted it.

Drinking from the little bottle of rum is easier if you sip some Coke after. The sweet soothes the scratchy.

The black hole glimmers.

The girl-bug approves.

Is this better than pinching your thigh cutting your skin punching Ellen Untermeyer is this better is this better is this better is this better is this better is this better is this better.

## 23 days

MY SISTER'S FACE IS an angry stone mask.

She's standing above me in the shed, holding the rum bottle and the empty can of Coke. The single bulb in the ceiling flares from behind her like a crooked halo.

"What the hell."

Her voice comes from far away, because my head is a series of firecrackers and explosions. I try to open my mouth, but it's so dry it sticks together.

And then I lean over and puke on the laundry basket full of clean clothes.

"Jesus, Tiger."

Shayna puts the rum and the Coke can down, swabs at the floor with a green bath towel. I roll backward onto the floor.

"I was so worried about you. I've been texting your friends."

I want to say, *I only have one,* but then I remember Thaddeus. He must count now, right? Yay. My mom is dead and my friend count has increased. Small miracles.

"You don't drink. Listen, you can't drink. I mean, honestly."

"Where did you get this? I thought you had group today. Tiger, what's going on?"

I grab her hand, shake my head. Black spots float in front of my eyes.

"No," I say.

"Well, this is bad, Tiger. What's going on here? Who are those kids? This doesn't seem like—"

*No!* I stand up, weaving back and forth. I'm afraid I might throw up again.

"They're the only people who understand," I mumble.

"Well, I felt that way about some of my friends when I was sixteen, too. Hell, last year even, but—"

"No, not that. They understand about her. My mom. Being gone. You don't."

She sits back on her feet, looks up at me. "I don't, but I'm trying my best."

She sounds defensive.

Now I feel guilty. I've made *her* feel bad.

All the rules of death and dying: Move On. Stay Strong. Be Brave. Time Heals. Don't Make Other People Feel Bad. I'll never learn them all.

It's dark outside. The big white moon is covered with clouds. I stumble to the back door of the house. Shayna gets up and follows me as I go in and make my way to my bedroom. "At least let me—"

"I have to go to bed," I say. "I have to go to sleep."

"Just leave me alone," I say.

"Tiger—"

But I close the bedroom door on her and she doesn't try to come in.

## 24 days, 10 hours

S HAYNA IS ON THE couch, texting with It's Just Ray again. I can tell because her face is scrunched up and she's swearing under her breath. She hasn't said much since finding me drunk two days ago. We've been quiet in the Jellymobile. She did call someone last night and talked to them for a long time in the bedroom. I wondered if it was my dad.

I spent yesterday afternoon in the shed, looking things up on my phone like:

What happens when you die?

Help me my mom died

How to live without your mom

My mom died

The most popular searches for the last one are:

*My mom died today*

*My mom died of cancer*

*My mom died now what*

I wish I had that on a T-shirt: *My Mom Died Now What.*

Maybe if I wore it long enough, someone would give me the answer.

There are apps and crisis lines and places to leave notes about your grief and to find people you don't even know to talk about your dead person. There's a whole world of dying out there that I didn't know existed. A whole world of crying and hearts with

Grand Canyon–sized holes. A whole world of people teetering on the edges of black holes.

I finish putting my books in my backpack. My sister looks up, her eyes red.

"Are you crying?" I ask softly. "Is he being mean?"

She wipes her face. "Just forget about it. You have too much to deal with, anyway. You don't need all my crap, too. You ready to go? I have an appointment after I drop you off."

When we pass by the table, she looks down at the manila envelope and swears under her breath.

"Maybe you should open that," I say tentatively. "It looks important."

She grabs it and stuffs it in her bag. "Yeah. Just one more thing, right? Like I don't have enough on my plate."


Mae-Lynn pokes me in Grief Group. Walrus Jackson isn't here yet. Taran and Alif are on their phones and Lupe is at a game.

"Where's my bottle?" she whispers.

I grimace. "About that. It's kind of . . . gone. I kind of . . . drank it."

"You drank the whole thing?" Her voice is loud and Taran looks up.

"There wasn't that much, I mean, but yeah. And then I passed out and my sister found me and I threw up. My mom's . . . the death certificates came."

Mae-Lynn says, "Oh. That's hard. Really final. A lot of medical jumbo, but what it really means is: yep, still dead."

"Yeah."

Alif pipes up. "Hey, did you guys keep their clothes? I did. Is that weird? I have one of Dad's sweaters, from this time we went camping, and it still smells like the campfire smoke. And him."

Mae-Lynn says, "I burned a lot of his sick stuff. I was so . . . you know. My mom keeps his dresser full of his clothes, though."

"My mom's clothes are in our closet," I say. "I feel weird giving them away. Like if I do, she didn't matter or something. But her clothes meant something to her."

Mae-Lynn says, "The person is gone, though. The clothes aren't the person."

Taran shakes his head. "But they smell like them. And they have memories, like the campfire sweater. You can't just give those up. They are . . ." He pauses.

"Last little bits of them. Last little bits of their lives with you," Alif says. "Like if you keep giving away their stuff, eventually you won't have anything left of them."

Alif rubs his chin. He's trying to grow a goatee, and it doesn't look like much is happening. "You know, Tiger girl, I gotta ask. The dress. What's going on there? I mean, you used to wear funky shit, but now you're just wearing the same funky shit like every single day. Plus a funky hat."

They all look at me. Outside the classroom, the janitor is running the mop up and down the hallway. There's a leak in a ceiling pipe. I can hear the wheels of the yellow bucket clanking on the tiled floor.

"My mom bought it for Memorial Days. The dance. Without telling me. And we had a fight. And then she died. And I'm never taking it off."

Taran looks like he might cry.

"That's hardcore love, Tiger."

His brother nods. Mae-Lynn smiles.

I was afraid they'd tell me I was crazy, that I should get rid of it, stop wearing it, but they don't.

"Thank you," I say.

Mr. Jackson lumbers in with a stack of folders in his hands. Sometimes I forget now that he's a counselor for all kids, not just us, and that he has a real job here at the school.

"Folks, we have a development."

He plops his folders down on the desk and slides into a chair. "We have to find a new meeting place for next week. This is our last day of school, after all, and then they're going to be doing some renovations. I thought we could meet at the county library, or maybe drive into Sierra Vista as a group, but then a wonderful opportunity presented itself."

He gives us a big grin.

"How would you like to spend a week with horses?"

Alif says, "What?"

Taran says, "Like, horse-horses? The big kind? No way. No way. I don't even know how to *ride* a horse."

"I don't have money for that," I say. "Camps cost money."

"Now, hear me out," Mr. Jackson says. "I ran into Randy Gonzalez the other day at the coffee shop and I was telling him about you all, and our little group, and he says he often has sick kids out there to stay, kids who have disadvantages and the like. They stay in a little house, visit with the horses and other animals—oh Lord, he's got ducks and turtles, goats, the works—they learn to ride, and how to take care of horses."

"Wait," I say. "Like, the *ranch* ranch? Caballo Dorado?" That's where Thaddeus works. I could see him for a whole week, practically.

I don't think I've ever seen Mr. Jackson, well, *beam*. "Yes, that one."

"I'm afraid of horses. And what do you mean, we'd be in a house together?" Mae-Lynn says. "Like, with them?" She points to the boys.

"There are two guesthouses on the property. You two could be in one, the boys in the other. Lupe will be at a U orientation event, so she wouldn't be joining us. I go back home every evening. No one has to pay. Mr. Gonzalez is going to put you to work. Mucking stables, feeding the horses. You'll learn how to care for one of God's greatest creatures. We'll have sessions, too. But I think being somewhere else might prove beneficial. Rejuvenating. Animals are therapeutic, you know. Even chickens, or so I've heard."

I think of the stony silence between me and my sister. The way the house seems so empty and cold and different. She'll probably be glad to be rid of me for a while.

And I could see Thaddeus. Like, every day. Because I miss him. Not in *that* way, but in a he-knows-how-*this*-feels way.

"I'm in," I say. "I'll do it."

Mae-Lynn sighs. "I'll try to convince my mom. But I'm not getting on a horse."

Taran and Alif look at each other. "Okay, we'll ask our mom," Alif says. "But is it okay if we leave a little early today? We've gotta get ready for the dance."

Mr. Jackson nods. "I'm thrilled. And yes, you can leave early. Now let's get started."

Mae-Lynn has her mom's car, so we drive to Cucaracha after the meeting to get blue Icees and then drive back to Eugene Field and park at the far end of the lot.

We watch as kids hang pretty golden string lights up in the mesquite trees out front, place luminarias along the front steps and sidewalks and light them up.

It's the Memorial Days dance.

Mae-Lynn slurps her Icee thoughtfully as we watch the van with the band arrive. They unload their equipment, hustle up the steps, arms full.

"Have you ever been to a dance?" she asks.

"No."

"We could go in together," she says hesitantly. "I mean, if you wanted to. No one would even notice us. We could just watch, inside. You *are* dressed for it."

She gives me a weak smile and pats my dress.

I think about that. There are some kids arriving in nice cars, probably rented, stepping out in pretty dresses, well-pressed suits, corsages pinned just so. In the fading light, the luminaria lanterns on the walkway look beautiful and magical.

"I think you have to have tickets, maybe?" I say. I was supposed to be one of these kids, though it seems like a long time ago now. "I don't know. But . . . no."

Cake is inside, I know that. The school band is going to play some songs first. We've still been quiet around each other. I feel like things are changing.

I pull out my phone.

*I know you probably got into the music camp. I'm really happy for you. I can't wait to hear all about it. It's okay to tell me.*

It takes a long time for her to answer.

*I don't want to leave you. I'm not going.*

*You are. It would make me feel horrible if you missed out just to stay with me.*

I pause. Mae-Lynn is watching me.

*And I already feel horrible. Right? Nothing is going to change that. So go. Because that would make me a tiny bit happy.*

Cake writes, *I hate you and I love you.*

I slide my phone into my backpack, breathe deeply.

More cars pull up, kids spilling out. The glossy dresses, the swinging hair. Girls in makeup, girls in tuxes.

Mae-Lynn says, "Those girls look really pretty. I like girls. I like boys, too, I guess. Does that weird you out?"

I look at her. She looks scared, like maybe I'm the first person she's ever told, and I probably am, since she's lower than me on the Eugene Field Ladder of Desolation.

"No," I say. "Just love who you want, you know? Life is so much shit. We should just be able to love who we want."

"I'm too confused to even do anything about it. But I keep thinking that's a thing about me my dad will never know. The biggest thing." Her voice gets very quiet. "I think he would have loved me just the same."

Her hand finds mine across the front seat.

"There's so much about me he'll never know," she says softly. "That's the hardest."

Even though I don't look at her, I know she's crying, and I am, too. I scoop her fingers tighter.

Music starts to pump out the school windows. Laughter.

321

Mae-Lynn and I sit in the car, not saying anything, watching everyone else have the best years of their lives.

Someday, when people ask us about high school, and dances, and kisses, and all that stuff, I know that what we'll remember most of all is how normal was stolen from us.

## 27 days

MY SISTER DOESN'T BAT an eye when I mention the ranch. She just keeps looking at her laptop, curled up on the couch. "That sounds nice," she says. "A week? That will be fun."

"It doesn't cost anything," I say.

She snorts. "Well, that's good, because we couldn't spare it, anyway." Her eyes flick across the screen.

"What are you looking at that's so interesting?" I ask tentatively, moving around the couch.

She snaps the lid shut. "Nothing." Picks at her cuticles.

I take a deep breath, just like Walrus Jackson said to when we wanted to talk about something we needed.

"I was hoping that maybe, when I get back, maybe we could talk about calling Da— Dustin." My heart's beating so loud I can barely hear my voice. "I feel like it's really important to me, to talk to him."

My sister keeps her eyes on her nails. Scrape, scrape, pick, pick.

"He's the only parent I have left." I pause. "I mean, you still have a mom, at least."

Shayna keeps looking at her nails. Scrape, scrape, purple polish drifting to the floor. "Yes and no," she says mildly. "I wouldn't say we were ever besties, but she's not speaking to me right now. Because I'm here. Helping you. I'm a traitor."

Her voice trembles.

I don't know what to say.

The girl-bug says, *Don't cry!*

My sister looks up at me. Her eyes are bright. "But you know what? Fine," she says. "It's fine."

"For reals?"

"Yeah," she says. "For reals. But it might not turn out the way you want. I just want you to know that. But okay."

"I'm not trying to take him from you—"

She stands up abruptly, the laptop sliding off her legs. "It's fine. It is what it is."

Clipped, done. That's her way, I guess.

She slides a scrunchie down her wrist and pulls up her hair. "I'm gonna go for a walk. Your turn to make dinner?"

Softly, I say, "It's always my turn to make dinner."

She chucks me under the chin before turning toward the front door. "You do it so well!"

She leaves.

I look down at her laptop.

I look at the door.

I open the laptop, tap.

The window pops up. *Beautiful Boise! A winter wonderland. Resort jobs, benefits, natural wonders.* I click on another tab. She has like twelve up.

*Come to Maine! Discover your Maine thing.*

*Make Minnesota your destination, ya, you betcha!*

All the tabs, different towns, cities. Everywhere but Mesa Luna.

I close the laptop.

*I think she wants to move,* I text Cake.

But Cake doesn't answer, because she's in New York, enjoying the sights with her family on vacation before music camp in Massachusetts. She left the day after the dance.

She's probably at a play or a concert. It's three hours later, there.

I go into the bedroom.

"I think she wants to move," I tell my Boxes of Mom. "This is the only place we've ever been."

No answer.

I'm getting used to that by now.

T HADDEUS IS THE ONE who greets us inside the big front gates. Walrus Jackson picked me and Mae-Lynn up; Taran and Alif followed in their pickup truck.

At Caballo Dorado, I feel it the moment I get out, the same as I did the first day Thaddeus brought me here: the smell of the horses, the excitement of movement, the sun hot on my face.

Thaddeus grins at me first, and that makes me feel special. Then he gets all serious, and leads us around, showing us the hacienda, which is the main house where Mr. Gonzalez lives, and the kitchen where we can get snacks and make food.

The guesthouses have neat, elaborately carved wood furniture and brightly colored pillows and blankets. Mae-Lynn whispers, "It's like we'll be college roomies or something," and even though I get a little pang for Cake, what Mae-Lynn says is kind of fun, and cool, because she's right, and I'm excited to have all of this.

Like, here is me going away to camp. Doing stuff. Like the other kids do.

At the stables, Thaddeus turns us over to a leather-faced guy named Marco, who immediately looks at Taran's, Alif's, and Mae-Lynn's shoes and clucks his tongue. "Y'all gonna get shit on yer shoes. I'll see if we can scare up some boots. That's a pity. Hope you're ready for hard work." He grins at Walrus Jackson, who laughs. Walrus is decked out in shiny cowboy boots and a tall hat and looks ridiculously excited to be here. I'm pretty sure he's not going to be getting his boots dirty, though. I think he just likes dressing the part.

Marco walks us down the middle of the stable. It's early afternoon, and the horses are in after their morning routine and training, he tells us. They need to be iced, and he shows us an interesting machine, kind of like a giant bathtub. You walk the horses inside, close the door, and turn it on, and cold water floods around them, soothing sore muscles.

The horses snuffle and stamp. Mae-Lynn looks nervous. Marco says, "They'll smell that, girl. They'll use it against you. They are smart and playful and they like to tease, but they're also big, dangerous, and heavy, and they take no shit."

At that, he turns to face all of us. "If I see any one of you, ever, mistreating any of my horses, you are out of here. No second chances. No explanations. You are *out*. There is no call to treat an animal cruelly or carelessly. Is that understood?"

We all nod.

"Good. The first thing is boots. Feel free to walk around, get to know our family, be gentle, and then when I get back, it's shit-shoveling time." He grins.

As soon as he's gone, Taran says, "Oh my God, this place *stinks*."

Alif covers his mouth. Mae-Lynn looks freaked out. "They're so big," she says, but she starts walking anyway, looking at the horses in their stalls.

I follow her. She's right. Most of them are regal-seeming, with kind of long and elegant necks. I remember Thaddeus telling me these were Arabians, a very old type of horse.

Mae-Lynn reaches out, slowly, to touch one horse. The horse

is utterly still, but as soon as Mae-Lynn's fingers reach her mane, she shakes her head violently and sneezes all over Mae-Lynn's hand. "Uhhh," she says. "So gross. Oh my God." But she laughs.

"She's so soft, you guys," she calls out to Taran and Alif. They're still standing by the doors. Walrus Jackson is busy nuzzling the face of a chestnut-colored horse down the way.

Taran and Alif look at each other and then start walking, shyly checking out the horses in each stall.

I keep walking, inhaling the smell of the stable, horses' sweat, all of it. Is this what my mom loved? The whole thing? Last night I spent hours looking up things like bridles, reins, saddles, brushes, boots.

At the end of the row on the right, a horse much smaller than the others stares at me.

There's a funny-looking kind of splint on one of her legs. She holds it a little above the ground. She flicks her eyes at me.

"Hey there," I say. I look at her stall gate, the sign that says her diet and name. "Opal."

Marco comes sauntering through the double doors, his arms full of boots. "Oh, you found our tough girl. Messed up her leg pretty bad a while back, but she's coming around. She's a little runty, but got a lot of heart."

Opal tosses her mane at him. He just laughs and heads toward the others with the boots.

Opal and I stare are each other. I reach out slowly and run my fingers down her nose. Is it called a nose? Or something else? I was so busy looking up horse *things* that I forgot horse *anatomy*. I make a mental note to look that up later, after dinner.

She's so soft, like velvet. And warm. We stand there for a

long time, just breathing, and I can feel myself kind of sinking into a warm feeling, like my bones are loosening ever so slightly.

Like things are okay, just for this tiny moment.

I look down at her splint. "I'm sorry you got hurt," I say. "Hurting sucks."

Opal leans her nose into my palm.

And then Marco calls out that it's time to start mucking shit.


Mucking shit is just as horrible as it sounds, and by the time we're done, our backs are sore and we smell to high heaven, or so Walrus Jackson says. He sat in the corner the whole time, reading a book, while we heaved horse manure, measured out food, and raked and cleaned stalls.

Outside, it's hot and flies are buzzing all around us. Marco looks almost gleeful as he explains the routine.

In the morning, we'll help exercise the horses, help the staff with riding lessons, and learn the ins and outs of working the stable. After lunch, we muck. After mucking, we help feed the ducks, the pigs (there are two), and take riding lessons in the late afternoon. "Nothing fancy," Marco says. "But you need to learn the basics of riding."

Randy Gonzalez has appeared, his wide-brimmed hat shading his face. He smiles at all of us. "Welcome to my home. I'm glad to have you as my guests for the week. I hope you find sustenance for your soul here."

The four of us look around awkwardly. Adults are weird. Always saying these giant things that you have to think about for so long, you usually forget what they said in the first place.

"There's a pool down that little path," he says, pointing. "You can use it, but please be respectful of noise. Most of us around here go to bed pretty early. Ranch life starts before the sun rises, after all."

He meanders off. Alif says, "That dude is like something from a cowboy movie."

Marco laughs.

In our guesthouse, in our tiny shared bedroom, Mae-Lynn snores deeply. Her hands are blistered from the muck rake. I had to dig around the pink-painted bathroom to find some Band-Aids and ointment. We were all so tired from the first afternoon we could barely keep our heads up over a dinner of posole and fry bread and iced tea.

I am tired, too, my bones aching, but I can't sleep. I feel rickety, loose. I get up and put my dress on, even though it's still damp from me washing it out in the sink. I slide my boots on.

The night sky is velvety black and the air is still. I can hear the pigs gently snuffling in their pen as I walk to the stable.

Of course, the doors are locked. These are important horses, after all. I walk down to the end, to where Opal is. Her Dutch door, which is what Marco called the half door to each stall, is partially open.

I hold my hand inside.

It only takes a minute, and then I hear her shuffle, snort, and then a long tongue reaches out and licks my fingers.

She appears, her eyes glossy and curious.

"My mom died," I say.

Soft snort, foot stamp.

She nudges my hand with her nose.

I talk to her for a long time, stuff about my mom, and my sister, until I can barely keep my eyes open, and then I say good night and go back up to the guesthouse, and fall into bed still wearing my dampish dress.

T HADDEUS IS STANDING AT the edge of the ring, a giant grin on his face. He's watched all of us struggle to get on a horse, stay on the horse, and make it around the ring in one smooth go.

There's a lot more to horse riding than just getting on, it turns out.

There's grooming, saddling, cinching, reining, and a kind of awkward-sounding thing called mounting. And then the feeling of terror at being so high off the ground on such a powerful, unpredictable animal.

You have to learn how to walk, halt, turn. All of these things have to be learned before you can jog or canter, which Mae-Lynn says she's never doing.

"Happy just moseying along," she calls out, as her horse, Fireball, meanders slowly inside the ring. Mae-Lynn is doing pretty well. Taran and Alif are struggling.

I've been circling the ring at a slow clip on Opal. At first, Marco didn't want to give her to me, because of her leg, but then he decided it would be okay. "You two like each other," he said. "I know you'll be gentle. No one likes to be forced to do things they aren't ready to do, and she'll let you know when she's had enough."

It's very bouncy being on a horse, and kind of painful on muscles and bone parts you weren't really aware of at first, but I like it.

I look down at Thaddeus as I make my third turn around the ring.

He gives me a thumbs-up.

I feel at home.

Maybe horses, like avocados and stand-up comedy, can be in your DNA, too.

## 30 days, 16 hours

R ANDY GONZALEZ HOLDS OUT the receiver of the stable phone. It's bolted to the wall next to the stacks of feed. We aren't allowed to bring our cellphones with us when we work the stables. Marco had said, "I don't need anyone not paying attention and then getting kicked in the head."

"Your sister," Randy says. "Don't worry, she says nothing is wrong."

I take off my smelly gloves and drop them on the ground.

"Hey, you," my sister says. "What's shaking?"

"Um, nothing? Just . . ." I look around the stable, at my friends—my friends!—shoveling horse shit and measuring food for the horses. "Working."

"Well, glad to hear it. Listen——" Her voice gets softer, but also quicker, like she thinks someone might be listening, and my ears prick up at the difference. "I know you're supposed to stay until Sunday, but it's summer!" There's a pause, and when she starts talking again, her voice is higher. "Aren't I supposed to take you on a summer vacation? We did that sometimes when I was little. Went to a cabin once on the Redneck Riviera. We lived in Florida then. Other places, too."

"I didn't know you lived in Florida, too," I say.

"Oh, yeah. Lots of places. Anyway, I've gussied up your mom's car and I can pack some bags——"

"We don't have the money for that, Shayna. Do we?" I lick

my lips. She seems weird, like something is wrong, but taking a trip can't be wrong, can it?

"Oh, don't worry about that. My grandpa sent a check, not a big one, mind you, but it'll cover some things, and hey, maybe we can even stop by and see them in Alabama on our trip. I love driving. It'll be a blast. Maybe you can take the wheel a little. Back roads and stuff."

"Um . . ." I look over at Taran and Alif and Mae-Lynn, their clothes wet with sweat. They're all watching me. "Well, I mean, I kind of like it here right now. Maybe I can stay? And you could do your trip. I bet I can stay with Mae-Lynn until you get back."

There's an eerie silence on the other end of the phone.

"Shayna?

"So, no. I mean, I hate to pull the guardian card, but you're coming with me. I can't leave you behind."

"I don't . . . you're making me go on vacation with you?"

"Yes. I'll be by at ten tomorrow, so be ready! I'll pack up some of your stuff here so we can just get started." She tries to make her voice sound bright. "A sister trip. Just you and me."

She hangs up. I listen to the dial tone before replacing the receiver.

Her voice, it had just the tiniest, sharpest quiver at the end, when she said *just you and me.*

When I turn back around, they're all looking at me, eyes concerned.

"Looks like I'm leaving tomorrow," I say. "Who's up for one more ride?"

. . .

I ride so hard and so fast on the trail that Tarin's and Alif's voices are lost in the wind. Opal is heaving herself forward, like she couldn't wait to try to go fast again. I can feel her blood pumping beneath my legs.

I want to go fast all the time now.

I want to go so fast I can't see, can't hear, can't be.

I was happy here, and now my sister is ripping me away from it.

But I feel better, riding Opal. Maybe this is our shared story: a fast horse, time stopping somehow.

I don't ever want to stop. I dig my heels into Opal.

I can ride so fast and far that when I come out the other side, everything will be different.

I'm crying.

She snorts. Her gait slows. She's telling me she's done. She tosses her head. I dig in. She whinnies.

She balks, and I go flying.

I land a few feet away, thudding so painfully on the ground I'm afraid I might have broken something. I have burrs and goatheads in my hair, in my hands, in my dress. I almost smacked my head into a rock.

I breathe in dirt and dust. Cough.

Opal snorts, limps over. She stamps a hoof.

*I didn't like that.*

*Okay,* I say. *I'm sorry.*

*Okay.*

She leans down, noses my face. Snorts, sending snot and spit on my cheek. I rub the side of her neck.

Taran and Alif ride up, sending another cloud of dust over me.

"What the hell were you doing! You could've killed yourself." Taran gets off Duster, kneels down and brushes dirt off me. "You're bleeding."

His brother takes my arm. "You just took off. Was it the horse? She get spooked or something?"

"It wasn't the horse, dude. It was *her*." Taran picks some pine needles off the sleeve of my dress. "We're supposed to be having fun."

"I just . . . ," I say.

They look at me. The sun is golden and hot, and even though we have hats on, our faces are sweaty and dirty and tired. Four days of mucking stalls and chasing ducks and trying to learn everything horse will do that to you, I guess.

"I'm sorry."

Alif's eyes are sad. "You don't have to be sorry, Tiger. But it's not going to do any good, hurting yourself like this."

I don't say anything.

Taran says, "Come on, let's go. Jackson will be worried. And the horses need water."

They help me back onto Opal. My body is starting to feel sore and stiff. I ride behind them. When I think they're enough ahead of me, I lean down close to the hot velvet of Opal's neck and whisper, "I am. I'm really sorry."

She twitches her mane, sending whips of thick hair against my cheek.


In the guesthouse, Mae-Lynn examines my cuts, pulls goat-heads from my hair.

"That was stupid," she says. "I mean, *so* stupid." Her fingers are rough in my hair.

"Why are you so mad?" I ask, swatting her hand away. "I just wanted to go fast. I don't *know*."

Mae-Lynn crosses her arms. Her cheeks are wet. She's looking away from me, down at the ground.

"I know what you were trying to do. You thought you could go so fast or far everything would change, or you'd die, right?"

She looks back up at me. Her eyes are streaming.

"Well, bully for you, then. And how dare you! I thought I finally found a friend. And not only that, a friend who understands this horrible hole I have inside, but you know what? I don't care. Because what kind of friend would leave me that way? What kind of friend would do that to me after I've had the *worst* kind of leaving?"

Her voice shatters. She's crying so hard her shoulders are shaking.

"I'm sorry," I whisper, leaning against her, wrapping my arms around her. "I'm sorry. I won't leave you. It was stupid. I promise. I promise."

"Don't," she cries into my hair. "Please don't. I've had too much already."

## 30 days, 23 hours, 17 minutes

M AE-LYNN IS SITTING ON the edge of the pool, her legs in, trailing her fingers through the water. "I'm sorry you're leaving early, but that seems cool, a road trip. Right?"

"Yeah, I guess. She seemed weird about it, though."

"Well, there's no turning back," she says. "She's it. She's what you have and you have to make the best of it."

"Yep."

I get up. "Hold on," I say. "I have to call her. I need her to pack something for me."

I've never been anywhere on a trip without my mom, and I don't want to start now. I call Shayna, but her voice mail picks up. "Hey," I say. "I know it's bizarre, but can you, uh, pack my Boxes of Mom? They won't take up much room. I just . . . I don't want to leave her behind. Okay. Call me back if you want, or text."

Taran and Alif start calling out *Marco! Polo!* and Mae-Lynn is giggling. Even though I'm just wearing a T-shirt and some shorts Thaddeus loaned me, since I don't have a real bathing suit, seeing them playing in the pool makes me kind of giddy, and not awkward or poor.

They make me feel hopeful even, with their voices ringing out in the night air, the stars perfect and sweet in the dark night sky.

I take a running start and when my body slices through the water, I feel as free as I did all those years ago in The Pit, my body weightless and ignorant of the pain to come.

S HAYNA DOESN'T COME TO get me.
I wait for her in the guesthouse, scrolling on my phone. The others are in the stable, working.

I try not to panic, like that one night. PTSD, Walrus called it. I tell myself: just because one person went away, doesn't mean another will. Deep breaths.

I send two texts and leave one voice mail before I go down to the stable and ask Taran and Alif for a ride after lunch. At least I can wait for her at home.

The first thing I notice when Taran and Alif drop me off is the dented black sedan in the driveway. Shayna never has friends over. She always says she's meeting people, but they never come over.

I walk slowly to the door, my heart sinking. First we go on this mystery trip, then she doesn't show up, and now she has friends over?

When I open the door, the second thing I notice is the mess.

Not that Shayna is a neat freak, by any means, but this is by far worse than anything I thought possible, coming from her.

Clothes all over the place, like they've been thrown and kicked around. Stacks of dirty dishes in the sink and toppling on the red counter. An open cardboard container of orange juice on its side, a pool of gelatinous pulp drying on the counter.

The smell of cigarette smoke, which makes my eyes tear up.

I set my pink suitcase by the door, my heart sinking. "Shayna?" I call out softly. "I'm home." I suddenly wonder if I should text Taran and Alif and have them come back.

The door to my—our—bedroom is closed.

There are beer cans in a pyramid on the coffee table in front of the television.

A full ashtray.

Shayna doesn't smoke.

My voice trembles as I call out her name again, a little louder this time.

No answer. I'm completely freaked out, and just as I'm turning to go, and planning to run down the dirt driveway and call Taran, or 911, the bedroom door swings open, and a gravelly voice says, "You must be the famous little sister. The one that up and lured my girlfriend away."

My fingertips go cold. My whole body goes cold.

*Ray.*

She said he was gone. She said he wasn't a worry. She said, *It's just Ray. He's all talk and no game.*

But maybe her voice had shaken, just the tiniest bit. Can I remember that? Did that happen? That happened. It happened.

*I'm telling you for the billionth time.*

It's Just Ray is leaning in the doorway of my bedroom, his flannel shirt untucked, his jeans greasy, hair hanging in his eyes. He has deep, dark circles under his eyes.

He smiles, but his voice isn't friendly. "Don't you want to say hi? I came all this way, after all."

Behind him, my sister is a lump in the bed, her long hair

spilling over the side, toward the floor. There's a tear in her pink Victoria's Secret pajama pants.

They were in my bed. Doing things.

My stomach turns. I might be sick.

I don't want to look at him in the doorway anymore, so I look at the floor.

And then he bellows, so loud it makes all the hair on my body stand up, "Shayna, your sister's home!"

My sister shoots out of bed, weaving and almost falling over. She catches herself with one hand on the bed before pushing herself back upright. She lurches toward Ray, who makes room for her in the doorway. When she takes her hands away from her face and looks at me, I see the dark circles under her eyes, too.

She's as pale as a ghost and her lips are dry, dry. There's a purplish shadow on her temple that makes my heart squeeze.

"Did he hi——" It comes out in a half breath before she shakes her head violently.

*No.*

But I don't believe her, because I remember that morning she left her phone on the bed and went to shower and it lit up. *You are not the one in charge here don't forget that.*

She starts talking before I can say anything else. Her voice is weird, like nothing is wrong, like this angry person in the house with us is not a weird situation at all, but completely normal. "This is Ray. I told you about Ray. He came to visit. You remember I told you about him. Ray, this is Tiger. My little sister. She's back."

Ray says, "I can see that."

My sister looks at the ground.

Once, she expertly shamed the landlord, the bill collectors, *and* my principal, her voice strong and confident, her pony-tail swaying.

But now, her hair is a tangled mess against her face and her voice is hoarse and shallow.

"He's going to stay for a little while."

Ray grins. I stop breathing.

My sister keeps looking at the ground.

I was at the horse ranch and I fell in love with a horse and fell in friendship with Mae-Lynn Carpenter and came home ready to be a family with my wild and unpredictable sister and now my sister is someone else. Someone broken and unfamiliar.

Maybe the broken was always in her and I just didn't want to see it.

Maybe she was good at hiding it.

"Aw, come on," Ray grumbles, lighting a cigarette and moving out from the doorway. His boots scuff the floor. "Don't look so grim, kid. I'm not so bad. I'm great at taking care of people, aren't I, Shay? I'm really good at it. It's your sister who isn't so good at it, are you, Shay?"

I don't know who to look at, It's Just Ray, or Shayna.

Shayna keeps looking at the ground, licking her lips. I think she's hungover, really hungover.

When it comes out, her voice is small, and pleading.

"Don't, Ray. Just don't."

He leans back against the counter, smiling. "But we're all family now, right, honey? We should know each other's secrets, start with a clean slate."

"Shayna," I whisper. "What's—"

Ray barks so suddenly the phone drops from my hand, clattering on the ground. "Don't. You. Talk. To. Her."

He moves up close to me, as fluid as a snake, his face inches from mine, his breath a terrible cloud on my cheek. "Did she tell you what she did? Did she tell you what she did right before she ran away from me?"

Shayna starts to cry. "Don't listen to him, Tiger. *Please.* I'm *going* to make a nice home for us, I promise."

She sounds like a little girl.

Ray shouts, "You think she really wants to take care of you? Really? She was just using you as an excuse to leave the island. She doesn't care about *you.* How could she? She's a *drunk.* She killed our *baby.*" His voice cracks.

Shayna screams, *Jesus, Ray,* and the sound is so painful I wish I could stop up my ears. Frozen, I watch as Ray begins shaking her, her face crumpled and wet with tears. *It's not what you think, Tiger. I can explain.*

His hands dig into the flesh of her bare arms.

I don't know who I become, but whoever she is, she tries to pull him away from her sister, clawing at his flannel shirt, because *blood is blood,* kicking at his jeaned leg. *Don't you hurt her.*

And then I'm flying, like I'm nothing, a speck, a feather or mote of dust, against the wall, still feeling the strength of his hands as they pushed me so hard, away.

And I'm looking at my sister look at me, her face stricken, and she doesn't help me, even as the back of my head is ringing from hitting the wall.

But I see her mouth move as Ray nears her again, his eyes clouded over with something I am too scared to think of a word for.

*Run.*

And then I scoop up my phone and tear out the front door, down the dirt driveway, into the bright day.

Cracks spider up and down the front of my phone. The charge says "5%."

I'm breathing so hard I think my ribs will break. My lungs will explode. My eyeballs will pop and bleed.

I had a mom and now she's gone. I had a sister and now she's gone.

I have no one.

I should go back. I can't go back. I'm afraid to go back. I'm afraid of everything.

My fingers don't even shake as I press 911, tell the operator a woman is being beaten up at 344 Morales Road, that they need to come quickly.


I just start walking. I have no idea where I'm supposed to go. I don't want to call my sister, and even if I did, now I don't have a phone. Maybe I'll just walk to the desert and die there, in the heat and loneliness, coyotes and jackrabbits tearing at my flesh.

I don't have any water, and I get tired and thirsty and hungry pretty quick.

I stagger at some point, and fall into a teddy bear cholla. The pain sears through my leg and I can barely breathe.

When I jerk my leg away, part of the cactus comes off in my calf. It dangles there, painfully, and I try to use my dress as a kind of mitt to pull it from my leg, but the needles are in too deep, and the spines of the cholla poke through my dress and into the soft pads of my fingers.

I give up. I walk, like a creature undone, slowly and haltingly, the piece of cactus bobbling in my leg. Wherever the black hole is, I am heading toward it.

I walk as far as I can, the teddy bear cholla hunk still dangling from my calf. Then I stop, because I can't walk anymore, and I don't want to, because there's no point.

My sister doesn't want me. My father doesn't want me. Cake is all the way across the country. My mother is dead.

I think if I had something right now, something to help me along the path to the S word, I would do it.

I sit down on the desert floor, gather my dirty mourning dress around me, and start to cry. I think about things to do to myself. I scratch my arms with sharp rocks. I hit my forehead with the heels of my hands. My body feels electric with longing and dread and finality. That's really the only way I can express it. I feel dark inside, and I feel something pulling at me, and I don't feel like resisting anymore.

I don't know how long I sit there. Time stops.

I hope when night comes, it swallows me whole. Whatever creatures live out here can eat me alive. It doesn't matter. They can nick at me slowly, they can leap with great flashing teeth and tear at me, it doesn't matter to me. Or I can die of infection from the cactus needles dug deep into my flesh.

I close my eyes. I might doze off. I rouse myself when my dress starts to itch from dried sweat. When the temperature is falling, the sun follows.

I listen to the sounds of the desert: the strange scratches, the odd caws and hoots. I become aware of a low rumble, too, in the distance. And the sound of something moving toward me.

When I look up, there are flames in the distance, great orange fingers licking the sky, and before them, a silhouette gliding silkily in my direction, hair fanned out like a black cape against the sudden orange of a large, luminous fire.

I blink, disoriented. I didn't realize I was so close to Rancho Luna, the old abandoned hotel, and it's the Friday bonfire, and soon, hordes of kids will descend upon the deserted hotel to drink beer and do nefarious things until the police break it up.

Gradually, I realize that the silhouette is my mean and beautiful and damaged friend Lupe Hidalgo, coming to me like a vision from another world.

I'm afraid maybe she'll kick me, or throw sand in my face, or at least make fun of me, because it's not like it's after Grief Group, when we all feel close and conspiratorial. That's over now. To tell you the truth, I relish the thought of her hurting me. Sure, do it. What do I care? One more thing isn't going to make much difference.

Still, I duck my head behind my arms as she approaches.

But she doesn't kick me. There isn't any sand-throwing. She gives a great sigh, shines her flashlight in my face, which hurts my eyes, and mutters, "Tolliver, you horrendous fool, what the hell are you doing out here?" She waves a hand in front of her face.

"You stink, Tolliver. That dress. Do I smell horse shit? Ah, man, you guys went to that ranch without me while I was at orientation, didn't you? You couldn't even *shower*? Oh, shit, what the hell did you do to your leg?"

She kneels down, carefully aiming the flashlight at my calf. She tsks. "Stupid," she says. She digs deep in the pocket of her sheepskin vest and pulls out a small pouch. She lifts out tweezers. Who has tweezers in the desert?

"Do you often feel the need for eyebrow maintenance in the

desert, Lupe?" I ask hoarsely. My throat is raw from thirst and crying.

"Shut up. It's for my smokes." She considers me. "That's what's wrong with you, you know that, Tolliver? You always gotta be so highfalutin about everything. You sound like a damn book all the time."

"I'm not the one who just used a word like *highfalutin*."

She grimaces and bends over my leg, considering her options. "Gonna hurt," she says. "Sorry."

Lupe works quickly, tweezing the larger piece out slowly, which makes me wince with pain, and then works to extract the smaller, nastier needles. When she's done, she licks the hem of her T-shirt and runs it over my calf. When she takes it away, little flecks of blood spring to the surface of my skin.

Lupe brings out a half-pint of peppermint schnapps from the pocket of her vest and regards me. She takes a sip and settles next to me, not too close but not too far.

"Thanks," I say.

"You shouldn't be out here. You should be at home." She pauses. "How's it going with your sis?"

"Quite poorly."

She hands me the bottle of schnapps.

"Her boyfriend came out," I say. "There was a fight."

Lupe tsks-tsks. "Ay, shit. You okay?"

I take a big swallow and it floods through me. I immediately feel better: warmer, braver, fierce and mad and important. I take four more big swallows in a row, and feel myself getting woozy really quickly, probably because I'm dehydrated and hungry.

Lupe thinks it's funny, I think, that I just start chattering, mostly about Thaddeus and the black hole and that maybe there's a person who lives in the universe who's turning the pages in the story of your life and you have no control over it.

Lupe scoffs. "That's some messed-up shit, Tolliver. I don't buy it. I believe we control our own destiny, you know? *I* make the choice, not some weirdo on a cloud. And I'm getting out."

I burp. "What?"

"Out. Of here. Mesa Messed-Up Luna. I got a scholarship to the U, you know. Softball." She gives a proud smile.

"Oh, right," I say.

The noise from Rancho Luna increases. Laughter, shrieking. Bottles breaking.

Lupe says, "My girlfriend broke up with me." She sighs.

"Oh," I say. I reach over and gently ease the peppermint schnapps from her grip. I feel woozy and wonderful and I want some more. "I'm sorry. That's terrible. She seemed nice."

Lupe and Breisha Walters often liked to make out by the entrance to the library, leaning against lockers, entwined tightly. It was hard to avoid staring; they were both beautiful, with dark hair and dark eyes. Together, they were weirdly like fantasy-novel heroines come to life, stalking the school with their flashing eyes and dancing hair. I half expected them to whip out swords in lunch period.

"I'm bereft," Lupe moans. She slurs a little. "I bet that's a word you like. I don't want to go to Rancho tonight. She'll be there. She said I was too controlling. I mean, what does that mean, even?" She reaches over and takes the bottle back from me and swigs.

"You going with anybody?" she asks me.

"No," I say decisively. "No one wants me." Briefly, I think

of Kai, but then I don't, because that doesn't matter anymore, either.

"Stop feeling sorry for yourself, Tiger. There's somebody for everybody. And even if there isn't, be a woman, for God's sake! Learn how to be by yourself. Like I said, control your own destiny."

I wonder how Lupe Hidalgo got so worldly.

We're quiet, listening to the shouts and laughter of the kids at the bonfire.

"Sometimes I get so mad at my brother," Lupe says softly. "For leaving me. I think it's so selfish. Like, he did it because he was messed up, and sad, and things got ahold of him that he couldn't control, it's a disease, you know, being that way, but now I'm the one who's left, and *I'm* messed up, and sad, and things are getting ahold of *me.*"

Her eyes shine.

"I mean, that's *fucked up.*"

She finishes the bottle and throws it. I watch it arc through the sky, pinned briefly against the darkening sky.

"We should go somewhere," she says. "Let's go somewhere. I mean, *somewhere.*"

"Like, somewhere, *somewhere*?" I ask. "For reals?"

"Yeah. Like, *gone.* I don't have any wheels, though."

At Rancho, a bunch of them are singing "Highway to Hell," deep and throaty voices slicing through the night. In my inebriated state, that seems like a fine thing to be singing, and an even more apt way to describe how my life is going at the moment, so I clap Lupe Hidalgo on the shoulder and say cheerfully, "I do."

It's going to be *great,* finally controlling my own destiny.

. . .

I'm not sure how long it takes to get to my house, because I'm drunk. We'd stopped by Rancho on our way so that Lupe could nick another bottle of something, at which point I vaguely remember Grunyon and Boots, tipsy themselves, raising their bottles to me. I raised an empty hand, which they thought was hilarious.

This new liquor is not green and minty and delicious. It's sharper and, frankly, kind of gross. It stings my throat and smells terrible, like gasoline. Lupe seems to like it, though.

My house is dark. The Honda and the black sedan are both gone. I wonder if the police came, and the thought of Shayna hurt makes my stomach squeeze.

Lupe squats at the edge of the driveway, by the backyard fence, peeing.

I squat next to her.

The keys to the Jellymobile are under the front seat, as usual. I dangle them in front of Lupe, and she laughs. "The jelly truck? You kill me, Tolliver. Let's go."

It sounds like *less goh.*

I don't have any thoughts like *Don't do this, this is bad. This is BAD.*

The girl-bug is remaining suspiciously quiet, just watching everything.

The world is kind of cloaked in a gleaming, desolate light, one that seems to moan, *Who cares?*

I mean, who cares? Everyone in my life is gone.

If Lupe Hidalgo wants to "go somewhere" to get as far away from her broken heart as she can, then by God, I will take her in the Jellymobile, because I simply have nothing left to lose.

It's a little hard getting it started, and we lurch forward a few times until I get us out on the road. Pretty soon, we're tooling down San Gabriel, one of the back roads in Mesa Luna, a long stretch of dirt and houses set far back behind cottonwoods and cacti. The windows are down, a warm breeze ruffling my hair.

Lupe is disappointed to find there isn't actually any jelly in the Jellymobile, but she finds a packet of Little Debbies in the glove box and that makes her happy.

We sing along to songs on the radio. On comes Taylor Swift's "Style". Even I know that one. Lupe knows the words to all the songs.

Lupe complains about the smell of my dress, we trade the bottle, I try to drive carefully, though my vision is starting to get a little wobbly at the edges, and I do, just the tiniest bit, begin to think, *I feel a little sleepy. Maybe we should pull over and rest for a bit.*

I don't know where we are going. "Lupe," I say. "Where exactly are we going?"

She hoists the bottle over her head. "To infinity and beyond!"

And I'm just about to say, "No, really, maybe we should go back now," when suddenly, a long, gray, furry jackrabbit appears out of nowhere, darting in front of the Jellymobile, and then stops right in the middle of the road, turning its head to us.

In the headlights, the jackrabbit's face is bright white, like a ghost.

Lupe Hidalgo screams, and I swerve, and the universe swerves with us.

## 32 days, 2 hours

Y OU KNOW, IN THE movies, when people drive off the road, lots of times the driver can somehow maneuver the car back onto the road, but this isn't so in real life, especially if you're an inexperienced and extremely drunk teenager.

The universe swerves with us very quickly, but then slows down almost to a crawl, as if to say, *I want you to see each and every minute of this as it happens.*

Something huge and square-shaped and metal strikes the windshield, splintering it.

Flecks of glass spray out into my face, my hair.

Lupe Hidalgo screams again. I think I do, too, and instinctively I draw my feet up onto the seat, put my head down, and clutch my knees.

The Jellymobile careens down a residential street in the dark, plowing over a lawn ornament, which flies up and knocks off my side-view mirror. The window is open and pieces of the mirror hit my mouth. I taste blood.

Lupe Hidalgo scrambles over the seat and jams her foot down on the brake. The Jellymobile lurches to a stop mere inches from a telephone pole. Lupe's head hits the dashboard.

Lupe is laugh-crying, holding her head in her hands.

"I'm so screwed," she moans. "I am so done for."

The doors of houses along San Gabriel Lane begin to open,

and cellphone lights begin to shine in our direction, voices shouting, gravel crunching. People run to us.

Lupe and I simultaneously burst into tears.

We are in deep, drunk shit, and we know it.

A lot happens when you drink, drive without a license, and mow down a mailbox and a lawn ornament. In a converted ice cream truck. When you are sixteen.

I sit in the front of the truck for I don't know how long, my chin warm and steaming from the blood pouring from my lower lip, listening to Lupe whisper, "Oh God, oh God, oh God," over and over, her voice shaking. I've never seen Lupe scared before, and I don't like it.

I whisper, "I'm so sorry," but I don't know if she hears me. My entire body is shaking; my teeth chatter like loose stones in my mouth. I feel like one of those Halloween skeletons dangling from posts on a windy night.

Bodies cluster around the truck, ask if we're okay, open the doors, peer in. I hear sirens in the distance.

"Don't move them," someone says. "They could be really hurt."

Lupe staggers out of the truck anyway, and falls on the ground. An old woman with curlers in her hair peers down at Lupe and asks, "How many?" and holds up three bony fingers.

Glass is everywhere. In my hair. Stuck in my dress. Shards in the blood on my chin. Someone undoes my seat belt very slowly. "Stay still," a voice says. "Help is coming."

The voice is familiar, but I can't seem to place it, and my eyes have grown so heavy I can barely see.

"What were you girls *thinking*?" His voice is sharp, but then softens. "You could have died."

I turn my head, trying to make the blurry face stabilize.

It's hard to make him out in the dark, with my alcohol-misty eyes.

The figure fumbles in his bathrobe for his glasses. My heart sinks.

"Grace Tolliver, my God. And is that *Lupe*?"

Walrus Jackson stares at me. He leaves camp every night after dinner to go back to his house.

The disappointment in his eyes is heartbreaking.

"My God, girls, what possessed you?"

The police come. An ambulance. A reporter with a camera and microphone.

J AILS SMELL. THEY SMELL like vomit and old food and fright
and anger.

They put Lupe and me together in a small room and ask us
questions. The incredibly bright lights sting my eyes. Things are
blurry and I don't understand all the questions. My head is starting to throb.

My stomach is jumping, but it's Lupe who throws up in a
trash can. They bring a new one and a napkin for her mouth.

"I'm so fucked," she whispers. "I am so, so screwed. My
scholarship."

I want nothing more than to go to sleep, but the female police officer has given us bottles of soda and I'm jittery and awake.

Lupe says, "My mother is going to kill me. I'm *dead*."

The female police officer scratches something on her yellow
legal pad and murmurs, "Probably."

The police officer, whose tag says *F. Ruiz,* clacks away at a laptop. "I'm showing an open case file in child protective services.
Is that true?" She raises her eyebrows at me. "Your mother is
deceased, your father is incarcerated, and there is no other relative to act as guardian?"

I lick my lips. My mouth is dry and dirty. I think I might
be tasting glass dust from the windshield on my tongue. "No, I
mean, yes, my mom is dead, but my sister, my half sister, she's

my guardian. Shayna Franklin. You can call her." I say her phone number.

F. Ruiz keeps typing. She frowns. "I'm not seeing it. Did you and your sister fill out your paperwork for guardianship and have your hearing? Nothing is firm until a hearing with a judge and a home inspection."

My heart drops. Lupe mumbles, "Oh crap."

"She said . . . she said she was doing the paperwork. Soon. Maybe it's just not processed yet? I don't know." *Things move slow,* Karen had said once. The last I saw the manila envelope from the state, Shayna had shoved it into her bag.

I feel the press of tears behind my eyes. The front of my dress is Rorschached with blood. Blood in my hair. Blood on my face.

I stammer, "Y-you can call my sister. Just call her. She'll clear it up."

But maybe she won't. My head is clearing. The 911 call. *Ray.* "Hey, you know, could you maybe check on her? I think something might have happened to her. I had to . . . call 911."

F. Ruiz flicks her eyes to me. "About what?"

"Her . . . her boyfriend was angry."

"A domestic call?"

"I guess."

She makes a note on the yellow legal pad. "I'll try to check on it. I still have to call your caseworker. I can't release you to anyone but a caseworker or legal guardian, and coupled with the infractions you've incurred tonight, I'm gonna be frank, it isn't looking good."

F. Ruiz gathers up her Styrofoam coffee cup, her laptop, and her yellow legal pad and leaves.

Lupe says, "You are in way worse trouble than me, Tiger. Oh man. Because you were driving. And where the shit did you learn to drive that way, anyway? Girl, you are lethal. God, my head kills."

Lupe and I stay in the room with the windowed door for seven hours. I know this because outside in the hall, through the window, I can see a round clock on the wall. The hours tick by. I have a tremendous headache and spots float in front of my eyes. Paramedics came after the accident, but they said we'd be okay.

Lupe sleeps, her head down on her arms on the table, like when they used to make us put our heads on the desk at Thunder Park Elementary, when we misbehaved.

At 6:04 a.m., F. Ruiz comes to get Lupe. She shakes her awake roughly. "Your ride is here. And a coach. Are you the girl I read about in the papers with the pitching scholarship to the U?"

Lupe nods slowly, sitting up. Her face is puffy and swollen and there's a bruise on her cheek I didn't notice before. Tiny Band-Aids line her forehead where she was nicked by minuscule pieces of windshield. "Yeah."

"Your coach looks pissed."

Lupe stands up. She looks down at me sadly.

"See you, sis. Stay cool."

Before F. Ruiz closes the door, I blurt out, "What about me? Who's coming to get me? Did you find out about my sister?"

She shrugs. "Nobody. There wasn't anyone out there when the police went to check on the 911 call. You're with us now, girl. Shoulda thought of that before you got drunk and took a joyride."

. . .

From 6:04 a.m. until 7:22 a.m., I do nothing. I can't sleep. I don't even get up and pace the room. I just sit, staring at things. The wall. The floor. My bloody dress. I rub my fat lip. It stings, and I bite back tears.

I miss everybody.

At 7:22 a.m., the heavy door opens and a woman I don't know comes in. She frowns down at me.

"Grace Tolliver?"

"Yes. Where's Karen? She's my—"

"Not anymore. I'm Luisa. I'll be your caseworker from now on."

"I don't . . . I want Karen. What's going on?"

Not-Karen says, "You know what's happening, Grace? Do you have any idea?"

I hang my head, tears swimming in my eyes.

"You didn't just take a car and drive without a license. You got *drunk* and took the car and drove without a license. And then you drove over a mailbox. We've got destruction of private property, driving without a license, driving while intoxicated *and* under-age drinking. Let's hope those home owners don't press charges. We're looking at serious stuff, Grace. You have a record now. We're going to see a judge as soon as they can find a hearing time."

Not-Karen sighs. "Look at your lip. Gracious. You probably should have gotten stitches for that. Why didn't the paramedics take a look at that?"

I ignore her and stand up. I'm wobbly and sick. "Where's Shayna? Is she outside? Is she mad?"

She gives me an annoyed look. "Is that the sister?" She opens the folder she'd tucked under her arm, licks a finger, and flicks some pages. "No, she's not outside, Grace, and she hasn't answered her cell. It doesn't even look like she's done the paperwork we sent her. I'm not surprised. Sometimes raising a kid is too much for people. What happened during your home visit?"

"What home visit?"

"You were supposed to set up appointments for home visits." She looks down at her file again. She shakes her head. "We contacted your sister on three occasions, it looks like, and never heard back."

"No, there must be some mistake."

This can't be happening.

My head is pounding. I lean on the table. I can feel sweat breaking out on my forehead.

Her voice is firm. "There's no mistake, honey. There's going to be an investigation into her fitness to be your guardian, after all this, if we can even find her. And I don't see an effort on her part to make this work, frankly."

She checks her phone. "It's time to go. I've got some other pickups." She raps on the door and the guard comes back.

"I don't . . . Where are we going? I want to go home." My voice sounds high and frightened, like a kid's.

Not-Karen is matter-of-fact. "You're going to juvenile detention, Grace. You drove drunk, stole a car, destroyed private property, and you don't have a legal guardian. You're going into the system."

I can't hold it in anymore. I throw up all over my shoes, and Not-Karen's.

H ERE IS WHAT HAPPENS when you go to juvenile detention, which turns out to be a low-slung, brick-and-cinder
building in Sierra Vista.

You ride in a white van with four other girls. Everybody
stares straight ahead, or checks their nails. One girl just cries,
but silently, tears running down her face and neck.

Not-Karen rides in front. She's in charge of all of you. She's
the one who gives all the paperwork to the woman at the front
counter, who sits in a kind of half-cage, half-desk contraption.
There is a metal detector you have to go through, and a pat-
down. Two of the girls have been here before, because the guard
at the metal detector says their names. *Hi, Raisa. Hi, Trini.*

When you look back, Not-Karen is gone.

They fingerprint you.

They make you sit for hours in a hot room with the other
girls. One by one, you're called out to sit in another hot room,
where you get photographed for an ID, asked questions about
your periods and health and *are you pregnant do you think you could be
pregnant have you ever been pregnant are you currently on medication are you on
drugs are you hiding drugs on your person are you withdrawing from drugs.*

The girl-bug stirs. *You are nothing now.*

They take you to yet another small white room, where a
woman runs her gloved fingers through your hair, your mouth,
your ears, looking for you don't even know what. Then you

strip, and they do even more horrible and embarrassing things in embarrassing places, and if you didn't feel like nothing before, you do now.

They give you a beige jumpsuit with a front zipper and plain slip-on sneakers, three pairs of underwear, two flimsy bras, and wait while you hand over the dress and change. You ask, *Will I get my dress back?* and the guard says, *You've got other worries now, girl.*

Another guard shows you your bunk in a huge room filled with bunks. They assign you to a sour-faced girl named Wee-Wee with lots of holes in her ears and she walks you around an entire building filled with sour-faced girls, pointing out the showers, the nurses' office, the psych office, the dining hall, the TV room, the tiny library. "Don't even try to get in to see the psych," she says. "The line is always too long. Better off seeing the nurse. At least you get to lay down and stuff. Take a load off.

"We got classes," she says. "Like if you're here a while. Math and stuff."

Bored, she ticks off her fingers what will get you demerits, what will keep you "in good." She looks around covertly and then leans close. She smells like old milk and pudding. Then she pinches your arm very hard, says, "Dig? That's as nice as I'm gonna get," and walks away.

You sit in your bunk trying not to cry, because you've seen television shows about prisons, which is the closest thing to where you are now, and you know what happens to people who show weakness. You wish you had the superpower to become invisible *right now.*

The beige jumpsuit is itchy. The shoes are too big. The bra is too thin and doesn't have underwire, so your boobs feel loose and uncomfortable.

You choke back tears, because no one should see you cry, here.

You wonder how you got from *there* to *here*. From a mom to none. From a friend named Cake to a girl named Wee-Wee. From ashes to darkness to ashes to foster to kid prison.

In a little while, you get up and walk to the library, because it's the only place you remember how to get to. You don't make eye contact with anyone. You stay there, in the stacks, holding yourself, trying to cry without making a sound. The smell of books is familiar, and makes you feel better, but not much.

Not much at all.

You wish like hell your mother would come to get you.

## 32 days, 15 hours

THE JUVENILE DETENTION CENTER is called Ignacio Ortiz Girls' Rehabilitation Center. I stay in the library the first morning I get there until a bell rings and another girl in the stacks looks at me and says, "Lunch. Can't be late. Get a demerit."

I follow her and just do everything she does. Show my ID card, get a tray, join the line, drink some weak Kool-Aid, nibble a cracker, wonder where my bloody dress is, and listen to the noise around me, girls chattering, shouting.

At another table, a girl jostles another girl with her elbow and the other girl stands up and slaps her across the head. The other girl shrinks away.

I move my elbows closer to my body.

There are guards, even though we are just kids. Guards walking slowly up and down the cafeteria aisles, faces set, eyes bored.

The Wee-Wee girl is down the table. She eats methodically: crackers first, sip of Kool-Aid, scoops of pudding, then the white-bread-mayonnaise-yellow-cheese sandwich.

It's pretty much like the school cafeteria, only some of us, I have a hunch, have stolen cars or punched our parents or stolen stuff from a store or maybe even worse things.

I don't want to know what those things are.

There are so many of us who've done something wrong.

There are probably a lot of broken-back stories in this place, too.

A bell rings and everyone stands up suddenly, trays clattering. Another line to put your tray in a bin, drop your utensils in a bucket.

I don't know where to go. Girls push into me, shove me out of the way, and Wee-Wee appears, exasperated. "What's wrong with you? Just *move*. You want to get hit?" she grumbles, taking my elbow and leading me out of the rushing pack of girls. "It's like school. We do something different every hour, okay?"

She takes me to a kind of gym, with rows and rows of girls doing jumping jacks. Touching their toes, reaching for the sky.

A burly man stands at the front, dressed in sweats. He blows his whistle at us. "Front of the line, ladies, if you get here late," and Wee-Wee groans, because now we have to be in front of everyone else, and I guess she likes the back, where no one can see your butt.

It hurts to do the exercises, because my body is sore from the accident.

She takes me to a class. "Health," she whispers.

We watch a video about taking care of your baby. The lady in the video holds a supremely fake-looking baby. It's a White baby and the Black girls in the room laugh. *That's not MY baby,* they shout.

The lady in the video shakes the fake baby. *Never shake your baby.*

She puts the fake baby in a giant bed and climbs in next to the fake baby. She pretends to fall asleep and roll over on the fake baby. *Never put your baby in a bed. Put your baby in a crib.*

She holds the baby with one hand, under her arm, and lights

365

a cigarette with the other and blows smoke and watches television. *Don't smoke around your baby.*

One girl waves her hand dismissively. "Shit, my daddy and mama smoked up around me all the time and I turned out just fine." She laughs and high-fives with another girl.

The lady holds a bottle of soda to the baby's fake plastic mouth. *Babies need breast milk or formula, not sugary drinks.*

Some of the girls cry. Wee-Wee whispers, "They miss their little ones."

"Where are their little ones?" I whisper back.

Wee-Wee shrugs. "Not here."

After dinner, I sit with Wee-Wee at the back of the rec room. The girls watch *Chopped* on a television hung high up on a wall. It's behind a cage.

Someone switches the channel to local news. "My auntie bought lottery this week. I wanna see the numbers."

And suddenly there I am.

*Mesa Luna Teens' Ice Cream Truck Spree.* "Two teens decided to . . . almost turned deadly . . . damage to home owner's property included . . ."

I can't even breathe. They don't show our photos or say our names, but they show photos of the busted mailbox that I ran over, a fence I flattened, and the Jellymobile, whose front is crushed beyond repair, and everyone in Mesa Luna knows that truck, so now they all know what happened. Or part of it. Probably.

#girlfelon #orphandelinquent #jellythief

My mother would be so upset, if she knew. If she could see this.

I went from regular kid to full-blown criminal in a little over a month.

I go back to my bunk. I'm afraid to turn on my side, so I stay on my back. I have to go to the bathroom so badly, but I'm afraid to. I try to be as still as possible so I don't jostle all the pee in my body.

No one talks to me. Girls buzz around, change into sweat-pants and T-shirts, brush and braid hair. At a certain point, a kind of alarm sounds and the ceiling lights shut off, all at once.

The girl on the top bunk leans down. She has large dark eyes. She says, "Don't let the bedbugs bite," takes out her wad of gum, sticks it on the underside of her bed.

I spend a lot of time that night staring at all the lumps of gum.

## 34 days, 10 hours

Two DAYS LATER, A guard comes to get me out of bed. "You got a hearing," she says. "Judge time."

The bathrooms are scary here, so I've been holding my pee at night. I can't hold it anymore and she lets me duck into the bathroom. There are curtains and not doors on the stalls. I have to wait in line, but I keep my elbows close to my body and my eyes down on the damp tile floor. Everything stinks.

Another guard drives me and five other girls to a courthouse in a van.

Not-Karen meets us in the lobby and takes us through the metal detector. The courtroom doesn't look like what I've seen on TV. It isn't stately, like in those fancy law shows. In fact, it's kind of dumpy. It's long benches and some tables and a tall, plain desk for the judge. It looks like a place you go to give blood or something.

Not-Karen takes my elbow and leads me to the front of the room. The judge asks me if I am Grace Maria Tolliver and I say, "Yes, that's me." She pages briskly through a file of my crimes and looks at me sternly.

She has a voice like her throat is full of gravel. "What's gotten into you? Where are you going? You are headed down a dangerous path, young lady. You could have *killed* someone. That's no joke, do you understand me?"

When she says that, I think of my dad. I guess I truly am

his daughter now. Maybe all his weaknesses thread through me, too. It isn't just a DNA coincidence of avocados and comedy. There's malice and stupidity and a whole lot of other shit, too, I guess.

The judge says things like *pending appointment of counsel, pending family services investigation, until such time as placement can be determined, until adjudication.*

Not-Karen says things like *mother's death, no priors, clean record. Bereavement.* But she sounds almost bored, like she doesn't care, and I guess, really, why should she? She'll probably see fifty other kids like me this week. Maybe even just today.

*Returned to the juvenile facility until counsel . . .*

My eyes blur.

I'm disappearing.

Not-Karen sighs and closes her folder.

The judge asks me if I understand, and even though I don't, I nod that I do, because nothing even matters anymore.

T HE GIRL THEY CALL Wee-Wee looks nervous and that makes you nervous.

She's in the hallway after you get processed and the guard sends you through the door. You are supposed to follow the schedule now, a piece of paper handed to you, a list of things you need to accomplish if you want to use the phone, take out books from the library, have a visitor.

*Remanded to*

*For a period of*

*Until such a time as*

You feel cold, so cold inside, like your heart has been wrapped in cloth very tightly.

Wee-Wee motions to you. She shakes her head.

Her voice is urgent as she pulls you closer, her breath hot in your ear. You can barely understand her.

*Just drop. Cover your head. Don't scream. Curl up tight.*

She keeps looking back at the double doors, the ones that lead to the dorms, where all our bunks are. Suddenly, there is shouting and screaming behind the doors.

You say, *Wha—*

But there isn't any finishing because the doors burst open and a stampede of girls appears, followed by fierce-faced guards, and Wee-Wee is pulling you down to the ground.

*Cover your head. Don't scream. Curl up tight.*

A horde of girls stomp over you and Wee-Wee, kicking and punching as they move to the front doors of the hallway, the ones that lead to the lobby. Alarms begin to sound as they break through.

Shoes in your face, against your cheek, down the length of your back.

You can feel so many things being crushed down in you.

Just like in the hospital, the night your mother died, you think, *This can't be happening.*

But it is.

Next to you on the floor, Wee-Wee's eyes are leaking. Her lips shake.

*Effluviam,* you think. *Maraschino.*

Out loud, you whisper, *Perpendicular. Entropy. Magnolia.*

Wee-Wee stares at you, shoes whizzing by her face. *What are you doing?*

*Ampersand. Sussuration.*

Wee-Wee whispers, *Lava. Sara Lee.*

The lights go out but the alarms stay on, and the words keep coming, from both of you, long into the night.

## 40 days

THIS TIME, IT IS Karen who picks me up. She's waiting for me after I come out of processing, wearing my blood-stained dress, the stains now washed to a grim, thin pink.

She gives me a sad smile.

"A lot's happened, I guess," she says softly.

I nod.

"Let's go, then."

In Karen's car, she hands me a cold hamburger in plastic wrap and a plastic bottle of soda. "Here, eat. I'll fill you in as we drive."

I hold the soda bottle between my knees. The burger tastes like cardboard, and I can only manage one bite. I lost what was left of my appetite in Ignacio. It didn't seem worth it to eat, after a while. Like Wee-Wee said, the line for the psych was long, and the nurse was often out sick.

After the riot, Wee-Wee said, "Sometimes bad feelings just build up. You'll get used to it. That word thing, that was cool."

I didn't get used to it. But I wondered about the girls who did.

Karen tells me I'm going to a group home for juvenile girls.

"The home is monitored," she tells me. "Most of these girls have been in juvenile detention and this is their first step after leaving. If they complete their stay without any infractions, they can go back to foster, or home, wherever they were before.

Some of the girls might become emancipated. The house leader teaches life skills, like keeping a bank account, getting a part-time job, how to manage schoolwork and emotions. All in all, it's not the worst place you could be."

"When can I see Shayna?" I ask slowly. I'm almost afraid to know. "Did you find her?"

Karen shakes her head. "I don't know, Grace." She pauses. "She's not returning my calls right now, which doesn't help our case. I did see the 911 call report. I wish I'd known that before-hand."

She pauses. "It could be that she's not ready for this. We might have to start investigating other options."

"What does that mean?"

"It means that for right now, the state is your parent. Eat your burger. You don't look so good."

T HERE'S A FEATHER ON the doorstep of the group home. It's gray and white and placed right in the middle of the step, too carefully to be an accident.

Karen and I step around it gingerly. "Pretty," Karen says.

She rings the doorbell. A sign says, *Visitors must have prior approval.* A video camera is mounted above the doorframe.

A smiling, cheerful Black woman opens the door. She sweeps back her hand. "Welcome," she says grandly, like it's a castle.

"I'm Teddy. You must be Grace Tolliver. I hear you prefer Tiger, so Tiger it shall be."

The house is a sprawling brick ranch, six bedrooms, two girls to a bedroom, three bathrooms, with a schedule on the door of shower times for each girl. There's a schedule in the kitchen, too; we help cook each meal. Some girls set the table and clean up. As Teddy walks me around, she explains that the girls like to cook things they remember from home: eggs and toast, baloney sandwiches, macaroni and cheese.

Teddy says, "Nanette makes the best Navajo burger I have *ever* tasted. Her fry bread is to *die* for." She kisses her fingers.

Teddy says, "Children need to learn skills. Cooking, cleaning, schoolwork, simple things to get by. You can cook for yourself, keep a clean house, get good marks in class, those are just little things that make you proud. You don't need a man to make you feel proud of yourself. I teach my girls to take care of themselves. A messy life leads to messy decisions."

There are eleven girls. Teddy passes by a room with a television and I count them, sprawled on the couch, on the floor. Some of them look up at me. Some don't.

This place doesn't seem as grim and gray as Georgia's or as light as LaLa's. But it isn't Ignacio Ortiz, either. Or something way worse.

It's not my home, either, but I'm guessing that's not an option anymore.

It's funny. I feel like I should cry, because this is very bleak, but I can't, because I don't have anything left. I literally have nothing left. I'm just a moveable object, like Leonard and Sarah.

I've become a kid chess piece.

Thaddeus was lucky. He found a home.

Teddy hands me a pile of clothes and tells me to go change. She says, "You start in my house with a clean slate. To me, you are the most wonderful girl who ever lived. You've done nothing wrong, ever. I believe in you."

She leans close. Her breath smells like peppermint tea. "Don't make me a liar. That's all I ask."

I nod and say okay, even though I don't mean it.


I got to the house after dinner, but Teddy made me a plate anyway, and I sit in the kitchen, dressed in too-loose blue jeans and a T-shirt, pushing chicken nuggets and peas around. She sits with me, doing paperwork. She glances up. The other girls are still watching television. *Pretty Little Liars.* Reruns of *Buffy.* Cake really liked those shows.

I wonder what she's doing in Massachusetts, at her music camp. If she even knows what's happened to me.

"You're like my babies were with food, nudging it around your plate. You act like a baby, I'll treat you like a baby. You can leave this table when you eat seven peas, two nuggets, and drink six swallows of milk. You are skin and bones, you know that?"

She pauses. "Do you have issues with food? That I should know about? I didn't see that in your papers."

*Your papers.* Like an animal from the pound. A file. A number. A girl with no face.

"I'm just not hungry," I tell her. "It hurts to eat. I was in a car accident and then there was a riot at the center. I got kind of banged up."

"Yes. And you lost your mama." Teddy breathes in through her nose, deeply. "That's very hard. But she would want you to eat. Your mama would want you to live, do you understand that?"

I eat two peas and nibble a chicken nugget.

"There. That's a start."

She puts her glasses on and looks at the papers again. "Your mama would not want you to be driving drunk down a road in a stolen truck, would she?"

I shake my head.

There are sayings all over the kitchen. On posters. On oven mitts. On coasters on the round table.

*Forget the mistake. Remember the lesson.*

*If it doesn't open, it's not your door.*

*Open your mind, open a book.*

I haven't read a book in what seems like forever.

Teddy says, "Then *don't.* From now on in life, ask yourself,

376

would this make my mama happy? And think real hard about it. Because if the answer is no? *Then don't do it.*"

She takes a sip of her tea. "I should put that on a T-shirt, shouldn't I? Make a million dollars. You can go watch television with the other girls now."

After four days in the group home, I get used to the routine. Every day I do math, English, and spelling at a long table in the basement with the other girls. Teddy tells us, "Even though it's summer and school's out, learning is not over."

Some girls roll their eyes.

There are some girls who seem nice, girls that seem mean, and some girls that are eerily, quietly broken, girls for whom this is going to be the nicest, kindest place they'll ever live.

One girl, Fran, tells me, "The weird thing is how attached everyone gets to Teddy. I mean, girls get let out and reoffend just hoping they'll get sent back here, you know? Fucked up."

Fran is matter-of-fact. She makes the best macaroni and cheese because she uses a lot of butter.

I fold a lot of T-shirts and plain white underwear and blue jeans of all sizes.

We journal in composition books and try not to cry.

I'm moving on autopilot.

Some girls get to make phone calls and I strain to figure out who they might be talking to. A girlfriend or boyfriend? Mom?

Cake is still at music camp. I wonder if I'm allowed to call her, or if she would even talk to me. Maybe I could call Thaddeus.

Teddy tells me I don't have phone privileges yet. Privileges take seven days.

The chart on the wall says you earn your phone calls and "days out." Some girls get to leave the house for two hours in the afternoon. They come back with bags of candy that Teddy spreads out on the table.

"Share and share alike," she says, sliding each of us a candy, one by one.

One day mine is sweet and tart, lemon-flavored, which is my mom's favorite kind of candy flavor, and the taste in my mouth reminds me of her so much I walk away from the table quickly and go into the bathroom, even though it isn't my scheduled time, turn on the sink water, and let the hard yellow drop fall from my mouth. I watch it clatter in the sink, wondering when anything will ever be normal again.

O NE DAY, LONNIE COMES to get me in the study room. "Boy out front," she says briskly. "Teddy says you got ten minutes in the main room."

Thaddeus is sitting on the couch, his hands on his knees, a wall of girls with crossed arms staring at him. Marisela bobs her head up and down. "This your man?" she asks me.

I laugh, not because it's impossible, but because I'm so happy to see him.

Thaddeus shakes his head. "Oh, no, no . . ."

Marisela says, "She's not good enough for you, then? You would be grateful for a girl like her, boy."

Teddy comes in, herding everyone out. "Ten minutes," she says. "And I'll be watching. No body contact."

I sit next to him on the couch. "How did you find me?"

"Karen. I begged her. You look . . . not good."

I shrug. "It's fine."

We look at each other sadly. There's too much to say and not enough time.

"I'm leaving," he says. "I'm going to Phoenix. I got a job at a Best Buy up there."

"Phoenix? But why?" My heart drops.

He takes a breath. "I'm gonna go up there and I'm gonna get custody of my sister. I have to have a steady job, a place to live, take parenting classes. And then I'm gonna file for custody.

I'll get it. My mom'll give her up. She's too far gone. I can tell you right now when I move there, she'll start leaving Jax with me so she can go score and then . . . she just won't come back one day."

He starts to cry, which scares me, because he's *Thaddeus*.

We can't touch, and even if we could, I still remember what he told me about being touched, that because he was beaten, it's hard for him. His shoulders shake.

"That's really good," I say, trying to be positive. "That's awesome and perfect."

He nods, swipes at his cheeks. "Yeah, and after that, I'm going for Leonard. I know where he is, I found out. It's not great. I can do this. That's what I keep telling myself, anyway."

I look at the doorway. No Teddy.

I slide one hand across the couch cushion.

Thaddeus looks down.

He slides his hand across the cushion until just the tips of our fingers are touching.

## 53 days, 12 hours

W HEN TEDDY TELLS ME I'm leaving, I assume I'm going to another house, probably the first in a series of houses, until the day I turn eighteen, when I'll be thrust out into the world, friendless and penniless, like all the girls here talk about. "You're just shit out of luck at that point," Marisela had said once. "Out on your ass."

Cake and Thaddeus will be just a dream. My sister and dad will fade into the background.

I don't even say anything, just nod. I'm a blank slate at this point, bereft and lonely. I'll go wherever they tell me to go.

She points to my clothes. "You can keep those. That dress you came in with? My God, that dress oozed pain. I could barely hold it, Tiger. Whatever the story is behind that dress? You are ready to write 'the end,' my girl."

She looks at the wrecked dress in her hands. "How long did you wear this tattered thing?"

"I can't remember now," I mumble.

"What on earth would make you do that, Grace?"

I don't know how to say it. It all seems far away now, why I didn't take the dress off. "She wanted me to," I manage.

"Who?" Teddy's voice is gentle, but insistent.

"My mom. She bought it for me . . . before she died. And I hated it."

Teddy frowns. "It's okay not to like the clothes your mama picks out for you. That's a story as old as time."

As long as I live, I'll always think that I *must* finally be cried out, and as long as I live, I'll always be surprised that somewhere inside me, more tears are being manufactured, because here they come, splashing on the lap of my jeans.

"I fought with her. I said I wanted her to just leave me alone. And then she did. The very last thing she heard from me was horrible. Can you imagine?"

My voice cracks.

"And the last thing she wanted me to do was to wear this dress. So I did."

Teddy is quiet for a long time. I can hear sounds from the television down in the next room. The show Shayna liked. *Chung, chung.*

Teddy's voice is soft. "Tiger, the last thing your mama probably wished for you was to be happy. Not to wear a dress until it's falling off you. Not to hurt yourself in her memory, and to lash out at others. No mother wants that."

She holds the dress to her chest.

"You don't honor your mother by wearing a dress, honey. You honor your mother by remembering her, and holding her dear, right here." She taps her heart.

I ask her if I can have it, though, and she wraps it in a bag and gives it to me.

I don't think I am going to wear it again, but I don't want to treat it like it's nothing, either. I don't want it to end up in a box on the side of the road, a pink-stained curiosity for a stranger.

The phone on her desk rings. She picks it up. "Yes," she says, her eyes grazing over me. "Yes, she's coming right out." She hangs up.

"It's time," she tells me.

I walk slowly behind her, not looking forward to another long car ride with Karen, who will deliver me to yet another house. Maybe I will end up with Brownie and Blondie again, way out in the middle of nowhere with Georgia and her late-night prayers and boiled meat.

When Teddy opens the door, the sunshine catches my eyes, and I close them briefly against the brightness.

When I open them, Shayna is standing at the curb, next to a black car I don't recognize.

"Come on, you," she calls out. "I'm starving. I'd let you drive, but that's not allowed for the next year, you stinking criminal."

She grins.

"Thank you," I say softly to Teddy.

I start to cry.

Teddy nudges my back. "You be a good girl, all right? Remember what I said."

I step over the feather carefully on my way down the steps.

My sister hugs me long and hard. "You didn't think I was just gonna up and leave you, did you? Nah," she says. "I'm in it to win it, Tiger."

Just before I get in the car, I turn back to Teddy. "I forgot to ask, what's the feather for?"

She smiles at me. "Blessings. All who come and go from

this house receive blessings on their life. This feather can change things."

She puts her hand on the doorknob of the house.

"Really?" I ask.

Teddy shrugs. "Sometimes you need to open yourself to the possibility of the miraculous, Tiger Tolliver. Sometimes you just do."

## 53 days, 14 hours

OVER GREASY HAMBURGERS AND too-salty French fries at the Triple T Truck Stop , my sister tells me everything.

"I'm an alcoholic." She gives me a sad smile "That's where I would go at night when I went out. To meetings. I realize now I should have told you right away, but I was afraid you wouldn't have any faith in me. Does that make sense? I mean, your mom died, do you really want an unreliable alkie coming to take care of you? I kind of know how that feels, after all."

She wipes her hands on her napkin. The truck stop diner is too cold from the air conditioning, and goosebumps prickle up and down her arms.

"I was sober for almost six months," she says softly. "And Ray, you could see, he's *not.* And when Karen called me about you, and then my dad, and he told me to come to you, that whole 'blood is blood' thing? It's weird, but I thought, this is my *chance.* This is fate. This is a reason for me to *be.* I have a purpose now, you know?"

She shreds a paper napkin.

"It was hard, being the only one with my parents. Taking care of my dad, watching my mom fall apart. And, like, now the universe was giving me a sister, you know?

"Anyway. *Ray.* I tried to leave him there, in Hawaii, but he found me. It's why I went to Utah, to try and throw him off the scent. But a friend of a friend told him where I was headed."

Her face has turned pink and her eyes well up.

"It's why I called you, about the road trip. I was going to make us run. I knew he was on his way. I thought I had time, but he was . . . he was farther along than I thought."

She starts to cry.

"What Ray said was true. I did have an abortion. And I don't regret it. Not at all. Because not only would I never have a baby with someone like Ray, I'm not ready to be a parent. And that was one hundred percent the absolute right thing for me to do."

I stare at her, hurt. She takes my hand.

"But that doesn't mean I'm not ready to be a *sister,* okay? Does that make sense? We can do this, together. I know we can. I *want* to."

"Does he . . . did he . . . hit you? That day?" The words feel thick coming out of my mouth. I'm scared to hear the answer.

She looks at me for a long time before answering. "He has, and he did. But someone called 911. I pressed charges. He's not going to bother us again. Please believe me."

"That was me," I whisper. "That night. I did. I'm sorry I left you."

Shayna's lips shake. "It's okay. That's why I told you to run. So he wouldn't hurt you."

"Okay." I take a sip of Coke. "Are they going to let me stay with you?"

"Yes, but we have a lot of work to do. I've been busy for the last couple of weeks." She takes a deep breath.

"I went to Tucson, and I rented us a house. I got some money from my mom and my . . . well, *our* grandparents. Dad's parents."

She pauses. "They're excited to meet you, by the way. They're a little sick, and old, but very sweet."

"We're moving? For real?"

"I can't make a living in Mesa Luna, Tiger. And I think we need a fresh place, a place for just you and me, you know?"

I nod.

"But I have some ideas. I've been meeting with Louise and Mary about the alpacas and the jams, and I think if we're careful, and make a good plan, it'll work. Obviously, the Jellymobile is inoperable, but I think we can join forces with Louise and Mary and sell our stuff together, on the Internet. A virtual store. Alpaca mittens and scarves, jams and jellies, you name it. We might have to learn some shearing and knitting, and you'll have to teach me your mom's jam secrets, but we're resourceful girls, we can do it, right?"

"Wow," I say. My brain is feeling a little overloaded. "That's a lot."

"I know. But you know what? We've already *had* a lot this summer. From now on, I feel like everything is going to be easy-peasy. I got a job in Tucson. Waiting tables. Grandpa Al's going to help out a little. I might go back to school next year. I was thinking of nursing. Which reminds me."

She digs into her backpack and brings out two books.

"I know I can never be a parent-parent to you. I can't be your mom. Your mom is always your mom, you know? And I didn't have the best role models growing up. But I'm going to do better. I swear. Look, I've already started studying."

She holds up *Parenting for Dummies* and *How to Raise a Teenager.*

I laugh. "Seriously?"

"Totally. There's good stuff in here! Like, I have to register you for your new school. And I think you might need shots, like immunizations. I'm not sure. I kind of skimmed that chapter.

And there's all sorts of stuff about college and savings accounts and peer pressure and sex. For the sex part I'll just rely on the wisdom of Tami Taylor in *Friday Night Lights*." She shrugs.

I suddenly feel overwhelmed. Grandparents. Moving.

After a lifetime of just my mother, it seems like I have more family than I ever thought possible.

The burger is sticking in my throat a little.

Shayna says, "There's more. Are you ready?"

"I don't know if I can take any more."

"Try. As per conditions of your release, you can't get a license or drive a car for a year. You have to do drug tests once a month, join another grief group, attend teen AA, and you have to write letters of apology to Walrus Jackson, because it was his mailbox you totaled, *and* the dude who owned that ugly lawn ornament, *and* you have to do two weeks of community service with that Lupe girl. Got it?"

Shayna reaches out her hand. We shake.

Her hand is warm in mine and her smile is hopeful.

I have lived through more than I ever thought possible in two months and come out the other side. It doesn't feel bad. It doesn't suck. It feels scary. But it feels doable.

It almost feels *right*.

I'll never not be sad. I'll never not be a girl without a mother. I'll never not have a ludicrously big hole in my heart.

But I am a girl with a sister now, and a chance, and I have to take it. I want to take it.

"Okay," I say.

"Egg-cellent," she says. "Now, let's finish dinner. I'm starving and we have a lot of packing to do."

## 60 days, 14 hours

IT'S SORT OF LIKE that poem: I thought I was done with death, at least a little bit, but death wasn't done with me.

I thought I was done with the details of grief, like viewings, and services, and caskets and songs to say goodbye, and which clothes to keep and which to give away. I've started packing for a new life in a new city. I shouldn't have any more last details.

But it's Cake, back from music camp, shyly sitting on my bed next to Mae-Lynn, as I fold and box clothes and throw out odds and ends, who reminds me that I've never written my mother's obituary.

Mae-Lynn nods. "You have to do it."

On Monday, Cake drives the three of us to the office of the *Arizona Daily Star* in Tucson. Mesa Luna has a paper, but it's a weekly, not a daily, and Cake feels sure we should do this properly.

"After all," she says, "this is like a public statement of love. On the record, for everyone to see."

In the parking lot, she says, "I'm coming with and don't argue."

"Me too," says Mae-Lynn.

Inside the *Daily Star* office, the secretary punts us to an older woman at a messy desk in the corner. "Esme!" she calls out. "We have an obit."

Esme looks surprised to see the three of us. "We usually do this online." She puts on her glasses, which rest on a shiny silver chain around her neck. "But here, have a seat."

She has to get up, though, and move a mound of newspapers off a series of chairs to make room for us.

I hand her the piece of paper I carefully typed up the night before and then printed out at the library at Eugene Field. Walrus Jackson let me use it.

He said, "I really like my new mailbox. It's very roomy."

Esme starts reading. She taps each word with a pencil.

"This is really nice," she says. "Did you write it? I'm impressed."

Cake says, "She likes words. She's a good writer."

Esme says, "I see that."

She punches out some numbers on an old-fashioned calculator, the kind with paper on a roll. It makes a sound like *chugga ehhh, chugga ehhh.*

"We charge by the word. Here's what your total would be."

My stomach sinks when I see the number. It's way more than I had saved from selling jam. My eyes fill with tears. How can it be so expensive to place an obituary? It should be free, practically, because it's *the last thing,* right?

Mae-Lynn makes a startled noise over my shoulder. "That's a lot."

I shake my head. "I don't have that," I tell Esme. "Maybe we could edit it, a little? Here's all I have. What can that get me?"

Esme takes the envelope from me and counts out my money. When she's done, she chews on her pencil for a minute. "I can work with this, because these are good words. Good sentiment. You'll definitely be a writer someday, yes?"

"No!" I say, embarrassed. "I don't think so."

"She will," says Cake.

"Listen to your friend. She's a smart woman," Esme murmurs.

She starts crossing things out.

As she edits, she says, "I've been doing this for quite some time and you know what? It's a shame that it costs so much to tell the whole world that someone you love mattered to you, it really is. And I know we want to put every little thing in here because we want to show such a good, full life, don't we? Even if it was a short one."

She draws lines through some sentences on the paper and erases others. "But sometimes . . ."

She gazes down, crosses out more words. "What's really important is the *essence* of the life lived. A college degree isn't going to tell me how well somebody lived, now is it? Does having a boat mean you lived a good life? Or a summerhouse? What about saving each valentine your son made or even working a roadside jam stand? A million, what do they call it?—selfies—on some silly website. What does it all mean, in the end?"

She says, "I knew your mom. Every year I buy five jars of prickly pear jelly and send them to my grandkids for Christmas. They live in Memphis, of all places. Go figure. And they are crazy for that jam."

"We still make it," I say. "I mean, me and my sister. It's going online. JunesJamsdotcom."

"Glad to hear it."

She pushes the paper back to me. I read it.

"Are you sure?" I ask. I'm trying hard not to cry, but then I think better of it. Like hospitals, maybe the people who work the obituary section at newspapers are used to tears, so what does it matter?

She nods. "Not to toot my own horn, but I think that's the loveliest thing I've read in nineteen years of this job. Now, do you have a photo I can scan? We have a charge for that, too, but I'll give you our special prickly pear discount. It's only good for—" She peeks over her glasses at the clock on the wall. "Two more minutes. Lucky you."

I slip the photo from my backpack. I'd stored it carefully between two pieces of cardboard, so that it wouldn't bend.

Esme examines the photo. She peers at me over her glasses again.

"Well," she says. "Wasn't your mother a lovely young girl."

She closes her eyes. "Your mother made a damn fine jam."

"She did," says Cake. She's crying a little. So is Mae-Lynn.

Esme dips her head, as if in remembrance, and so do I.

H ERE IS A SHORT list of the things you will wear and find when you are performing community service with Lupe Hidalgo, or perhaps some other person, on the side of a road for two hours:

A bright orange vest that makes you look like a deflated pumpkin.

Heavy work gloves.

A brimmed hat and reflective sunglasses, provided by the County Detention Center, that kind of make you look like a covert operative *or* a drug dealer, and which, you are sad to say, kind of make you feel cool and important and mysterious, which is good, because:

You will pick up some disgusting stuff.

There will be the usual smashed beer cans, tossed from cars. Some of these will still be a little full and you should know that beer in cans in 115-degree heat smells like the worst possible pee ever, so don't spill it on yourself. Assume every can is loaded.

There will be cigarette butts, some lipsticked, some not. They, too, smell horrible in the heat.

There will be odd papers, Post-it notes with strange scribbles.

Candy wrappers.

There will be ID cards, like driver's licenses and debit cards and EBT cards, strewn in a kind of line along the road, which makes you think of the mystery of how they got there. Lupe is interested, too, and whispers, "Bet there's bodies out here they haven't even found yet," and raises her eyebrows. That makes you shiver, but the foreman glares at you, so you keep spearing cigarette butts with the stick.

There will be underwear. Also disgusting.

There will be diapers. See above. These are difficult to pick up properly if they are fairly fresh, and you never want to think of it again.

There will be makeup, pens, lone shoes, socks, hats, needles. And packets of what might be drugs, which have to go to the foreman immediately.

Sometimes, there are animals, but you aren't allowed to touch them. The foreman has to call animal control.

"Disease, yo," says Lupe knowingly, leaning on her pincher. Lupe is working hard to keep her scholarship. She wrote letters of apology to Mr. Jackson, the owner of the lawn ornament, the neighbors along the path the Jellymobile traveled. You go to teen AA meetings together that meet in Sierra Vista and you're surprised who else is there, but you keep it quiet.

Lupe says, "Not my business. Not yours. Move forward, Tolliver, not back." After the meetings, you go to Los Betos and gobble tacos. You swear you'll never drink again. You like Lupe now, her humor and her hardness, her big heart and big mouth.

When she gets to the University of Arizona this fall, you're going to meet up at the student union for coffee once a week. You made a promise. Your new house isn't far from the university, just a bus ride and a short walk.

## 64 days, 16 hours

O NE DAY, LUPE DROPS me off at my house and I'm tired and thirsty and sweaty and annoyed, and not looking forward to packing more boxes, choosing one memory of my mother over another.

My sister is waiting inside, and she has a very serious look on her face.

I drop my ugly city-issued hat on the floor and grunt, "What? What did I do now?"

She answers, "Go shower. Dad's calling you. In exactly twenty-three minutes."

I stare at her, my heart soaring and falling all at once. Her face softens. "Hurry. He only gets ten minutes."

My heart thud-thud-thuds like a hammer in my chest all the time I'm in the shower. I pull on my clothes, nice ones, simple stuff. Tank top, shiny basketball shorts that feel great, and comfortable. Shayna got them when she went to Tucson to get the utility stuff straightened out and to open a checking account. She stopped at the mall on a whim, she told me.

"Next time," she'd promised, "when we're there and settled, you'll come with me. School clothes, right? Probably not all at the mall, because that's pretty expensive, but I found some good thrift stores. But you can pick your clothes yourself, okay?"

I wait by her phone. She's discreet, staying in the bedroom, cruising her laptop.

The phone rings. A nasally voice says, "You have a call from the Springer County Correctional Facility. Will you accept the call?"

I say, breathlessly, "Yes," just like Shayna told me to.

Dusty Franklin says, "Hey, Grace."

My *dad*.

*My goddamn dad*.

I say, "Hi."

There's a big pause.

He says, "I'm sorry about your mom."

He says, "It's all real hard to talk about, you know?"

"I know."

"I'm sorry about everything. Grace. That's a pretty name. Your mom had a good way with words, you know?"

"I know." My hands are shaking so badly the phone is knocking against my cheek. There's so much to ask, but I don't know where to start, or what to ask, exactly, and we only have these few minutes.

"I hear you're a reader. Your mom was a big reader, too. Me too. I read a lot in here."

"Yeah."

Silence.

"You used to be a teacher," I say.

"I did. I was good at it, too, until I wasn't." He pauses. "Things get away from you sometimes, and you can't get them back."

I don't know what to say about that.

The silence is hard. It almost hurts.

"Will you tell me about her sometime? Can I . . . can I talk to you again?" I ask.

His voice is gruff. I think he might be crying.

"I would like it if you'd call me, Grace. I'd like that very much. I can tell you some things you should know. Yes."

A voice cuts in. *Two minutes.*

I blurt out, "Tell me, Richard Pryor or George Carlin? Kiwi or avocado?"

And he's off. His voice brightens. He says "Oh boy, that's not hard for me. I mean, Pryor, all the way, am I right? I love Carlin, he's so bright and angry and spot-on, but something about Pryor was so intense, you know? Especially after the burning thing. And don't get me started. Avocado all the way. Kiwi is an aberration."

He takes a breath. "How do you know all that stuff, anyway? The comedians. You're way too young for them."

"I don't know. I guess it's just in my blood."

He laughs, but it's kind of sad sounding.

"I've got to go, Grace."

"Okay."

"You take care."

"You too."

The line cuts out.

I know he's done bad things. Hurt people. Messed up a lot. But that doesn't mean he doesn't matter to me, to the puzzle of my life. He has a place somewhere with me and within me, he's a piece.

My sister comes out of the bedroom.

"All good?" she asks.

"All good," I answer. "It's all good."

O N THE DAY SHAYNA and I are finishing up the packing for the move to the new house, I find The Video.

Bonita thought it might be a letter, one on crinkled paper, that my mom would leave me. A letter Cake scoured the closet for.

But it's not anything like that, at all.

Shayna's out to Cucaracha for carne asada burritos and Cokes and she left me in charge of cleanup. The moving company, or, as Shayna prefers to call them, "the Three Amigos also known as Grunyon, Boots, and Chunk," are set to arrive any minute, ready to bumble around, break our lamps, bend our curtain rods, drop boxes and shatter plates, and mostly destroy whatever else we own while shoving it in a truck Grunyon bought on Craigslist, determined to start his own business.

What they don't kill putting in the truck will surely die a thousand deaths on the trip to Tucson, where our meager belongings will be installed in a corner adobe of a six-unit courtyard in a run-down neighborhood near a Pep Boys, a bowling alley, and a bar called the Bashful Bandit.

At that very moment, Cake and Thaddeus and Mae-Lynn are in the adobe house, scrubbing toilets and cabinets and doing some last-minute painting.

Cake has declared the house "cute as all get-out and I can't wait to stay over and go thrift shopping on Fourth Avenue with you!"

I stand in the front room, boxes piled against the wall, broom in my hand. Mr. Pacheco certainly isn't going to give us our deposit back, I'm sure of that, so I'm not entirely set on how much cleaning I really want to do. The little pine kitchen table is piled high with boxes; my bed's been taken apart and the mattress and frame are leaning against the wall.

This leaves the couch. The last thing in this world—in our house, anyway—that held the body of my mother.

We aren't taking the couch. Shayna and I haven't discussed it, exactly, but after she signed the lease on the house and took an inventory of what things we'd need to get at thrift stores and on Craigslist, and what we should leave behind, she casually said, like it was no big deal, "The new place has a pretty big living room—I mean, compared to this one—with one of those round fireplaces, what are those called, the cute ones—"

"Kivas," I'd said. I'd been stacking books, sorting ones to go to the Bookmobile. Rhonda was going to drive the bus now. Cake would be her assistant.

"Yeah. So, I was thinking, maybe a sectional? You could have space to stretch out, and I could have space? All at the same time? I mean, I think you're cool and all, but I don't want you on my lap."

And as casually as she said her part, I said mine.

"That sounds good. Perfect. Roomy."

I heard her breathe a sigh of relief as she crumpled a package of Little Debbies and went on sorting dishes and cups. I didn't know if she could hear my sigh, too.

I'm glad to leave the couch. I'm glad to move, to be honest.

I take a deep breath and push aside the couch my mother died on to sweep beneath it, and that's when I find her cellphone.

The one we haven't been able to find all summer. The one I keep leaving voice mails on, because I'm lonely, and want to hear her voice.

I sink down to my knees, my heart in my throat.

I scoop the phone up in my hands and scramble around my backpack for my charger. I practically stand above it, willing it to charge faster. I mean, I don't know what I'm looking for, maybe I just want to see her photos, or our texts, or something, but as soon as I start scrolling the gallery, there it is.

She didn't write me a letter telling me everything she'd kept from me. She made a video. And there it is, plain as day, the only video on her phone. And when I press the white arrow, my mother floods back to life.

*Hi, Gracie,* she says, and my whole world shivers and splits.

There she is, my pretty mom, her spiky blond-and-gray hair, her pink cheeks that always got pinker when she was upset. She'd propped the phone up on something in the red kitchen and was sitting on one of the barstools. I can tell by the cookbooks behind her on the kitchen counter.

My mother takes a big breath and her eyes get really wet and she says, "Baby. Tiger. If you're watching this, I'm gone. And if I'm not gone, and you are watching this, you have a very, very macabre sense of humor, my dear girl."

She says, "Before I start, I need you to know, wherever I am, I am *with* you, Gracie, I promise you. I will always be right next to you, even if you can't see me, okay?"

I feel the way characters do in fantasy books and movies.

Like when tremendously powerful forces move through them. Like, giant lightning storms or thunder clouds of electricity or power, or something like that, whips through the person, momentarily paralyzing them, and then when it's done, they fall to the ground, hollowed out, and usually another character rushes in to find them, and picks them up, and takes care of them, and looks all around, like, *What the hay just happened?*

That is happening to me.

I *am* paralyzed, watching my mother, hearing her voice, her words thundering through me, a great and powerful force filling the comically huge hole in my heart.

My mother has been gone for exactly 94,620 minutes, and yet she's been *right here* all along.

And then something else happens.

Teddy said at the group home that sometimes you have to open your heart to the miraculous.

When I reach a trembling finger to touch my mother's face as she talks to me from the past, the screen kind of *ripples,* and she pauses, smiling in an amused way, and moves her head just so, right at the moment when my finger touches her cheek on the screen.

Like she can feel it.

She says, in an entirely different voice than moments before, a voice that sounds like she is right here in the room, and not 109,270 minutes in the past on a cellphone video, *Hey, you.*

Like she's *here.*

The life in her voice races through me.

And the whole force of touching my mother, and seeing her eyes glisten as she feels *me,* too, rips through me, and I crumple to the floor, carved out by the universe and my sorrow and this whole new world that Mae-Lynn calls Grief Life, in which I can touch my dead mother through a cellphone *and she feels it.*

That's where my sister finds me, the video still going. She drops the sack of burritos and sinks down next to me, feeling my head for blood or a fever, breathlessly asking me what's happened, until she sees the video, my mother's voice a tinny, ethereal thing, still talking, as she tells me everything I ever wanted to know and they are so many words filled with pain.

*Died when I was eleven, not in college. Nobody wanted me. Passed around relatives for years. Just a shoebox and a suitcase.*

*Never rode a horse again. Never wanted to lose you. Had to keep you close.*

My sister says, "Oh. June."

She turns off the video and wipes away my tears. She pats my back and hugs me as I sob so hard I think my ribs might break.

I will never be able to tell her my mother was alive again, for just one moment. She'll never believe me. But that's okay.

My sister says, "It's too much, honey."

And she's right.

Sometimes you're so hungry, so thirsty for something to fill you up, you've craved it for so long, but when you finally have it, it hurts going down. It's not a medicine for what ails you. It might just be the thing that is keeping you sick.

All the things I wanted to know about my mother are right here, and I'm not ready.

Shayna says, "I'm here, Tiger. I love you. I'm gonna take care of you, okay?"

And then she tugs on my hair gently and says, "Come on, kid. Let's get out of here. Let's go home."

*Now*

O N THURSDAY NIGHTS, I sit with twenty-six other people in the basement of Our Lady of Guadalupe Church. I'm writing this, *this,* well, whatever it is, or will be, I guess a *primer,* because the woman who runs our grief group says we need to find outlets for our sadness. Our grief. Our ghostly feelings.

So I'm filling composition books, one so far, with things I want to remember.

Twenty-seven of us sit in the basement of Our Lady of Guadalupe, twice a month, on hard and squeaky chairs, clutching teddy bears.

Lupe Hidalgo comes with me. I still don't know the whole story of her brother, Crash, or what led to his suicide, but one thing I have learned from this group is that people need time to say what they need to say.

When people die, it's like they kind of take your ability to form words with them. You come up empty a lot of the time.

The very first meeting we had, the leader, Felice, asked us, "What would you say to your loved one, if you had just one more chance, just one?"

The basement of Our Lady was dim. The bulbs in the ceiling lights needed replacing. The children's chairs for Sunday school were stacked in the corner. Plastic bowling pins and balls spread across the floor. I didn't know what they were for, exactly. Were we supposed to bowl for salvation? I was still a little confused by my new life, to be honest, and sometimes, frankly, my thoughts drifted.

Lupe and I are the youngest people in the group. There are people who've been going here for years, who've lost more than one person, which I can't imagine surviving, then or now, because after someone dies, what more do you even have left inside? What more can possibly be taken from you?

I mean, *for God's sake.* Come *on.*

Some people started to cry after Felice asked her question and some people ducked their heads over cardboard cups of coffee or tea. It was always someone's job to bring the coffee and tea. A platter of tiny and sugary cookies. I was still new, so I hadn't had a turn yet.

People murmured, *I forgive you.*

They whispered, *I love you.*

They said, *You don't have to worry about me.*

My fingers trembled in my teddy bear's fur. I always picked the same one: a grungy-looking brown thing who was missing one eye and had lost a leg. Where the leg was, there was just a tiny patch of denim.

The last thing I said before they took me away from my mother was this: *Please come back. Please don't leave me.* I will always remember that.

I didn't say this out loud in the group, though. At that time, I hadn't said anything yet. Felice told me that was okay, too. "Words come when words come," she said with a shrug.

There was a silence and then Alice, the oldest person in the room, cleared her throat. Alice has watery eyes and fluffy white hair and favors sweatpants and sweatshirts with glittery stars and flowers. Alice lost her mother when she was ten. That is a whole lifetime without a mother, to get used to not having a mother, and yet here she is. All these years later. Still grieving.

Alice said, "Write me a letter telling me how to live for the rest of my life without you." She paused.

"That was sixty-four years ago, and I still would like to know."

I'm writing this down because someday I will be Alice, with a whole lifetime spent without a mother, a lifetime of walking around with a Grand Canyon of grief in my heart, and people should know what that feels like.

Shayna's AA meeting is next to the church in a run-down office building. A dental office is on the ground floor, a tax person on the third. Her people meet on the second floor.

After, we go to dinner at Denny's. Lupe always gets the Philly cheesesteak. Shayna gets the Caesar salad and a giant ice cream sundae, at the same time. I usually get a bowl of soup and some crackers. I'm eating more, but not a lot.

My sister and I, we can be quiet together, eating, and it feels okay.

It's a little family, but it's ours.

Sometimes Shayna and I drive around the city, trying to get our bearings. She waits tables in the morning, and when I get home from school, she's still wearing her apron, counting her tips.

We go to Eegee's and get brightly colored icy drinks and

drive. She likes to drive toward the Catalina Mountains on a series of curvy roads with long wooden fences and lots of trees.

There are horses there, grazing, and a sign that says *Lessons.*

I miss Opal with a fierceness that feels hot and alive, and someday, I am going to come back to this place, and get a job, and be with horses again.

Because that is in me, for real, and I got it from my mother.

My new high school is a lot bigger than Eugene Field. Sometimes I feel really lost, walking the halls, my books against my chest. I wonder about all the kids, and what kind of homes they go back to, the people who are supposed to care for them. Are they like Thaddeus and Leonard and Sarah? And me? Cobbling together families with what we've been given? Making homes from scraps.

Parents shouldn't die before their kids get old, but they do.

Parents shouldn't beat their kids, and break their backs, or lock them in dog cages, or let them live in cardboard boxes by the 7-Eleven, but they do.

I don't know how to live now, knowing what I do, but I have to keep going.

Sometimes I feel like those guys in that weird play Hoffmeister made us read.

I think about what those two odd guys said.

*You must go on.*

*I can't go on.*

*You must go on.*

Because what other choice is there, really?

You have to make friends with the dark.

. . .

I feel like I was one girl before my mother died, and another girl after, and now, at the end of this story, still another girl, crawling out of the jar, but keeping her wings close.

There's so much I wish I didn't have to know about living.

ONE NIGHT IN GROUP, we talk about what I was wondering about, way back at the beginning of the summer.

If your dead come to you. That.

Phil is in his thirties. His face is gutted from teenage acne and he wears a black leather vest bearing the insignia of his motorcycle club. His forearms are a testament to ink and time spent in jail. But he cries when he tells us about spooning vanilla ice cream into his mother's mouth just before she died, because she wanted to taste sweetness one last time. Her cancer made eating incredibly painful, and nearly impossible, at the end.

Phil says, "A few months later, she showed up in my dream. She was sitting on the couch in her old living room, her feet up and her circulation stockings on, watching *House Hunters,* and she said, 'Oh, Phillip, sit down. Look what I have. I can have all I want now.' And she had the biggest barrel of vanilla ice cream in front of her, and a giant spoon, like in a cartoon. And I knew she was all right. And I ain't even had anything to drink that night, and there she was, and we had ice cream and watched television and when I woke up I cried. I could taste the vanilla ice cream. I really could."

One by one, the others weigh in. A woman named Trisha, who'd lost both her mother and her sister within a few years of each other, says her mother showed up in a dream the very night after she died. "She'd been in a wheelchair for a long time, and we were in a room somewhere, it was very bright. And she didn't have the chair! She was walking! She hadn't walked in years and there she was, up and about. I remember she said, 'I'm going to go look for your sister now,' and she walked out of the room." Trisha pauses, her eyes wet. "That made me feel better. Thinking they would be together. And that my mother could walk again."

I still haven't seen my mother, except for that video on her cellphone. And part of me hopes it's because she's busy with people she hasn't seen in a long time, like her parents, or because she thinks I'm okay and I don't need her, or maybe she's worried she'll frighten me. I don't know, but I still hope, every night, regardless.

I think I'll tell my group about the cellphone thing sometime.

I know they would believe me.

And I do find it comforting that maybe when you die you get back all the things you've lost, like your legs, or your parents, or your daughters, or even your mom, and you get to eat all the ice cream you want, finally, and it doesn't hurt one bit.

**June Frances Tolliver** passed away on May 13, 2019, at the age of 45, in Mesa Luna, Arizona. She is survived by her daughter, Grace Maria Tolliver. They were a well-oiled, good-looking, and good-smelling machine.

June was loved, now and forever.

# AUTHOR'S NOTE

No one really knows the story of their parents. After all, as Tiger Tolliver says in this book, "It's very hard to think of your parents as people, full of bad checks and bad decisions, fistfights and broken hearts, all of it." Our parents pick and choose what to tell us about how they grew up and became, well, those people telling us what time to go to bed, or when to study, or why we can't go to that party.

You quilt the story of your parents through small patches of memory, some bright and hot, some so faded the truth of them is almost invisible. Maybe in the end, through photographs, you finally have a semblance of a whole. You can piece a parent together this way.

But what if your parent's whole life fits into one shoebox? What if there are tremendous gaps in the story?

The story of June Tolliver, who loses her parents as a child, was partly inspired by my own mother. Her mother died when she was seven, and my mother and her brother were sent to an orphanage. A baby sister was given to relatives; no one knows why they didn't take the older kids, too.

Her father remarried soon after. A nice family adopted my mother and her brother. They grew up comfortably. Photos of clean, smiling kids in cowboy chaps, my mother's hair curled just so. A shy smile at thirteen, but a hint of sadness in her eyes, a look she would carry her whole life. A friend painted her portrait. He called it *Sad Lady*.

She didn't like to talk (at least to me) about her days in the orphanage. Sometimes the smell of boiled cabbage would set her off, or a scene in a certain movie, but her outbursts were brief. Once or twice I asked what her mother's name was. She couldn't remember. Perhaps that was something she had to bury, in order to go on.

Before I was born, my parents took in foster children. Later, they adopted my brother. Perhaps this was something my mother carried, too: a need to help kids who needed family just when their lives were darkest, just like she once had.

Tiger's story is what can happen when one child finds herself at the mercy of strangers.

On any given day, there are almost half a million kids in foster care in the United States alone. Almost 2.5 million children are now homeless in the United States and one in twenty-eight kids has an incarcerated parent. More kids than you know are being raised by a non-primary relative.

These children are all around you: in your class, on your team, in your neighborhood, your camp, sitting quietly among the stacks in your library. Do you know them? Like Tiger, do you only realize how many broken lives are around you when you have a broken life of your own?

No one story can encompass all the experiences and minute details of foster care and juvenile detention. Or even grief. In this book, I've tried to tell a story about lost kids. Kids who have found themselves without parents, or family, for a variety of reasons: death, addiction, neglect, abuse.

Not all kids have safe home lives. To not show Thaddeus's experience does a disservice to every kid who's ever been abused by a family member. Sometimes that abuse happens in foster care, too, as we hear from Blondie and Brownie.

But I have also tried to show the LaLas, the Teddys, and teachers like Walrus Jackson, who try hard to make kids' lives better. There are people working valiantly in foster care, in homeless shelters, in teen homes and hangout centers. There are teachers and school counselors and librarians and grandparents and aunties and half siblings who open minds, homes, and hearts. These people fight the good fight each and every day to try to lessen the Grand Canyon–sized hole in kids' hearts.

*How to Make Friends with the Dark* is, above all, a book about grief. This is a book about learning how to go on, about finding your way in the dark. Mae-Lynn's father dies from cancer. Taran and Alif lose their father to a car accident. Tiger loses her mother to a brain aneurysm. And Lupe Hidalgo's brother dies by suicide, the second-leading cause of death for young people ages fifteen to twenty-five.

We must do better by our young people. We must engage in open conversation about depression and mental illness. Our schools need more resources, more support.

Once, I posed a question to my friends on Facebook: "What would you tell someone who's died if you had one last chance?" Lots of people said things like "I love you" or "I miss you." One person said, "I forgive you." Another person said, "I just want you to know I'm happy now." And a lot of people messaged me privately because not everyone has good things to say about the dead, and that is a true and valid thing, and we need to listen to these people as they grieve in their own way, too. And one person said she wished her mother had written her a letter telling her how to live without her, because she didn't know how.

That stopped me in my tracks, because it's true. There is no manual or primer for grief. There are lots and lots of books, but there's no minute-by-minute manual that lets you know the smell of Pond's Cold Cream will cause you to burst into tears at Walgreen's, or a certain song on the radio will make you pull to the side of the road to cry. And that these things last the rest of your life.

Within three years, I lost my mother and my sister. I don't have the answers; there's no blueprint for grief. What there is, is a lot of stumbling around in the dark, looking for a warm hand to hold on to.

I can't explain the Grand Canyon–sized hole inside me, so I wrote a book about it instead. I hope that if you are wandering that dark road of grief, Tiger's story helps you in some small way.

*Kathleen Glasgow*

P.S. My older brother undertook a hero's journey to piece my mother's story together through Ancestry.com posts, locating old neighbors, county files, and even old immigration records. He found that baby sister, now a grown woman, though my mother had already passed away.

But just before that happened, he did find out her mother's first name, which she had long forgotten.

It was the same as her own.

# RESOURCES

If you are feeling suicidal: suicidepreventionlifeline.org

If you need grief counseling: dougy.org/grief-resources/help
-for-teens/

If you are a homeless teen, or know someone who is:
nationalsafeplace.org/homeless-youth

If you are a child or teen in foster care, you have a mandated
bill of rights. These may vary from state to state, but you
can get more information here: childwelfare.gov/topics
/systemwide/youth/resourcesforyouth/rights-of-youth-in
-foster-care

If you are an LGBTQ youth:
thetrevorproject.org/#sm.00004zcgdcu9kfl8s8s24qwbinvh5

If you have an incarcerated parent: sfcipp.org

If you are the victim of sexual assault:
rainn.org/about-national-sexual-assault-telephone-hotline

# ACKNOWLEDGMENTS

A lot happens when you write a book.

You think you have one story, and then it turns out you have an entirely different story.

And even after *that,* there's one more story inside that one waiting to be trimmed, polished, painted, buffed.

And a lot of people are responsible for shaping my scraggly first idea of a girl and her mother and grief into the thing you are holding right now.

Krista Marino is, hands down, the best editor on the planet. Even when I do entirely uncool things, like, uh, rewriting an entire novel while she's out of the country on vacation? She rolls with it! I mean, she said, *"Put it back,"* meaning everything I'd taken out and replaced, in the nicest way possible, when probably she didn't have to be so nice. But she is. And she's also funny, and very good at making me face my fears and write the story that needs to be written.

Everyone at Delacorte Press and Penguin Random House makes my writerly dreams shiny and wondrous, especially Barbara Marcus, Beverly Horowitz, Monica Jean, Mary McCue, Kristin Schulz, Jennifer Heuer, Alison Impey, Kate Keating, Cayla Rasi, Elizabeth Ward, and Kelly McGauley. Thank you all so much for the time and care you've taken with Tiger's story.

A couple of years ago, an agent told me she couldn't possibly take on my first young adult novel. "You need to find a champion for this book," she said. And I did. Julie Stevenson has been my champion since she plucked me (and that book) from her plethora of daily queries, and I'm forever grateful that she understands my writing style and the stories I want to tell, and that she's with me every step of the way, being her usual joyful, funny, strong, and superb self.

Sometimes writing is exceedingly lonely, especially when you write about difficult topics that have a personal edge. I missed my mother and my sister so much while writing this book, and excellent humans like Janet McNally, Lygia Day Penaflor, Bonnie Sue Hitchcock, Sandhya Menon, Jeff Giles, Robin Roe, Julie Schumacher, Karen McManus, Julie Johnson, and Shannon Parker talked me through hard moments, even when they might not have realized that was what was happening. Thanks also to the Sweet Sixteens for continued support.

Tiger's story is about grief. Part of how I fought through writing her story was to ask people about their own Grief Life (thanks, Janet, for coining that phrase), because no one grieves in the same way. No one's Grief Life is the same. Special thanks to Susan Moger, whose response to one of my Facebook posts, about what you'd say to someone who has died if you had one last chance, inspired the character of Alice in this book.

Many thanks to Holly Vanderhaar and Elizabeth Noll, and to my front-desk pal, Mitch Gerson, for sharing his horse stories with me.

And thank you to Nikolai and Saskia, who have the biggest hearts and the best laughs, for always letting me hold you just a little tighter, a little longer.

# ABOUT THE AUTHOR

KATHLEEN GLASGOW is the *New York Times* bestselling author of *Girl in Pieces. How to Make Friends with the Dark* is her second novel. She lives and writes in Tucson, Arizona. To learn more about Kathleen and her writing, you can visit her website, kathleenglasgowbooks.com, or follow @kathglasgow on Twitter and @misskathleenglasgow on Instagram.

Praise for *Girl in Pieces*

**A *New York Times* Bestseller**
**A New York Public Library Best**
**Book for Teens, 2016**

"*Girl, Interrupted* meets *Speak*."  *Refinery29*

"A dark yet powerful read."  *Paste Magazine*

"One of the most affecting novels we have read."  *Goop*

"Breathtaking and beautifully written."  *Bustle*

"Intimate and gritty."  *Irish Times*

"A haunting, beautiful, and necessary book that will stay with you long after you've read the last page."
Nicola Yoon, bestselling author of *Everything, Everything*

"Equal parts keen-eyed empathy, stark candor, and terrible beauty. This book is why we read stories: to experience what it's like to survive the unsurvivable; to find light in the darkest night."
Jeff Zentner, author of *The Serpent King*

"Raw, visceral, and starkly beautiful, with writing that is at times transcendent in its brilliance… An unforgettable story of trauma and resilience."  Kerry Kletter, author of *The First Time She Drowned*

"A breathtakingly written book about pain and hard-won healing… I want every girl to read *Girl in Pieces*."
Kara Thomas, author of *The Cheerleaders*

"A *Girl, Interrupted* for a new generation… The story of the mad girl is ultimately a story about being a girl in a mad world, how it breaks us into pieces and how we glue ourselves back together."

Melissa Febos, author of *Whip Smart*

"*Girl in Pieces* is like the friend you wish you had by your side for every hard choice and every time you›ve felt lost or alone. It›s fearless and uncompromising, but overflowing with heart and wisdom." Anthony Breznican, author of *Brutal Youth*

"Dark, frank, and tender, *Girl in Pieces* keeps the reader electrified for its entire journey. You're so uncertain if Charlie will heal, so fully immersed in hoping she does."

Michelle Wildgen, author of *Bread and Butter*

"*Girl in Pieces* has the breath of life; every character in it is fully alive. Charlie Davis' complexities are drawn with great understanding and subtlety." Charles Baxter, author of *The Feast of Love*

"Charlie Davis has been damaged and abused after several years of living on the streets, but she is fiercely resilient. Though it will appeal to readers of *Ellen Foster*, *Speak*, and *Girl, Interrupted*, *Girl in Pieces* is an entirely original work, compulsively readable and deeply human." Julie Schumacher, author of *Dear Committee Members*

"In this sharp and beautiful portrait of eighteen-year-old Charlie Davis, Kathleen Glasgow illuminates not only the anxiety of youth but the vulnerability and terror of life in general. What a shock it is to engage with such a sensitive, sad, rage-filled soul: Glasgow›s rendering of experience and emotion is so succinct and honest that I kept catching my breath in recognition, and admiration for her sensibility and empathy which glows on every page. *Girl in Pieces* hurts my heart in the best way possible.»

Amanda Coplin, author of the
*New York Times* bestseller *The Orchadist*